AF552562

THE ULTIMATE MISSION OF DEVIL

<u>An extraordinary novel sparking excitement with every single line</u>

PRAKASH MAKWANA (SATHWARA)

ISBN 978-93-5288-825-2

Watch video trailer of "the ultimate mission of devil" here :

Prakash sathwara the ultimate mission of devil.

To contact for ask the film's rights, Translation rights for other languages and obtaining a license to publish in other countries: 09824427867 / evilumbrellaa115@gmail.com

Ph. : 09824427867, 09898818405

Email – evilumbrellaa115@gmail.com

Written by – Prakash Makwana (sathwara)

Editing by - Prakash Makwana (sathwara)

₹ : 279-00

First edition: January 2019

Since the novel is spread out over a very large panel, a plethora of characters are also associated with it. Along with the names of characters clarification of their identity have also been frequently given so that confusion is not created in the mind of the reader: Publisher's Note.

FROM THE ANCHOR

"Extremely interesting…" But after reading this novel even this adjective proves to be weak for appreciating this great story. While reading, a tremor of panic does not stay without inducing this thought... whether the author really has close contact with the other worlds or not? as a person having contact with our world only cannot give such an accurate, ghastly and extensive description as that in this masterpiece.

It appears that the mysterious protagonist of this 'life changing novel', the protagonist who is trapped between two dangerous women is born from the terrible screams emanating from the hearts of not just you, me and more than seven billion people living on this Earth, but also the creatures having an existence on other planets.

Usually a novel created with one or two layers of mystery, kindles extreme thrill, but there are so many surges of mystery in this story, and there are so many nets woven that it is difficult to understand the nectar-quintessence of the story without venturing into it with overall concentration and complete intellect.

There is one sign that exposes our foolishness, through that belief of ours, in which we feel that the thoughts we get are our own. But in fact, Lord de Ros, the New-God of some colony like *'Cons Lydia Dyaan'* implants such thoughts through his *'Mind Cataclysm Machines' (a device that fires thoughts)*, in the minds of certain people so that his favorite dramas can be composed on this Earth.

New-god's two groups exist on Galaxy L-Three, *'Off Idiotic group' (A group that providing a governance and creating an environment like heaven for the residents on the planets owned by them.)* and *'Vio-Crazy group' (A group of colonies who ruling the residents of their planet in a cruel manner.)* The colonies of both groups have many precious planets. Discerning at first sight, it appears that all the gimmicks of the *'Devil Family'* and S.O.G. (Devilish Institute) are being contrived to usurp this new-god's colony. however, the Ultimate Mission of the Devil challenges the IQ of the best experts. If you realize the Ultimate Mission of the Devil right in the middle of story, then consider yourself to be extraordinarily brilliant.

The meaning of running away in our world refers to escaping from one city or country to the other, but the meaning of running away in the world of *'The Ultimate Mission of the Devil'* is death to quite an extent... *'On the other side is a Secret Society that makes arrangements of rebirth for you on your desired planet in your desired city, through a mysterious ritual. Along with getting back the old memories as well.'*

At one point of the story, when it feels that the New-Gods are the ones who are supreme, then the mystery of the new rulers of the 'Master Galaxy', who holding lordship on these six galaxies and new gods, is revealed. And again when it appears that these rulers are the final emperors, then a completely unique secret of a mysterious power ruling over that rulers and creatures of every planet of all six galaxies in this local group and all such New-Gods who are the so-called owners of all those creatures is revealed. This most mysterious protagonist of the universe, who has known the terrible truth of the ultimate sources of power, develops one such unimaginable conspiracy to uproot the base of that power from its roots and throw it off through the *'Mission Walk of Life'*.

Then, *'Striado Unit' [The department that does the root record of the non-residents (A person who is not a citizen of the Master Galaxy) who enter Director Apotheosis' part of the 'Master Galaxy' through their aura]*, *'Devilet Again'* the scripture written about the mysteries of the Devilish existence, *'Book of Bell'*, *'Thought Steal'* and *'Memory Thief'* machines that steal the thoughts of other people, description of such wonderful things, and with that *'Signature Band'*, *'Chargeman'*, *'Warlord'*, *'Evilstock'*, *'Win Maker'* and *'Liquor Mine'* such armies holding various characteristics, and an universal organization named Channel 'S', that has made the journey of our infinite universe accessible in a way that even the speed of light that has the highest speed does not come in any comparison to it, such a novel that represents such unimaginable things and opens up new doors of probabilities, for which the word excellent also appears to be pale, I welcome to you with the highest level of happiness and excitement in it.

"DEDICATED TO THE SUPREME GOD ALMIGHTY WHO GAVE THE INSPIRATION"

"DOMINUS ANTONIO'S MYSTICAL CASTLE IN THE HIMALAYAAN REGION OF NORTHERN INDIA"

"Oh..! Today is the last day for both of us in this world, and finally, the question as to who she loves is equally mysterious..!"

On the shores of the Rebel Lake, in the boat anchored beside the Top of the World sign board, Elvis said with the intention that Paras would now keep his oar at one side.

Today, the lotuses in the lake looked so happy as if they had not blossomed as per their daily routine but out of sheer joy. They were also proclaiming the reason of their happiness, but where did both these navigators have time to spare from their tittle-tattle of damsels...

"This is the thing that is called a girl, my friend." Paras, who looked like the Prince of Attraction, whom the whole world would gladly choose and send forth to perform in the Mr. Universe contest, said continuing to carve on the oar with a piece of glass. "Before you open your mouth to tell her after years of studying her that *I understand you now...*, prior to that she will say, I have changed now buddy, I am not the same as before."

"Hey... A Shooting Star..." Raising his finger towards the sky, Elvis said sighing, "Alas! I wish! I had worn my lucky underwear that day. To tell the truth, I feel scared even today that she will come looking for me all the way to the Earth."

"Seeing every *'shooting star'* you should indeed be scared as she will never cease to chase you."

"Whom did you miss out on enticing with the help of your lucky underwear, Elvis?" The euphonic words capable of captivating in an invisible fascination whilst dancing, such a melodious voice was heard from the edge of the bridge.

"Where were you, Susan? After tomorrow, you will not find anyone waiting for you here to go boating." Elvis said, extending his hand.

"History of Bikini-Day... What talks were going on?" Susan came into the boat holding Elvis' hand. A magnificent light, like the reddish glow of the dawn that is formed due to the process of interaction between the solar-wind and the Earth's atmosphere, was shining on her face.

"That foolish girl had come to the classroom with my photo stuck on her pink panty, and that too, a totally stupid one." With these words, Elvis' face, as he was releasing the anchor, turned scarlet.

Blowing on the engraved carving of the oar, Paras said, "The photo was stuck on the panty in the form of a small pocket. From that she pulled the ring in a dainty manner and proposed Elvis right in front of thousands of students. That Bikini-Day has become memorable in the history of *S.O.G.*" *(S.O.G. - An Institute run by the Devil family for some special families having faith in Satanism.)*

"Can we expect a decision today, from the mysterious minded lady, whose thoughts cannot be deciphered even a wee bit by all the experts around the world vying to do so?" As Paras started moving the oars and asked this, the all time desolate lake that was feeling good about this one and only boat splashing on its surface during the evening hours, raised its ears.

Susan said, raising a face that created an illusion of innocence, "It is not easy to penetrate the tight security of Susan's heart. But anyways, as a solution to the situation of having similar feelings towards both of you, Susan will not be able to stop herself from being dedicated to the one who exceedingly affirms to the definition of greatness. So the ball is now in your court." She pressed the blue-colored knee length summer dress worn beneath the jacket, between her thighs.

After all three of them listened to the music created by the oars for some time, Elvis said, "The kind Susan, who cannot see the pain of humans, wishes that when it has been unquestionably proved that the *'Government'* of every country has failed in establishing stable peace, these circumstances are now demanding an alliance that can establish an *'Alieonic Scope'* to face evil people on this Earth. Susan will devote her heart at the feet of the one who will be successful in bringing about a *'New World Order'* from amongst the two of us."

"And if this indeed is the demand, then I have won Susan, Elvis." Although Paras quickly said this, he shrugged his shoulders to show that he did not know the answer when he realized the questioning eyes of his companions were asking, *'How will it be possible?'*

When the boat reached close to the scaffolding in the middle of the lake, Susan held on to the carved pier of the platform while Paras got up and spread the grains in it. His glance fixed on the picture carved on the column in the middle of the canopy in which a brutal animal was giving human sacrifice by piercing a spear in his chest. He moved his fingers there.

"What is it?" Elvis asked as he stood up.

"It is weird."

"What?" Elvis came closer.

"*Graphic conversation...*" *(A dialogue taking place through an illustration)* Paras said in a lost voice.

As Elvis narrowed his eyes and looked there attentively he appeared to have lost his senses. He said quickly, "We should return instantly."

"Why...?" Susan asked leaving the pier.

"This symbol made to keep the divine powers away, suggests that the Devil is dwelling somewhere around the lake. We are near *Terror-Street.* My father has a book from the restricted library of S.O.G. in which I had vividly seen the same portrait." *(Terror-Street - One of the numerous transitory residences of the Devil)*

"Devils Tip...? Interesting....!" Susan commented, pulling down the trilby from her head, "I am a fan of the Devil. Any guesses, why? One of the best things of the Devil is that he never pretends to be good. It is now imperative to find that terror-street."

"This is not a joke..." Elvis mumbled as he sailed the boat to the Western shores of the lake from where the jungle was commencing. Paras jumped down first and stood holding out a hand for Susan.

"What are you going to show? Devil?" Susan asked, grinning.

Anchoring the boat on the coast, Elvis led them across the coastal stones and stopped near the trees lined up in a queue. "Some of these trees have moved by approximately three feet in the last two days." He said, sitting down and measuring the distance from a rod he had inserted in the ground some days back, up to the tree.

"So?" Paras asked.

"So the trees do not do this naturally!" Elvis said as he stood up.

Susan said, "It is noted in many places in Central America that wherever the trees could get more nutrition from the sun-light, they move towards it."

"But here, every tree is going far from the lake, and there was no deficit of sunlight even where they were earlier."

"Who knows, there might be a habitat of the Devil even around the moving trees of Central America. Let us ask Antonio." Paras said extending the cigar box towards Susan.

*

They walked towards the mountains, where the mysterious mansion of *'Dominus Antonio'* was situated. Made from black rocks, the castle looked like an ancient monastery from the foothills. An edifice was being formed by the amalgamation of a cluster of shacks with small and big tetragonal peaks that were constructed by carving half the portion of the mountain top.

"Antonio is not going to be present for the dinner." As they entered the high porch of the castle after crossing the tangled pathway, Rayan's high tone also attracted their attention along with the bells around the neck of the brown *yak* grazing on the left side. *(Yak – An animal found in the North India)*

Placing the lantern on the last one of the high columns that was in the barnyard, Rayan came towards them and inserted a slip in Paras' palm keeping his glance fixed on Elvis, who was bidding farewell to Susan as he set the tresses of his hair that were flying due to the wet winds coming through the lake.

Clenching the slip in his fist, Paras climbed the corridor stairs and reaching inside he opened the paper given by Rayan.

A map leading towards some secret portion of the fort was drawn on the page. Paras's eyes could not refrain from lighting up electrically with the thought- 'Is it possible that this map has a relationship to the hidden location of the 'Book of Bell'..! Before coming to the Earth, the conversation of father and son was grasped by his ears from a corner of the S.O.G. library. Luiciano had said, "Elvis, if you want to become a 'New-God' of several valuable planets without labor, then track down the Book of Bell. No matter what the world says, but there is no doubt that Antonio has hidden that strange book."

Here, from the time he and Elvis had stepped into this fort, they were searching for the 'Book of Bell'. And as if Antonio himself wished to offer him that book, he had called him there by sending a message to him through Rayan in a secret manner.

He felt that the third part of the night is too far away.

*

"You are not going to come to stroll up the peak today?" Susan asked Paras at the dining table while Rayan was arranging the new stand decorated with blue candles.

Taking a brown colored sauce, Paras said, "I still have to complete the packing as well. Elvis has already sent the signal-image to take us from here, and we do not get any straightforward punishment to keep the air-ship of S.O.G. waiting."

"Well, today I have brought a poem written to express gratitude. I felt that today I must express my respect towards Antonio."

"Oh… Elvis! My father will certainly like it." When Susan told Elvis beholding him with gentle eyes, a young rose from the flower-vase on the table looking at its cheeks, smoothened its scattered petals due to molestation by the wind.

"My Lord and Emancipator help us with the power of the Holy Spirit. O Lord, open the doors of our self-realization to your glory and for the expansion of your empire. Amen."

After a minute of having started dinner, Susan said, "Recently, in a few days, I have seen this sixth pair coming here for the purpose of study, although, I don't even know which technique Antonio knows. After all what is your special experience here?"

"All this is very complicated." Elvis said, "A special force is being prepared to defeat the special army of *Lord De Ros*, the New God of Colony Cons Lydia which is known as Gardi-Force. These soldiers are known as the *'Energy Warriors'*. That's all about the project of preparing the Energy Warriors."

"But that is just an excuse." Paras retorted, "Based on the doubt that Antonio has hidden something that belongs to him, *Dervil (A member of the Devil family and the Dean of S.O.G.)* keeps sending his spies here under the pretense of training. Well, I need to do some preparation." Paras started eating quickly and wiping his lips with a napkin with his other hand, he watched the reaction on Elvis' face on being called Dervil's spy.

*

In the dilemma whether he should believe that scene or not, Paras was pacing back and forth in the bedroom. A few days ago, while purchasing goods with Elvis in a city situated quite far from Antonio's castle, he had suddenly glimpsed a face which intuitively, he felt resembled

Clesta's brutal agent, Telon's. But what would he be doing here on Earth? And there was also no such disaster on this planet that a well-known agent of a top-rated agency, hired by the owners or enemies of Planet Earth, should be seen here. It had been heard that he had been banned from getting a license to enter most of the planets of many colonies. If he was here, then it was surely a big thing. He had seen him only once in Luiciano's party.

The whirl of Paras' thoughts stopped when he saw a figure moving far away on the Guru Shikhar on the glass of Antonio's room's window. The curtains that always remained closed were open today. He ran guessing it to be Elvis' shadow. He was lost in his thoughts and who knows how long Elvis had been searching for the 'Book of Bell' in Antonio's room. (Guru Shikhar - A peak of the Himalayas)

*

It was not as much by seeing Paras panting, as it was by the way he had pushed open the door, that the three people present there glared at him with a facial expression as if asking- *'Where has the fire erupted?'*

"I just thought that someone barged into Antonio's room."

Jerking his head instead of laughing as expected and reverberating the black cloak he had draped from head to toe, *'Dominus Antonio'* got up. After staring for some time in a strange manner at the walls shimmering in the yellow illumination of the flambeau as if his lost memory had just come back, he told Paras, "It is good you came. I was about to send Rayan to call you."

"This way, please." Signaling with his first two fingers, Antonio hinted them to follow him and told Rayan something in the language of the eyes.

Rayan, who had a rhinoceros-like strong and stern physique, bowed his head in response and started walking towards the door. His dirty, leather gown was dragging on the floor.

After leading them to a room right behind the drawing room, Antonio said, "Our towers constructed on countless planets of many colonies which can steal the energy from the human bodies from far off, looking at the capacity with which they are currently working, we will get enough army of our Energy Warriors ready to exterminate the Gardi-Force of Earth's New-God Lord de Ros, in just a few days."

Looking at the narrow manner in which Antonio's drawing room was designed, Elvis and Paras were still watching all around the room like fools as if unable to believe that it could also hide this next-generation lab behind it.

Ahem.... Antonio cleared his throat and say, "Today I am about to reveal the mystery of such a midpoint that is situated in our body in which the energy being stolen from countless human beings can be stored. This knowledge can be a destructive weapon in the hands of miscreants."

The ears of both of them rose up like monkeys.

A Gardi-Force soldier of Colony 'Cons Lydia Dyaan' that owns the toy-planet 'Earth' on which we are currently sitting, could be killed just by opening the belt on his neck and chopping off his neck in one stroke. But the opponent would have to go near him to do that which is impossible while being alive. A weapon that could kill him had not been discovered till date. Hence they acquired a reputation of being immortal in the world. But now, the matter is different. We have discovered that strange weapon which is somewhat like this- '9+s–ye (KN) 5.' It is only the machine in the form of the human body that can generate this energy structure throughout the world. This is the sole 'human power weapon', an attack with which can eliminate a Gardi soldier. However, no one will forgive us till Lord de Ros' infinite army is eliminated with the help of the energy stolen from billions of people on this Earth and many other such planets and good governance is not established by us."

"Why is it so damn difficult to kill a Gardi soldier?" asked Elvis.

"According to the prevailing natural rule, a man needs to depend on the digestive system to heal his wounds and in turn the digestive system depends on food. A boring process..! But the inner-system of my unique army unit use those infinite atoms from Space, that is Ether from which all the physical things are made and can immediately join a broken body again. Whoever has the link connecting ghosts and the body in his neck," Antonio said as he took his hand to the belt tied to his neck, "We are the ones who are the combinations of such ghosts and living human beings together." *(Antonio himself had also been a Gardi soldier and the former Chairman of Lord de Ros, but was now working on the Devil-Family's mission of eliminating the Gardi-Force and capturing Lord de Ros' Colony)*

"This might be a stupid question, but forgive my ignorance, what role do we have to play in this mission, Antonio?" Paras asked.

"In order to prevent this technique from going into the hands of miscreants, a small part from here is handed over to the manual." Dodging Paras' question, Antonio pushed him in a high chair and pierced a syringe filled with a pain killer on his neck. Pulling the *'thread tube'* hanging on top of the chair, Antonio pierced it in the middle of his chest.

"Ahh…! After the thread-tube entered Paras' body with a slight groan, he took Elvis to a small cabin a little away, in which two people could not enter without pushing each other, Antonio showed Elvis something in the monitor.

Driving the *'thread'* in Paras' body, Antonio murmured, "Every substance has its gravity center point. Each and everything whether it is a heavy substance or living beings like humans. A cycle, that can load a huge amount of the human energy that is stolen and stored by our towers exactly behind the place where nature has established this center point in the body, has been discovered. You will not be surprised to see millions of armored soldiers of Ros' army falling on their knees once the energy stolen from thousands of humans is loaded in each and every warrior of our army. But the problem is that this cycle in our body can load the pure energy prepared by the human body only. It has been ages since nature has sent everyone with this great possibility, yet till date, it has not been used even once."

After staring into Elvis' eyes for some time, Antonio said further, "Nature's objective may be that a weak person can get rid of his deficiency by taking energy in limited quantity, from another person who is stronger. but we are using this phenomenon for making a big change in this world, by eliminating the *Uncontrolled Emperors*." Saying this, he closed the monitor.

And moreover, Antonio had given Paras the card to lock the lab. Paras controlled his anger with great trouble. Elvis had been made the *Main Energy Warrior*, who had the knowledge of that epicenter in the human body, instead of him. Not only that, the other meaning for this was that Antonio might now select Elvis for Susan. *(Main Energy Warrior – One, who knows the whole technique of the process of loading pure energy in the human body.)*

*

A prideful smile was playing on Elvis' face as if he had won battles that would proclaim him as an oil king on Earth.

"Antonio, may I take one of these Aakrids tomorrow?" Elvis asked, glancing towards the two shining fishes emanating light in the fish tank placed on the table near the door opening in the gallery.

"Only an individual at a Chairman's position can keep things that provide this level of protection against infernal forces..." Saying this, as Antonio suddenly faltered, Paras, subject to such hysteria as if a black shadow had gone floating out from the balcony, slowly stepped towards it. *(There are many colonies on Galaxy L3. Every Colony owns fifteen to three hundred or more planets. The owner of the colony is referred to as a New-God. Those having less authority are referred to as Chairman and President in the descending order. Mostly, five to eight Chairmen and sixty or more Presidents working under each Chairman are designated in one colony. A group of three to ten Presidents handle the administration of any one planet. Prior to this, Antonio held the position of a Chairman in New-God Lord de Ros' owned Colony Cons Lydia Dyaan. Colony Cons Lydia Dyaan holds the ownership of fifty planets. In which even Planet Earth is included.)*

Pushing aside Elvis' hand extended for support, Antonio balanced himself with difficulty and reaching the aquarium, he opened the lid and threw some blancads.

"No problem, it should be possible to obtain another Aakrid like this from somewhere, right?" With his hand kept at the edge of the fish-tank in such a way that it would not attract Antonio's attention, Elvis scattered poisonous particles in the tank and shouted loudly at Paras who was groping in the balcony, "Something is out there, Paras?"

"Oh...This..." Looking at the light gradually vanishing from the fish's body, Antonio growled in a shaky voice. When the black carcass of one of the two fishes surfaced, Antonio pushed Elvis who was trying to reach there and instantly pulled out the other fish that was circling around the dead one. The death of the Aakrid in this manner was akin to a danger alert because even though Antonio's group was working hand in hand with the Devil family in this mission to gain victory over Colony Cons Lydia, but their ultimate intention was to betray the Devil family and usurp the whole Colony. And he was keeping these holy fishes with him for protection against the Devil in case their ploy was exposed.

After looking continuously for sometime towards Elvis, who was stealing his eyes to hide his cheekiness, Paras raised his steps towards Susan's room.

*

"Activated with the power of the 'Host of Hell' (Devil), who bestowed the lease of life to the 'Milky-way' (Galaxy) wavering on the brink of devastation, Dervil has removed the last cover of the Aakrid and made arrangements to kidnap one more President, Telon will be reaching there with that President shortly."

After compulsion-induced cajolery, Dervil stood holding the phone. *(The enigmatic meaning of Dervil addressing the Devil as the Host of Hell who bestowed the lease of life to the 'Milky-way' wavering on the brink of devastation was that according to the book, 'Devilet Again' that was written on the Devil, the mysterious scientific rules based on which this universe is surviving, can bring an end to it for two reasons, when all the people become either outright good or bad. It is mandatory to have a balance of both good and bad for the world to survive. And in a way the Devil's presence also prevents the end of the universe by stopping preventing the entire human race from treading on the path of righteousness.)*

["And hence, from time to time, to prevent all these worlds from being totally demolished, that externalization of the disliked element (Devil) begins." – Devilet Genesis Scripture]

"One more useless effort…" The black shadow that had come out from Dominus' balcony had assumed a distinct, corporeal appearance and was now moving around on Terror-Street that was made in the abyss of the lake. Its voice that echoed was as copious as if all the seven seas were roaring together and one that could frighten any Dictator with Total Power over the Country. With just these words from him, the boisterous *Alcohol Festival* that was going on, transformed into mourning, and the Devilishs started moving away from there, one after another. The Devil said further, "Never, at any given point of time, I don't want to hear such news that due to the over pressure of the *Memory Thief* or *Thought-Steal* the neurons containing intimation of the Book of Bell in the skull of anyone have been burnt." *(Memory Thief - A device that steals the information stored in the mind of any person. Thought Steal - A device, that along with copying the memory hidden in the mind, it also converts the thoughts going on in that person's mind, into explicit information.)*

"Alright." Dervil said in a submissive tone.

"A newest God whom people distraught by traditional religion have recently discovered, such a God who can confer something that is not there in destiny and is known in the world as Devil, that Misguiding-Prophet himself is experiencing helplessness today in the biggest mission of his lifetime."

"The President kidnapped today claims that there is one more way to find out the whereabouts of the Book of Bell. On release of *Robrelco Fero's* soul captivated in that book, the sky in that vicinity will be filled with red waves as a result of a large scale immersion of energy taking place in the form of electro-magnetic waves which can easily be noticed by our satellites." The line went dead with these words of Dervil and the Devil looked towards Telon who had just arrived in Terror-Street and stood there. He was wearing an armored leather jacket and there was a remarkable cunningness in his eyes. *(Robrelco Fero – The head of the Devil family who had been imprisoned in the Book of Bell. It was said that the Devil needed Robrelco Fero so much for the success of his Ultimate Mission that he would be ready to give Colony Cons Lydia that was to be won after some time without any thought in exchange of Robrelco Fero.)*

After lighting a cigar made of bear's skin and taking a deep puff, Devil signaled with his first finger to bring that President.

Telon bowed his head in consent, brought the President wrapped in an overcoat, inside and removed the mask from his face. Pushing the President into a chair lying in front of the Devil, he announced in a loud voice, "News has been received about a *'Ventricle Chamber' (Secret Place)* at one side of Antonio's Castle. The Book of Bell might be there."

*

"If Antonio gets to know that I had brought you into this chamber, then he will kill me." Susan said as she walked briskly through the corridor covered with a dim light.

"I want to live in the lap of luxury..." Walking behind Susan, Paras said removing the stick from the violin, "That moment will never come. If the Book of Bell is found from the chamber, the two of us will elope from here, tonight only. Witch, you should have asked Antonio emphatically about what we are doing in this desolate place on Earth? And what type of collaboration he has with Director Dervil of an institute like S.O.G. that is located in the Northern *'Draco'* Constellation of L3 Galaxy?"

"You should be asking this question to the S.O.G. who has sent you here."

"*Witch*," *(A hag who does black magic)* Paras used to address her by this name whenever the two of them were alone. "Antonio will soon give you the news that I have cleared your confusion."

"I did not understand what you said."

"Today, Antonio has made Elvis the *Main Energy Warrior*."

"And as it is, you yourself had said that the average span of life, of people living on the planet Elvis comes from, is more than three hundred years. So, now you tell me whom should I choose...?" Giving a flirtatious smile, Susan winked.

They lit a lantern with the lamp flickering in the walled-bower near the steps in the basement and removing the cobwebs they pushed the brass door and entered the tunnel.

In contrast to the tunnel, the 'Cave' was absolutely neat and clean.

"But how long will it take me to learn the language of your planet?" Susan enquired picking up a book on ancient architecture made of birch bark, from the shelf.

"One minute." Paras said turning the books propped up against the right wall of the chamber.

"Meaning?"

"Meaning, sixty seconds. If a resident of any planet of the highly developed colonies of Group SP would get lost on the Earth by mistake, and would look at the students who work hard year after year for any course such as doctor or engineer, then the helpless fellow will not return back without going mad."

"Why, how's that?" asked Susan.

"Instead of school, college or university there are Knowledge Booths over there. A candidate who qualifies in terms of the age criteria determined for the syllabus of choice goes into the Knowledge Centre, and within a few minutes the entire course is installed in his brain through the most modern computers of the Galaxy. S.O.G. and other such institutes have the technology bought from the colonies of Group SP. Any language can be pasted in the brain in less than a minute. Our world has already overcome the hurdles against changing things like the physical appearance, fingerprint or iris identity, long back. People there, see one and the same movie that is very good, then they delete it from their minds with the help of certain devices and then see it again and again hundreds of times with the same thrill."

"Wow... All you Gods...! We will also choose a planet of Group SP only to set up our new world. There is something below here..!" Susan's leg had impinged a hollow object. A six feet long *casket (case like a coffin)* had been secured with boards and buried in the ground.

The noise of nails being pulled out became horrifying screams of a witch and frightened the quiet desolation of the night.

Removing the dust, Paras was just about to open the casket when Susan said with a throbbing heart, "Did you hear something?" Before they could ascertain the distance from which that noise as if a pigeon was fluttering in a hunter's hands was arising, on noticing someone's shadow, they blew off the lantern and quickly moved towards the back of the chamber. At the back of the cave, there was a rift between two big rocks behind the sharp gorge hanging down from the roof. The rocks moved away on pushing the gorge. As the rift opened, a narrow passage unveiled in a miraculous way.

When Telon came into the cave and took off the small wings from his back, Susan said, "What is this?" Standing in close proximity right behind Paras, Susan's lips were brushing Paras' ears.

"Clesta's neoteric human wings."

“Human wings? And what is Clesta?”

“An Intelligence Agency. And there isn’t much traffic on the roads out there.”

“Wow, I also want to fly...” Susan said in an excited voice.

“Ssh.. ssh.. ssh...”

“He will have to be taught a lesson.” Susan nudged Paras angrily as she saw Telon expeditiously scattering the books all around.

Telon pulled a laser-gun from the jacket and melted the chain wrapped around the casket. Paras started shivering imagining his hand in place of the chain while Telon came and stood beside the rift in front of them. He drew his face close to the rift and started peeping inside in the flashlight.

Holding their breath, Paras and Susan slowly stepped behind softly.

Putting the flash aside, he lit a cigarette and blowing the smoke inside the rift as he stood reclining on the hanging gorge, instantly the stones moved away in the opposite direction. After the end of the statue-seconds of Paras and Telon, staring at each other as if they were seeing a marvel, Paras said, “Hi Telon...” Before Telon’s hand could come out of the jacket pocket, Paras’ powerful punch had made it necessary to get an imitative nose for his face. The whole cave shook up as Telon crashed onto the floor with a bang.

Paras pulled Susan by her hand up to the far corner as he sensed her thought of opening the casket after taking the laser-gun lying in the armpit of the recovering Telon, and murmured, "Witch, not as dangerous as you, yet he is believed to be the most precarious agent in the world..."

Walking backwards until Telon disappeared from their sight, they reached the tunnel and ran closing their fists. After closing the door from outside, they put their hands on their knees and started panting as if a prey had been saved from a cheetah.

"Antonio will have to be told...!" Paras said as the breathing became normal.

"Are you mad..?" Susan retorted, "If we had to die through Antonio's hands, what was the need to escape from Telon. He had warned to stay away from this cave beforehand."

*

When they reached below, they saw Elvis coming from the opposite direction. Paras said in a soft tone, "It is time for me to go to the strange place at which Antonio had called me. For how much-ever time I stay there, Elvis should not move from your sight."

"Hum... Hi Elvis."

"I wish, I would have never met the shimmering knife that gives light to thousands of shining stars in this drunken night..." said Elvis as he came closer.

"Bo! Elvis, you are a poet…!" Susan said giving a lovely smile.

"When a *ghazal (a type of musical composition)* itself is standing right in front, who will be so pernicious not to become heady in a poetic way?" Saying this, Paras waved his hand in encouragement.

"I have something for you, Elvis." Holding Susan's hand as she mumbled such words, Elvis turned towards the summit, and Paras moved forward towards the long, inaccessible rocky path denoted in the map provided by Antonio.

It was quite evident that the 'trek' (path) that would give a glimpse of the Book of Bell would certainly not refresh the memories of excursions. Large swarms of black clouds, holding each other's hands were eager to cover the sky. Crossing a long rugged path, he reached the castle constructed on a *mountain-crest (one of the small and big peaks of the mountain)* in the Western area of the castle. Reaching the castle's balcony constructed towards the valley, he looked around with an *infrared-stealth (Binoculars with which one can see in the dark)* and climbed the balcony's rail. As such, apart from him and Elvis only Antonio, Susan and Rayan were staying in the monastery. The expectation of the human population was till very far far away, yet Antonio had called him alone.

After opening the climbing kit and rubbing his hands with the chalk, he climbed about fifteen meters with the help of the chain hanging on the stones towards the right side and stopped to take deep breaths. When he looked up again, after glancing down at the hundreds of feet deep valley covered by the oak trees, he saw something like a gentle light of the torch in a mine about five feet ahead. He started climbing again after removing the worm that had clambered on his hand.

When he reached the cave after crawling through the mine on his knees, he could see Antonio seated on a stone with a serious facial expression.

Getting up, Antonio slowly pressed the eye in Petroglyp's face carved on the right wall of the cave and stood there. Opening a safe hidden behind the stone wall, he took out a chest from the safe and coming near Paras. he fished out two books from that and keeping the chest at one side, he said, "Protected at the Sweden National Library in Stockholm, 36 inches tall, 20 inches wide, made from the skin of 160 donkeys, weighing 165 pounds and written in a medieval manuscript, the '*Codex Gigas*' which is also known as the 'Devil's Bible' on Earth, that entire scripture will not be able to give as much knowledge about the mysteries of the Devil as just one paragraph of this book can provide."

"Antonio, is this the *Book of Bell*...?"

"No, this is a small part of the book *Devilet Again* written about the Devil. And this is the Book of Bell." He mumbled as he showed one more book.

Antonio, swirling a chip-detector on his left shoulder, suddenly stopped and drawing a knife from his waist, he pierced it at a specific spot on Paras' shoulder. Paras felt as if his eye balls also had fallen down due to extreme amazement, along with the Positioning Chip that had come out of his shoulder's flesh and bounced onto the floor. He also did not have any clue as to when and who had loaded this chip in his body to know his live location.

Wrapping a cloth on his wound, Antonio was murmuring sheer nonsense, "Paras, I do not know to what extent the influence of the Book of Bell will corrupt the background image of yours and Susan's personality, yet, what can I do? It is not safe to send the Book of Bell there in this form." An appeal for mercy appeared in his eyes for his state of mind.

"What are you going to do?" Paras asked as he stepped behind with a fearful face.

In response, shouting, "Quiet…" with a murderous face when Antonio signaled him to sit between the Magic Pentagram Plate, a cat had suddenly come and sat at his feet spinning its neck with alertness with no clue as to when and from where she had come. Saying that it is for preventing the damage to the body due to radiation coming out from the Book of Bell as he showed the syringe, Antonio gave a beautiful oil-painting of Susan to hold on to in his hands and pierced the syringe on his arm.

*

"Ah...!" For one whole second, he feel pride not less than a world winner in facing those eyes glaring in a horrifying way. The President's hypnosis had been started through Devil's dangerous eyes in Terror-Street situated below the lake near Antonio's castle.

"Rihon, the new Chairman of *Earth Eleven*, yes, any President from amongst his loyal Presidents could currently be a short term owner of that *'Book of Bell'* book…!" The President spoke further in a trembling voice, "Everyone except Chairman Rihon who takes it from one President and hands it over to another is oblivious to when, where, that ominous book..." *(Earth Eleven – A cluster of eleven planets of Colony Cons Lydia Dyaan on Galaxy L3 holding the ownership of total fifty planets including the Earth and other planets more prosperous than that was referred to as Earth Eleven. Rihon had replaced Antonio and had become the new Chairman of these eleven planets cluster, Earth Eleven of Cons Lydia. It was Rihon who had imprisoned the Devil family's head Robrelco Fero in a book which had been named 'Book of Bell', further details about which have been given in the forthcoming chapters)*

"Ahh.. hh.." Terror-Street echoed with a frightening scream. The President only had to be impudent enough to move his eyes from the Devil, and Telon standing next to him, would pierce a steel-tube embedded in his ring, right into his chest. An acidic fluid would be injected push down into his body, and outcries of unbearable pain would be augmented.

"Then perhaps the time of your choice by Rihon is going on now...? Devil said.

"It is said that Rihon, the creator of the Book of Bell, has lost that book now." The President said.

"You can make me happy with some new information. Ask him what I want."

"Where is the Book of Bell, now?" asked Telon.

"It is not with me."

"Who has it?"

"I don't know."

"Who could have it? Who had it before it came to you?"

"Last, it was stolen for some time in Japan." The President's head was hanging down.

Telon looked towards the Devil, the flesh of his scary face had started dangling.

"After that book was salvaged from being stolen in Japan, it remained with me for some time. Rihon took it from me and handed it over to some other President in the general assembly of my group." As the Devil placed his hand on the tattoo visible on the President's open shoulder, his black eyeballs instantly turned white like cotton.

*

"We both are alike, Susan. Such people are not born to match the society's rhythm. Either they stay away from everyone, or with everyone as their boss." Elvis smiled mysteriously and continued, "I am excited about the forthcoming years that we will spend together as the owners of the inhabitants of this Earth and other planets like that."

"I think that I am clear about my choice now...!" Susan said, turning her face which looked as if beauty itself had made its abode, away from Elvis to the other direction.

"Carefully sweetie, you don't know, but I can even become an animal to get what I want, and right now, my priority is you." Elvis said and extended his hand towards her, but before the sense of touch could register the feel of Susan's skin, she collapsed on him.

"Susan..!!" Elvis got up patting her cheeks and picking her up, he directly rushed towards the Guru Shikhar.

*

Indents were forming in Antonio's ribs as he was pronouncing the spells with lots of power. As if the air wanted to escape from there and hang the vacuum on the cross, a black storm rising from all around Paras who was sitting with Susan's photograph in his hand and was blowing towards the outside. As if retouched by some invisible element from Antonio's spells inspiring the transformation, thin layers of the soul came out from the Book of Bell and transformed themselves into a reddish light rotating around Paras and started creating sharp spheres of flame.

The coverage area of the fierce red light that had intensely filled the cave came out of the tunnel and spread up to thousands of yards.

As soon as the deadly light that had come out from the Book of Bell went down Paras' chest, his lifeless body fell on the candles burning at the corner of the Magic Plate with a bang. He was visualizing Susan in a strange world. As those with divine powers can feel the colors and flavors of sound, similarly their souls were tasting the flavors of the undiscovered elements of each other's personality. Gradually, as the light of the abrasive fire became smaller in the pink light of the harsh storm, he slowly started gaining consciousness.

Keeping aside the happiness of being alive, he said raising angry eyes, "Actually, if I would not have heard from *Luiciano (Elvis' father)* that the Book of Bell is a soul of a cruel dictator, then you would have really succeeded in making us believe that you have done a big favor by imposing it on us. Why did you do this to me, Antonio? And with Susan...? It will take our lives at any moment and if it doesn't, then we will become murderers till that point of time."

"Don't worry. Not so soon at least." Antonio said with ease. "Only a small part of the spirit of Robrelco Fero, the so called father of the Devil and the head of the Devil family, was in the Book of Bell. The same is now imprisoned with your and Susan's soul. No one else can be trusted with this thing that can be used to negotiate with the Devil in case he hesitates to give us our share at the time of dividing it after winning over the Cons Lydia Colony. My faithful *Benedict* is coming to take you. Today, before the night is over, he will free you of this part of his spirit after reaching the underground world out there." *(Benedict, Levi and others were his faithful Presidents at the time when Antonio was the Chairman. They were spying on Lord de Ros and his loyal ones for Antonio.)*

"And the remaining portion?" asked Paras.

"The remaining portion of Robrelco Fero's spirit is imprisoned with the souls of Rihon and his four companions. The liar, Rihon spread the news that Robrelco Fero had been released from their souls and imprisoned on the bodies of other Presidents. And those loyal Presidents of Rihon are hidden in such a place where the Devil cannot reach even in his wildest dreams. But the Re-built Tune required to complete this process has been destroyed with Daarck's death."

"If that is the case, how will Robrelco Fero be released from our souls, and who is this Daarck? And what are you eventually trying to prove by provoking the Devil family?" There was a probability that the questions of Paras who was speaking anxiously could become endless."

"Anyways. Antonio said, "Before your curiosity to know what all is going on becomes deadly…" He paused a little and continued, "In very ancient times, thousands of years ago, the matter was very different. At that time the 'Master Galaxy' was not holding rule over all the six galaxies named L1 to L6 that are situated on our local cluster. That was an era when not only the contact of the creatures of one galaxy with another galaxy was extinct but they were also totally ignorant of the existence of many other colonies in their own galaxy and that innumerable creatures resided on its countless planets. The way short term travelers 'common people' are totally oblivious to the existence of Colonies and New-Gods even today. And if that silver age had prevailed, then the fire of turbulence started by the religions of temper would not have been able to destroy the exhilaration of those years."

"The fact that they are not alone in this universe kept on revealing itself in front of those colonies. But just like shopping for the happiness of any relationships irrevocably brings with it the price-tag of persecution, as the relations got established amongst the owners of the colonies known as New-Gods, their hands hidden in closed gloves kept on moving forward for the destruction of the New-Gods of other colonies."

"A mutual relation kept on developing amongst all the colonies of all these seven galaxies. After that as centuries passed, slowly and gradually all the colonies situated on Galaxy L3 where we are currently sitting, got divided into two fanatical groups. One *Vio-Crazy* (*A group of colonies who ruling the residents of their planet in a cruel manner)* and another *Off-Idiotic (A group that providing a governance and creating an environment like heaven for the residents on the planets owned by them.*) Changing the mind-child of the rulers of all the colonies of these two groups being similar to waiting for the birth of a white crow, both these groups started conspiracies to eliminate each other. (*Because the New-Gods of the 'Vio-Crazy' group wanted that the New-Gods of the 'Off-Idiotic' group should be just like them. And the New-Gods of the 'Off-Idiotic' group wanted to make the Vio-Crazy New-Gods kind like them.*)

"The colonies that developed extremely in the scientific and other fields were given rank SP, medium developed were ranked Q and less developed colonies were ranked R."

"There is a stubborn perception that baffles me till date." Paras said, "How the New-Gods who are enjoying the ownership of 15 to 300 or more planets and the special waves arising in the two-three brains possessed by them, would be generating space in their brain for more enjoyment by interfering in the colony of some other New-God..?"

"The mentality of a New-God is a matter of a very high level of nature." Antonio said, "As such there is no sense of guilt in the Vio-Crazys, but over and above that, they think of the Off-Idiotics who think about the happiness of billions of people living on the planets owned by them, as a disgrace to the dignity of the New-God. As per the strong belief of the Vio-Crazys, why should the New-God be deprived of the fun derived from violence and playing with feelings of humans, just for the sake of upgradation of humans who are nothing more than worms that die early? Although on many Vio-Crazy group colonies, like our Cons Lydia Dyaan, Chairmen like me who are partisans of the heavenly-rule also exist. If we take the example of Cons Lydia, then the quality of life of total 165 billion people of all its toy-planets including the Earth depends on the choice of one person named *Lord de Ros (New-God of Cons Lydia)*. If Ros would not have a zest for seeing lives with *'Testing Ones Ability'*, then today the competition to become the best heaven would have been prevailing between his fifty planets."

"And you have to say that the belief of the folks (common people) of this planets owned by the Vio-Crazys, that their good or bad situation is a reaction of their own sins and righteousness is just their imaginary confusion…?"

"The value of this belief does not come into existence before the second stage. The *Mind-Cataclysm-Machine* for the creation of a desired society is available with nearly all the New-Gods. As an example, in case of the Earth on which we are sitting, if even a little change would have been done with Mind-Cataclysm on the thoughts of the cruel dictators who ruined the lives of millions of people, then the pages of history would be dripping with *'laughter'* instead of tears today!"

*

Telon took out a Three D-Pocket–Projector from his blazer and started it. The display of the Presidents' photos started on the screen one after another. As the sacraments of the awakened situation moved rapidly in the form of a dream, the President, in an entranced state, tried to identify the face of the person he had seen with Rihon when he was returning the Book of Bell to him. The slide kept on moving forward and with that, the hope on Devil's face also kept dissolving slowly, gradually into the valley of death.

In the end, the disappointed Devil restarted the slide of the Presidents' photos that had already passed through before his hypnosis session. But it was not so surprising to see that *Levi's (Antonio's loyal President who was spying on Rihon)* face was responsible for the change in the eyes of the President sitting in front of them, than to know that a person hypnotized by *Beelzebub (Devil)*, had impersonated and escaped successfully from his clutches. "Traitorous Antonio…." The Devil roared in a horrifying way.

Before Telon, who was closing the projector, could open his mouth, the emergency tone of the *'Image Machine'* roared. The redness filled celestial area in the pictures sent by the satellite, had moved somewhere far in the distance surpassing the mountain range of Antonio's castle. Seeing the small flames of fire rising on Devil's eyelashes as he observed the candles extinguishing in the chandelier, the skeleton like girl who had come to wake up the President, knocked him off from the shoulder in horror.

The shadow of Devil flying away from there, covering his body with a black cloak, was conjuring up a motion picture of a dead body rising and running away from its funeral.

*

Antonio said. "Many organizations including the Devil Family and Rihon are fighting for their own benefit in this whole mayhem. But my group has only one objective, to release the aggrieved creatures of Earth and many other planets like that, who are trapped in the authoritative grasp of the Vio-Crazy New-Gods, from the brutal clutches of those cruel New-Gods and bestow the gift of a heavenly life to them."

"Why are you not taking the help of some *agency* to do this?" Paras asked. *(There are private intelligence agencies on every Colony that are hired by the colonies to fulfill all kinds of their missions.)*

"This task is beyond the scope of the agencies."

"Antonio, it is very clear that the planets are maintained and survive only through the great and mysterious powers of a New-God. Do you intend to destroy all the planets by rebelling against the New-Gods?" Paras spoke up.

"Huh…" Antonio growled. "The fact is that neither are these New-Gods the owners of the planets and neither the planets are surviving on account of their mercy. They are just self-proclaimed owners. At first glance you feel that these New-Gods have miraculous powers with which this living creation is surviving. But they have only very advanced scientific techniques. They have conducted research on the *Five-Elements (Panchmahabhut)* and have acquired several such powers through which they can protect their planets from disasters like tsunami, famine, earthquake, moving of the Techtonic Plates to some extent. However, the headache to figure out the survival of the existing lives is not meant for the common people but for the New-God. Just imagine if no employee survives, how will it be proved that the owner is actually an owner? These colonies also help the scientists of their toy-planets by inspiring them for new inventions by sending several thoughts in the minds of the scientists without their knowledge. They are the ones who have implanted the ideas of discovering destructive equipment like nuclear weapons in the minds of the scientists. And if something that could give relief to the human race is being discovered at any time, then they stop that as well. Their interference in forming the government that would work wearing the uniform of their intentions in the countries of the toy planets, starting or stopping all the big battles is only to watch the drama created in these planets that would entertain them."

"But Antonio, what do I have to do with all this mess...?"

Antonio spoke up, "And one day, as if there is an end to the sufferings of countless human beings living on planets of the Vio-Crazy group, there was an advent of a person named Daarck on Galaxy L3. He had brought with him a horrible conspiracy like the mission *Walk of Life.*"

"Was it a strategy to shift the inhabitants of the Earth to a heavenly planet of the Off-Idiotic group?" Paras asked with a serious countenance.

"Hmmm… The armies of all the colonies included in the Vio-Crazy group have, are such that it is an impossible task to defeat them with conventional weapons. The way we have discovered this pure energy and are preparing an army of Energy Warriors to kill the Gardi soldiers of Lord de Ros' army, similarly, he had come with a project to prepare entirely new weapons as a resolution to conquer the army *'Fifty Carat'* of colony *'Runcap'*, *'Winmaker'* of *'Nebel Shift'*, Chargeman, and other armies of total 11 Vio-Crazy colonies. That was named Mission Walk of Life..."

"Do you think that I am Daarck...?"

"Not only that, there is every possibility that Daarck's girlfriend Filipa has been transformed into Susan. Everything was going on just fine, the eleven Project-Discs were ready for making eleven different armies. We were equipped to beat the eleven New-Gods of the Vio-

Crazys and bestow the gift of heavenly life to billions of people, and suddenly through the killer-painting Filipa tore Daarck that is you, apart. Yes, the traitorous woman who murdered you was none other than Susan, which means that it was Filipa herself."

Antonio spoke further after a short pause, "There are very few men, hardly any, who can comprehend a woman's pretense of false love. But Filipa's love for Daarck actually seemed to be true. I fail to understand why she did this. It is not that she did not know that we are using the Devil Family for Mission *'Walk of Life'* and after completion of the mission our plan was to betray them by imprisoning the Devil with *Devilet-Again*, I had heard her saying a number of times that- *'The creation of my existence is done only for you, Daarck.'* These words are the ultimate statement of love, still don't know why..?" *(Devilet-Again - the one and only book in the world written on the mysteries of the Devil, through which he can be imprisoned.)*

"It is not very difficult to understand." Paras said. "Big wars keep taking place here for one small *asteroid (small planet)* and when the question is of the ownership of eleven colonies, and its countless planets, then why would Filipa not expel Daarck from her way?. As the project discs were ready, she did not require Daarck after that. She also must have preferred to die so that no one could find her after taking rebirth through the ritual. Then in that case how did Susan come to you, and how did you know that I am Daarck and she Filipa? And who is responsible for the rite of my reincarnation?"

"Hardly two years must have passed since that incident in which Filipa killed you and died herself. You and Susan were kept on the Glips-Treatment imported from Colony Metal-Casting which increases the mental and physical growth by twenty-five years within 1.5 years after a new birth. An unfamiliar President suddenly arrived one day with a few days old children. He had to say that the President under whose care these children that is you and Susan were had told him to hand you over to me at the time of his unexpected demise. And also that it is very important to use the *Discovery Copperhorse* on you at the stipulated time. That's because these are Daarck and Filipa only. So that those project discs can be recovered. You were sent to S.O.G. without anyone getting to know about it." *(Discovery Copperhorse Engine- A machine that gives back all the memories of every single second of the last two-four births)*

"It is very risky to make use of the Discovery Copperhorse until the Nerve Strength is not developed to a certain level with the help of a special vaccination course. But anyways, now the time has come. Benedict will release Robrelco Fero from your souls and will take you to the Metal Casting Colony, where the Discovery Copperhorse Engine will be used on you. The Discovery Copperhorse Engine which accurately gives all the memories of past births is only available with New-God 'Lon' of Metal Casting and Colony Nebel Shift on Galaxy L3. After that, the deadly mystery of why Filipa did something like that will not remain a mystery."

Antonio who was preparing to leave just paused as if he had conceived a doubt that they would not meet again after going from here and affectionately putting his hand on Paras' shoulder, he added, "Paras, it is possible that Lon himself is your godfather. At every level and at every time, nature keeps on creating characters that might have the revolutionary bug for astonishing drama. And Lon, the New-God of *'Glee Metal Casting'* Colony and Leader of the Off-Idiotic Group is a classic example of the same. It is said that he was the one who hired Daarck through a deadly Intelligence Agency of the Master Galaxy because Lon is staunchly committed to transforming the planets of all the Vio-Crazy colonies that are there on Galaxy L3 into heaven."

It appeared from the moving muscles of Paras' neck that he wanted to ask something, but words were not getting unleased.

"All this is very complicated." Antonio said feeling pity on him, "Something that is not easy to understand. Although I am trying to make you understand it in as short and easy to understand words as possible. As you are aware, there are total seven galaxies in a local cluster that is present in one corner of this universe. Six galaxies, with names ranging from L1 to L6 and one Master Galaxy that holds a dominant position on each one of them. The Master Galaxy is three times larger than these six galaxies. The ownership of the Master Galaxy is divided between two directors *'Prestige'* and *'Apotheosis'*. Each of the two Directors holds the ownership of three Galaxies. Amongst them, Apotheosis who is the owner of our L3 Galaxy, usually never interferes directly in the regime of governance of the New-Gods, yet in the interest of the Vio-Crazys, if he somehow manages to stop this war, then the entire Walk of Life project of eleven armies prepared after such hard work would have become useless. And hence, along with Project Discs, Daarck that is you had discovered things like the Re-built Tune, Tie-in Tune, Mummy-Ointment and *Transmission Germ*. It was possible to win these eleven Vio-Crazy colonies with the help of these four things without the need to go to war." *('Transmission Germ' – A recult-mapping virus that could give an identical Aura-Structure of any one individual for a few hours to another individual)*

Antonio started speaking quickly as the strange voices started at the foothills, "During the time the Tie-in Tune is played on the violin, the body and soul of the individual standing on the magic plate melts through its sound waves and gets imprisoned with the soul of the other individual. It was our plan to discreetly deceive the New-Gods into listening to one of the sensational tunes of the violin and imprison them straight away by kidnapping them. Nobody would even get a whiff of where they disappeared. And after that, releasing them again with the Re-built Tune, the bodies of our loyalists had to be exchanged with those eleven New-Gods with the help of the Mummy-Ointment, whose characteristic is that it exchanges the bodies of two individuals. Now during that time, our loyalists introduced in the bodies of the New-Gods would be transferring the colonies on our names, the Master Galaxy would check if they are the genuine New-Gods or not through their Aura Print. and the Transmission Germ is that thing that can give an identical Aura Structure of any one individual to another. With that we were going to give the Aura Structure of the New-Gods to our loyalists. But the way we did not get any support from the favorable luck right from the opening of the action, before we could make use of the Tie-in Tune on Lord de Ros and imprison him after going to Mahanabh, the tune reached him and Ros re-programmed his body in a way that the tune would not have any effect on him. Now, in order to imprison the re-programmed body, we prepared a spell book named *'Contrus Affair'* with the help of the great *'Word Scientists'* of the Master Galaxy. It was decided to re-program Robrelco Fero's body and test the spells of *'Contrus Affair'* on him, but before the test could start, Rihon and his companions attacked and snatching the Contrus Affair, they imprisoned Robrelco Fero. The strange thing was that, one part of Robrelco Fero's soul could be imprisoned by Contrus Affair into the Book of Bell and the rest with the souls of Rihon and his companions through the Tie-in Tune. The *spells (incantations)* to release the part in you and Susan is available with us. And the part that is imprisoned with the souls of Rihon and his companions can be released only with the Re-built Tune which was known only to Daarck..."

They looked towards each other with the terrifying sound of a blast that took place outside.

"Remember Paras, since a part of Robrelcofero's spirit is within your's and Susan's bodies, you will now have to grapple to stop yourself from becoming dangerous. Saying that, he quickly put a Surahi (glass bottle), in Paras' hand. "This is the Mummy-Ointment, the thing that exchanges the body of an individual with anyone."

"But Antonio, where is Benedict taking us...?"

"This time is scarce, Paras, that cunning Rihon has a bird named *Dhwanibodhak (Sound-imbiber)*. Whenever any kind of paternoster is applied on the Book of Bell, this extraordinary bird instantly grasps the chanting of these sound-waves in whichever part of the world it is..."

"But Antonio, Elvis…" Before Paras could speak further, a second blast took place." He ran.

*

Galaxy L3, towards thirty thousand light-years North from the Galactic bar. On 'Climate Canopy', a home planet of Colony Cons Lydia (On Galaxy L3, they refer to the planets like Earth that are occupied by common people as 'Toy Planets' and their own resident planets as 'Home Planet')

"Emergency conference. Subject- Regarding the Book of Bell that has been emptied. A large amount of radioactive light had been seen in the sky at some location in Northern India on Earth." These words coming from Antosa struck again and again in the minds of Chairman Rihon and his three Presidents. They usually made use of this network only to send messages to each other through thought waves, which was limited only to the five of them.

After a few minutes in the video conference room, Rihon placed the pictures captured through the satellite on the desk and removing his coat, he straightened his blonde (golden) hair hanging down up to his waist.

"Can it be a nuclear reactor leakage?" Asked Leonid, speaking from the last of the four screens opposite him.

"There is no nuclear leakage. This is a catastrophe of that bloody book… The atomic plants of any country are miles away from this jungle." Another President spoke up, "Can we send some of the Gardi soldiers there before a report of some radioactive material existing around that location comes in? In case they are not busy with some specifically important work?"

"There is no need to be perplexed." Rihon said, "Before I personally meet the team reaching there in eleven minutes, let me just check Dhwanibodhak's cage."

"Oh! Our miraculous Chairman and his magical tricks."

Rihon switched off the conferencing equipment. Coming into the sitting room and moving the desk in the adjacent small library, he reached between the rough walls after climbing the circular stairs. The Dhwanibodhak bird having supersonic hearing powers to hear sounds of frequencies up to 55,000 Hertz per second, raised its neck slightly above the floor.

*

Galaxy L3, Draco Asterism based S.O.G.

"Ultimately, Robrelco Fero is now looking through someone else's eyes." Luiciano's treacherous eyes were swiftly moving all around while talking on the phone in the corridor lined-up with rooms. "The loathsome Dervil had manipulated Elvis into going to Antonio in search of the Book of Bell. But my Lord, the Intelligence of *'Cons Lydia'* is running quite slow here due to some weird cause. Otherwise Antonio, who has hidden on one of Earth Eleven's planet Earth, would have been found long back. His location has been sent to *Gosha (A guard of Lord de Ros).*"

"Where is Luiciano's murmuring going on...?" *'Dervil'* who had suddenly appeared in a way that would surprise even the ghosts, stood there extending his hand.

"Elvis' mum's," Luiciano said as he gave the phone in Dervil's hand and calmed down within a fraction of a second.

"I should say Hello to her," saying this, Dervil put the phone to his ears. "Hello, Senora Barrison."

"Como Estas, Senor Dervil!"

"He recognized the voice..!! Shocked on hearing the voice of a girl when he had expected it to be Lord de Ros, Dervil laughed pretentiously and the diamond embedded into the cross carved on his tooth, sparkled.

*

"This is the address-code of Asteroid 'Bobcat' which has to be given to Benedict. The *airbus (A small spacecraft)*, is in the Eastern Chamber and the voice command is *Dark-Matter (The voice password used to start the airbus)*. The airbus will drop you at the South Pole *S. Station* within sixteen minutes. In a shocking mental excitement, Antonio put a bag in Paras' hand. Don't be impudent to return here even by mistake. Benedict will be there to receive you. Elvis, you are going back to the S.O.G." *(S. Station - An intermediary to travel anywhere in space. Address Code – A code to be dialed in the S. Station to go to any selected planet in space. More information about S. Station has been given in the forthcoming chapter)*

The sky was bewildered to see human shaped vultures hovering about.

"And you?" Susan asked.

"I will have to deal with those savages. But don't worry; my life is essential for those monsters. I'll surely meet again." Saying this, Antonio held Susan's face in his hands as she disappointedly glared at him and kissed her on her forehead. "Both of you, you and Susan, are now a Live-Key to open the door to the world of Sorrows or Happiness. Before Antonio, glaring with eyes that could get mysteries accepted, could finish his talk, Susan feinted and fell down as a result of arteries that had become breathless from relentless running. Before *'Cassia Soferra' (A special alcohol having medicinal properties to stop the soul of Robrelco Fero from controlling them)* mixed with precious metals, could be poured between her lips, *Clesta's (Telon's agency)* rubber bullets laden with a drug to make one unconscious, clashed with Antonio's cloak that had the characteristic of Ballistic Nylon. "Run awaaaaay... If you want to be saved from a life that is spent crying out for death..." Turning towards Paras, Antonio screamed threateningly and moved forward towards the Devilishs.

Antonio's Castifo (A high speed laser gun of the Gardi-Force) was pouring havoc as he was slowly getting defeated in an attempt to fight against the Lord of Evil (Devil). Electrical Whips (Laser-Beams) were passing through the bodies of Clesta's agents tearing them apart. Even then, currently, the enemy was better. Seeing massive damage of his agents, Telon who had become ferocious, drew out a 'Metal Blast Rifle' to open fire on Antonio but before his murderous intentions could be fulfilled, Devil's deadly claw tore his neck apart. Telon continued to have difficulty in breathing. His eyes continued to shrink. He pressed both his hands on the blood flowing from his neck. After death took away the collapsing Telon, his murderer moved towards Antonio and seized him in his arms.

Elvis who was standing duty folly, slowly moved backwards... "Coward..." With her widened eyes and sore throat, Susan shouted at the escaping Elvis.

A divine fairy who had come with Lord de Ros' Gardi-Force was standing in front of the Devil who was proceeding towards Paras. The éclat of *'Arina'* dressed in skin-tight blue leather garments was more lethal than her battle-skills. Paras was a little sad with the thought that he would now have to fight with her. Looking at the Gardi soldiers moving forward with boxes of *Aakrid (A sacred fish that weakens the powers of Devil)*, when the Devil moved backwards like the end of the wicked was near, Antonio's helpless mind trapped between the binding layers rising from Devil's body, was running like a deer to give Paras the last moment's final hint. Suddenly he signaled step-by-step towards the Book of Bell's chest that was lying on the ground, the trees and the direction in which Elvis had run and with that, the *'Majesty of Darkness'* disappeared with Antonio.

It was possible for them to get just about one minute or so to take the benefit of the deadly fight between the Gardis and Devilishs in order to escape from Arina. Paras forcefully picked up Susan who was using all her might just like a witch to save Antonio, and ran towards the airbus. The shock of losing a loving father had broken the walls of the reservoir in her eyes and that waterfall of tears was wetting Paras' arms.

*

"What exactly had happened over here..? I am asking you like a monk." Rihon took off a light purple colored brocade overcoat and sat on the ground near the struggling Rayan.

"Since how long was Antonio hiding here? Anyways, let it be, I am only interested in knowing who else was staying here with him? I promise you, I will leave the Chairman position if I am unable to convince our owner *Lord de Ros* to include you in Gardi-Force."

"A person expecting such mysteries from an employee becomes a Chairman...! A very clear sign of the downfall of Cons Lydia..." Rayan's deadly sarcasm as he slid backwards on his back proved to be unbearable. Rihon's eyeballs changed, Rayan had very few moments to run away from the painful life he was about to get from now onwards. He got up and ran towards the valley. Paralyzed with the stroke of Rihon's eyes, Rayan suddenly put a hand in the pocket as if he had remembered something.

Seeing Rayan remove a small *'Killer-Painting'* from a leather wallet, Rihon's face lost the readily available self-confidence. Rayan's glance had collided with the killer-painting before he could reach close to him.

Abusing his helplessness, he kept on kicking Rayan's distorted dead body for quite some time. Finally, vigilantly, in a way his glance should not fall on it even by mistake, he pulled the killer-painting lying on the eyeball that was hanging outside, and folding it, kept it in his pocket.

*

One week later. in a small town near Ladakh in North India.

Knock, knock...

"Oh..." After looking into the CCTV and swiftly opening the door, Elvis' open lips instantly started doing sit-ups again, "Who gave you the address of this tower?" Quickly pulling Susan inside from the freezing cold and atrocious darkness, he closed the door.

The dam of tears from Susan's eyes could be seen breaking down in the dim light and walking a little hastily, she embraced Elvis. "Paras, is no more..." She said in a stammering voice.

"What had happened to him?" Elvis asked, as he separated Susan.

"According to Antonio's advice, we took the airbus and reached the Southpole's Dummy S. Station. Benedict was not present there to receive us. We waited there for him for almost three hours. We had no other option but to come back. Paras had already been badly injured at the time of escaping from Antonio's castle. A farmer gave us shelter in a town situated approximately about ninety kms away from here. He could not live anymore."

"How did you get to know about this place?" Moving his eyes around the inside portion of a windmill structure constructed in the nineteenth century, which had now been transformed into a tower to steal energy, Luiciano repeated Elvis' question. He was sitting on a chair, a little distance away. It was not difficult to identify the suspicious expression that was there in his eyes for Susan.

"There in a small local newspaper, I saw some totally dried up, blackened corpses of people who died suddenly as a result of some weird illness for the last few days in this area. I understood that they were the assassinations done by this tower."

"Oh yes, this tower has been started just a few days back. Some people along with First Shadow had been killed. The technical deterioration due to the disorder in Energy Amount Functioning has now been rectified. Now this tower will steal human energy only in the quantity where they will not feel anything more than a little weakness."

"Just one minute, Susan, Elvis, will you come out?" Luiciano said, going towards the door, and stopped as Elvis started talked in a private language. After both of them talked for about five minutes or so, and as Luiciano went away, Susan said, "I have left some of Paras' things there. The road is not good. It will be morning before I can get back here."

"There is no need for you to go alone. I'll come with you." Elvis said.

"No, that kind man has come with me. He is standing outside." Susan moved the curtain from the window, a man looking like a primitive was staring at the door from an old Roadster.

"Isn't a farmer with a *Roadster* looking strange?? Anyways, I'll wait for you." *(Roadster- An open vehicle without the back seats)*

*

The radiance of a night between the full moon and no moon nights had dispersed out there. Pretending as if she was totally ignorant of Elvis' spies following her, Susan knocked on the door of the grass warehouse and stood there without looking around her.

"Will this run-down airbus be able to take us to Romania within an hour or not?" Quickly getting inside as Paras opened the door, Susan said, pulling the cover from the airbus and throwing it aside, while she started gathering the luggage.

"What has happened?" Paras asked as he started switching off the lights.

"Destiny is clement on us." Susan said as if she had found a treasure, "Luiciano was right there, Elvis thought that I would not know that private language. After one hour a special devilhood gathering is going to take place in the *'Romanian Palace'*. Special for that because Devil himself is rendering his presence in that Gathering. There, *Benedict* is going to meet, what was the name of that scoundrel, yes Dustin. Benedict will have an upside down cross made on his right cheek." Don't know if we will be able to reach Benedict before this Book of Bell's catastrophe stuck to our throats will take away our lives? *(Benedict- Antonio's person, who had not come to receive them. One who was going to release them from Robrelco Fero's spirit.)*

Taking a sip from one of the last two left over bottles of the alcohol that stopped Robrelco Fero from dominating them and taking their lives, Paras extended it towards Susan and said, "Dustin- A Chairman of the Nebel Shift Colony," and going near the window, he peered far with the *Infrared-Stealth (A binocular with which one can see at night)* and continued, "Don't you find it strange that Elvis let go of the *'Book of Bell'* that he had in his hands and especially you, so easily...? This is one of his tricks." Saying this, Paras diverted his attention from Elvis' agents who had surrounded the place from outside and dialing a number, he started the airbus.

"Hi Eddie..."

"Hi." Eddie said, "See Rihon has currently hired total six agencies to search for the *'Book of Bell'*. Among them, the owner of the agency exploring on the Earth is *'Kendrick'*. Send Elvis' location to Kendrick and the entire Gardi Force including Rihon will be chasing him within just a few minutes. I have informed Kendrick that this boy of Luciano was present at the time of the Book of Bell's experiment."

"Thanks. We will be meeting in a few hours." Saying this, Paras disconnected the call and when he connected to the number given by Eddie, Susan said staring at him with a strange look, "Are you doing this because you feel that some day after, they winning over Cons Lydia, when Elvis will gift a planet at my feet, I will go to him, right?"

"Stop talking nonsense." Paras said and added immediately, "Oh not to you Mr. Kendrick. Kill that mongrel Elvis and bury him in that tower itself. But tell Rihon that the immortality of the Gardi soldiers is now useless in fighting against him." Saying this, when he threw the satellite phone at one side, Susan said,

"What is the need for you to mess around with these people?"

"It is necessary, sweetie. I would not have done it if it wasn't." Saying this, he loudly read out the report calculated by the airbus, "At maximum speed the approximate time to reach Romania that lies towards 44/25 North 26/06 East in the European Union is seventy-two minutes."

He flew the airbus straight out bursting the top of the warehouse into the sky at ultimate flying speed. Before

Elvis along with his agents could understand anything, their small *'airbus'* had disappeared from sight.

*

North Romania

Standing near the main gate of the royal palace just vaguely, for sometime, they kept staring at the palace. Fire was burning on the waist high brass stands everywhere in the large garden in front of the palace and in the upper balconies.

Their walk slowed down a little, looking at the Devilish checking the invitation passes at the palace entrance.

"All this is going on exactly on time." Seeing the expensive cars still arriving there and stopping on the porch, Susan said and added giving a charming smile to the man standing on the left side of the high door. "Mr. Benedict is coming here with it," Without even waiting to see the guard's reaction, Susan caught Paras' hand and pulled him inside. However, Paras could not stop himself from turning to look behind him. The man, stopping the gateman following them to check the pass by putting a hand on his stomach, gave Paras a weird smile. Paras looked there but the right cheek of the man dressed in a black suit was totally clear.

They went into the adjoining room where the gathering was going to take place and picked up two black cloaks wrapped in plastic.

"Witch, tell the truth, had you ever imagined becoming a woman having two men at once..."

After staring for a couple of seconds at Paras who was wearing the black cloak from the feet upto the head, and seeing his face now shrinking and becoming lifeless just like her own, Susan said, "No but I hate the men with two women at once for some incomprehensible reasons right from the beginning." Both of them knew in their mind that any moment from the forthcoming moments could be coming with their death message. And hence they were trying to overlook the moment that would separate them forever by talking in a roundabout way.

"And I have forgotten to tell you this, before leaving the tower, Luciano had gestured towards me with his eyes and said that, 'This treasure should not get out of our hands. *Billion Couple* is going to start there in just a few minutes. I did not have any intention to participate in that till now but Lord de Ros is going to set a trap for Malesty.' What is the meaning of that?" Susan asked.

They had now entered the gathering hall. At the opposite end of the hall, a stage, short in height had been erected and the long queues of the Satanics' secret organization standing with their faces towards it were waiting for the ceremony to start.

"Oh, this means that our troubles are going to more increase." Paras said, "So now New-God Lord de Ros will himself be chasing us for the Mummy-Ointment. Antonio has made adequate arrangements for our miserable plight before going. Luiciano might be expecting to use the Mummy-Ointment, given to us by Antonio to strike a deal with Ros. The matter is straight-forward, a New-God cannot be imprisoned without a volumetric war, and hence at the time of this Billion Couple congregation, after inviting Colony *Nebel Shift's* New-God Malesty on *Mahanabh* with some trick and exchanging the body with him through the Mummy-Ointment, the ownership of Two Hundred and Fifty planets in Ros' lap in a single stroke..." *(Mahanabh – Lord de Ros' residence on Cons Lydia)*

"Ssh.. Ssh.. Ssh…" Getting exasperated, one Satanic told Paras to talk softly and when he moved closer to Susan, his ears focused on the sudden frightening weeping that had started from all the six directions of the Queenly-Castle. This was an indication of the Devil's advent. The layers of ebony fog went through the luxurious windows of the Twilight-Chamber and gathered next to the high backed *easy-chair* lying near the fire-place in a corner of the hall.

*

'Billion Couple' had just dispersed at ten thousand light-years North-west away from the Solar System, on *'Area M21'*. The New-Gods of the Vio-Crazy group Lord de Ros, Malesty and their Chairmen were moving swiftly towards the *'Reaction Lounge'* with the New-Gods of other *dominions (colonies)*.

When *'Lon'*, the New-God of the ultra-developed Colony *'Glee Metal Casting'* of the group of benevolent New-Gods was seen coming towards them, Gosha said bending towards *Arina's* head, "It is being said that Lon has recently developed such a technique that his body can move at a speed of sixty-five thousand kms. per hour like a chemical rocket,." *(Arina – Lord de Ros' commander-in-chief.)*

"I will let you know if I need a guide." Arina moved away giving a scornful look to Gosha who was transmitting a perception of proximity.

Shaking hands with Lon, Malesty said, "Incessantly, endless, even though it may be benevolence, doesn't the indication of boredom that lies in its basic characteristic make you vomit?"

"Honestly speaking, looking at this world from a gaming perspective, yes." Dressed in a dark blue colored hunky-dory suit Lon winked and said, "But in the end, the nature of goodness should dominate us." His eyes were cherry colored. He was currently in a shining transparent form to protect his physical body from potential injury. Everyone followed him below the open sky full of wandering bright groups of the nebula.

Malesty started with the topic that was chosen to organize this Billion Couple convention, "On a planet of the Vio-Crazy Group, A whimsical person demanding to build a paradise on that planet by establishing a cult, and In the form of its rebellion he will make millions of toys (common people) to remain childless by taking an oath and the Master Galaxy will get upset with such tactics and remove the New-God of that colony and hand over that colony to an Idiotican New-God..? Never… The Master Galaxy is just pretending to be impressed with the Billion Couple event and enjoying the thrilling battle of the Off-Idiotics against the Vio-Crazys. Otherwise it does not have any interest in establishing the good governance." *(Some time ago a person named Kundali had started a weird cult on a toy planet Opti-L. Making the invisible natural powers responsible for all the small and big hardships and chaos in life, he had influenced millions of couples to revolt against these all powerful elements by remaining childless till the time a sorrow-free environment like that in the heavens does not get created on his planet. His success was unbelievable. As such this convention organized to solve any kind of issues of the New-Gods on Galaxy L3 was referred to as a 'Joint Colony Organization' but here since this unique case was going on it had been given the Billion Couple pseudonym.)*

A smile kept playing on Lon's lips during the entire narrative. "You also do the same thing by instigating people to fight against each other on your planets." Lon showed a mirror to Malesty in an ardent voice.

Ros' attention was on the colors changing in the pupils of Lon's protectors. The world's smallest computer. These advanced organisms had created a laboratory in their body with gene editing and development of new cells. Not only would it send the report of the detected bacteria and virus infections transitioned by air, water and food to the Pupil-Screen, but it also knew how to create disease resistant molecules to fight against complex organisms. The Pupil-Computer of every *Protector (Army)* was connected to the main server, which operated with their thoughts. The big buttons producing invisible rays of protection on the surface of the body were melting in the belt on the neck. Ros was mentally bowing down to these patrons of genetic engineering.

Coming and standing in front of him, Lon's Chairman *'Simbal'* said, "Shuttle is ready." Displaying the humor of the Idiotic governance, Lon laughed and waved his hand in farewell to the New-Gods of both the groups while Ros quickly turned towards Malesty and said, "Perverted, abusive language is constantly being heard from the beauty of the Mahanabh. And the Mahanabh secured by a majestic temperamental nature will continue to function until it does not receive appreciation from someone like Malesty.

Dangling a carrot in front of Malesty, Ros bent towards Gosha and said softly, "You will find the Mummy-Ointment from that lad Paras soon, isn't it?"

Shivering with the thought of him searching for Paras in a deplorable condition on the innumerable planets of the many colonies of the six galaxies, Gosha warned Ros with his eyes that he was rushing up. However, just like the intoxication of some other world, Ros' impatience had made him helpless. The *'Take-Off Strip'* of Channel S. was not too far away now and Ros wanted to ascertain it was done before they reached it.

"I am eager to welcome Malesty on Mahanabh through the gift of the Gardi-technology...!" Ros said.

"A lot has been heard about Mahanabh." Hearing the name of the Gardi Technology, affirming to Ros' expectations, Malesty's melted smile yielded a cheerful effect. He said, "But on this occasion, I want to decorate time with favorite colors. If you are offering this monopoly thing, then you must be expecting some invaluable thing in return?"

Ros said, "If great Malesty is eager for the presentation of the gift, then I will look forward to seeing the latest *Discovery Copper Horse Engine* on Mahanabh." (Discovery Copper Horse Engine- An implied memory consciousness device that bring back all the memories of the previous births.)

*

As always, even today, mysteries of undiscovered powers were hanging down from Devil's fluttering fleshy face. To acquire which such powers, numerous secret Satanic cults, on innumerable planets, are perpetually vying to find the solution to different types of Devilish riddles everyday. As a famous personality from a devoting clique of a creed giving the credit of his success to the Devil, in whose Palace this gathering had been organized, came forward and welcomed Beelzebub with a Black Rose, Susan said softly in Paras' ears, "Where should we search for Benedict in this crowd of Satanics?"

Susan delicately elbowed Paras at his waist who was glaring at the man who helped them inside and was now settling down behind them slowly, said again," You start from the front row, I am going on the back side."

Before the whispering could start to connect the Devil's presence exhibiting some specific reason who generally ignored many such gatherings, the high door behind the stage opened imitating the droun...droun... noise of innumerable toads. A fear destroying frank-incense made of bear's fat was burning in the hands of the rich Devilish community who stood facing the immobile platform on the other side of the hall. Every Satanic was dressed in a black muslin cloak. Except for a Satanic standing in the front_row, there was a falcon-like bird in his hand. The bird's eyes were moving all around the hall as if it was brought to visit a *'Museum'*. Its blue colored cheek had been pierced and a small sphere was swinging like a pendulum at the edge of the chain hung onto it.

The dimly lit talismanic hall shook as the boot's soles made of horseshoe thumped on its maple flooring. Appearing from the door behind the platform, as the *Apostate Speaker* opened a book and started the *'Holy-Corrupt' action (A devilish actus that crushes the belief and religious tendencies present in humans)*, the mob standing in the queue transformed into a pulsating human flow. Removing the mask, Dustin, the Chairman of Nebel Shift had immediately jumped up and leaping on the speaker, he had snatched his book.

As the rapidly-flaring velvet curtains along with the frank-incenses bouncing out due to the stampede, lit up the dimly lit gathering hall, the Satanics enjoying the thrill, quickly grabbed Dustin as well as the speaker and flew towards Terror-Street within those minutes. Paras, who was looking out for Benedict, felt a pointed object pricking his back and in the next instant he lost his consciousness and fell backwards. For a moment before his eyes closed slowly, he saw himself swinging in the arms of the man with the black suit.

*

Lon's (New-God of the Idiotic colony Metal Casting), luxurious space vehicle Daddy's Woolybear flying at the speed of a modern Ion Propulsion Rocket, was making fun of any

Mega City. The aircrafts floating over the innumerable high buildings of this flying city, the roads near the huge lakes and the sodium lamps shining near those roads, the casinos within its atrium, advertisement boards shimmering with neon lights and just about everything... was giving an absolutely firm realization of the peak of luxury and development having been reached.

Seeing a chopper coming towards the direction of Lon's office from the direction of the Focal Point Parks, Lon's transparent body started hiding behind the corporeal molecules.

Simbal brought the person named Kundali who had churned up this Billion Couple mess on planet Opti-L and making him stand in front of Lon, he threw some photographs on his table and said, "That Diaboli Couple through whom Filipa had done the rebirth ritual has been found, but in the form of decayed bodies. We could have gained some information from their brains if the cerebral region of their corpses would have been even in slightly better condition." *(Simbal - A Chairman of Metal Casting's New-God, Lon)*

Nodding his head in bewilderment, Lon said, "You mean to say that having taken the tremendous risk of opposing Apotheosis' policy of not interfering in the modus-operandi of the New-Gods, I should now forget my plan to overthrow those eleven Vio-Crazy New-Gods after getting those Eleven Project Discs prepared through the Mission Walk of Life by someone like Daarck?" I fail to understand how a cunning player like Daarck could put his trust in a woman like Filipa in such confidential matters…!"

"Please have mercy on this old man… What kind of a thing have you blocked me with?" Kundali spoke up in between. His weak and shaking voice was becoming stronger amidst his disbelief. "Am I being given mental instructions? I have never even imagined about such magic. Youth... My youth.....!" He pulled his space suit in excitement.

"You had been made to wear this special attire with the objective to protect you against the life-growth barrier coming from the High Radio Activity of the Galactic Centre." Lon said, removing his suit, "I do not have any particular hope of getting back Daarck, Filipa and along with them the Discs that they have disappeared with. Hence if you are successful in creating one more Billion Couple fruitfully on Earth as on your Planet Opti-L, then there is hope that Apotheosis might give some firm decision against the Vio-Crazys." Lon came forward and gave him a Dragon Fruit to eat. "I hope that you are not angry about our kidnapping you like this!"

"Once again, a leadership of the Billion Couple...? But now I was… gaffer... what is this you have done?"

"The vaccine given to you is capable of cocking a snook to your old age for the next ninety years."

"It's quite delicious. The taste of this is different where we live." Kundali started relishing it under the reversed age cycle's effect.

After some moments of silence, Lon said, "The little bit of Metal Casting technology that you will be given to make the successful Billion Couple that I expect to create on Earth will leave the inhabitants of the Earth with no other option but to believe that it is a miracle. As a result of that, even the educated people will become your devotees along with the illiterate ones. On just one indication from Kundali, millions of followers will commit to remain Childless throughout their lives. It should look as if this is happening in an entirely natural way."

"What did you say first? Earth...?"

"Yes, on one planet Earth, you will be living that memorable period once again by repeating upheaval of the Billion Couple there." Saying this, Lon taking out Metal Cards that looked like playing cards and piled them up on the table. He pulled out one card with a magician's grace and inserted it into the I-Book Drive, after which he typed *Neuron Chip Order of Restricted Agenda Setup*. The first atomic dissolution of the card took place in the process seen on the I-Book screen. After that, with the restructuring of the separated molecules, it was re-created in the form of a small chip.

"Now a compulsory order form will be fitted here." Putting his hand on Kundali's brain, Lon loaded the chip in a Tido Gun and gave it to Simbal.

"Ah…!"

After a slight moan ceased, Lon said further, "This is an order form that you will be able to break only by begging for death. When you will fail to maintain total secrecy of this contract between us that proves the Billion Couple to be a pre-planned conspiracy, this chip fitted in your brain will automatically blow your skull into pieces."

"Are you willing to be bound by this contract in such a terrible way…? Kundali does not even deserve to make such a question seem necessary…"

Pointing towards the door, Lon said to the mumbling Kundali, "Alright Kundali, you are now going directly to the Earth from here. As such, Simbal is presently coming with you. He will make all the arrangements for you to establish a society named *Fight Club of Earth Renovate* in Mumbai city which is towards the East."

*

North India

When Susan's eyes opened, she found herself once again in the same tower where she had come to meet Elvis a few hours ago.

"Do you really think I am so foolish to believe that Paras would not have taught you this common private language of the S.O.G…?" Elvis lifted Susan's chin while she was tied to the chair and added as he looked towards Paras imprisoned right next to her, "I wanted that you and Paras would go to Romania. That's because, I wanted to reach Benedict through you and through Benedict, to the site where those *Body Programming Machines* are kept. Through which Ros and other New-Gods like him have become immortal."

"His father Luiciano will rest only after making him a New-God, think about it Susan? Anyways," after Susan turned away her glance, Paras said further, "I appreciate your passionate love, Elvis. You also should appreciate such feelings that Susan has for me. Instead of winning over this Earth by stealing the energy of a few million people and then gifting it at Susan's feet, it is easier to forget her. If you cannot become soft towards another woman, how can Susan be at your side?"

"Uh.. Huh… Even though you see feelings in this deceitful woman, she is only in love with herself." Elvis said.

"Even someone who loves herself so much would never display such cowardice as to run away from Antonio castle, Elvis. I hate you." Thorns, like that of a penguin, had grown up on Susan's tongue.

"If I tell you that Antonio is still alive and Luiciano can certainly help you reach there… But you will have to come with me. Then you will feel that I am negotiating with you. But I am actually saying this because this orphan, whom you have chosen, is not at all eligible for you." He said looking at Paras as if he was a worm.

Paras felt like going near Elvis and twisting his neck, but the bonds were rigid.

"The end of these discordant relationships is at least not near." Susan turned off her face.

Before one more crooked smile could emerge on Elvis' face, Paras saw the man with the black-suit from Romania who had helped them get inside the palace, coming down from the top floor. Giving Paras a smile, he gave a Low-Light Polarizing Microscope in Elvis' hand and signaled towards the right window. Elvis moved the curtain to one side and peeped outside. The uncontrollable crowd advancing with burning torches from the direction of the new streets made on the town's boundary had reached up to the tower compound. Elvis removed the binoculars from the side of the mob smashing their hands on their chest like hammers and moved it towards the right hand corner. Finally *Seagram* that Kendrick had been waiting for came and stood there in the frightening influence of this catastrophic faced night.

Reaching Seagram's descending glass, Kendrick said to Rihon who was seated inside, "All three of them are inside the tower right now. Apart from Rayan, these three also were present near Antonio during the time the Book of Bell's experiment was conducted."

"Not even one of them should die." Rihon said.

Kendrick spoke, "The Devilishs have made a bullet-proof jacket of the town residents. *Titus (A member of the Devil family)* has instigated the town residents and brought them here. He told the town residents that- *'Deaths of one citizen after another are taking place because of one Dibukk who is hiding in the tower.' (As per the Jewish mythology, it refers to a malicious possessing spirit of a dead person who moves around in search of someone else's body)*

"Hmm... The fools feel that I will not attack this tower directly in order to save the lives of these *toys (inhabitants of the Earth)*, the responsibility of whose protection is mine?" Rihon asked descending from Seagram.

"This civilization of your planet Earth, living in the superstitious techniques…" Pausing for a moment, after glancing at Rihon's exclusive colored collaret exhibiting the respectable position of the Chairman, Kendrick continued with a stammer and with eyes seeking forgiveness. "Instead of witch-craft, destructive magic or an epidemic which was assumed to be responsible for the ruined and broken down bodies of the victims passing from the vicinity of this tower, the source was actually some kind of *Occultism (Mysticism)* that was at work…" Saying this, he quickly flashed the search report in the air.

"There on the top of the tower, an antenna with the competence to tow human energy has been planted. Any person or group coming in its range withers and falls off like a dry leaf within a second. This *'Power Tuber'* Electrical Attraction Antenna fitted on the rooftop of the building builds up an overwhelming magnetic field within itself. These electro-magnetic waves play the role of Energy Transporters. After the energy stolen from the humans is loaded in the body of the suspect in the bottom level of the building…"

Lifting a hand to say enough, Earth Eleven's new Chairman Rihon moved forward to take the report.

"Finish off all this soon. I do not want the residents of our toy-planet to notice any miraculous events generating their surprised exclamations that would result in the reduction of points and consequently taint the tenure of my regime." *(According to a new order of the Master Galaxy the practice of giving points to every colony had been started. As per that, if due to any activity done by the New-God, his Chairmen, Presidents or any ordinary members of the colonies which would reveal the existence of the colonies would be revealed in front of the common residents of the toy planets, or else the activity that appears to be a miracle to the common people, with any such event the points of that colony would be instantly reduced. And as a result of this transgression, arrangements had been made for punishment that could uproot and throw off the New-God of that Colony.)*

Hidden far away in the jungle the Satanic Titus aimed Rihon on target in the long-range rifle binocular and pressing the high-frequency *Ear-spot (A cell-phone communication unit)* a little more, he said, "My Lord, Elvis' bastard Meriano has seized Paras and Susan and brought them into the tower just some time back."

Devil said, "That crook Rihon has blocked all the S. Stations of Earth. We are currently on '*Pendigyunra 06*' *(An asteroid of the Devil)* and since it has to be reached there by *Dummy (Dummy S. Station)*, it is feared that this will turn out to be a useless trip. *(The Devil meant to say that there was a possibility that it would take them six minutes more to reach there and before they could reach, the Gardi soldiers would already have seized Paras and Susan and gone away from there.)*

After reaching close to the tower, when Kendrick raised his hand giving a Gardi-soldier fighting about 150 feet away on the front, an order to fire a missile on Elvis, Titus shredded his fingers into pieces with a rifle. Half of Kendrick's scream echoed whilst the rest was swallowed by the missile blast. Elvis' agent Meriano started sucking the souls of the crowd with the help of the '*Power-Tuber*' that was at the top of the tower. The body of the person on whom the magnetic waves of the tuber fell, dried up and became green. Hearing the screams of the people getting crushed below the crowds running helter-skelter to save themselves from the shining shells, a Gardi-soldier fighting in the first layer of the Mission Area, yelled... "What is this thing…?"

"Healing, a reversed form of healing…" Shouting, his companion briskly fired rockets with the 225 mm. multiple launcher on Elvis. As the right side portion of the tower broke down with an explosion, pushing up the *'Ultra Night Vision Glass'*, Kendrick showed him a thumbs-up sign.

Figthing there against the Gardi-soldiers with an Orbital Strategy, Elvis entered this new doorway and sat down slopping against the wall. As Elvis who looked like the descendant of a wealthy lineage despite his ash laden face, glanced towards his gashed right shoulder and gave Susan a faint smile, *Lessie (Elvis's agent)*, said in a stinging voice, "These damned people are the ones who have got Rihon and his Gardi soldiers here." She quickly opened Susan's bonds.

Before the dripping drops of blood could leave his cheeks, Elvis wiped them and got up. Leaving the compromising demeanor aside, he went and stood outside with a nonchalant attitude as if he was oblivious to something called death. Both his hands could be seen rising upwards as he started the dance of devastation under the effect of the disastrous electrical-thunderbolt emanating from the edge of his hand paws. *(At this point of time, the energy of humans had been loaded in Elvis' body and he had been made an Energy Warrior.)*

The Gardi-soldiers were being consigned to ashes and getting scattered all over the place. A stampede of the city crowd took place amidst their blood showers. The city was oppressed with the screams of the town residents who were throwing the torches and running away. Seeing the bodies being crushed in haste, Elvis came in laughing dreadfully. Since a large portion of the pure energy had almost drained from his body, he was not in a position to continue confronting any longer. And the new convoys of Rihon's Gardi soldiers were still pouring in.

Explaining to his companions to pretend that they were surrendering, he pointed in the direction where the spacecraft hidden below the curtain of bushes on the other side of the wooden bridge was ready for take-off. The spacecraft having a color changing characteristic had now discarded the sky-blue color of the day and covered itself with darkness.

Paras, Susan, Elvis, Lessie and Meriano slowly came out with their hands behind their heads. Looking at the strange birds circling overhead in the sky, Kendrick said "I do not like these birds." Standing beside him, Rihon looked towards the sky and said, "Tamed Pitohuis. The one and only poisonous bird in the world... Hooded Pitohui... Its feathers are also filled up with poison. It pecks with its beak just once and it's over…"

"Kill them… Burn them…" The requiem like uproar of the town residents is echoing. Yet surrounded by several gun-points, they are standing silently with their hands on their necks. Some of the agents are trying to disperse the rally. A torch thrown by one portion of the crowd came and fell near their feet, when suddenly Susan, hearing a beep-beep voice chiming in the *G3-Electrode* attached behind her ear forced her eyes and looked behind towards the jungle. She felt that she again saw the beggar-like man who had been standing in the Romanian Palace with a falcon-like bird. Probably there was someone who intended to capture the information hidden in her brain through the *Thought-Steal* or *Memory-Thief* Machine.

Susan instantly remembered Antonio's words, "The Dark-Matter in which you have been pushed, the audacity to store thoughts and memories in a block devoid of any lock can accelerate defeat." *(The 'Memory-Thief' machine that captures all the memories stored in the human brain from far away, awakens the memories in the form of thought waves by churning the neurons through waves-fire. The powerful receiver of the Memory Thief is capable of receiving such thought waves even at a distance of 950 meters. The G3-Electrode attached behind Susan's ear is capable of creating turmoil in the broadcasting frequency of micro waves of the nerve spot process. As a result of this, the recording that is done by 'Thought-Steal' or 'Memory-Thief' is not converted into a clear language. And in this manner the information hidden in her brain remains safe.)*

The night had now come to be aged. Rihon was instructing the local police chief to submit an investigation report about an attack done by some private army.

"Move…" After an insulting gesture done with the neck by a Gardi-soldier, the agents took the prisoners behind their backs and slowly traced their steps forward. Rihon was about twenty feet away from them when a rocket fired from Devil's war-crafts that had suddenly materialized, blew up Rihon and his Seagram with an ear-splitting explosion. Paras who had become motionless just stood there watching the fragments of Rihon's and Kendrick's body that had spread in the air, slowly and gradually getting connected once again. Susan shook him up.

The ratio of ten Devilishs against one Gardi made Elvis' path easier. One moment he was seen shredding the remaining Gardi-soldiers whereas in the next instant, he was seen somewhere far away. Making way between the catastrophe of the *Castifo (A high speed laser gun of the Gardi-force)* versus the Laser-Dazzler Gun of the Devilishs, when Paras looked at the compass and started running, Susan who was running behind him shouted and asked,

"Do you need to see the direction even while running?"

"Every aircraft is in an invisible mode here. The aircraft's fuel chamber is made of magnet. Hence, right now only the needle of this compass can save us by taking us towards it."

Titus who was pursuing them with a trap-gun, fired impatiently and the net wrapped all around Susan. The tactics applied by both the fighters, Paras and Titus, who were trained at the same institute, S.O.G., were boring. Neither of them was ready to be defeated. In the end, struggling like a pigeon to free herself from the net,

Susan lost her senses thinking that the *tranquilizer gun (A gun that knocks off unconscious)* Titus was pointing at Paras was life threatening. "Elvisss…" she screamed to distract Titus's attention. Titus looked behind, although the one to take advantage of the situation was not Paras but Rihon who had suddenly appeared on the scene. Titus was thrown far off as he was hit on his chest with Rihon's round-kick zooming through the air. Titus hit the butt of the tranquilizer on Rihon's head while he was engrossed in staring at Paras keeping the leg with which he had kicked suspended in the air, and Paras ran towards Susan.

*

"You don't have any idea what kind of mess Antonio has put us in by imposing this Book of Bell on us." Paras said as he started the engine in the cockpit, "It is not just the fifty planets of Cons Lydia, Antonio has not left even any surrounding colony worth living for us. Anyways, Eddie has made some arrangement for us." When the shuttle arrived outside the Earth's atmosphere, saying this, Paras comfortably relaxed in his seat and slowly closed his eyes.

"Antonio would frequently discuss such things that could not be understood," When Susan started talking again after taking a sip of Cassia Sofera, dim lights could now be seen a little away on the landing strip of Morphic, a small asteroid on the Western Asteroid Belt. "Every person finds the manufacturing of their own thoughts to be totally pure and that's where the mysterious games start off. He never accepts that whatever good or bad thoughts he gets are actually playing the role of a puppet-lace. That creates the favorite drama of the puppeteer."

Swiftly descending from the shuttle, they walked towards the S. Station. Susan gave the address-code to the Station in-charge.

Closing the door of the cottage, the in-charge led them across a small ground that looked like a church graveyard, to a high hall that looked like a jumbo-jet service station. Susan looked behind, the in-charge's assistant was drawing their damaged shuttle to the hall.

"Oh my God, really… on another planet, but which is this place…?" Susan asked in an excited voice.

"At the other end of Galaxy L3, One of the few agencies on a planet of the Asteroid Belt named 'Pioneer Mound' is run by senior Eddie of my S.O.G. There is no comparison of his agency in terms of creating fake identities."

"Wow. This somewhat long journey of one hundred thousand light-years with you will be thrilling." Susan said liberating the naughtiness inherent in her nature to play on her face without any impediment, "Antonio had never taken me on the S. Channel journey. I am excited about this journey that contradicts Einstein's theory of no other object in the universe potentially having more speed than the speed of light…!"

"This is not any royal railway. Whose, hours of royal journey, you can enjoy. We will be with Eddie in less than a minute. The Master Galaxy that holds dominion over the galaxies L1 to L6 established a universal travel agency named Channel S. This channel has sweep away the distance between the places. The neighboring galaxy of the L3 galaxy that the residents of your Earth have just found is 54 million light-years away."

The station in-charge now pushed them into a chamber and closed the door from outside. The brown walls of the chamber were absolutely clean. The opposite wall was fully occupied by a camera-lens that had been fitted over it. Apart from that, it was totally empty.

Settling down in front of the camera, Paras continued further, "Anything in the world whether it is a text or a voice message, telephonic video calling or else the human body, each of these things are made from the basic molecules of infinite light. And this camera that is connected with universality has the capability to identify the manner of the basic structures in which each of these things are made. The type of file identified here by this camera is exactly re-constructed at the dialed address-code location, In just a few seconds… As the basic particles are the same in every place. Otherwise, the journey in this infinite universe would have just remained a dream. A closed room is not required for arrival S. Station."

Susan asked, "How long will it take them to find out the location on which planet and in which place we have gone by gleaning the record of the address-code dialed by us from the Channel S. headquarters on the Master Galaxy?"

"In this respect, the Master Galaxy is strict in a terrifying manner. It is almost impossible even for a New-God to procure the record of travelers' arrival and departure from any of the numerous S. Stations of the six galaxies and the Master Galaxy, put together. Now that we have already stepped inside the station, just suppose, if Lord de Ros himself also comes here, he will not be able to do anything more than helplessly look at us from the other side of the door. Yes, if you travel using a Dummy S. Station, then the owner of that S. Station would certainly be able to know which specific location you have gone to."

"The numerous colonies on all these six galaxies, the mysterious New-Gods of these colonies that hold the ownership of fifty to three hundred or more planets and the billions and trillions of inhabitant of the toy-planets who are totally oblivious to all these facts... Don't you find the change, Walk of Life, threatening the existence of these inhabitant, to be an imagination of idiots, *Levi*? I had overheard the whispering discussion of *Dominus Antonio* with a President who had come to meet him secretly." Susan said, "On the home-planets…" There was a click of the Station camera and her consequent words eventually got submerged with their bodies' atoms that were getting separated and floating in the air.

*

The Devilish gang had now returned to Pendigyunra-06 where Shashira, the speaker who had been seized from the Romanian Palace and Dustin, the Vio-Crazy Colony Nebel Shift's Chairman were captivated.

"So… Where have you hidden those Project Discs, Dustin? My *Lord* cannot wait any longer for the ownership of all the eleven colonies together." *Malachi* said in a loud voice. The Devil looked at him and Malachi instantly bowed his head. *(Malachi – A member of the Devil Family)*

Turning his glance from the branch on which the *'falcon'* bird was seated eclipsing the big moon that looked as if it had arisen right near the garret, on the castle, Dustin spoke, "Hmmm... If it would have been with me then wouldn't I have become the New-God of Nebel Shift in place of Malesty by now? Everyone except me and Antonio was killed in that lethal pestilent meeting with Daarck, does not mean that the Project Discs are with me. And that I was the one who killed everyone, including Daarck and Filipa, and became the sole owner of the Discs."

"How…! Means by which finesse that modest girl deceive someone like Daarck who fooled the great Chairman of a colony holding the ownership of two hundred and fifty planets and take away those Project Discs?"

"Bloody hell-borne. That Filipa should go to hell." Dustin said with hiss, "I can put myself at stake, if there is anyone here who is not trapped in her deceptive illusion. One day she suddenly came with *'Daarck'*. Introducing herself and *Daarck*, she said- "We are the owners of an intelligence agency that was based on the Kwaiper Belt but was later transferred to a planet of *'Cons Lydia Dyaan'*.""

Satan turned his face in another direction as if he was getting bored hearing something that was already known.

"This dangerous person Daarck established the Mission Walk of Life by selecting eleven Vio-Crazy colonies including Cons Lydia and gathering each of those Colonies' Chairmen, who were heartily engaged in bloodshed through several conspiracies since ages in order to remove their owners and become New-Gods themselves."

"His horrible plan in his own words…" Saying this, Dustin projected a video on the opposite wall with his field-phone.

Dustin was seen sitting next to Daarck's girlfriend, Filipa amongst the eleven Chairmen who were seated around the round table in Daarck's conference office. Daarck's puzzling voice was heard as if coming from the darkness, "You have been dreaming of becoming New-Gods for centuries. Dreamers who have known my glory, yes, there is not even single day that arises in which they would not be able to see the soil of my threshold on their forehead. He looked towards Filipa and spoke further, "You have been conducting research for decades to penetrate the peculiar security system obtained by your colonies' New-Gods and their armies and prepare the material for their death. I will give you the answers to the questions you have about penetrating the protective layers of your New-Gods."

"And how will it be...?" A man, sitting in front of Daarck asked keeping his head raised.

"I have a special type of *10-6 (A type of conditional agreement)* with the scientists of one of the *Harmony Planets (A home planet is referred to as a Harmony Planet on the Master Galaxy)*. They will help you create such a soldier who will not only be able to fight against the immortal warriors of your New-Gods, but will also be able to win against them. We will make use of the Devil Family to prepare a battalion against the armies of these eleven colonies. The incalculable Satanics residing on the six galaxies will become our troops."

"Oh God...!" Dustin said, "He really had the second part of the book *'Devilet Again'* that was filled with numerous holy-dolls imprisoned in crystal chains. He said that we will imprison the Devil with this book after that. As a result, the question of giving a share to the Devil Family would just not arise. After seeing Devilet Again, it was possible to take an oath for whatever guarantee he had given." Looking towards the falcon bird that was sitting on the branches that had grown on the broken border of the castle, Dustin said quickly, "This falcon-like bird, there in the hands of the wandering vagabond in Romania..."

But Dustin had been late in beckoning. In the blink of an eye, the bird took the shape of a mobile-launcher rocket and piercing through *Shashira's (The speaker who had been seized in Romania)* abdomen with the speed of sound, it disappeared in the darkness on the other side of the castle.

Before the climax of the mysteries being revealed by a beloved victim of failure could come, the audience came with Shashira's dead body into the safety panel of the castle. "This Shashira, who had been hiding in the guise of a *Devilish (Satanic)*, ever since Daarck's death, was the foundation of Daarck's conspiracy syndicate. He was a special man of Daarck." Dustin said with disappointment.

Post the murderous interval that had proved to be more thrilling than Dustin's story, Dustin started once again. "After the Project Discs prepared in the form of this ferocious conspiracy Walk of Life's course of action were completed, a meeting was again conducted at Daarck's place. "It was discovered that pure energy was required to eliminate Ros and his Gardi-Force. The complicated mechanisms of the towers stealing the human energy were developed. An entire plan, on how to remain safe from the sight of the colonies during the time the energy was getting collected, was also laid out. And in the same way, projects were also prepared for the elimination of the other ten New-Gods and their armies who held a totally different security system from one another. And in each of those projects the technology was entirely different from one another."

Dustin paused for a moment to drink from the goblet of wine that Sierra had given him, and spoke again, "A killer-painting has been prepared in our world. I wish I would have exfoliated and seen through this rumor." New video-waves were now being transmitted to the black wall of the castle from his tele-projector. "This was the same conference room, the birth-place of the Mission *'Walk of Life'*. Filipa appeared from the door behind

Daarck's rocking chair. She put one envelope each in front of all the ten Chairmen sitting on the table in a circle, in which she had kept the killer paintings. And she came and sat beside Daarck. The *'Magneto Optical Discs'* on how to prepare eleven different type of armies was lying ready in the center of the table. Daarck's plan was to kill all of us and take away those discs. But the unblessed Daarck lost by trusting Filipa. Filipa exchanged Daarck's and her envelopes in which the killer-paintings had not been kept with mine and Antonio's and coincidentally, the share of the painful moments of death that had to come to us, were endured by Daarck and Filipa." Dustin spoke in a tone as if he was not happy about his life being saved and played the paused video again.

As always, today Filipa did not put the cigarette packet into the pocket without offering Daarck. As Daarck pulled one cigarette and smiled with an undertone of sarcasm, Filipa instructed, "The *map keys* taking you to the locations for accurate implemention of this project are closed in the white envelopes in front of you." She lit the tip of the cigarette with the lighter and picking up the two envelopes lying in front of her, she gave one of them to Daarck. Everyone present there including Dustin opened their own envelopes.

"This weird thing…" Some exclamations that could not be understood were heard and before anyone could understand anything, the fatal imprint of the *'killer-painting'* had passed through their eyeballs and had opened the door that riddance their souls. Dustin jumped forward and pounced, but before his hand could reach, the hidden *'Panama Blockade'* in the table had opened and swallowed the eleven *'optical discs'*. Taking pity on the distorted bodies wallowing with merciless suffering in the chair and on the floor and clamoring for death, Dustin killed all of them one by one and brought an end to their increased suffering. And hence he tarnished the Vio-Crazy nickname acquired by his group in this way.

"From that very moment, it might be this Shashira only who was going around trying to save himself in the guise of a Satanic … the one who might have taken the Discs and run away going through the underground path coming out near the public swimming pool below the conference-hall. It is a strange thing," Dustin exclaimed, "When Antonio and I returned all our backup-discs had disappeared. There was only one left with Antonio. Thanks to which you have been able to prepare the pure energy warrior army. They had been spying on every Chairman right from the beginning of the *Walk of Life*."

"Then the question still same as to where the key to that vault will be right now, in which the Project Discs to confiscate those ten great colonies have been hidden?" Devil asked.

Luiciano, who had been quietly listening in a steady position till now, spoke from one corner, "We are forgetting this, my Lord. This *'X-Out'* conspiracy of Daarck was against the great New-Gods. Wouldn't one of the New-Gods successful in attaining Filipa's loyalty, be the owner of these eleven discs now? Anyways,

Rihon's group is going to be the guest of Mahanabh today. Ros has called an emergency meeting to immediately look out for the whereabout of that ostentatious Paras and Antonio's girl who has suddenly emerged on the scene from who knows where, and bring them from wherever they are."

"And the closing of Rihon's Mahanabh-meeting should be done in a spectacular way, Luiciano." Hearing Rihon's name, Devil said with a tightened jaw.

*

After six hours. Galaxy L3 North, on the edge of the Stellar-Disk, in the Crown-Pok area, Mahanabh Mountain, Lord de Ros' residence…

"A few minutes have passed since Rihon's caravan descended at the arrival station in the foothills of such a measureless Mahanabh mountain whose resistless formation is incomparable and makes the whole world envious with its appalling beauty. They had preferred to get down at the bottom to elicit some pleasure from the journey of this immobile, rocky terrain overflowing with the magical lakes and rivers. And that is what they intended to show as well. They had to wait only for some time. Luiciano's airbus could be seen descending from the sky and raising his neck in the direction of the numerous shuttles flying on Mahanabh, Elvis climbed down the steps of the airbus' ladder and quickly came towards them.

"Okay, coming straight to the point…" Elvis said as he got there, "I do not have any Book of Bell."

Luiciano who had come behind him said, "Gosha is investigating with all his might. But if you can get into the control tower of the Mahanabh and get me Gosha's progress report before he reaches Paras, the Devil Family is not only willing to forget your audacity of imprisoning Robrelco Fero but is also ready to help you become the king of Cons Lydia. In return, the Devil only wants Robrelco Fero who is imprisoned with the souls of the five of you and now with Paras and Susan as well."

"I had captivated Robrelco Fero with the expectation that I will be able to grab something big from the Devil in exchange of Robrelco Fero. But anyways, we will manage with this much help from the Devil for now." Rihon said mounting on the *Dectilon (An animal like a soft fibrous dinosaur)* and with that everyone started mounting up. Apart from Chairman Rihon's four Presidents Damitri, Leonid, Antosa and Ekaksh, the other five attendants also had fortunately got an opportunity to reach New-God Ros' habitat today.

"I will imprison Lord de Ros by the Tie-in Tune. And who is going to be able to stop you from becoming the New-God of Cons Lydia after that." Responding in a creamy voice, Luiciano looked towards the peak where Lord de Ros' massive palace was located. The periphery of the series of mountains spread afar seemed to be endless. The concealing of Mahanabh by the abating evening was like a shying bride hiding her face slowly in the veil. And the volatile fog covering the display of dim captivating colors of that evening was also participating in that impressive competition of elegance. Only the eyesight of someone having a divine vision could reach up to the crown jeweled peak of the mountain.

"If you think that I am insane, then What you said is right. Otherwise, that tune has been with me for quite some time. Wait…" Stopping a Gardi who had rapidly come near him from talking, Rihon said further, "If I would not have doubted that Ros had indirectly sent me this tune and the address on which the testing of Robrelco Fero was to take place, then you wouldn't be talking to the king of Cons Lydia, now..."

"Annihilation… we can hardly stop this tsunami even relaying the volcano hit…!" The Gardi, who had again come near to give the alert of the upheaval in the North American Tectonic plate in the next twenty four hours said.

"A more important issue than saving the lives of some smart toys is currently in discussion here." After sending him away, Rihon turned towards Luiciano again, "And the other fact is that the Re-built Tune releasing Robrelco Fero from our souls is not with me." Saying this, Rihon smiled at the *'Guest Relation Lady'* as he got down from the *'Dectilon'*.

"Chairman Rihon…?" As a young girl standing near the boundary of the lake spoke moving her attention from the guest list, it felt as if shrill wind-chimes waves had spread out with the air. The penchant of appreciation of the beautiful women welcoming those deserving the dignified hospitality was not just superficial. Lord de Ros' guards were negligently walking past Rihon as if they were ignorant of the dignity of his Chairman's position.

But those flirtatiously laughing delicate curvaceous beauties finding several new ways of erotic playfulness with their intellect were bringing forth feminine feelings on their face that were making him forget that negligence.

Gesturing the excited Rihon to remain calm, Luiciano said, "I will play that tune for you in tonight's feast and imprison Ros. If Ros is aware of this tune then the ones whose well-being will be at stake will only be Elvis and me. You just pretend to be ignorant about it till the very end. But yes… it is you who will have to figure out a way to create the magic plate below Ros' throne. *(Any individual can be imprisoned by the Tie-in Tune with the souls of other individuals only to the extent that he is within the limits of the Magic Pentagram Plate.)*

"I will take care of that." Rihon said, and added, looking at that young girl, "We have changed our minds to fly upto the summit. One airbus, please... Quick." The darkness was deepening and with that Mahanabh was continuing to enunciate its heavenly shadow more and more. And hence the rest of the faces were disappointed with this proposal of Rihon.

"I just hope that Elvis reaches Paras, before Gosha arrives." Luiciano said and again under the pretence of enjoying the beautiful scenery, he became engrossed in thinking about the mistakes of the conspiracy.

As if the environment here had become addicted to the heady feeling of appreciation, it was always ready to seek appreciation by regularly assuming new forms in a tireless way. The atmosphere overflowing with rosy winter hues was creating a sense of attachment. On the left side, an all-encompassing vacuum also prevailed in the hundreds of feet deep valley filled with ravines. Small dynamic view points could be seen everywhere with the flames of fire. There was a lake on the right side. Attractive couples in luxurious boats could be seen enjoying pleasure trips as they passed through the *'Wool-grass'* and *'Blue Flag Iris'* flowers.

*

They were passing through thousands of feet high walls of the castle taking them to Lord de Ros' residence, when Antosa said, "Aren't we forgetting to take the violin, are we…?" A salty precipitate had burst forth from the high stoned walls and attentively beholding the mysterious words emerging from that salty precipitate, everyone looked towards Antosa as he said this and chuckled.

Once the butler had taken off the boxes of Aakrids, they settled down in front of the scanner.

'Identity Confirm'. After the *'Aura Print-match Scanner'* had confirmed their identity based on the specific imprints of their individual aura, they entered the enormous Basilica, where Ros, dressed in a dark brown overcoat, was gossiping amidst the crowd of moody entertainers who had been brought from different places. Probably no one there liked sharp lights. The huge room lighted with lamps spreading fragrance for controlling the mood, presented an image of conservatism having forcefully covered itself with modernism. *(Moody entertainers – Individuals making the ambience vibrant with their eminent styles.)*

Ros got up and came in front of them. "You are welcome…" He said. The face shining with the brightness of thousands of stars in the eyes, to define which the word *power* had been discovered, was welcoming them in a speech overflowing with reverence and guestship. All faces had bowed down in front of that. Although, there was a coagulation of the valuable things of many planets, the prime aspects of the Basilica's attraction were the antique and unearthly things.

*

"Sorry..." Antosa said coming and sitting at the dinner table when the delicious finger licking banquet was almost over.

"hunm…" After Ros removed his hesitation with a slight gesture of his neck, Antosa bent near Rihon and talked a little bit.

"There is an emergency." Rihon said looking at Ros, "The President of the Nation on *Coolen (A toy planet of Earth Eleven)* has lost his mind. If his thoughts are not interfered with right at this moment, then a nuclear war will be about to end there within three hours or so."

As soon as Ros raised a hand to grant consent to Rihon who was contemplating his mood while Ros enjoyed the sapor with relish, Rihon got up and went away.

With a thumping heart, he reached the parlor to make the Magic Plate below Ros' throne. "But if the meeting-place gets changed, then who knows for how long the aspiration to become Cons Lydia's emperor would remain buried in the valley of disappointment." Thinking about this, Rihon instantly stood still. But now, he did not have the time to bother about the surprise. The door that opened with Ros' distinguished footprint identification was open as if particularly welcoming him.

He thrust Ros' seat aside. And engaging one hand to pull out the Magic-Plate contour from his waist, he used the other hand to remove the carpet. "As if the scene that emerged on moving the carpet was a reflection raising a curtain from the mysteries of the scene of creation, he was compelled to sit down on Ros' high throne to maintain his balance. After sticking there like an iguana for quite some time, he put the map of the Pentagram Plate back in his pocket. Adjusting the seat in its original position, he started marching directly towards Mahanabh's control tower.

*

In the parlor's late night feast, as the other four Chairmen stared at the attendants who had come in with Rihon in a curiously culminating glance, Rihon who had entered hurriedly directly slid towards Luiciano.

"I did not see any specific reason not to grant this meagre wish of those five Presidents from my dominion, whose loyalty I have heard is worth appreciating..." Giving a fake smile to the mumbling Ros, Rihon bent forward towards Luiciano's ear, "Those fugitives Susan and Paras are currently on Colony Studium. Someone named *'Eddie'* from S.O.G. is helping them. Gosha is just preparing to leave because they are not going to live any more now. How will Eddie be able to guess that Paras was compelled to board the vehicle of Kendrick's agency to reach his asteroid? Poor Eddie, he will never again be able to help anyone."

Luiciano immediately turned towards Elvis, "Isn't it taught at the S.O.G. that even after abolishing the entire *'Flight Transponder'* series, the vehicles of such Intelligence Agencies are also possibly equipped with a *Hidden Black Box* through which their location can be easily traced. *(Hidden Black Box – A device that broadcasts a coded identity in response to the enquiry related signals via S. Channel)*

Elvis said shrugging his shoulders, "In the situation, when it is necessary to escape for survival, the mind might not even be able to keep so much caution." And looking towards Ros he got up instantly. Glancing towards him with permission seeking eyes, he bowed his head slightly in farewell.

*

After ninety minutes. Galaxy L3, Paras' new residence on one of Colony Studium's planet Opdrazen's country Infiltam.

Walking on the arched portico of the Estate House's park, when they reached *'The Nude' (A naked statue of a man and woman)*, then ultimately getting bored, Elvis picked up Luiciano's phone once again.

Luiciano said, "I just want to know what stupidity you are going to do that will bring an end to both of us?"

"My strategy is full proof." Elvis said, "It is now impossible that these Paras and Susan who are about to die will find Benedict to release them from Robrelco Fero. They have only one way to live their life ahead together in the future. It is to copy all their memories in the Memory Machine and then find a Diaboli couple to conduct their re-birth ritual. Pasting the memories from the Memory Machine again in their minds after a new birth, that's it… The traditional procedure of our world… But adopting this procedure also is impossible for them at the moment. That's because, they cannot even dream of immediately getting the unbelievable amount the Diabolis charge for such a ritual. But I will entangle them in a net by showing them that dream. I will present myself in this manner- I am Liam and Cons Lydia has assigned the mission to find the blue print of the energy stealing towers constructed by the Devil Family on the *'Koll Your Highness'* asteroid that is near the Earth, to my agency. And if you will fulfill this mission for me, I will pay you a big amount. They don't have any other way left but to accept my mission."

Luciano's voice speaking with scorn and reproof was akin to the highest note of the sound box. He said, "Even an aspiration to become a New-God of Cons Lydia requires immense passion and you intend to send the moment that has brought the gift of toppling its throne to the pier of death..? There is no need to do any such thing. Just simply imprison them and come back here."

"Toppling the throne of Susan's heart is more important for me." Elvis said in a cold voice.

"You fool…" Luciano fumed, "After the experiment of Discovery Copper Horse on them, in case Paras turns out to be Daarck, which is entirely possible, then he is the only one who can remove the lack of knowledge of the Mission Walk of Life Discs that have disappeared and you want to put the kingdom of eleven colonies that is going to come in our share, by leaving them free like this..! What is this thing called love..? One day, Paras' name will be gradually erased from the plate hung on the room of her heart and Elvis will be written instead."

"You don't know anything about love. Hence stay away from giving advice in this matter. For the mission I am going to hire them, they will have to exchange their bodies through the Mummy-Ointment with the authorized people to reach the towers made on that asteroid. In order to acquire the tower's blue-print by spying easily. They will perform *Parkaya Pravesh (Parkaya refers to 'another body' and Pravesh means 'to enter' Parkaya Pravesh refers to the soul of an individual entering into the body of another individual)*, and after that Sebastian, one of Eddie's loyalists who is now Paras' manager will use the Memory-Machine to install their previous memories in the minds of Paras and Susan again. Till the time the memory machine has not been used on them they would be oblivious to each other's existence and I can only make Susan mine with all her heart while she is totally blank about Paras' existence before Sebastian uses the memory machine on Susan. As soon as they do the Parkaya Pravesh, I will instantly kidnap them."

"Intense yearning, for anything whatsoever, is capable of shutting off one's intelligence in the coop of foolishness..." Elvis cut off the mumbling Luciano's phone and once again turned a warningful ferocious face towards Eddie who was walking beside him.

"I hope our problems have not reached Eddie, somehow?" Paras, who zoomed the face of the man clearing the security layers with Eddie and took it nearer to the monitor, finally got up and walked towards the door.

"This is a totally useless effort…" As soon as Paras opened the door, Eddie quickly got inside and addressed Susan who was removing things for the new house from the cartons dispersed all around.

Susan, carefully reading Eddie's face, opened her mouth with her hand on her waist, but before she could say something, Eddie said, "I am sorry to be contacting you like this." He said further in a serious voice pointing his hand towards Elvis, "Mr. Liam came to me with an offer and instantly I got the thought that this offer can become a possibility for you to get rid of Robrelco Fero's torment. The mission is somewhat like this- An asteroid that is near the Earth repeatedly crosses its own sphere and slides close to the Earth. Being suspicious that the *'Devil Family'* has constructed receiver-towers stealing human energy on this asteroid, *'Earth Eleven'* has handed over this mission to *'Irato Corps'*, which is Liam's agency. If Lord de Ros wants, he can destroy this asteroid of *'Koll Your Highness'* in a minute. But the proposition here is to acquire the Broadcast and Receiver Tower's technology. That's because, it is not possible for Ros to reach up to even one of the other towers. All of them have been built on the Idiotic colonies. The only one that was on the Earth has been destroyed just a few hours ago. Anyways, the matter of significance to us is that, Liam will pay you an extraordinary amount for this mission." *('Irato Corps' – Earth – An angry squad)*

"Would it suffice to easily hire *'Krech'* for the rebirth ritual...?" When Paras said this, there was a hint of an old time Roman soldier in his smile. *(Krech – A reputed member of the Diaboli secret society)*

"Absolutely," Eddie said, "It will be better to join hands with death that has suddenly come through Robrelco Fero who is imprisoned with your souls, in our favor before that death becomes horrible enough to push you and Susan in different worlds forever. This will be just a little cumbersome. As it is, the whole world is chasing you. You might probably be able to free yourself of Robrelco Fero only after passing through just this one door of death which is open for absconding...!"

"But there is no such guarantee that even after rebirth Robrelco Fero's spirit would get separated from our souls." Susan expressed doubtfully.

"Witch, this is the only option we have." Paras said turning towards Susan.

"Don't be concerned about the amount to be given to Krech for arranging to take re-birth at the desired place. Once the mission starts, I can make arrangements for you to get cent percent payment within an hour." Said Liam, alias Elvis, who was watching Susan with an affection seen while meeting a person for the first time.

"Apart from that, *'Krech'* has the high quality breed Diaboli couple of the Nebel Shift Colony, who will give you a strong and healthy physical structure in the new birth. And with that we are also getting acquitted from the slow and tedious process of development here." Saying this Eddie extended his hand towards the right side and Elvis put a small box in his hand. Giving Susan a packing portraying a comic strip of a man rising high on the time graph, Eddie said, "The medicine that develops the whole foetus in less than one and a half months and through the *'Glips Vaccination Treatment'* you will have acquired physical and mental growth equivalent to twenty-five year old youngsters after 1.5 years. What do you say?"

"I don't doubt your loyalty, Eddie..., but why should I not believe that Mr. Liam, is not an ally of Ros' or from the Devil family's side and he has not held your family hostage...?"

Eddie quickly took out his phone and extended it towards Paras, "You can leisurely speak with my family."

"There is quite some efficacy in Eddie's talks." Elvis said, "Will you make use of some technique like Parkaya Pravesh for spying...? I have been inspired to hand over this mission to you for that characteristic."

"Absolutely... and after that our troubles related to *spying (espionage)* will become trivial." Susan said giving a glass filled with whisky to Elvis.

"Your devotion towards work appears to be more suggestive of enhancing your impression in the eyes of someone special rather than ambition…?"

Looking towards Paras in shock and returning to his composed disposition the very next moment, Elvis said, "Yes, that traitorous woman was so special at one point of time that the hearts of both would be throbbing together and if one's would slow down, the other would miss a beat in order to match the rhythm." Before the uncontrolled emotions could sink the boat near the coast, Elvis said, coming back to business issues, "May I meet your manager Sebastian?"

"Alas." Susan pressed her lips, "Sebastian has disappeared from the time he saw the name of a person named *'Gosha'* in his appointment note."

"From amongst my opponents rarely some promising one can show the maturity of leaving the arena, but anyways…" Taking one deep breath, Paras washed down the *'Cassia Soferra'* remaining in the glass in one single gulp and extended his hand in front of Liam alias Elvis, "I agree to it. Tonight, exactly at eight thirty, we will be on Koll's asteroid." He added turning towards Susan, "Salisa, you tell Krech to start making the *'Gerifuna Stagi'* *(Gerifuna Stagi – A 'magic plate' holding the power to pull the souls of them for whom the rite is being performed from any part of the world after their death, wherever it is made.)*

"Can you do Parkaya Pravesh on someone's request in front of their eyes?" Elvis asked rubbing his fingers on the shining suit button.

"If our sense of vulgarity would not have been linked to nudity…" Saying this, Paras took them towards the door.

*

On Mahanabh

"This *devotee (worshipper)* of Lord de Ros aspires to present a tune in the service of his Lord…?" Standing in front of Ros, Luciano spoke in words reinforced by etiquette and sent this message typed in his mobile to the Devil- "Only this much information has been received from Rihon regarding Paras' location- Currently they are on one of the planets of Colony Studium," When he looked up, Rihon's eyes were abusing him for his foolishness of being so hasty to play the tune. The magic plate was already made below his throne and if Ros would have stood right there near the balcony during the time the Tie-In Tune was being played…?"

"Yes why not?" Responding in a juicy voice and going to sit on the throne, Ros said in a strange tone, "Whosoever can solve the puzzle of The Ultimate Mission of the Devil with this hint, I will make him the owner of Cons Lydia, this very instant- *The condition of the Devil is like the drug addict with an irritable nature who is under rehabilitation.*"

Scratching his head like everyone else, Rihon noticed Arina who had suddenly come in, bowing towards Ros' neck. Ros, who was about to get up again after he ceased fondling the peculiar animal without ears that heard with its hair seated next to his throne, stopped. And looked up.

"If luck is in our favor in this manner, then that lad Paras will be on Mahanabh by evening." Saying this Arina put some documents and a *Lazo* {*A pen, that keeps the live aura-identity of the signatory connected with the Manithus Office of the 'Master Galaxy' through the S. Station medium during the signature process*} in Ros' hand.

Ros said, raising the hand with which he held the document, "Liquor Mine, Glee Metal Casting, Antpatic, Adopt Baby…" "These are all the Off-Idiotic Colonies where we can never reach. Where, the Devil has erected towers producing the Energy Warriors. Let's see with how much seriousness Master Galaxy will take our complaints against the Devil Family."

Signing and giving the document to Arina, Ros spoke further in an ironic way, "Daarck went, but his conspiracy is still alive. Why is someone not showering contempt on us for losing that *master-card of Antonio (Paras)* with the kind of resources we have?"

Gesturing Luiciano as he was about to open the violin box to wait, Lord de Ros said, "I do not think that until the Devil is taking a challenging breath against this colony, we will ever qualify to be called guardians holding the responsibility of billions of people living on the fifty planets."

"Devilet Again," Now Ajar, the Chairman of *'Stuvet Twenty-One'*, a group of twenty-one planets of Cons Lydia, said, "Is the one and only remedy… that mysterious book written about the Devil in which his deceitful nature and ultimate intentions have been highlighted. His absolute dismissal is possible only through that. But… anyways, the issue which is not less worrying than the one I have brought."

A motion picture emerged in the Bascilica from the Three-D Projector kept on the table by Ajar. A shadow of a Chairman of one of Group SP's colonies could be seen descending from the sky. He poured some chemical from a thin necked *surahi (glass bottle)* on a huge stone at the brink of the city and a vibration instantly started in the stone. He kept on pouring the chemical on one stone after another. As if someone's spirit had entered the big rocks, bouncing like ostriches the rocks were hurled towards the city. The image after this was taken through the satellite. Roads, shops, buildings and the market crowd; the rocks destroyed everything that came in the way and ruined the entire city.

"They are conducting the experiments of their new chemical weapons by ruining our cities. The stones are using their inner energy." Ajar gave his commentary pointing towards the shrinking stones.

"They have discovered the mind of physical substances." Ros said as he signaled Luiciano to start and as part of the very last state Rihon, Antosa, Damitri, Leonid and Ekaksh brought their entire strength up to the palm of the hand and steadying it there, went and settled down near the other Chairmen inclusive of Ajar, so that even they could be finished after imprisoning Ros.

Opening the box, Luiciano took out a high strata violin and started playing the entire *gamut (A whole series of recognized musical notes)*. Consecutively a storm arose in the auditorium with the increased heartbeats of the ten

Presidents. Apart from being bland, weird and old, there was also nothing special about the Tie-in Tune's musical series, yet Ros' face kept on swaying in appreciation.

"What nonsense is going on…!" Rihon rubbed his eyes, but Ros was still sitting there having fun as if he was *'happy with the hare-brained comedy'*. It was now impossible for Rihon's attendants to keep on their fake smile imagining that Ros was melting with the Tie-in Tune and getting imprisoned with their souls. The faces were on the edge of becoming permanently distorted with the storms of emotional tensions, when ultimately Luiciano withdrew the stick from the violin.

"Praise Worthy …" Looking at Arina, Ros said in a knotty voice. Before the suppressed laughter would burst forth from her stomach, Arina quickly fled from there.

*

"Was there any mistake in playing the tune? Is it that Rihon has made an incorrect magic-plate in haste? After all, what was it? Not even one of Ros' nails could be melted." Antosa asked with a serious face like that of a man who has set out to find the meaning of life, as they directly descended to the foothills to reach the travel room, on their return journey.

Rihon said peevishly, "Antonio turned out to be incredibly cunning."

"How…?" Everyone exclaimed together.

"Someone had already made a magic plate below Ros' throne, and whose work can that be, other than Antonio's. I wish I also had two minds like Ros. While one always remains scared, at least life's pleasures can be enjoyed with the other." Rihon said as he reached the travel room with heavy steps and stiffened his neck.

"Ohh muffish…" As Luiciano addressed himself, everyone turned in his direction and watched him with flashing eyes, "At the time you imprisoned him, the test being conducted on Robrelco Fero was not of the Tie-in Tune but of *Contras Affair*." Luiciano said hurriedly and gave the '*address code*' to the station in-charge, "They tried the Tie-in Tune on Ros and just like today, as Ros could not be imprisoned, they might have prepared an ethereal spell book like the '*Contras Affair*'…

"Welcome to the hell…" With the vanishing of the S. Station camera's flash of light, some strange words echoed. Speaking in an enticing voice, the Devil raised his hand towards the sky hitherto pointed towards Rihon's group as they groped all around to guess where they have reached and once again the black clouds eagerly waiting for his decree stopped the return of the rain.

An extraordinary non-verbal music capable enough to transform even a powerfully pious soul into an emperor of evil, echoed between the blurred walls of Terror-Street, based on *'Pendigyura 01' (A small planet of the Devil)*, which had two soft suns rising side by side.

"An angry mist spread in Rihon's eyes and behind that mist two flaring embers which very clearly held the intention to burn Luiciano to ashes could be seen. "Adieu Luiciano." Rihon said, "In your performance, not getting a glimpse of your attempt to act was truly commendable."

"My Lord," Malachi, who had entered hurriedly, bent his neck in front of the Devil and said, "Forgive me for the audacity, but now we have prepared more *'Energy Warriors'* than necessary to easily defeat Lord de Ros' army. They are awaiting just one signal from my Lord. If it's your verdict, a war can start within the next thirty minutes. My Lord will be on the throne of *'Cons Lydia'* on the third day."

"No, no… not at all. This has been happening right from the beginning of this world. One of the emperors attacks another, defeats him, wins over his empire and feels proud. But do you think that the Devil is so ordinary that he can be kept in the category of those foolish emperors? Even after the victory of the Devil-Family over Cons Lydia, Lord de Ros should continue to be its New-God. Of what use is the ownership of the colonies for us?"

"What….." Rihon asked expressing a deadly surprise, "A super boisterous conspiracy of preparing this huge army of Energy Warriors, an uphill battle of so many years, so many inventions and sacrifices, after which a terribly awful war takes place and after won that war, *'Cons Lydia'* is given back to Ros..! Which Devilish will believe that he has been worshipping someone so insane till now?"

"H..ha..ha..ha… that is the latest and greatest mystery of all. *'Lord de Ros'* continues to be the New-God of Cons Lydia and yet, the hiding place of that thing making it possible for me to get all the benefits of its ownership, is only known to Robrelco Fero. So now, please attach the

Memory-Thief to Rihon's mind and start investigating whether or not the information of the Re-built that can release Robrelco Fero imprisoned with his soul, is there in his mind or not." Saying this, the Devil standing near his seat made on the grave, suddenly pulled Rihon in his arms, threw him onto the enshrined tomb and pulling the *belt (that always keeps a Gardi safe from death)* from his neck, threw it afar. The Devil said in an ambiguous voice, "You don't have any idea to what extent you have disappointed *'Beelzebub'*...!"

"Ouch..." Amidst Rihon's screams, Antonio, who was hanging on one Devilish's shoulder, spoke as he tried performing the tiring activity of raising his eyelashes, "I am also vehement to see the functionality of the Re-built Tune."

"This son of a bitch, Antonio is instigating you." Rihon said rapidly, "Just like Luiciano, he is also so good at lying that even the helpless lie-detect machine would get confused. I don't have the Re-built Tune."

Going and standing in front of Rihon, Devil said raising his right hand, "Victory over these eleven colonies without the release of Robrelco Fero is like expensive bottles without whisky." As Malachi put a sword made of a blade sharp enough to cut a stone into pieces in his hand, Antonio looked excited today after a long time in the far corner. Following a fierce scream heralding a slogan of dismemberment of the connection between Rihon and his struggling leg, the Devil slowly slid his fingers into Rihon's hanging fleshy lumps. The Devil suddenly penetrated his fingers deep into his blood dripping foot. As soon as Rihon's mind lost control over the code of secret information in his mind due to the effect of brutal pain, Malachi quickly connected the Memory-Thief with his mind and attached it to his own brain.

*

That same night at 8:30 near the Earth on 'Koll Your Highness' Asteroid

This was the third time that Elvis had connected the phone to Meriano while listening to the live audio telecast of the Parkaya Pravesh ceremony going on in a space vehicle that was parked about six hundred feet away and hidden in the area having natural caves near the jungle, on his satellite phone. He said, "The continuity of your life is now dependent on your assurance that Susan will remain safe even after the blast…!"

"In the demonstration, the paint on the walls of the cockpit also has not fallen off after a blast of this level."Getting bored, Meriano disconnected the phone and pointed the rocket launcher in the direction of the space vehicle.

Susan, who had become speechless noticing the exposed glamour of the huge thighed *Yaara* as she dragged to the bathtub in one corner of the aircraft's fire-proof cabin, stuck a tape on the screaming Yaara's lips and throwing her into the thick water of the Mummy-Ointment, she stripped off even her last clothing, "If you promise to remain quiet, then I would even open your hands…?"

Susan said childishly looking into Yaara's big eyes staring amidst densely laden beauty.

"Hmm… Hmm…" Yaara shook her head at once as if she was taking an oath.

"Hmmm…!" As Susan slyly laughing at Yaara who was creating a fuss in vain, pulled her out of the tub, Yaara immediately ran towards the closed door and started kicking the door. Pushing the bell-button on the wall behind the tub, Susan entered the tub, after which, Paras who had come after one minute, opened the door and pushed Yaara behind. Taking deep breaths on seeing Yaara's *'Forty Twenty-six Forty'*, Paras gestured to Susan and Susan clutched Yaara in her cruel embrace. Paras quickly covered the two bodies that were like overflowing beauties with a shining black garment and set it on fire from outside. The eerie odor arising from the Mummy-Ointment with the ignition of the fire opened up all the physical bonds. Immediately the two *spirits* that were inevitably running attracted towards the scent, exchanged their bodies.

Far away, Meriano heard Elvis' trembling voice, as he was wondering what plan Paras' manager Sebastian's agents who stood surrounding this aircraft had for the time of exigency, "Just twenty seconds, Susan has entered Yaara's and Paras has entered Viter's body. Under any circumstances, Susan should be out of the shuttle before Paras enters her world again."

Entering the soul changing room with the Memory-Machine, from amongst the two leaping beauties who looked like courtesans of heaven, Sebastian caught the hand of Susan who was in Yaara's form and pushing her towards Viter standing in Paras' personation, he said hurriedly, "Taste her lips and say how sweet they are…! Yaara's and Viter's bodies are now yours. However, you will live the memories in the minds of these bodies until your memories are not installed in the brains of these bodies with the Memory Machine. This means that you will continue to be Yaara and Viter. " He was holding a gun in the other hand. But before Sebastian could pick up the *'Memory Machine'*, being hurled with an overwhelming blast, he went and fell straight away on Paras. Similarly troubled theologians present in the aircraft, looked towards each other and ran directly towards the emergency exit.

"Yaara…" Whistling gently, Viter alias Paras gestured towards the west side to Susan alias Yaara and Yaara remembered the t*antrik's (practitioner of black magic)* cave floating on the violent desert ocean that was spreading to the edge of apperception. Just a few minutes before these strange aliens kidnapped them, she and Viter were there. It was the only nearest cave holding a human population in this barren territory awaiting the opportunity to soon become a city. *(Here they have addressed each other in this way as Viter and Yaara. Yet their original names have now been continued after this so that there is no confusion in the minds of the readers.)*

"I am feeling quite weird and very strange." Susan said running on the rough and rugged road holding onto Paras' hand, "Certainly my nervous system is going to crash…"

"This is the limit." Paras spoke gasping between breaths, "I am also feeling exactly the same. As if I am just a machine filled with information. It feels as if I have just been born, became an adult within a minute, and someone crammed my brain to the brink with unknown memories."

A little further, they could see the light emanating from the tantrik's cave. Running parallelly on the hillock of the hunting den with steps matching their tired steps taken with puffing breath, Sebastian now descended towards them. As soon as he came down, Sebastian shot the *'Disposable Butterfly'*, that was flying over their heads to transmit video and sound recording signals to Elvis' satellite phone, blowing it into small pieces. When the tantrik's cave was about fifteen feet away, Elivs' agent Meriano's long range rifle echoed on Paras' back. Before the nine mm. bullet could penetrate his back and come out stabbing his heart, the sacrifice of one of Sebastian's agents had saved him. If the agent would not have worn a Mail-Coat, the bullet would have come out piercing Paras as well.

"I will take you to see a dying man again some other time." Paras had picked up Susan who was glued to the spot watching the struggling agent. Fortunately with the luck being in favor the cave's door was in a welcoming mood.

Coming and standing in front of them, Sebastian admonished Paras in a threatening voice, "Put her down and kiss her." He held a Memory Machine resembling a hairdryer along with a gun raised high. "Don't be scared, this machine is just to establish your real identity in your brains."

"Nobody will ever offer such a sweet condition for leave out..." As Paras mumbled and came near to kiss her, Susan shoved him away and said to Sebastian, "Are you a *Nunki-Bunki (A person who gets excited with perverted sex)*?"

"Hurry up, if you don't prefer death over and above one passionate kiss." Sebastian shouted angrily.

"Is *'Dion'* aware of everything?" Paras who was living with Viter's memories, enquired apprehensively. *(Dion – The prince of the king of this asteroid 'Koll Your Highness')*

"I am not Dion's spy."

As Sebastian standing with a gun pointed between Paras' eyebrows, was compelled to turn around for Elvis' agents approaching closer, they took advantage of the opportunity and entered the cave. The cryptic-cave illuminated with burning embers appeared as scary as some'Dirty-Dream' (Night Mare).

"What is it now?" The tantrik asked as if seeing the cards of a big lansquenet opening up and tightened his grip on the bag picked up in his hand. "Be rest assured," The tantrik said in a sweet drawl, "Your task will be accomplished in an excellent and immaculate manner. I am especially known for successful accomplishment within the stipulated time in a faultless way. Viter's soul will never realize that Prince Dion's body is not his own."

"Stop nonsense." Paras said excitedly, "We just want back those *'Rubeptic'*... If, there is no other exit to get out from here...!" *(Rubeptic – The currency of Koll's Asteroid)*

"Who is chasing you... Eh...? Dion's accomplice ?" The tantrik turned back as if death had come to embrace him. "I shall show this *'wealth'* to Prince Dion and shall personally expose the betrayal of these traitors. Viter has forcefully involved me in the conspiracy of entering Dion's body and taking away this asteroid after easily killing the king of *Koll Your Highness.*"

"Oh... Oh...!! This is not Dion's army." Paras said widening his eyes as he looked towards Susan who was standing in Yaara's body, "Do you think that Dion will ignore this universal beauty and trust a wraith like you?"

The tantrik opened the door that led to the valley.

"You disingenuous inamorato..." Beating the tantrik on his chest, Susan went out.

"It was expected, but not that Elvis would deploy the whole army." Holding the front behind the cover of rocks in the turmoil taking place outside, Sebastian was consulting someone on the phone. "It is not possible to re-load my weapons. Had you thrown the note correctly...? Those people are certainly obstinate to kill Paras."

"*Lessie* had also picked up the paper after I kneaded and threw it." *Nurai* said, "Don't know why, but by any chance did we make use of very difficult language in that note?" The second division of the infantry came out of Meriano's shuttle and marched forward crushing the skeletons of Sebastian's guards as they moved forward towards the Tantrik's cave. *(Lessie – Elvis's agent. Nurai – Sebastian's agent)*

"As they came out from the back door of the cave and escaped towards the city, Paras commented, "Looks like my potential murderers believe in chivalry."

"Why?"

"Didn't you see, I was the only target every time?" The little strength their rescue journey had gained after seeing the daylight of the bright, sparkling city now seemed to be futile. Because the agents with human wings descending from the sky one after another had surrounded them to quite an extent. The small working figures of the *'Grochs'* and *'Littons'* could be seen at the threshold of the city. *('Grochs' and 'Littons' – Two tribes existing on the Koll Asteroid)*

"Who knows whether our destiny will enable us to enjoy this *Holm* or not?" When they crossed the grounds and stepped onto the closed campus of the Knowledge Booth Depots, the *'Holm'* had started with a spirited announcement. *(Holm – A jollity collective festival)*

"It's alright, if you can't see him dying." Meriano aimed towards the left side at Sebastian's chest as he stood there shielding Paras and pressed the trigger, but before it could be completely pressed, Lessie descended from the sky like a meteorite, coming and standing directly in front of Meriano. She slipped a wrinkled wad of paper into his hands. "New research…" Meriano was finding it difficult to read. "Duplicating… Some male-female can also assume bodies of the opposite sex. Meaning it is also possible that Susan can be in the body of Viter whom we were inclined to kill…!"

"Oh…!" Meriano glared at Paras and Susan, one by one from top to bottom.

"My best wishes to Elvis for some other time, the function of this thing is over." Sebastian said in a loud voice showing the Memory Machine to Meriano.

"Come back…" Elvis' voice echoed in Meriano's ears as he signaled his colleagues to put their guns down. Walking a little backwards, they flew away in a falcon's style.

"What is the intention of this angel of ours…?" Paras asked, shifting his glance doubtfully from Sebastian to Yaara, alias Susan.

"Absolutely not… it's not like that. I cannot even think like that about this enticing thing of yours."

"So then..? How does your mysterious desire become known?" Paras asked.

"A kiss… A kiss that surpasses, the extreme limits of insanity."

"I don't mind." As Paras said this taking his lips towards Susan, she thrust him away.

"I'm saying this for the last time." Susan began trembling with Sebastian's roar. He pressed the hot spout of the gun on Paras' forehead.

Looking at his dangerous eyes, it appeared as if he would actually kill.

"I am not going to leave this perverted, stubborn, maniac." As the mumbling Susan took her lips forward, Sebastian pressed the trigger alternately putting the *Memory Machine* on the back portion of her and Paras' necks. After noodles injected in their necks, Paras' manhood was dripping from every cell in his body and as he took Susan's luscious protruding lips in his, sparks of electricity rose up all around. *(One Memory Machine holds the capacity to store the memories of the life events that took place during the whole life of two people who lived for two hundred years.)*

"It looks like I will have to explain the meaning of suck-madness by actually doing it." Sebastian threatened and the luscious lips started rebelliously merging with each other with a fierce intensity. The existence of the rest of the world was forgotten and when they came in contact with that world once again, the wonderful world looked very familiar.

The lips separated and "Oh, how is all this…!" with a similar type of melodious laughter, both of them kept their foreheads on each other. Continuing to laugh, they again pressed lips to lips, but this time the kiss was full of a potent attraction. After returning the pistol to his holster Sebastian now laughed shaking his head and grimly removing the bag from his back, he extended it towards Susan and said, "You really want to do this...? There is still time."

"You don't know how it feels to wake up in the morning and be anxious that this might be the last day of your life. I don't want death to separate Susan and me. I am aggrieved that I cannot hold you back any longer to take our lives when Elvis makes the payment after an hour. Susan and I will have to do this thing for each other." As Paras said this, Susan, took out a small remote from the bag and giving it to Sebastian, she said.

"I feel that if we do it in this manner, it will also be much easier to blow up Elvis- The king of this *'Koll Your Highness'* is infatuated to Yaara. Koll is eager to show Yaara the receiver tower that prepares Energy Warriors where even the Highness Family is forbidden to enter. After the meeting with Elvis that is scheduled forty minutes later, I will convince Koll to show the tower to Paras. These are the account numbers of *'Obiaahno'*…" Susan handed him a chit. "By the time Paras and me shoot each other in the tower, Elvis will have known that we diverted his attention on *'Krech'* and got this ritual done by some other Diaboli and when he personally comes to the tower to take our dead bodies which would be invaluable to know on which planet we have taken a rebirth, with the use of this remote by Nurai, this entire tower will blow up through the bomb tied to my waist." *(Obiaahno – The Diaboli couple that was actually hired by Paras for the rebirth ritual)*

"Do you know how dangerous this ritual is?" Sebastian asked, "If there is even a slight mistake the souls of both you and Paras will be permanently lost in the depths of hell. You will hardly ever be able to meet each other throughout eternity and apart from that, I do not think that Elvis will make the payment after the failure of this act related to the relationships of the heart…! Obiaahno is not going to start the ritual until he gets the payment."

"We have thought about every possible move of Elvis. As you rightly said, he will definitely refuse to make the payment. But before that he will offer to deploy us onto another important mission after disengaging us from this mission. So that he can get another chance to kidnap Susan… But on our remaining adamant, he will not have an alternate choice and will then focus his entire attention on kidnapping us one hour later after our new birth from Krech's place. Till the very end, he should be under the impression that this ritual of ours is happening on a planet of Colony Nebel Shift by Krech. Apart from that, you know what you have to do further."

Sebastian said handing over a strip to Paras, "As such this medicine is under experiment, yet it is effective to crash your *'Aura Structure'* for a few hours. It will make you ill or might even kill you. The Devil must have procured the Aura Print of both you and Susan from Antonio. I will not recommend that you take this until you face the situation where the Satanics are coming right in front of you with an Aura Monitor."

"It has become late," Susan said glancing at the watch, "Au revoir, we'll meet again." They had some hasty conversation with Sebastian and after holding each other's hand, they started running towards the city-fencing that was made of glass.

"The headman's messenger is searching for you since quite some time." The *'Coast-Guard'* said as he saluted him.

Viter alias Paras smiled and gave a Fifty Rubeptic note to the police officer.

Holm's long parade could now be seen. The groups of convergent women, who had taken the initiative to go for a rendezvous with their lovers, were haughtily frolicking around as they passed by the extremely supernatural inns that were built everywhere.

"If it were really possible, I would have loved to experience being in a man's body." Susan said.

"But I would never, ever…" Paras said now, leisurely raking his glance over Yaara alias Susan. The curves of her rotund figure were so alluring that is looked like a whole troupe of sculptors had spent their whole life dedicatedly to sculpt her. Paras spoke, "Nothing better than this will ever be found."

"Meaning…? I was quite good earlier?"

"Our definition of beauty is attached to some invisible thing." Paras said, thinking about the death that was going to come after some time as ostentatious colors of excitement spread and sunk in his eyes.

"Oh.. Oh.. Oh… Ridiculously awesome conspiracies are going on between the two communities of this asteroid to eliminate each other." Susan's exclamations kept on increasing as she laughed holding her head. "I wish we had some more time to gain an insight into the lives of Viter and Yaara."

Straitening Susan who had huddled down with embezzling laughter, Paras said as if he had suddenly remembered, "Hey, damn it, my wellbeing is at stake."

Susan raised her eyes giving a questioning look.

"For keeping the secret congregation in darkness… If my new father does not kill me, then I'll meet you near the gate of the *'Skeleton Museum'* exactly at nine fifty-five. You buy two cheap pistols." When Paras said this, Susan turned her face in the other direction to hide her moistened eyes.

Extending a One Hundred and Fifty Rubeptic note towards the vendor on the footpath in front of the road selling *'slabs'* of small and big batteries producing electricity with a working capacity of sixty minutes to *'six'* months, Paras said, "*One yam (A piece of battery that could work for about twelve hours)*"

"Only half yams are left." Saying this, along with two small *'blocks'* of batteries, he also gave a smile that made it appear valuable.

*

Thrusting open the door as if he intended to break it open, Paras had further offended the *'Re-cook Council'* that was sitting in darkness. He stood there turning his head as he saw headman coming closer. *(Re-cook Council – An assembly of the Litton community that was engrossed in destroying and throwing off Koll's authority on the asteroid. Headman – The head of the council)*

"Have you got the battery?" The headman asked roaring furiously.

Paras gazed at the Litton head looking barely like a twenty-five year youth as he drew on the pipe. Although, his age had crossed the one hundred and sixty years mark. "Oh… Yes." Paras quickly fished out the block and attached it with the *'Power Precept Unit'* behind the door. He saw the view of offended faces increasing his restlessness in the brightly lit hall.

"When will you grow up?" The anxiety of the headman was demanding a quick solution.

"Once Dion's informers stop chasing..." Paras responded with the memorized answer like a parrot and not having any interest in the progress of Litton or the downfall of Groch, Paras looked at the watch to estimate when he would be able to get out from there and said, "I do not trust Eliza. Yaara has promised today. She will follow my instructions, even if it requires her to keep her mind aside."

"If you don't trust me, then why am I getting an invitation from this *'fellowship'*?" Moving restlessly, as Eliza enquired with slanted eyes, Paras looked at her attentively, *'If Yaara wouldn't have been there, Eliza could be given first rank in terms of beauty on this asteroid.'*

"He is wasting the chamber's time with his fairy tales." Roared Viter's father *'Fazil'* from a seat on the right side as he continued to frown at Paras, "That universal beauty is in love with you as a form of benefit of the beautiful women's indolence in making a choice, but not so much that you can convince her to betray her own *'Groch'* community. Paras saw the love for Viter hidden in his eyes and brooded on what he has become. A repulsion for himself burst forth for snatching Viter's body.

It was now difficult for Paras' eyes to handle the burden of the tough rush in the last twenty-four hours. He went and sat in a corner. The sounds melting after reaching his ears were opening his half closed eyes again and again… "How can I let my death win without seeing the crowning of a Litton King in the *'Kingdom Fête'* that is going to take place tomorrow..!" So much excitement had compelled the ill headman to cough for quite a long time. "At the end of this Kings Royale, the shadow of Litton's authority will have spread across the entire asteroid. One multiple message, circulate… The Slug sign will be an indicator of the powerful-Polk…"

"Haaaaa…" When the council shocked by the sound of Viter's yawn looked in that direction, the soft buffets of Eliza's hand were falling on his cheeks.

*

After Gosha returned empty handed a few hours ago from *'Trojan Asteroid'*, a small asteroid of *'Pioneer Mound'*, the residence of Eddie who had suddenly disappeared with his family, the doubly agitated Lord de Ros had deputed the intelligence of all the fifty planets to leave everything aside and only look out for Paras and Susan.

In the urgent search conducted comprehensively by the intelligence of all the planets, one strange fact that had earlier been overlooked had surfaced. Sometime after the establishment of the organization for Mission *'Walk of Life'*, the owners of several private intelligence agencies of the eleven Vio-Crazy colonies that had been targeted had suddenly started changing. And this was because with the beginning of *'Walk of Life'*, their first move was to *'commence at short intervals, the 'take over' proceedings of all these reputed Intelligence Agencies of the eleven targeted colonies, to whom these colonies usually assigned important missions.'* They were also successful to quite an extent. Thereafter, these colonies engaging in their adverse propensities had started assigning missions for spying on this organization of Daarck to agencies owned by Daarck himself. Their budget for this activity was enormous.

"*Cons Lydia* has recently handed over the assignment to acquire the blue print of the *'Gravity Machine'* and *'Receiver Tower'* that is on the Koll Asteroid to *'Irato Corps'*, which is one of the forty agencies that had been taken over at that time." An operator, seated at the end of the round top in front of the control panel whose rotund face always portrayed him as stupid, which was in sharp contrast to his intelligence, drew their attention.

When Gosha pulled his chair near this operator, he flashed the preliminary report sent by Irato Corps from Koll's Asteroid on the screen.

"Koll has attached huge gravity engines to both ends of this asteroid of his and has transformed the entire planet into a Jumbo Airship. The cost of using the heat from the lava that is in the abyss of the asteroid as fuel to operate the gravity engine would only be affordable to Koll if the asteroid has been launched with the real intention to take it in any direction in order to be able to experience the desired season and under the pretext of keeping the sky glowing for hours in the political celebration, absorb the energy transmitted to the receiver towers on this asteroid of Koll by the broadcasting towers constructed on Earth, that suck the human energy…"

Gesturing the operators of the Mahanabh Control Tower who were rising when he entered, to sit down, *Lord de Ros* came and sat near Gosha.

Gosha said in an apologetic tone, "As Eddie was associated with a reputed agency his outsider call list is quite long. However we have identified a person from Colony Studium's planet *Opdrazen* of *Group R* whose New God was recently thrown out, with whom Eddie was in regular contact."

"And what was he?" Ros asked.

"A *'radio jockey'* of the national radio channel of the *'Opdrazen'* country having a population of six hundred and fifty million and an area of six million square kms."

Ros bent his head forward with interest.

"Establishing globally famed fugitives under the *'Fugaceous Protection Program'* with a new identity in a new life is the specialty of Eddie's agency. There were several ordinary families available with the agency residing on Colony 'Studium' whose Aura Records have no importance at all. The client is replaced by transforming the appearance, finger print, tongue print and iris-identity into one of the members of that family. The agency does not contact the client directly under any circumstances. This *'radio jockey'* was a mediator in the guise of a friend especially for the purpose of contacting, whenever required. Whenever, the agency has to deliver a message to this fugitive, a story is composed for that radio program. The secret message is hidden in the events of the story. Some code words are enunciated at the beginning of the program on the day of delivering the message. The client's reply is received by the radio jockey through a letter with an anonymous address. Eddie had allotted Paras the vacant house of this radio jockey to reside as he had been murdered just a few days ago." Gosha said gesturing towards the last screen of the panel board, "This is live."

As Ros watched the scene where Arina was investigating the radio jockey's house that had been burnt to ashes, Gosha said, now gesturing towards the third screen, "This person Liam who had been talking to Paras and Susan in the video recorded nine hours earlier by the peephole camera on the front door, was seen a few hours ago in the headquarters of Irato Corps and is now on Koll's asteroid. This means that Paras and that dame are also right there."

Staring at the fate with an enticing gaze, Ros said, "As if we have just got to know that the asteroid was frequently brought near the Earth so that the mysterious tower situated on Koll's asteroid can come in the range of the energy transmitted through the broadcasting tower constructed on the Earth by the Satanics and as we want to think a little about the lives of millions of innocent people residing there before we crush the asteroid straight away, accordingly issue a mandate to block all the *'S. Stations'* taking Koll Your Highness out of his asteroid, at this very instant. Once it is done, several people from Koll's end will take their aircraft and a nasty kind of rush towards such S. Stations on the *'Earth'* and the *'Western Asteroid Belt'* that can be reached by means of a shuttle will start… But these S. Stations will also be already blocked. This time if these kids sneak out of our hands than the whole world will condemn Cons Lydia."

*

The *boulevards (paths)* often exhibiting a brush-off for the destination by the crowd, noise and music of the Jollity Collective Festival, are jam-packed. Pushing aside the multitude of masses, when Paras reached Susan who was restlessly waiting near a colossal marble *'palace'*, a procession of youthful old men carrying a sign board of *marry-me* was passing in front of them. The music of the band leading them was unique. Probably like the forceful rhythm of the music resembling Jazz.

"Everything will be alright. There is just no existing scope to separate us in any way." Paras held her shoulders in a comforting manner.

Susan said thrusting a gun in his hand, "We have not let the Devil reach the first place. I will never be able to forgive myself for taking away Yaara's life." The buoyant Susan, who had disappeared behind the eclipse of guilt, swayed Yaara's velvety neck to and fro in repentance.

Paras spoke as he sighed, "We have become sinners thanks to the deleterious favor bestowed on us by your father."

Susan looked at him with squinted eyes.

Paras said, "Yes, even I am feeling the same way since I met Viter's father… but ultimately, after the curtain is withdrawn from the mystery, this vice that emerges as the foundation of the heavenly world might be able to destroy our vicious tendency."

A slight smile spread on Susan's cheeks, "Oh wow…! You are an emperor." She said.

"Am I not?" Paras winked moving his hand on his finely designed overcoat printed with high quality Tintonic.

"Holm's whole parade also seems *test less* in comparison to this romance…"

Shocked, they looked in the direction of the arrogant voice. Just like a picture being made rotationally visible by a disintegrated *'holographic-projector'*, Liam, alias Elvis manifested from invisibility and removing his *'Thistle Cap'*, he stood there. *(Thistle Cap – A gadget that makes a person invisible)*

"So, even though the beginning was disappointing, it looks like this country of youngsters has enchanted you..!" Elvis appeared calm. However, that calmness was not genteel enough to hide the suffering born out of defeat. "This asteroid has not proved to be very lucky for you." When Elvis said this, a thirty feet high circle was seen rushing exactly in the middle of the road. As a result of the screams reverberating in the sky, the romantic intoxication of the herb Susan had taken to forget the moments of death was reduced into half. The culprits associating themselves with a selfish-life had been tied to the top of the circle as if they had been proved guilty of the crime of selfishness. Watching people throwing useless, rancid, stinking things on them, Susan also looked around. Elvis extended his skulking *'thistle cap'* towards Susan who was getting disappointed. Susan tossed it but it did not succeed in even colliding with the prisoners' shoes.

"This deadly welcome on the asteroid was not shocking for us." Paras said and Elvis' heart missed a rhythm, *'Has he recognized me?'* Elvis thought.

Before Paras' sardonic questions could spoil the plan, Susan said changing the topic, "Man on this petty planet has been conferred with such a unique gift. A charming miracle like this is not there on any other planet across the entire L3." She also added some coquetry to make the discussion more effective. "The age that increases until juvenescence and stops after that. Oh! What must be the sin which these people have not committed, which has given all of us the curse to become old and die…?"

"Miss Yaara, sorry *'Salisa' (Susan)*. Nature keeps creating such miracles for diversification. Well, I am glad and aggrieved to say that you are being taken off from this mission." Displaying streaks of regret Elvis fished out the *'Dismissal Agreement'* and said, "A more thrilling mission is awaiting the services of this passionate couple. *Mr. Fargus (Paras)*, such a mission after which one need not execute any more missions to maintain the extravagantly lavish lifestyle filled with fame and aristocracy." Elvis glanced at the watch, "After several agencies failed to find Benedict, a powerful President of Cons Lydia, Lord de Ros' great Chairman Ajar is personally waiting there for me with an agreement to hand over this assignment to me. You and Yaara, sorry Salisa, can come with me if you want to…!"

"You have missed, Mr. Liam." Paras said.

"What do you mean?" Elvis asked and added immediately, "There will only be an increase in the amount determined to be given to you…!"

"Mr. Liam…" Paras said looking at the watch, "One hundred and ten minutes have elapsed since we stepped on the asteroid, and still I have not received the confirmation message that the amount has been deposited in my account!"

"I apologize. The final decision in Irato Corps is not solely mine. But as I said, can you give me one more chance? We are offering you double the amount?"

"Okay, I just need one day." Thinking of a new plan with Elvis' unexpected change in attitude, Paras said, "We have heard a lot about this asteroid's Kings Royale that is going to take place tomorrow. The Holm would not even have finished and we would be on your new mission."

"But as Eddie had said, what about some Book of Bell that can kill you anytime?" Elvis asked making a face.

"Probably you are not the mediator to rescue us from the Book of Bell, Mr. Liam." Paras shrugged off the discussion with a laugh.

Elvis' silence was abusing Paras. As a rainbow would develop with the electrification of light, the colors on his face kept changing and it was easy for Paras to understand the language of those colors.

"Anyways, we will find some preferred way." Saying this, Elvis put on the *Kirlian Glass (Spectacles with which a person who has become invisible by the Thistle Cap can be seen)* and turned his back.

As there was need for more land in the festival, the parade path had been covered with transparent hard resin and converted into a street. When Elvis reached the jam-packed crowd assembled on this street, Meriano who had come in a new form said in a shaky voice, "This is the time for us to bid farewell. Cons Lydia has found out that Paras and Susan are here. All the departure S. Stations of this Asteroid and those of the Western Asteroid-Belt as well as the Earth that can be reached from here via shuttle have been blocked just two and a half minutes back. A plethora of Gardi forces have already started arriving here."

"This means that we will have to escape through an aircraft and hide on the Earth or the Western Asteroid Belt, till the S. Stations are not activated again. Get me to talk with Luiciano." Elvis said, "Mahanabh Control Tower will have to be stopped from paying enough attention over here and the Diaboli couple in Krech's black-house should not be moved out of sight even for a second."

*

"Dion, my heart has been quenching to meet you in solitude since today morning...? It looks like arrangements have been made to expose me…?" Saying this, when Eliza came towards them flirting with the men strolling with their hands on the hips of rebellious women who had crossed the limits of repulsive ugliness, Paras blew something towards her neck in a way that no one would see it.

Talking to Susan standing in Yaara's form, Dion turned towards Eliza and Nurai who had suddenly appeared removing the Thistle-Cap, extended his phone towards Paras, "Obiaahno." He said in a voice filled with tension.

"Mr. Obiaahno, I am not asking for additional twenty-four hours to determine a convenient time." Paras said.

"Mr. Fargus." Paras heard a voice speaking incoherently, "Believe me, I have not called to remove the misconception from your mind that this ritual is some kind of a redundant witchcraft."

"Just extend it by one more day..!" Paras groped around for a soliciting voice.

"That's alright, but this delay will be with an increase of fees in our interest."

Paras returned the phone after five seconds of its getting disconnected in a nasty way.

"Ouch….." Eliza hit on her neck and threw away a blood thirsty insect that was sucking her blood for who knows how long. Making a face as if a favorite dress had got spoilt, Eliza cleaned the drops of blood from her neck with her delicate fingers. When an heir leading the goons flying on the *'air pedal'* in the sky parade, looked at Eliza standing amidst the plump girls and whistled, the laughing Dion took the intoxicating accessory from Eliza while she was mixing it and offered it to Paras, "There is so much intoxication in life itself..." Refusing as he said this, Paras picked up the weird insect shaking its innumerable legs a little farther from the footpath's edge and putting it in a small plastic bag, he pulled Nurai and Susan, taking them far from there, "We have been trapped in a very bad way."

"Not only that." Looking refreshingly fresh, Nurai spoke, "Gosha has reached right up to your residence on Studium. They have also found that shuttle on the stony-land and the signs of the use of the Mummy-Ointment in it. All the S. Stations of this asteroid have been blocked. It is dangerous to wait here any longer."

"Oh God! I am fed up." Susan said, "What is going to get impaired if we give the Mummy-Ointment to Ros and surrender to the Devil? At least those wretched people will stop chasing us. They are interested in the *'Book of Bell'*, not in our lives. And the Devil will surely have some knack to release Robrelco Fero off the bonds with our souls?"

"Probably he may not even have it and then it might also not be so simple." Nurai said, "In the rumors that are currently hot in the market, you and Paras are being connected to the Walk of Life creators Daarck and Filipa. Ros wants Daarck and why only Cons Lydia... Within a short time, Ros is going to arrange an assembly of the New-Gods of those eleven colonies, against whom the conspiracy of the *'Walk of Life'* has been done. And after that all eleven colonies will be chasing you together."

"Oh Devil...!" Paras said in a soft tone, pressing a hand on the lips with an expression as if narrating deep mysteries of character, "This commotion is such that there will be no scope of escape even after getting the citizenship of the Master Galaxy. Anyways, after our rebirth on Earth we have to wait for three months for the nerves to get matured before the Memory-Machine can be used on Susan and me. During that period, just suppose, you, Maya and Sebastian are not there… I will have to go to the Earth once more in order to arrange for more resources to use the Memory Machine on us." Saying this, pointing his first finger towards the ground, he gestured right now to Susan who was talking on the phone with Koll.

Adding stubbornness in her voice now, Susan said, "Koll, I can no longer bear the burden of proving that disregarding the most powerful person of this asteroid, was indeed my childishness..! We can get together right away..?"

Disconnecting the phone, when Susan showed her thumb, Paras said addressing Nurai, "Koll is a fox. I don't think we can grab such a big sum from him. Keep the *'airbus'* ready near the Palanquin Stand. I do not see any other way except to escape from here now. Whatever has to happen will happen, we can conduct the ritual sometime later." And as if he remembered something, he said raising his head, "I will cancel the deal with the tantrik and come back… Now we don't want to put Viter in Dion's body anymore."

"Of what use is that fractional money received from cancelling the deal with the tantrik for us?" Susan asked.

"After all this ruckus we don't have enough left to buy even a begging bowl." Saying this, he looked around and wore the Thistle-Cap. He took Nurai with him and departed towards the tantrik's cave.

Stopping Susan as she was about to go to meet Koll Your Highness, *'Dion'* wrapped his hand on her arm. "Where were you throughout the day today..?" Signaling Dion to pay attention to Eliza who was pulling his other hand, excited by the female accessible madness of shopping near the markets created by the *'employment-nomads' (vendors wandering around the world in search of employment)* of the progressive planets, Susan said, "I was at home only." and started walking again.

Walking behind Susan as he took a *'typewriter'* from one person who seemed to have a head screen with a barcode for worldwide transport license that could be read with a laser, Dion said, "You beautiful ladies do not bother to do even a little hard work before you tell a lie. If your lie would be even a little bit logical, we men would at least be spared from putting up an act to show that we have been fooled..."

"This is for you." Saying this he put the typewriter in Susan's hand.

"Undoubtedly... This should be fulfilling the typing requirements of the current ultra-modern offices in a unique way." Susan said looking at the strange kind of gift.

Dion smiled and gave a manifesto in her hand.

'An annotation that gives the ideal timing to type for obtaining a favorite thing' Susan quickly surfed through the index and opened a page, something that looked like a gramophone pin was shooting the typed words and melting them in the air. Along with photos, the pages in the back had a narration of the experiences of people who had been successful in becoming billionaires and fulfilling other desires of their mind with the magic of typing.

"We will meet at your mansion within a short time." Susan said, thinking of seducing Dion in case Koll did not get beguiled, and increased the speed of her steps.

*

"What is this story of the tantrik?" Nurai asked when they reached near the cave.

"Hmmm… The couples have been made inaccurately." Paras said.

"Means?"

"The two communities living on this asteroid, *'Groch'* and *'Litton'*, are so uncompromising that in order to keep the blood of each of their races pure, they have invented a strange vaccine. A vaccine given to a child instantly at the time of birth. After this, a physical relationship between a Groch and Litton will result in death for both of them. Dion loves Eliza but Eliza is a Litton. That is why he wants to put Eliza's soul in Yaara's body. Viter is a Litton and Yaara a Groch. And Yaara wanted to put Viter in Dion's body to get her hands on him. And the tantrik, who claims to hold the power to exchange bodies, a deceitful imposter."

Just when Paras had reached the exasperated tantrik and told him in his ears that Dion was coming, the voice of the front door opening once again was heard. "Our deal is getting cancelled." Paras said lifting up the bag of Rubeptic from the corner, "But don't worry, Dion doesn't know anything." As the tantrik turned towards the door, he and Nurai quickly wore the Thistle Cap again and stood in one corner.

Taking out a Hobo styled purse from her nape, Eliza pulled out a letter from it and gave it to the tantrik. Put his hand on his chest the tantrik took the *'Rokrey Letter'* with the specific sign and welcomed Prince Dion. *(Rockrey Letter – A pasta letter that can be eaten after reading)*

"How could the person giving the recommendation have an idea that this dangerous work is going to drain out my lifetime accomplishments..." The tantrik started negotiating as he chewed the Rockrey Letter.

"All that will be taken care of later, but what if there is a goof-up while pushing Eliza's soul into Yaara's body?" Dion asked transferring the heavy bag of Rubeptics from one hand to another.

"Be assured, your work will be accomplished in an excellent and immaculate manner. I am especially known for accomplishing within the stipulated period in a faultless manner. Eliza's soul will never experience that Yaara's body is not her own."

A smile surfaced on Paras' face.

"And what about Yaara's soul?" Dion asked.

"It will keep on wandering. Or otherwise, if there is some path determined for it, then it will walk towards that."

"Can it be imprisoned and retained?" Dion asked again and Eliza looked at him with eyes opened wide.

"Umm.. It is not impossible for people who are not afraid of atrocious risks. Risk, especially when the presence of that soul is around its own body." Saying this, the tantrik extended his hand to take the bag of Rubeptic.

"I will send *Collin* tomorrow morning, and he will help you get the things required for the ceremony. *(Collin – Dion's loyalist)*

"I will be present at your mansion tomorrow night at the time of the *'Kings Royale'* national festival. Imprison and keep Yaara ready. But remember, the work will stop if just five seconds differ from here to there. These five seconds will be our slave. Between that, Eliza's life should be taken away by hands inspired by a heart of steel. If some weak hearted person panics and gets stuck, then Eliza's soul will get lost in such depths of hell from where it will be almost impossible to find it again."

Dion, who was usually oblivious to fear, felt as if his heart will tear his chest apart and come out in order to escape. Eliza's face also was like that of a tender hearted damsel trapped in the jaws of a crocodile.

"In short, luck has remained adamant on its stubbornness to make me wealthy today." As the tantrik murmured putting the bag given by Dion in exactly the same corner from where Paras had taken his bag, his abominable face looked extra ugly.

*

Gosha, facing *Lord de Ros'* questioning eyes asking *after blocking the S. Stations of the minor planetoids of Koll, what strategy has now been designed to find out from amongst the sixty million people living there, two people Paras and Susan whose being there is just a blurred possibility and whose Aura Print also is not available* finally relaxed with Luiciano's advent.

Luciano, captivated in the hands of the Gardis said bowing his head "I beg your pardon, my Lord, for kidnapping Rihon for the Devil, but my professional ability was not giving me permission to counsel with anyone about it before the success of this move of mine. I had no other way apart from this to reach Antonio. When Rihon was seized, I had quietly slipped a GPS dot in his pocket. The Devil does not have an option except to get Rihon and Antonio under one roof."

When Lord de Ros gestured the Gardis who had seized him to leave, suddenly Luciano's whole body started trembling with a jolt as if a spirit of the Devil had entered his body. Gaping into Ros' eyes with glowing red eyes, he said in a killer's voice, "This is very convenient for you… Rihon, Antonio, Paras and Susan… Seizing all of them from one single place, that too, from *'Earth'*, a planet of Cons Lydia only…"

When everyone including Gosha swiftly came forward to overtake Luiciano for this great audacity, he said in a gentle voice, suddenly returning to his normal behavior as if he was not responsible for his actions, "These whereabouts based on *'Moutier'*, the distant town of France on our toy planet Earth is actually Rihon's sanctuary." After Ros raised his hand and indicated that everyone should move behind, he said firmly, "They have reached there just some minutes ago to acquire the *'Contras Affair' (The book that containing the spells required to release Robrelco Fero who was imprisoned with the souls of Paras and Susan)* that Rihon has hidden there But probably, here the Gardi-Force might have to face *Beelzebub (the Devil)* himself. They will not wait there any longer. They are going with Antonio towards some secret *bogmack (den)* of Daarck to look out for something like the Re-Built Tune."

"Ohh…" Ros said, "And the aura print record of Paras and Susan might be with Antonio on *Moletan*." *(Moletan – A site that maintains the online records of the aura structure)*

Catching Luciano pressing his tongue between the teeth for his foolishness done in a hurry, Gosha threw him into a chair.

*

Within the fourth minute of Luciano giving Gosha the information of Rihon's live location and *'The Mahanabh Central Commanding Station'* giving a green signal for the mission, three thousand Gardi soldiers had descended at the Northpole S. Station on Earth.

Coming out of the station, they embarked onto the *'i698'* shuttles that were waiting for them on the *'Channel-S'* takeoff strip amidst the desolate icy deserts. In the next second after the geographical co-ordinates became Latitude - 46° 05" 30 North, Longitude - 02° 03" 18" East as per the land based tactical venue navigation, their aircrafts disappeared. They had lost less than sixteen minutes to reach *'Moutier'* of Central France from Mahanabh that was millions of miles away.

"Ten Thirty pm." Matching his worldly watch with the clocks of Moutier's houses, *'Lord Meyer' (A Gardi Commander)* released man made spy flies from a small box. After the energetic flies sent the March-Clearance signal from all four sides of the roads leading towards the Devil's site, three thousand Gardi soldiers who had become invisible with the help of the Thistle-Cap fabricated in such a way that it would not be possible to see them even with a Kirlian Glass, started moving forward along the edges of the green houses that were based touching the seams. Whether the Devil needed to breathe or not, but possibly the cool fragrance of the lavender flowers had fallen in love with November and even continued to violate the seasonal-term..?

Moutier was now left too far behind. The Gardi-Force is standing silently in front of the territory constructed in the wild terrain. Their feet that had frozen with the load, now gradually started trembling with the imagination of the Devil. Lord Meyer is watching the video broadcasted from the brown eyes of the *'spy-bees'* that had reached every corner of the row of wood-tiled houses on the left side and a house that was located at a thirty feet distance on the right side. Lowering the *castifo (A high speed lazer gun of the Gardi-Force)*, he gave a commentary to the Gardi soldiers who were aspiring to see someone like Rihon and Antonio amidst the security of some other world-

"Antonio is lying with his eyes closed in a delicately carved chair. Rihon's other companions also have been tied up in the same room. In the same chamber, a Satanic wearing a *'battle dress',* like that of an old French soldier, who is sitting in the opposite direction of the temporary control display is shoving a *'spy-bee'* flying in front of his nose. The guest-houses are empty. There is no space in the foundation of the building, but still it can be a deception. Surrounded by six energy warriors on the top floor, *'Rihon'* is typing the password on the key-pad of the safe." Saying this much, Lord Meyer who was about to cross and enter the three feet high cactus fence at the edge of the courtyard clad with shining ice, stopped to read the *'Come in one's way'* inscription written in French on the nameplate tied with a wooden prop.

When the crowd of operators agitated to know the reason of this minor security of Satanics grouped there together in front of the *'Mahanabh Control Station'* screen, the five Gardi soldiers who had reached the back door heard a weird jingling noise.

As the eyes of the Gardis were about to tear apart the lashes and come out with the thought of the Devil having come and stood behind their neck, there was a terrible attack of pure energy on the back of three out of five Gardis. The nose of the Gardis was grounded. In a hurry, the remaining two Gardis made the mistake of targeting only one *'Satanic Energy Warrior'* the other Energy Warrior who had survived, got an opportunity.

Claws could be seen coming out of his *Amavasya (the night of no moon when it is pitch dark)* like black cloak worn by him and with the help of the violently dancing electricity that was coming out of his toes, the hungry death also got a chance to ogle the other two Gardis.

The Gardis were now introduced to the different types of strategies made by the Satanics. Passing through the battle area in the sky at lightning speed, the Satanic shuttles had suddenly appeared on the scene one after another from who knows where to wreak havoc on the Gardis. Due to the time taken for the restructuring of the broken bodies of the Gardis, this attack had been done through an aircraft with the motive that the Satanics would be faster. Despite that the Gardis astonished the energy warriors by counter attacking them with *'the S220'*. A large part of the *'Satanic Warriors'* were either killed, or taken as prisoners. *('The S220' - A polonium gun, invented by the Colony 'Glee Metal Casting', that had the capability to make a hole in the protective layer of the Gizmo Belt. 'Gizmo Belt'– Its cover made with invisible waves on the body's surface, produces movement in the light particles and is able to resist any form of energy that moves physically, like a 'bullet', in a way that is even stronger than steel. A kind of electronic armor.)*

Going towards the chamber where the five energy warriors had hidden themselves after crushing Antonio's and Rihon's groups, *'Lord Meyer'* stopped on seeing the new information that had flashed on the *in-head camera glass.*

The Earth Eleven headquarter controller who had barged into the air traffic control of every country on the

Earth said, "The possibility of such a Satanics battalion that might have been kept outside the range of the enemy's gun for a surprise attack cannot be denied. Apart from that one of the two airplanes having identical alphanumeric registration is currently taxiing on Paris' *'Charles'* runway. There can be a backup team of the Satanics in that. This airplane will be there in approximately six minutes."

The Satanics, who only had the permission to injure Antonio and Rihon's gang, were questioning each other with their eyes, the weak looking Antonio, held the claws of one of those Satanics and bent it with so much power that the condition of his broken wrists became like a witch's leg. As the Energy Warriors coming in their real Satanic temperament, raised toes splattering deadly waves with a ripping expression in front of him, exactly at that very instant, Antonio experienced bullets fired passing over his shoulders.

Gesturing gently with his head in front of Lord Meyer's bent head, Antonio slowly came out. Behind him while two Gardi soldiers were supporting the limping Rihon and bringing him outside, far away, sweet symphonies of *'One garden on Earth… only one insignificant mistake…'* in the voice of *'Serj Llama'* were echoing from the calm villages of France that were saying *'get out'*.

*

When Susan who was bored waiting was thinking of returning back, she saw *'Koll' (The king of this asteroid)* coming from the opposite side of the palanquin stand.

He had worn Kirlian Glasses. Susan's shy smile responded to his stalking smile.

This area also was not free from the revelry of the annual national festival. One part of the road was for the buggies and palanquins, the second for the infantry and the third had been designated for modern vehicles.

"Our asteroid was awarded the *'Gravity Machine'*, because Highness wanted to make it a *'Maverick'* asteroid moving in space, right? Hmmm…" When walking beside Koll the invisible Susan, said softly, they took a turn in the lane near the *'Fire-Protective System'* factory and entered a house giving them access to a tunnel that would lead them to the tower. *(Gravity Machine – That which releases the planet from the effect of gravity and makes it independent to relocate.)*

Susan entered a dirty room behind Koll. She had never seen such a dirty place earlier. Carefully drawing Susan from amongst several artisans standing in the big room, when *'Koll'* stared at her in extreme astonishment, Susan said in a serious voice, "Koll, this asteroid of yours and both the communities residing here are about to be destroyed very soon. Except until the Cons Lydia is convinced that the receiver tower, preparing the energy warriors was constructed here by *Devil family* through threatening and terrifying you and also that you do not have any contribution in this war against Cons Lydia."

The back door of the room had opened up onto an open space. After passing through a small lobby, leading her into a room where tools had been arranged, Koll spoke peering into her eyes without moving his glance for some time, "And how do you know about all this?"

"It's not necessary" Susan started laying a trap to extort the amount for the ritual. Koll slid his wrist behind the big showcase on the opposite wall displaying the old tools. Mostly his habituated fingers dialled a password. The wall decorated with the tools slid open and oxygen-bags attached with masks could be seen within the space that was enough to get inside comfortably. Now as Cons Lydia has compelled you to block your departure S.stations of the asteroid and Gardi forces has started to arrive on this asteroid, I don't need to provide any proofs for whatever I say.

When they descended about three floors below in the dim light, a six-seater trolley like a bullet train engine was seen at the head of the high tunnel in which one could stand comfortably. "It is true, that there is no other thing as dangerous as the confluence of intelligence and beauty in the world." Koll murmured pressing Susan's seat belt while she was thinking that the trolley standing on shining steel might probably be running on a magnet. Estimating that the trolley was running at a speed of at least three hundred kms. per hour from the walls that were passing by, Susan looked at the watch and precisely at that moment, the trolley knocked at its destination and stopped there. This was an eleven minutes journey.

"Listen to me very carefully now," Looking at the soft music emitting drops falling from the points of the protruding gorges hanging like the corners of her eyes from the ceiling of a very big cave, Susan said, "The strategy I have in mind certainly asks for the sacrifice of your ambition to expand your empire with the help of the Energy Warriors, but with that, it also saves you." Wading through ankle high water they reached the sail shaped tall door of the tower. As Koll pressed just one button three times in the piano designed on the right door, a glass cup came out from behind the key-pad. After gulping down one sip sizing of the pink liquid from the cup, Koll put his thumb on the same spot for the sample of blood. After the completion of the investigation of the reaction of the chemical mixed with the blood, the door automatically opened and welcomed them.

"What does *this best mediator weapon (Yaara)* who can destroy anyone's loyalty ultimately contemplate to do?" Koll asked.

"The only way to prove yourself to be innoxious in the view of Cons Lydia is that you have to blow up this tower preparing the energy warriors. This will prove that you are not involved with the Devil family and in order to execute this, our communication satellites shall be out of order suddenly within few minutes." Susan said.

"Means?"

"Now when your confrontation is with the Satanic warriors who have declared themselves as the owners of your own army, we can only defeat them in this manner- Tomorrow night since there is the *'Kingdom Fête'* there will be an urgent need to replace the communication satellites that we will disrupt. But we will launch *'Killer*

Satellites' instead of them. That will strike every location of your army that has been transformed into Energy Warriors like a thunderstorm. On all locations, at the same time! You just have to see to it that this asteroid is near the Earth as much as possible throughout the day tomorrow. I will take care of the rest. Now tell me how soon you can deliver the *Rubeptic (Koll's currency)* to Earth's currency convertor point?" *(Killer Satellite – A war-craft firing dangerous laser beams in the guise of a communication satellite.)*

Seeing Koll scratching his head, she said, "See all this happens in this manner- Since the S. Stations here have been blocked…" Susan suddenly stopped and asked, "Do you have a Dummy to get out of here?" *(A Dummy S. Station connects to the 'Channel S.' of Master Galaxy in an illegal way and becomes deadrest after being used for about three times. Every New-God has constructed numerous Dummy S. Stations on hidden locations of their own and other colonies' planets to be used in situations when there is a need to spy or for war.)*

"I do not have any Dummy." Koll said.

"It's alright. As the S stations here are blocked, we shall use the currency convertor point situated near San Francisco for making the payment to the weapon dealer of colony Noble Shift from whom we are purchasing the Killer satellites. *(The financial transactions and the video, audio communication of not only all the planets of the colonies of Galaxy L3, but also all the six galaxies of the local group and the Master Galaxy are done through the S. Station Communication Towers only.)* Within thirty minutes of the payment getting transferred, they will deliver the satellites and the launching vehicles to the launching site owned by a *'San Francisco'* company *'Parli Scope Corporation'* which is based in the *'Democratic Republic of the Congo'* in Central Africa."

"Is the launching site of Parli Scope situated in Central Africa because a Dummy S. Station is constructed there?" Koll asked.

"No, no, the owners of Parli Scope are the inhabitants of the toy planet. This is for what they call *Escape Velocity*. The *'Democratic Republic of the Congo'* is near the Equator. A speed of seven miles per second is required to send the rocket into space with enormous speed against the gravity. And in order to get this speed, the residents of Earth make use of the booths based in the countries near the Equinoctial Line so that they can also get the benefit of the speed of the Earth that rotates around its own axis. When we are making use of the most modern launching vehicles, it will take less than one and a half hours for the satellites to reach the orbital level of this asteroid from Earth. And these satellites will be roaming over the skies of the war zone from the orbital level in about twenty minutes whenever we require them. Although our arrival stations have not yet been closed, hence we will directly get the control bags that drive and operate the Killer Satellites delivered here from Nebel Shift." Haassh… Susan thought as she paused to take a breath, "After all this hard work if Koll says no, I will strangle his throat right away."

After staring continuously at this dangerous mind wrapped in beauty, Koll said, "Alright, but my loyalist Orian is not present here on the asteroid. He was going to come here on the night of Kings Royale. Well, I will call him right away. I will send him to Parli Scope Corporation with the Rubeptic. Orian will personally pay the amount to Parli Scope and come to the currency convertor point with your *blue coat (detective*). There, he himself will transfer the money to the *'Nebel Shift's'* weapon dealer and provided that during the time Orian makes payment and up to the time the towers are blown off, you should be in front of my eyes."

Susan, looking angrily at Koll, finally said, "I don't have any objection. A person named Sebastian will be waiting for him at Parli Scope."

How the hell can a person be considered a king when he avoids to express his beliefs to the others? "If the controversies of the deceptions by beautiful ladies would not be echoing in my ears, I would not have waited for Orian against such a huge amount." he finally ejaculated.

*

As Lord de Ros paced forward toward, Antonio seated in a chair near fire place shivered, he blurted, "This traitor conspires to become the New God of Cons Lydia by captivate you with Tie-in-Tune." The finger pointed towards Rihon who was taken outside was trembling like a seismograph needle.

Turning towards Ros, Rihon said in a humble praising voice, "My Lord, angels know what nonsense Antonio is uttering. However, the *'Devil'* had captured me for something like a Re-built Tune."

Gesturing Rihon to get out, Ros said, "Antonio, do you know, I am always eager to take the risk of keeping several enemies amongst us to check my talent. And, Rihon also has the right to take steps to save himself."

Nebulous voices were rising from the underside of the castle, as if it was built on a waterway connecting two big streams of water.

Antonio folded his hands, because ultimately he was sitting in front of a highly respected personality In front of a New-God Who alone was the owner of fifty planets... And who did not have the compulsion to depend on any Chairmen, Presidents or Gardi-Force to sustain the ownership. Antonio said giving the password to acquire Paras' and Susan's aura-print from Moletan, "But I have already given this password to the Devil and if arrangements are made to send me safely to Colony '*Metal Casting*', then probably I can provide the address of the Mummy Ointment enough to make Ros Malesty'." He did not have any strength left to tolerate further complications anymore.

"Your misfortune is really stubborn." Ros said in a sophisticated voice, "just a day ago, Master Galaxy has already implemented these rules that were pending for decades. One of those rules makes the Mummy-Ointment useless till such time I do not make my Aura Print exactly the same as Malesty's Aura Print. This means that even if I change my body with Malesty through the Mummy-Ointment and infect my aura through the virus, yet the '*New-Gods' or 'Chairmen'* with such an aura disorganized by infection that not matches anyone's Aura Print in the world are now useless for governance. And apart from that, you do not know what kind of a dangerous enmity I have with the Devil and Paras alias Daarck."

Absorbing one more shock, Antonio closed his eyes and started transferring the information of the location of the Mummy Ointment he had transferred from the spinal clot to the slot in the brain at the time of leaving Central France again into the spine through the neurons-network.

"We have all of this infinite life for remaining questions and answers but presently there is just one question for the solution of which I may cross any limit. It is not possible that Daarck who furnished an excellent idea to invent the Mummy Ointment to removing the 'Vio-Crazy' 'New-Gods' along with the Armies prepared under Walk Of Life without any commotion (big battles) would not be aware about the Master Galaxy's motive to implement this rule regarding the 'aura', from almost an era. He must have gone through a lot of trouble regarding the discovery of the 'transmission germ' and I need the Mummy-Ointment with the pair of this transmission germ.' *(Transmission Germ – A re-cult mapping virus for giving the exactly same aura-structure of one individual to another individual, for a few hours.)*

*

As Susan returned to Holm festival's main parade path area, the place could be seen surrounded by *Gardi soldiers* and *Satanic Warriors* roaming with aura monitor. As they watched the army deployed by Ros with aura monitors on this asteroid preparing the pure energy warriors, Devil family had not to consume much time to understand that they were searching for Paras & Susan. (*Aura Monitor – A device capturing the human Aura Print identifying it from a distance of some feet*)

The Thistle Cap he had worn was useless in preventing the magnetic fluid (aura) from capturing. Far away in the distance, wherever the glance could reach, the whole sky of the asteroid had been filled with small and big airbuses of the Gardis and Satanics. It was not difficult to conjecture that both *'Ros'* and *'Devil'* would have deployed hundreds of thousands of their soldiers on the whole asteroid to find them. They were opening the restaurants, bars, casinos, small and big shops and each and every house and were holding the aura-monitor in front of every individual and investigating their aura-print. She was now tired of searching for Paras. She had forgotten to take the phone back that had been deposited before going into Koll's tower. A situation of war had almost been created on the asteroid between the Gardis and the Satanics. In many places conflicts were created between the Gardi and Satanic warriors to investigate the aura of an individual together at the same time. She saw Dion standing between two young girls who were doing coquetting in front of the camera. She went and stood under the cover of a tall pillar in order to save herself from his glance, the speakers hanging on the stype of the pillar roared up… "The length of the day will be six hours tomorrow, and the temperature will be approximately 25 degree Celsius."

Looking at this awful trap, Susan's head had started reeling. Her mind had stopped working. She herself did not realize when her left hand removed the Thistle Cap from her head. She moved further and further in the colourful crowd of the festival like a living corpse. It was impossible for her awesome beauty to prevent all the roaming glances from focusing at one place. She came to her senses as she saw two Gardi soldiers raising the aura monitor and hurriedly rushing towards her. Quickly turning her back, she started walking in the opposite direction, but having walked just a few steps she saw a big crowd of Gardis approaching her, she felt like a panic button pressed. She swiftly turned her neck towards the left and right, the situation in all directions was the same. Amidst her diminishing hopes, when she was approximately one inch or so away from the range of the aura monitor, Nurai firmly caught her hand and pulled her towards the footpath.

Gently shoving Susan to take her to the opposite side of the road, Nurai quickly opened the door of a classic Lando and pushed her inside.

"We have escaped from Elvis' spies after a lot of trouble." Uncertainty was peering from Nurai's baggy voice as he fearfully looked here and there from both the sides of the Lando's window.

Susan frowned and looked towards Nurai.

Nurai said, "Finally revealing himself in front of Elvis, Paras threatened him that, 'How Luiciano and Elvis shredded the loyalty towards the Devil Family into pieces to safeguard their interests and had the terrible audacity to keep the Devil away from Robrelco Fero, that is from me and Susan, if you do not wish me to call up the S.O.G. and describe the overall scene at this very moment, then take all your detectives and move back right away.' And 'after all, one day the Devil Family will not be ignorant about the fact of this treachery.' Saying this Elvis ordered his spies to seize Paras and me. but a squad of Koll's Peace-Officers was passing by and we were successful in slipping and escaping from that one sided scuffle."

"Elvis is not among those who accept defeat. Even now, he will be designing a new strategy. Where is Paras?" Susan asked.

"He is safe." He said, clearing the concern from Susan's face, "And I think that in order to remain safe it is now necessary for you to take the risk of the aura-medicine. (A drug generating disruption in the Aura Print in order to prevent their Aura from getting identified) Nurai spoke further,

"It has been heard in the discussions of the Satanics wandering with the aura-monitors in hand that the Devil has come there personally. With his mysterious powers, he is being visible in all directions at ones. And He has engaged his full powers to realize the thoughts of success broadcasted from the minds of Lord de Ros' or anyone of his own soldiers as soon as your aura-prints are matched. And it will not be surprising if the king of 'Cons Lydia' himself would come here looking out for you within a short time. That's because ultimately, it's a question of the ownership of countless planets of these eleven colonies." (*Because those eleven projects discs giving victory over these eleven colonies were with Daarck and Filipa*)

After crossing several turns during the continuous twenty minute drive, the *'Lando'* finally came and stood at the corner of a dark lane. Five floor tall buildings were there on both sides of the lane. Nurai led her to a small terrace through a dilapidated house formerly used as *Operational Command Quarter* situated at the end of the dimly lit lane resembling the drunkards' den.

"Soon We shall be talking on the subject which shall not be related to how to break forth from the "*Book of Bell*". Susan said to Paras, who was assembling a small two-seater aircraft beneath a black pavilion on the terrace.

"Koll agreed…?" Paras asked turning his head quickly.

"Yes, but there is a problem, Koll's minister Orian will personally be making the payment to the dealers at both the places, *'Parli Scope'* and *'Nebel Shift'*."

"That will not make any difference." Paras said, attaching the last parts of the aircraft. For the first time after the rush that had started since the hasty travel from Romania, he was looking a little healthy due to the sound sleep of about an hour that he had managed to get.

Orian is not so foolish that he will transfer the Rubeptic before conducting an investigation related to the weapon dealer's account."

"It is not a big deal, Sebastian will handle it. Susan, I shall have to leave now." He said as he got up and wiping hands, started getting down.

Susan squinting under the pretence of watching the nail at Paras rushing here and there in room collecting his travel gear asked, "You are not forgetting something that you should be taking with you, is it…?"

Putting Eliza's blood sample in the bag, he came to Susan and wrapped his arms around her neck. Taking his lips forward as if pulled by a vacuum-cleaner, he kissed Susan and said, "There is a possibility that each and every bird flying out from here would be probably followed. It is not rational for us to go together."

"Is it necessary for us to be together during our death?" Susan asked.

Paras said, "I spoke to Obiaahno. After the payment is transferred, would there be a problem if I discard my body there on the Earth and you here on the asteroid? But his response was evasive. He stated that he does not have any experience about the outcome of this type of violation in the rules of such rituals. Now you tell me..!"

"Oh, these spurious Diabolis... Forget it, as it is I want to die in your arms only." Rubbing the part under her eyes with her ring finger, Susan gave a faint smile and put the cover she had with her into the bag filled with Memory-Machines that Paras had to take with him and came to the terrace behind Paras.

*

Sabastian was standing in front of the headquarter of a private organization manufacturing the related to Space systems and Space crafts located in the forests near *San Francisco.*

He removed his goggles as he saw the slanted reflection of the Ice coated trees of coniferous on the opposite side, in the embossed letters of *Parli Scope Corporation* on the building cladded with silver colored glass.

Parli Scope was quite enthusiastic as it was new.

"Mr. Sebastian, we do not claim our name to be on the top in that companies, who give International Launching Services, but suppose we imagine this company to be working from the long past when even the Apollo yan was in the experimental stage yet this private organisation should have the capability to manufacture *Communication satellites* which I have realized in my neutral analysis."

In the chamber of Parli Scope, Chairman was busy in getting the signature of Sabastian sipping the coffee on the *Launching Deal Agreement*, He smiled to the chairman and said, "No, no, you are taking this in a different way. Our satellites are getting launched from the Parli Scope Launching Stations, which proves that I am not at all doubtful about Parli Scope's capability."

"It is not that we are bound to use the territory not controlled by America for transport.'

"It looks like Mr. Orian has arrived." The Chairman stopped and looking inside the door, he went towards the window behind Sebastian after bidding farewell to the man who had come to deliver the message.

One more person along with Orian got down from the Orchid coloured long van below bearing the logo of PS merging to each other. He had *Muzzle Twenty One* in his hands *(a high speed Gun)(Orian – Koll's loyalist)*

Orian opened the door before the half bent chairman could take his seat. Arranging the camera hidden in the pin caught in a clumsy way in the *'blue'* colored tie that was a mismatch with the *'Grillo-Grey'* colored suit, he shook hands with the Chairman who was standing behind the table and Sebastian.

"I am happy, Mr. Orian that you did not have to go through a lot of trouble to make the right choice for launching." The talkative Chairman started talking again, "But if those satellites would have been made in Parli Scope, then the matter would have been something like this : Best in every performance, adaptive rotational mechanism, jam free steering system, solar drive mechanism, ozone monitor, climate surveyor, topography mapper, the best in every technological process."

It looked as if Orian was getting bored and taking advantage of this welcome situation, Sebastian kept the agreement in front of him. After hatefully reading about three pages of the agreement spread over multiple pages he glanced once towards Sebastian who was sitting beside him and bent his head indicating consent in front of the Chairman. The Chairman gave him a cover which had the account details to transfer the dollars.

The words of the Chairman, who had come to leave them till the door, could be heard until they climbed down one floor, "Do not worry at all, our *'Carrier Rocket'* is not inferior in level to Delta-2 of NASA, in any way."

*

One reason for choosing Parli Scope was also that its headquarter was near Earth's hidden Galactic Currency Convertor Point. Towards which Sebastian and Orian were driving. Through the signals broadcasted by the bolts of every registered note from the bundles of Rubeptics touching the roof of their van, in a way, *'Koll'*, who was seated on the asteroid, was also going near the Currency Convertor Point.

After a thirty minute drive, at the Convertor Point that was based in the basement of an old timber yard amidst the jungle, they were given a *'slip'* in return of the Rubeptics that were deposited on its counter. After Orian was totally satisfied regarding the account of Nebel Shift's weapon dealer, he had transferred the amount to buy six killer satellites.

When they came out, the driver of the taxy called for Sebastian was lounging with his back on it and was smoking. Orian waited watching taxi of Sebastian disappear. After some time, he rode the van and drove away towards the air bus parked by him. Before the conversation with the driver with a Scottish features can prolong further than exchange of the names, Sebastian returned there and went inside the basement of the Currency convertor Point once again.

"But at the moment I don't want to discuss about how this has happened." Sebastian said with a fake bewildered voice, "I apologize for troubling you but one out of six *'Satellite Weapons'* that I am not cancelling is not our requirement but indicates our feeling of embarrassment. I am sending the detail of the accounts in which the balance amount has to be transferred. A little quickly. Please."

*

Paras had checked the radar screen in his modern Cockpit several times during the journey of three hours and fifty seconds starting from the asteroid from which he flew the air craft and up to the vision of the lights of New York city. Still his belief that every shuttle flying from Koll's are surely followed by Gardies had not been confirmed. The hands of the clocks in New York were showing nine twenty of night. He selected a sixteen storied building just little far from Time Square out of numerous tall buildings and landed his shuttle on its terrace. After holding the aura medicine in his hands for a short while, finally he gathered courage and put it in to his mouth. He felt his whole body drenched in perspiration as he waited with throbbing heart for five seconds. He looked at his right hand which was hanging loosely like a pendulum of a clock as if paralysed. Finally he jumped out of the shuttle accumulating all his power. He stood up with the help of the door handle after dragging on the floor to reach the cabin at the top of the building. He came down to the sixteenth floor with trembling steps. He checked the display, the lift was still at the first floor. He quickly started descending the stairs.

The shuttle of the Gardi force landed on the sixty floored tall building casting its shadow on the building where Paras had landed. They were lagging by forty seconds and the commander of these immortal Gardi soldiers was not concerned at all about their pain. He pushed down six Gardi soldiers one by one from the terrace. A stampede aroused suddenly among the mob enjoying the comfortable treat at the adjoin footpath restaurant due to the six serial blasts. Gardis ran aggressively after Paras bumping off some of the people proceeding in the direction of blasts with their classic Cocktails and coffee cups.

"Ohh! Damn it!" Paras exclaimed in grief looking towards a signboard as he continued to walk in a way that could be termed as running, towards the Time Square that looked as if Energy Day was celebrated there every day. He was still nine hundred meters away from the venue that had been decided to meet Devdan and he did not have any strength left to walk upto that place. The first thing that the Gardis who had become invisible through the electronic device – Thistle Cap worn on their heads did was to check Paras' magnetic flow with the Aura Monitor. Although his Aura-Print did not match, there was no decrease in the caution of the Gardis. They were explicitly chasing him. The Aura-Medicine had totally clenched him in its vicious effect. The flamboyant lights of the shining advertising boards from all four sides of the tall buildings were now becoming intolerable for him. He showed his hand to a taxi and connecting a call to Maya, inserted the infrared-dot in his ear.

The Gardis' speed of running was challenging that of the taxi.

"There is one bad news." Maya said, as she stood in a firing position with a speedometer like instrument pointed towards the road in one corner of the footpath near Time Square, "The tanker that was coming for the *re-fill (shuttle's fuel)* has met with an accident. You are not going to reach the asteroid on time."

Time Square was exactly in front of him and leaving the taxi, Paras started walking again. Before the taxi driver swirling around the Rubeptic note in his hand in amazement could start shouting, two Gardies having entered from both sides snatched away the note from his hands.

"Who is this..?" Taxi driver asked narrowing his eyes.

"Soldiers of your actual owner..." The Gardi sitting on his left knocked him unconscious by giving him a shock on his neck with a *'Stun Gun'* and started tearing apart the taxi for investigation.

As Paras reached near the N.Y.P.D. building, Maya standing with an instrument to measure the frequency of Human Magnetic Fluid and having confirmed that Paras was shadowing by invisible Gardis, she pulled out a pin of only blast creating grenade on explosion and threw it in the middle of the road.

It took a second for the thoughts of the terrorist attack to show its wonder whirling in the top layer of the every brain roaming there. Paras quickly took of the bag from his shoulder and taking advantage of the situation where Gardis were entangled in a stampede and taking out the Memory machine from it, he threw it in to a passing Garbage truck. He noted the number of the truck and connected a call to Devdan.

"Mr. Devdan, I believe in those past stories of your loyalty narrated by Eddie and trust me that there is one and only one way to survive from those unbelievable forces against whom you are assisting me is the way to abolish your existence from their memory. The garbage truck proceeding towards south is now passing just in front of you." Paras quickly got him to note down the truck number and said, "If I do not turn up to collect this packet within next one and half year then the user manual showing how to use the memory machine on us and the details of my new identity are placed with it. Besides, you have to take care of the container which will be handed over to you by my manager Sebastian within a short time."

Paras, who had been expecting to hear some words that would guarantee trustworthiness, got to hear something totally different. "Forgive me, but since my base is in New York nowadays, you had to deal with this unknown city." Devdan said, "As if this world is not an adequate medium to provide dangerous hardships, some mysterious germs have become eager to send my wife into another terrible world through the path of death. Actually I have come here leaving India as she is suffering from a disease like cancer. Eddie had recently promised to send her to some other planet for treatment."

"Oh, I'm sorry. But we will find the remedy for that. Sebastian will be able to solve this issue easily." Paras pulled out the Infrared dot from his ear and threw it far away as he saw Obiaahno seated on the footpath little far in a Burgundy coloured ragged suit looking like a demon of some other world. He quickly pulled out the hand that held the worm with Eliza's blood from his pocket and flung it behind that sign board of Obiaahno, on which it was written in big letters -

"Can I have a burger, man?"

*

The day that had brought the scent of Kings-Royale on the asteroid that looked as if Yaara had adorned herself with the best ornaments of her lifetime for her beloved, had now set on the horizon and the *'Kingdom Fête'*, that was going on in the foothills of the tower located amidst the mountains where the energy warriors were being prepared, was in its last stage. Yet, there was no clue whatsoever of Paras' whereabouts. Twelve hours had passed since he had been last contacted on phone.

The winding-up of this festival that was known as the *'Kingdom Fête'* or the *'Kings Royale'* was one of the main attractions. In which during one of the *'Kings Royale'* in his lifetime, every Highness had to perform a feat that would prove him to be different than the rest. After a lot of thinking, Koll had finally decided to fulfil this huge responsibility by fooling the inhabitants of the asteroid with the marvel of the Gizmo Belt. Years ago his father had prepared a Leaf bear expert over the asteroid's wild animal leaf bear in a secret manner. After discovering that the sensory system of this animal can be provoked and controlled by some specific posture, the feat of subduing this deadly animal was attributed to the magical power of Koll's father.

"Whether this wretched Yaara is not the one, whom the militants of Cons Lydia are frantically searching?" Standing between Dion and the tantrik beside the stage prepared for Koll to show off the feat of taking bullets on his chest, Eliza said in an intoxicated voice, "And Viter also has disappeared."

"I think you should prepare yourself for the days to struggling with the agony of failure. Forgive me but once the time elapses, I would not be able to do anything." Tantrik said and suddenly Yaara was seen coming out of the door of the tower behind the stage with Koll. She looked sick.

Patting the cheek of *'Eliza'* who had done so much intoxication since morning that all consciousness apart from being able to stand would be lost, Dion said, "I am bringing Yaara here. Don't be unconscious." Eliza opened half her eyes and looked all around.

Susan's glance, as she was standing ready with the *'Peep of Night'* gift to be given to His Highness, was roaming all around in the crowd for Paras. It was compulsory for the personalities close to Koll to give him three gifts in the morning, afternoon and night as a token of their love for the *'king'* on this day.

"Yaara, come with me." Dion said holding her hand.

"Not now." Susan said relieving her hand.

The glance of that man roving behind the crowd was riveted on Susan. Even though he had taken the *'Revert Pill'* (*After the effect of this medicine that changes the entire structure of the body in terms of height, size, appearance within a few minutes, wears off after a few hours, the person again comes back in his original form.)* and come in an altogether new appearance, Susan had immediately recognized him. Elvis pointed his thumb towards the sky and gave an indication of the throat being slit. This gesture of his would not have been successful in creating a doubt of Paras' murder in Susan's mind, but Dion again said holding her wrist, "Viter has been badly injured, he is taking his last breath. He is waiting for you at my mansion." If she wouldn't have seen Sebastian standing on the other side of the mob, near the new bakeries with a *'mobile control bag'*, the violent thoughts tearing the shroud and fighting about Paras' survival would have taken her life. In one corner of the crowd, Sebastian had worn street-styled attire.

The Killer-Satellite had been launched in the orbital level of the asteroid. Before the team employed in the *'Satellite Operations Center'* could understand anything, Sebastian standing in one corner of the crowd had brought the Satellite in the sky right above the tower through his mobile control bag.

"Aren't you out of your mind?" Dion said as Susan was firm. She finally got rid of the grip of Dion trying to pull her forcefully and reached the two beautiful ladies in Spanish Carmine on both sides of Koll fanning him by hand fan. Dion returned and remarked, "No problem, we will do this ceremony right here. In front of all. Come what may.

The tantrik, who had been grumbling about doing this in public, finally out of Dion's fear pulled out the sack hidden in the *'gowncoat'* and started laying out an assortment of malicious material next to Koll's stage near the candles burning in the multi-colored glass bottles, at the place where Eliza had to be executed.

Putting his hand on his waist, Koll's loyalist Orian came and stood in front of the tantric and raised his eyebrows questioningly.

"Hmm.. hmm.. hmm…" The tantrik, who had bent down laughing awkwardly in a loud voice, straightened. He said, "So that the completion of the Kingdom Fête turns out to be pleasant."

Dion had started creating a barrier of his soldiers all around to be safe from potential hurdles.

The last part of the *Kingdom Fête's* closing of that had to take place with some special courageous display of the present king, started with the tunes of a state-instrument. Exactly at the same time, the sick Paras struggling to reach the main party area was proceeding towards the stage. Thanks to the aura medicine, boils had sprung up on his whole body. As he came forward making way amidst the acrobatics who were throwing knives on the small fruits pressed between the teeth of their assistants who were standing far and the artisans who had made colorful illustrations on their body, betting had started on his staggering walk as to whether or not he will fall.

A music band of one of Cons Lydia's home planet, that was famous for its heavenly art of music, was currently playing music here. The pure musical notes flowing from the countless bayonets, hand instruments and mandolins were mixing with the most complex vocal paraphernalia of the pure tune assembly singers and producing heavenly music.

It was not as if total silence was required to hear this music, but since this entire spot of the festive event was intertwined in the vortex of fountains, lakes and mountains, it was only necessary to consume the '*toffee*' converting the mental chemicals of the band in order to experience the wonderful sounds of music coming out from the countless instruments arranged there around the gorges and on the shores of the lakes far, far away. And no one in the swaying 'crowd immersed in joyous interest' after liberally eating it, knew with what kind of terrible blast they were going to wake up.

The flow of the melodious music from heaven has now reached the foothills and the universal star started her dance and wow…. the hearts having forgotten the senses with the nectar of her eyes cried out… "That's all, this is the paramount pleasure of the constellation world. Prior to this, Paras had never seen Susan engrossed in the dance with such passionate vitality before. Perhaps this was the dance intended to win over the extreme pain for which the word unbearable shall be insufficient. Susan moving her eyes extensively with a budding posture of Pallavi became steady as she saw Paras. Her spirit experienced relief as she saw him safe and sound.

Taking out things to achieve the successful functionality of the ceremony from his sack, the tantrik forcibly diverted his glance from Susan's subduing whirlwind dance and started creating *'dark magic circles'*. Once Dion killed Eliza, a small trolley had to be passed over Eliza's body lying in the circle and taken onto Yaara's body. Holding a trolley loaded with many types of charismatic things with a trembling hand, Dion's loyalist *'Collin'* was looking at the tantrik, but instantly taking away the trolley from him, the tantrik put a stick looking like a billiard-stick in his hand and said, "Stay close to Yaara. As soon as I give a hint, push her gently on her back with this stick."

While Orian was preoccupied in arranging the *'Peace Officers'* standing with the *'Portable Rocket Launchers'* on their shoulders, in a manner that they would be able to fire exactly on *'Koll's'* chest when he would get down from his throne, suddenly getting pushed by one officer, the *'tantrik'* stumbled and fell down. Dion snatched a pistol and pierced that peace officer's leg, after which the *'arm of law'* picked up and took him outside in a way that there would be no interference in the celebration.

"My lord, let me match this last rhythm with you before dying. God knows whether I'll get this opportunity again or not…" Susan said slipping a pistol in Paras' pocket when there was an announcement of the last Salsa Competition from the stage in which the one crossing the circle's border at the time of full speed after the slow speed union gets defeated.

The Salsa started with a languid speed. Without any reluctance, as Paras and Susan entered the magical circle created by the tantrik and started spreading dancing colors, they saw Elvis coming towards them with his whole troupe exactly from the middle of Gosha and

Arina hovering around him like forest demons. Getting soaked in Susan's kisses pouring like the clouds of the holocaust period, Paras started gathering cruelty from every corner of his mind. The drums of the Salsa music became faster, and with that the feet striving to see the competition between the favorite couples also started dancing. The victory smile that had burst forth breaking the limits of Elvis' face was shaken up by Paras' smiles that were striking back in return. Within the sixth second of snatching an aura monitor from one of the Gardi's and moving it once again on the couples who were taking part in the Salsa, *Arina's (the bodyguard of Lord de Ros)* eyes shone up. The aura medicine that Paras had taken had lost its effect.

When the breaking threads of life and the instruments raised the speed of the Salsa to the final tempo, as if the whole universe had slid down into a slow motion, Paras saw Arina running towards them with clenched fists. Saw Dion patting Eliza's cheek to keep her conscious in a circle that was eleven feet away. Saw the tantrik signaling Dion to kill Eliza. Saw *'Collin'* moving towards Susan with a stick raised in his hand. Watched Susan's eyes that had assimilated oceans and shut off…

According to popular belief, it is said that the hard and fast nature of time never waits for anyone. That's because, it has seen so many and such dramas during its lifetime, that now it just does not have any hope of a new type of incident taking place which can make it awestruck. Yet the time that itself had chosen to become a representative for despair, also was motionless as it watched the game of fate for this couple that had been made for each other in a peculiar sense.

In the last part of the moments together, Dion simultaneously unloaded bullets into Eliza's body, all at once and with the pistol, Paras hit Colin who had come closer with a raised stick as he smiled at Arina who came near. And with this divine laughter as if giving permission to death that was fearfully standing far, he gashed the body of Susan who was saying *'My infinite love is only for you…'* with her closed eyes. The shock that rose up on Dion's and Elvis' core horizon was enough to transform even the oceans into fire. Standing totally empty, Dion was sometimes getting pulled by Eliza's lifeless figure and sometimes towards the dying Yaara. *'Susan'* was asking *Yaara's* father for forgiveness with supplication filled eyes. But the guilty enlightenment of Susan who was in Yaara's body would never understand the cause of manifestation of this incomparable beauty: Yaara.

Before Arina and Elvis who had jumped together could reach Paras as he put the pistol on his throat, Dion pulled a *'Muzzle gun'* from the hands of one guard and eased Paras' task. The bloodshed fingertips, of every Satanic including Sierra, Dervil, Malachi, Titus, who had come there crushing the crowd that had been creating an uproar, had been raised up towards the Gardis. Just like minuscule particles flying near a big waterfall, the drizzle of blood flying around started a new music of destruction as the *lighting beams (pure energy)* tore open the bodies of the Gardis and passed through them. There was a destructiveness of all the men in the world in Elvis' eyes. All the blood arteries in his body became tough, raising both his hands, he roared so fiercely that even the stars in the sky started changing their own place in fright. After reaching the destination, dragging himself on the path leading towards Susan with the torch lighted in his heart, the corpse at the destination was now in front of him. He ran before the pure energy flowing in his veins would tear open his blood vessels and come out, *'Lessie' (Elvis' agent)* was confident that the habitats of those residing in the direction that he had disappeared would have been transformed into ruins by now.

Falling down on his knees, Paras' glance fixed onto the sky. The Gardis targeting the Satanic Warriors from the sky with *'Castifo Guns'*, resembled messengers of death who had taken the form of ferocious birds, amidst that, a demon came hurtling from the tip of the tower like a meteorite and stabilized himself. Operating a Killer Satellite from a far corner, Sebastian blew off the door at the tower's summit as he condemningly gestured- *What are you doing...* to Nurai. Pulling the *'Hero Trilby'* from his head up to his eyes, for his final task, Nurai lit a fire with the lighter in the truncheon filled with petrol and a copious voice like the one that is heard when the anchor is released from the niche of a big ship was heard once again. With a laser beam, the *'Killer Satellite'* melted one more door hiding the *'energy receiver antenna'* and rapidly fired missiles in the tower. But before the dead bodies of Paras and Susan could be consigned to ashes by Nurai, the Gardis who had come flying in a cyclonic manner, had picked up their corpses and flown away towards the *'Cons Lydia'* war-craft.

The noises of a crowd of more than two hundred thousand people saving their lives and escaping in this assembly adorned with corpses was echoing. Thrusting her lips in Gosha's ear amidst these noises, Arina said, "It looks like the Satanics have blown off the Gravity-Machine. The *'Early Warning System'* sirens of the *'Gravity Block'* could be heard shrilling far, far away. We should get out of here before this asteroid loses control on the speed and goes missing in the sky or collides with some other satellite and gets destroyed."

*

'One and a half months later'

The negative approach developed from frequent failures was not allowing Elvis to focus his attention on the aspects required for success now. Elvis was sitting with Lessie on one cold morning on his affluent estate in a city of *'Climate Canopy' (a toy planet of Earth Eleven)*. He was enjoying the view of the flowing river that could be seen through the transparent walls of the drawing room. Running his glance on the rows of flowers that had blossomed on the shores of the lake, he said, "Finding them is almost an impossible task now. They might have contributed to an increase in population on any of the fifty planets of Cons Lydia."

Laying out the breakfast made from the liver of *'calflid' (an animal of the Climate Canopy)* on the dinner table, Lessie said, "If we think about the warning expressed by *Krech*, that an excessive distance between the souls and the magic plate of the *'Gerifuna Stegi'* certainly affects the results of the ritual to quite an extent. And hence wouldn't it be possible that they would have been inspired to take rebirth on Earth only?" Lessie would always present an argument with the same kind of excitement. *(Krech – A Diaboli)*

"Even if we believe that, how much time is left in our hands?" Lighting a fire at the end of the smoke-pipe and taking the cup of coffee extended by Lessie, Elvis said, "The fiftieth day for those who go through the pregnancy journey on the Glips Treatment is considered to be the final limit. According to my calculation, they should be in this world once again and if Sebastian has taken them to one of the planets of Galaxy-L3 using some Dummy on the Earth, then this search of ours will become an infinite one."

"This thing can probably confirm that Paras was on Earth during the hours he had disappeared from the asteroid…?" Due to a decrease in the brightness of the drawing room Elvis looked towards the door, Mirashi and Meriano were standing with a bundle of newspapers. Throwing the bundles of newspapers on the couch, Meriano said further, "As such Alieonic activities had been recorded in many countries of the Earth on that night. It is clear that fearing the possibility of war, guests of a high stature had escaped with their shuttles from Koll's asteroid to the S. Stations on Earth to return to their planets. But this news should be read." Meriano said presenting a local newspaper as if he was removing smoke from the front of the mirror.

"Instant death of the driver as a tanker passing from the Westside highway overturned. A stampede that took place without bothering to take care of the people trapped in the vehicle in order to save themselves from the deadly chemical that had scattered around." In one corner of the news, a crowd could be seen near the gate of some geological park on the other side of the highway.

"So?" As soon as Elvis asked, loosening the fingers of his palm, Mirashi, who was standing with an English straw hat pressed in the armpit, quickly put a report paper between his fingers. "A report of the *'National Nuclear Security Administration Agency'* of the *'United States of America'* – The energy generated by the chemicals scattered from the tanker was observed by the American satellite that provides the signal of frequency that is used to detect signals of the Global Nuclear Detonations Detection System as well as other infrared incidents that generate a high amount of energy, in order to keep an eye on the Nuclear Test Ban treaties between the Satellite Frequency X3 – countries."

"We had been taught to assemble a special kind of shuttle in S.O.G. This small shuttle can be assembled in just a few minutes. This is an ideal shuttle for escaping by showing a boar's thigh to the spies keeping watch while in house arrest, during any mission that had to be successfully accomplished. Immediately after Eddie and I would have come out of their residence on Studium, they would have instantly delivered the content of the shuttle on the asteroid through Sebastian. The fuel carrying capacity of this type of vehicles that fly with chemical energy is less. They need to take fuel from the Earth for their return air journey."

"You are proceeding on the right track. This misdeed has been contrived on Earth itself." Luiciano said, immediately on entering, "The Satanics are conducting a meeting on Simla's Mall Road with the person who will be giving the exact location of Paras, after one hour. Gather the goods quickly."

"Who…?" Having asked this much, Elvis' open lips started trembling with fear.

Luiciano said, "Who knows by what means the Devil has trapped *Almuro (Almuro – The chief of the huge and highly mysterious secret society spread over the local groups of all the six galaxies)* into helping him in this task. Otherwise it is quite impossible to get any kind of information about the Diabolis' ritual, under any circumstances. Almuro has acquired information about six rituals of this type currently being conducted on Galaxy L3 from his strong contacts. One of them is being done on Earth."

"Oh, on Earth…!"

"No one can provide the specific location." Jangling the rocks in the glass filled with neat brandy Luiciano said in an equally rattling voice.

"Then what?"

"According to Almuro's confidential information – For the rebirth ceremony at a desired location on a desired planet, in order to perform this ritual for the announcement of impregnation, it is required to remove and use a heart of some unsatisfied and fierce person. The heart is a factory of desires. Unsatisfied desires give birth to an unmatched force of attraction. Through this force the souls get pulled towards the magic plate Gerifuna-Stegi. In order to find out the location of such a distorted corpse whose heart has been removed, the Satanics are publishing advertisements in every newspaper of every country on Earth since the last one month."

"What is going to happen with that? Would the Diabolis have retained such a corpse in the courtyard of their house?" Elvis said.

"'The Devil Family has purchased a satellite based *'DNA Matching Kit'* from *'Milky' (A Home Planet)* of Group Q. If they trace the corpse from which the Diabolis have removed the heart, they will find out the location of the heart of that corpse from its DNA sample within a short time in this manner – The system's test-kit identifies the corpses DNA and sends it to the satellite after labeling it with a specific coding. The satellite broadcasts signals on a specific microwave frequency. Its waves have the capacity to penetrate deep into the skin. With the help of these signals, within a few minutes the satellite's *'receiver'* will determine the location of rest of the parts of the body and in case they are being taken somewhere then the speed also can be determined apart from finding out where the heart has been kept." Saying this, Luiciano touched his fist with all the other fists in which a *'revert pill'* was clenched. *(A medicine that changes the height, size, appearance and the entire structure of the body for a few hours within a few minutes)*

"My plan was absolutely straight forward." Luiciano said in a disconsolate voice, "After using the Discovery Copperhorse on Paras and Susan who are with us to bring back their memories of Daarck and Filipa, then gathering the information of those ten *'Project Discs'* from their mind, and after that, acquiring those ten colonies by preparing ten armies like the Satanic Warriors. Anyways, destiny does not become favorable again and again. When Lord de Ros offered me to spy on the Devil family, I was a loyal Satanic. After accepting Ros' offer with some reluctance, I immediately approached the Devil family and revealing the conspiracy of this agreement, I said that now I am spying on them for Ros. And I was actually successful in proving myself to be loyal to both of them by conveying quite a few secret matters of the Devil to Ros. I have taken a lot of risk in doing this. But with this foolishness done by you, my tenure as a mediator between the Devil family and *'Lord de Ros'* is over now."

"But then how did you get to know about all this?" Elvis asked.

"His name is *'Dominic'*. One of the special spies of the Devil family. Who actually works for Ros. We have never hidden this type of secrets of ours from each other. But now that I have become useless for Dominic, he says that this is his last assistance. Since he has also conveyed all this information to Ros, the possibility to seize Paras and Susan from amongst the Satanic Warriors and Gardi-Force is next to impossible. Yet we will try albeit keeping ourselves out of danger. Because you know that at the time of Daarck's existence, I was employed in his agency. And spying on the dangerous Daarck, I have acquired a trump card, which has the power to extort several planets from the winner of the eleven colonies very easily." Luiciano paused and staring at his foolish son, he became quiet.

"When did Dominic give this news to *'Cons Lydia'*?" Elvis asked.

"Not much time has elapsed since then as yet." Striking the clock with his first finger as he pointed towards the five airbuses standing on the archway of the empire, Luiciano spoke, "We have only a few soldiers against the large armies that can seize a complete town sent by the Devil family and Ros."

*

'India, Mall Road Simla. Nine thirty in the night'

At the moment, they had reached Simla by one of the five *airbuses (small space vehicles)* that had got down at Luiciano's one and only Dummy S. Station in the mountainous forest of East Nepal. Elvis was marching forward with his agents since it was not possible to take a car on Mall Road. Since they were the last days of the calendar, the tourists were heating up the markets with their hands in their jacket pockets. Even the looped hands of the new couples were not uncovered. Smoke could be seen emanating from the chimneys on some of the terraces of the shops with the Victorian terraces on both the sides.

A man looking like a beggar was standing in the corner of the shawl shop was taking in deep puffs of cigarette. His open legs below the half pants were enough to put him in the fraternity of bears. As soon as Elvis' glance fell on him, he displayed impudence as if he wanted to blow the smoke on Elvis' face even from such a long distance. Elvis who had gone ahead a few steps stopped as if he had remembered something and observed as he turned, the smoker's smoke pointed on the other side of the road towards a café that was at the corner of the stick shop. Elvis thinking *'Who was that man who looked like a ragamuffin'*, advised his agents to get busy in purchasing while he himself, looking at the shoes of a man near the coffee shop who was talking arrogantly with a person who looked friendly, crossed the road and stood turning his back towards them as he reached there. He looked into the screen of the aura-monitor hidden in the hat pressed in his armpit, even though the *'aura print unmatched'* signal was flashing on the screen, it was a wonder that Dervil, seated at a table a little away, looked like a health statue. Elvis thought, "Would he have taken some advanced aura-medicine of the *'Master Galaxy'*?" Despite having taken the appearance changing *'revert-pill'* he could be easily identified through his body language.

"The matter is something else." Said a policeman standing in front of *Malachi (A Satanic of the Devil family)*, "You have published an advertisement, not just once but several times, in several newspapers… It is difficult to find a person matching with your sketch not just around Simla, but in the whole of *'Himachal'*. Finally, what can this matter be?" He said rubbing his forehead, "This is the weirdest thing I have ever seen in so many years of my service."

The temper of the atrocious Satanic *'Malachi'* who had been listening silently was pulsating. It could clearly be seen from the tightened nerves on his face that he was not used to listen to this type of language.

"Giving this kind of an advertisement to contact on this number in case any kind of corpse is found in a distorted condition is just a straight forward pretense. Such an excessive amount is not paid even for a living person. You have now become a criminal. Hooligans are killing the poor people living on the footpath and distorting their corpses as much as possible and bringing them to you. I will have to take you to the police station for interrogation."

Turning his head, Malachi glanced behind towards Dervil and Sierra who were seated a little away at a table on the back side and confining his anger with a deep breath, he spoke, "Your intention for this secret meeting clarifies how much interest you have in law maintenance. Pick this up and leave from here." Malachi said throwing a big bundle of money on the table.

Dressed in blue jeans and a purple top, as Lessie came and wrapped her hand on Elvis' arm, they occupied the seats on the table next to Dervil and Sierra in such a way that they could hear their conversation.

"Who knows whether the satellite based DNA Matching Theory will work accurately or not?" Sierra said taking a deep breath and giving an order of *'Salmon Bacon'* and Coffee to the waitress waiting for the conversation to get over to take the order, she turned once again towards Dervil, "Change of time, determination of a specific location, and relative speed… Whether the satellite receiver will succeed in bridging these three dimensions accurately or not? What about the possibility of jamming? They are not giving any guarantee even after purchasing such an expensive system." Before Dervil who was snuffing out the cigar after taking the last puff could respond, a person whose whole body was wrapped in a silky shawl, as if hiding leprosy, could be seen coming from the same direction in which the inspector had fled with the bundles of notes.

"This Ron (imposter) like costume of yours is one that raises a doubt, Mister *'Shashang'*. Couldn't you come in some simple attire?" Sierra said.

"What..? Why..?" After uttering words, coming out in panic generally, Shashang quickly handed over a sealed packet and said, "If you do not find this sample of the flesh and hair of the corpse as per your advertisement to be enough, then I have mentioned the exact location of where I had found this corpse in the note." He had worn dark goggles on the face that was completely covered with the shawl.

"But what were you doing in such a desuetude place in the jungle?" Dervil asked and got up gesturing to Malachi who was sitting at a far off distance.

"You should be concerned with your own business." Saying this, Shashang ran his glance around him. "The money is on the way." Saying this, Dervil went away, and after some time Malachi came and sat in front of him with a bag. Behind them, Lessie pretended to make Elvis stand up by pulling his hand forcefully.

After following them upto the *'State Museum'* located three kms. away from Mall Road, Elvis saw a big van parked in the area behind the museum. He was approximately half a kilometer away from there. After one of the Satanics came out from the van and took from Dervil the packet that had been given to hi by Shashang, Elvis reset a 2.3 mm gun and fired a *'microphone bullet'* a little away from the feet of Dervil who was rapidly knocking on the van. There were several Satanics investigating the presence of some invisible enemies all around with the Magnetic Fluid Frequency Measurement Monitor. Glancing all around the open fields with Kirlian Glasses, Elvis could not feel any signs of the Gardis. He thought, "What will be the exceptional spying method of the Gardis..?"

Thirty-five additional minutes elapsed without any incident. Bored, as Elvis was contemplating on the next course of action, a Satanic disembarked from the van after completing the chemical test. Looking at the compass, he said "Signals are received from the Middle East direction. India, we are in the right place…"

"Is there anything else you have to say except India..?" Sierra asked moving up and down.

"It will take 30 seconds for the next frame to come." The Satanic said.

Showing Dervil the celestial area covering the Earth on her *Tolmi (Mini Brain Pad)*, Sierra said, "Our satellites have not recorded any *waves (speed waves)* which may emanate from the invisible war-crafts of the Gardis."

"Even then," Dervil said lighting a cigar, "I will be rather surprise if they do not reach Kangra to induce some alertness in our lazy Energy Warriors. Ros possesses a unique series of Dummy S. Stations on all of his fifty planets through which he can deliver one hundred thousand shuttles filled with Gardi soldiers to any location on any planet of Cons Lydia within twelve minutes. But Earth being a toy planet, keeping in mind that the existence of the colony would not be revealed, he is only going to be able to send a few war-crafts."

"Frame-two, powerful signals indicating the existence of one part of this corpse are being received from Kangra hill station located on 32° 06'N 76° 16'E. The target is exactly 241 kms. away from here." The same time at which the Satanic uttered these words, at the far end of the Kangra hill station of North India, a woman's shadow was silently but hurriedly marching forward on the edge of the road. Shuddered by the roaring bright flashes of piercing lightning, the masses had fled away from there and were still trembling in their houses. But some big anxiety keeping her oblivious to this wolfy-atmosphere was making the daring shadow continue stepping forth further and further.

When a dim light started showing up just opposite on the upper floor of *'Manjri Farm'*, she pulled down her sari border to hide her forehead. That unfortunate, miserable young woman shoving aside the back gate of the farm densely filled with voodoo-dolls and intruding did not even have a wild guess as to whose den she was entering.

"Nurai, five minutes have elapsed since the Farm's *Motion Detector* has shut down. Yet how much of your pissing is still left…!" A Toast Factory was located on the opposite side of Manjri-Farm that had been built on a wallowing street. Standing at the closed door of the factory, Sebastian was knocking on agent Nurai's mind through the phone. *(Motion Detector – A speedy thing, especially a device ringing a warning bell by itself after finding the person)*

"You should be able to see me in ten seconds, dear." Nurai said.

"Don't forget," Sebastian said in a serious voice, "You are going on a Diaboli's site. If required shoot with a Muzzle gun and escape. In case any Diaboli dies even by mistake, the entire *'Secret Society'* will start chasing behind."

The old Mercedes tumbling in neutral came and stopped puffing in front of Manjri Farm's gate. Noticing the filthy dolls tied to the gate as started the engine again and got down, Nurai asked, "What kind of decoration is this..?"

"Thank God, I had totally forgotten…" Sebastian said taking a breath of relief, "It's a disillusion of the Diabolists. Whoever crosses the cursed limits of the voodoo-dolls tied on the gate and enters in it, bad luck does not stop following the destiny of that person until it ruins him. If you would have entered the building without removing those dolls from there, then Mumbai would have remained far removed from us forever." As *'Sebastian'* frightened Nurai by bowing his head to wish him *'All the best'* from the opposite side of the road, a person looking like a foreigner passed by on the street with an umbrella. He glanced once towards Sebastian. Even though this deadly atmosphere of the night and a person standing all alone like this was signifying that something weird was taking place, he just turned his gaze and walked away as if the word *interest* had been destroyed by life's bitterness.

As that lady crossed the stairs with soft steps taking her to the upper floor and reached next to the glass elevation, there was a terrible bolt of lightning outside. Her sacraments inspired by religious beliefs were trying hard to pull her far away from this abetment. She thought of turning back but *'greed'* had taken an upper hand over fear. She slowly pushed the first door that was open by about two inches on the left side of the corridor, a little more and peeped inside. The same woman, whom she had seen her during the surveillance of the farm just a few days back, was sound asleep on the bed. She had smiled strangely at her but had made a sinister face as if it had been eaten by rust and had gone inside immediately after that. The other brown eyed woman who remained aberrant, whom she had seen only once was not present.

She closed the door and carefully proceeded towards the room in the front.

Cutting the black dolls flying in the air with a knife, Nurai's attention was naturally drawn towards the window of the upper floor. He saw a reflection of a child being picked up by a woman on the transparent glass window and keeping his glance there, he started cutting the dolls with more speed.

Cramming Paras between her left hand that woman picked up little Susan with trembling hands and put her in a sack hanging on her chest. The heavy pendants hanging in their necks must be expensive, besides the chance of awakening them by swinging and hence removing the pendants, she wore them in her neck. Blood stained hooks were hanging in the ceiling in such a manner that drops would fall exactly in between the star scribbled on the floor. Thinking that the room that had become impure with signs of a very evil ceremony would bind her there itself, she ran non-stop from there. When she passed from near the kitchen, she started getting nausea due to the foul stench that could result in vomiting. As she pressed her mouth with the other hand and closed the back door from outside, Nurai pushed aside the front gate and stepped onto the driveway of the farm.

"I checked just ten minutes back, they were sound asleep...!" The brown eyed Diaboli woman was crazily searching the empty room. Nurai stood motionless staring at the barren cradles along with three other Diabolis standing in a statue position. Sebastian's explosive uproar assaulted his ears again in the Bluetooth attached to his ear, "Nurai, you can go there again some other time to drink coffee. The transporter waiting here is a hired one. He has to take Paras and Susan and reach all the way to Mumbai. The increasing rain and if the roads get closed then…"

"Sebastian, you will have to come here to see this awful view." Nurai said and Sebastian ran towards Manjri Farm.

"*Kedepsiz'* oath … If we turn out to be liars then a horrible curse will never stop chasing us." *(Kedepsiz – A downcast deity of the Diabolists)*

Sebastian's voice as he stood holding one Diaboli's collar was more gruesome than the lightning that was flashing there. "Mix of an unholy breed… If I do not get them back right now then I will show such a dance of death that even your *'Kedepsiz'* will have to go in search of God. Nurai, run towards the back road, it looks like the *Sons of hell (Satanics)* have arrived." Saying this, he took off to check the farm's video recording.

The drops of rain were now starting and stopping. From the time she took the wild path on the left side of the road, half a dozen dogs had started following her. The children had woken up with the voice and started crying. But she had gone very far. She had been walking with all her strength since the last eight minutes. Tired, she now sat on one stone. It was not possible to hold the delicate bodies twisting to free themselves from the grip, more tightly. She got up again with the challenge to get them to keep quiet. "The *'master'* should have come by now."

Blabbering, she glanced around once again, "It is the same place. Would he have come and left?" She also checked around behind the big tree trunks.

After walking for another four minutes or so, she came and stood in front of a bungalow. The children were again lost in completing the challenge for refreshing the body and mind. She opened the gate just enough to pass through and came inside. Slowly knocking on the door, she came near the window. The furious discussion, that was going on inside, fell on her ears.

"I am sick and tired of sorting out your sins. I beg of you, stop it." Shashang was roaring.

"This is the last time. Please agree.. I am promising, let my affection be satisfied…."

"It is never going to happen witch, scoundrel.. Oh God, I also became a partner to your sin."

"I am giving a promise, giving a promise…" The woman clamped to Shashang's leg could be seen as the curtain moved for a couple of seconds. She said in a voice like a helpless lady, "Our children will also grow up with time." But after that, instantly as a witch would expose her real shade, she asked in a haughty voice, "Where did you get so much money from, rogue?"

"Well, there is no need for this as well..!" When Shashang did not give any response, there was a noise as if she had thrown something heavy and instantly a crying voice of a boy about ten years old could be heard.

Frightened, that woman again went to the door and knocked the door frantically. As soon as he opened the door, the man entering middle age from youth gestured to talk softly. In the view from the half open door, his wife who had plunged down was seen getting up and sitting on the floor. There was a chopper in her hand. "Who is at the door?" She bellowed sitting right there.

Shashang closed the door and went outside.

"Master," As if she had not seen or heard anything, she went near Shashang's ear and said in such a soft voice that two people could barely hear, "I have kidnapped and got such a lovely heir for you that you will fall in love as soon as you see him. The baroness will just go crazy seeing him. So much radiance on the face as if you would see the son of God himself personified." Shashang opened his mouth, but that woman said again, "Master.. And if you do not want to lose your consciousness looking at the inhuman brilliance then glance at this moon only after making your mind strong." She said removing the cover from Susan's face, "But why did you not come there to take them?"

"What was the need for you to come here?" Shashang covered little Susan's face again without even glancing at her.

She said despite feeling that the sentence had a double meaning, "Well, well, take them quickly now, and give me my reward…!"

"Don't even want to see and don't even want them. Go and put them back from where you picked them up. You will get your reward."

The woman's face drooped. "What are you saying..!" Scratches formed in her eyes. "Is this some kind of a game! Turmoil must have started there by now."

"We have now decided to adopt a child in a legal manner."

"So this has happened today itself..!"

"Ssh.. ssh.. ssh.. Keep your voice low. Yes… Take this money and get lost from here…"

"Hey, but everyone out there would have got to know about it by now."

"Then keep them somewhere else."

"Master, I became a thief, on your behest. But I am not so merciless to leave these tender children on the road to die."

"Ask for some more money if you want to, but do not pretend to be truthful. It is not too late as yet. It's night time, and there is a possibility that no one would have got to know about it out there."

Wiping his wet eyes, he removed the cloth from Susan's face as a last attempt. Big jet black eyes, a childish face as if created by melting the innocence of the whole world… Shashang kept staring in the dilemma of whether to keep a girl who looked as if beauty had manifested itself to be born donning a spiritual body. Reading the shining words on the tag attached to the thumb of her small foot, he said, "Fine, I am ready to keep Susan." Susan's calm eyes began to stare at Shashang.

As if he had visualized a demon's shadow in the eyes of that beautiful flower in the flash of lightning, Shashang who was watching without taking off his eyes, finally said, "I'm coming." When he opened the door, a wave of foul smell came from inside and pushed that woman behind.

"You will be able to spend the rest of your life comfortably with this money. Leave this state and go elsewhere. Decisions inspired by feelings do not generate anything apart from remorse. Emotions are transient and grief is substantially permanent. Give the girl to me." He picked Susan up and flung bundles of notes in the sack in which she had got Susan.

Shashang stood there and kept watching her until she went prattling out of the bungalow.

*

"Of what is this light..?" Sebastian could see bolts of intense light descending behind the window as if lightning was falling on several places at the same time. He quickly ran there and opened the window, "Aw shucks…" Arrays of Satanic shuttles were landing in front on the whole street. He ran towards the window on the other side of the hall and pushed the curtain aside, there also the scene was the same. Far, far away in the distance, all around Manjri Farm, he saw Satanic shuttles hovering on the terrace of every house, and the strange thing was that all of them had not been kept on invisible mode. Sebastian remembered the Master Galaxy's rules of points that would uproot the New-God of the planet if there was any blunder like revealing the mystery of the

New-God or Colonies in front of the common citizens of the toy planets, although in this case since the Satanics had made a start, there was no possibility of Lord de Ros' points going down. Maybe the Satanics wanted to provoke the Master Galaxy…? He came back to his senses on hearing the humongous noise of a shuttle landing on the terrace. Glancing at the Diaboli couples running down, he pulled the sheet from the bed. Wrapping the cloth to make it appear as if he was taking Paras and running away, he came to the balcony and jumped onto the lawn below. He saw the view of the living room from the ventilation of the store room next to the kitchen.

"But what is so much hustle and bustle about… Working in haste is the work of the Devil…?" Hmm.. hmm.. hmm… Dervil stood laughing sarcastically opening the door from outside for the Diabolis. Dervil roared almost as if he was screaming, "Where can your little clients be found now?"

One Diaboli said with a throbbing heart, "Our commitment was to give them rebirth at this location, not for the security for the rest of their lives. You do whatever you want to, it does not make any difference to us now. So get out of the way, Dervil."

"There is no one here." Malachi said coming down from the floor above as he threw a glass jar filled with hearts onto the floor.

"Where is he..?" Dervil asked, getting hold of one of the Diabolis who were speaking in gestures and putting poisonous claws of a paw on his throat.

"Don't know. But still even that much time has not elapsed for them to have left Kangra." Streams of thick green colored blood had started flowing from his throat.

"It's of no use, these are Diabolis." Reprimanding Malachi who was using the Thought Steal for the memory hidden in their minds, Dervil slit off the throats of all four Diabolis one after another with an agility of a magician having hand skills that could get one dumbfounded within seconds.

"The Gardi-Force has arrived." As Sierra repeated the instructions received on the headset from the outdoor unit, a Satanic warrior let out a scary scream from behind Sebastian who had been staring at them from behind the window. Sebastian ran tossing the cloth into the Satanic's hands that had risen for striking but stopped seeing the cloth shaped like a child in Sebastian's hand. A terrible air battle had started between countless war-crafts of the Gardi-Force and the Satanics in an instant. Numerous Gardi soldiers and Satanic warriors jumping from the shuttles on both sides with human wings, attacked in the direction of the Satanic warrior who was groping for the cloth. The protection layer of the Gizmo Belt of the stumbling Sebastian running wildly was weakening with several strokes of Pure Energy and the Castifo.

She was already frightened with this type of embezzlement committed for the first time and this weird, strange and horrible view seen on the road leading towards Manjri Farm frightened her even more. She also looked doubtfully towards the sack hanging in her neck once or twice. The woman walking like a mad beggar suddenly realized that she was still flitting around with trouble. When she bent down to hide the bundles of money on one side of the road, someone shouted horrifyingly from behind. For a while, she was unable to hear anything apart from her own heartbeats.

Approaching closer, as Elvis was pulling the sack from her chest, she gestured with the bent first finger towards jungle track where she had left little Paras. Before Elvis could ask anything else he was flung and fell far off with Gosha's kick that had hit him in the back. A battlefield was resurrected on that venue within a short time through the *sky-blaze (A rocket released in the sky from the ground to indicate the targeted war area)* that was released by the Gardi soldiers who had reached there. Using the *'Multi-Barrel Machine-Gun'* that could fire five hundred rounds per second, the Satanics had penetrated the protective layer of the Gardis' Gizmo Belt and after that, with destructive strokes of pure energy, they were blowing off the Gardis to ashes in the air.

Leaping towards Elvis at the speed of a cheetah, Gosha jumped on him with all his might, but before Elvis could offer the empty sack tucked under his chest, to Gosha, they found themselves laden under a huge heap of the Satanics and Gardis. When the crowd of the *'Satanic warriors'* and *'Gardi soldiers'* increased there to grab the little Paras to such an extent that it would be impossible to move even a hand or a foot for fighting, a huge aircraft colliding into the shuttles destroying each other in the topmost level of the sky, appeared. The anchor shaped aircraft was encrypted with *'M'* in big, bold letters.

Solon (A Chairman of Apotheosis who was the owner of half of the Master Galaxy), who had come with an aircraft that could not be encountered with, came flying down and stood there laughing in front of everyone in a way that could make them feel like worms and spiders. *'N.X.C. Wing, Master Galaxy'* was inscribed on the crest of the wings he had harnessed. His soft voice echoed in the frozen silence.

Turning towards Gosha, he said, "Due to the forceful waves of surprise that have risen here by the residents as a result of this open spectacle of the Gardi-Force, the *'Master Galaxy'* that is hundreds of thousands of light years away, has been compelled to send a memorandum to *'Cons Lydia'.* Even though the Devil Family compelled Cons Lydia to do such a thing, a person who does not have the capacity to stop such events from taking place in front of the common people of their toy planets is not eligible to continue being a New-God. Several points are certainly being reduced today itself. It is necessary for Lord de Ros to maintain the remaining points to continue to stay at the New God's position." Gesturing Dervil and Gosha who were standing amidst the crowd to come behind him, Solon flew towards his aircraft.

This *'alien visit'* had been bad to worse for the innocent inhabitants of Kangra.

Lessie said raising her thin eyebrow as she bent her neck towards Elvis who was kicking the corpse of the grotesque woman with his foot. "This is so strange! The reports of the blood-samples found on the Diaboli's site are very odd, it was a mixture of the blood of three individuals. Paras, Susan and with them even some third person's…!"

"What…!" Elvis' mouth remained open in bewilderment as if he had seen the sea going to meet the river.

*

After fifty minutes, India, South Mumbai

"I thought in every way, but this matter is not understood in any way. Leaving Paras safely on the wild road in this manner after kidnapping him from the Diaboli's site? Who could have done this?" Nurai said while waiting with Maya and Sebastian for the house owner Qadir near the door of *'Bension House'* that had been constructed in the British era.

"Who knows whether the trouble of the *'Book of Bell'* has receded or not even after having gone through so much fuss?" When Sebastian said this, a procession dancing in front of a band could now be seen. A smile forcefully surged forth on Sebastian's worried face. Till now, he had only heard about the wedding of the toy planets. In which manner women and men make a commitment for permanent alliance by means of some unique customs and traditions while their friends mostly dance in a haphazard manner and rejoice.

It was difficult to say whether Qadir's newly-wed wife was more beautiful or the *'Bension House'* that had been decorated like a bride. The pleasant warmth of the in-laws house had now replaced the sad traces of farewell on the bride's face. *Qadir* had to force the dancing party reluctant to stand straight even though the newly married couple entered the porch to stop the dance by clapping frequently, after which he conversed a little with a family organizer and approached Sebastian's small group. Qadir quickly completed the congratulating ceremony and led them to the guest room inside. Remembering something, he opened the door and called out to his permanent serviteur. "One large scotch for me."

"Not one, two." Nurai said, putting a hand on his shoulder.

Sipping the whisky, Qadir went near a cupboard lying in one corner and opening the cupboard, he dialed the combination code in the dialer behind the hanging suits. They descended the steps revealed by moving the sofa of that bulky sitting room to sixty degrees and entered a small room containing a lift. Looking at the lift's display showing an oxygen level of ninety percent, Maya asked Qadir who was pressing the depth button in the lift, "What if this lift breaks down midway?"

"Even then, it will certainly deliver us somewhere. If there is an issue, then its conveyor capacity will increase by several times, upto the other world." Before Qadir's laughter could finish, the door of the lift that had reached ten floors downwards, opened in the living area of a dome-apartment furnished with facilities like that of a nuclear bunker.

"We only have one way left to reach Susan." Sebastian said as he extended Paras towards Qadir, "Pray that they would not have been released from Robrelco-Fero's soul.

Both have one part each of that in them. And hence it is the only thing that will now attract them towards one another. Rest of it depends on their destiny. The Diaboli has applied Glyps on them. Within six months or so, after Paras accomplishes a mental and physical growth of about twelve years, you will have to take him wherever he wants to travel following his inner instincts. You have already got the brain operation done to get relief from the *'epilepsy'* strokes. Your history will reveal that your brain had been opened for epilepsy, yet the Satanics or the Gardis would not know that your brain has been opened twice. The desired thoughts and memories can be kept safe by the micro version of the G3-electode that has been implanted in your brain. Only the thoughts and memories that you want to provide can be captured through the most modern device, yet you have to be alert every moment."

"And what about the hypnosis?" Qadir asked.

"This G3 cannot stop hypnosis, but it automatically gives a command to the safely lock the folders when such an attempt is detected. Me, Maya and Nurai shall be around, but may not be there always."

"Is this enough?" Nodding her head in denial, Maya expressed a doubt.

Qadir said, "The stones used in the construction of this basement-dome have the unique characteristics to misguide the needle of the compass so that it points in the wrong direction. They have the natural properties of jammers. And however powerful a satellite, it cannot find the cosmic hidden beneath it."

"I will return soon from *Woolybear.*" Sebastian said turning towards Maya and Nurai, "But remember, there is no scope for even a single mistake. *(Daddy's Woolybear – A mega-city sized space craft of the leader of the Off Idiotic Group and New-God, Lon of Colony Glee Metal Casting. Where the Discovery Copperhorse Engine was installed… With which the memories of the past few births could be recollected… Sebastian proceeded forward to make arrangements to try the use of the Discovery Copperhorse to check out the extent of the truth in the say so that Paras himself was Daarck.)*

That same night, Mahanabh Mountain

"Arina," Ros said, "Will you please deploy some Gardis with hot iron rods around the Diaboli who is looking out for those dogs of the Devil (Paras and Susan) before we get our luck in our favor when Malesty agrees to visit Mahanabh daily?"

"Dogs of the Devil…?" Arina said getting shocked, "Just a minute, when Paras alias Daarck died, Devil was nowhere on the scene of the Mission *'Walk of Life'* …? Devil had nothing to do with Daarck even remotely, right…?

"You will get to know all those mysteries some other time. But right now, please…!"

"Are we in a position to extract all this information from Paras' brain through the Copperhorse Engine during this premature condition of his body? I mean to say that his body is just a few days old." Arina expressed doubt.

"It will be easier." Ros said, "Once his brain gets developed, we will only get the information he wants to provide us unless we place a chopper on the throat of his beloved Susan and threaten him." Malesty has received the latest model of the Copperhorse. The talks like using the Copperhorse engine before the nerves have been strengthened through the vaccination course have now become old.

"I take to task that Diaboli." Saying this, Arina went away.

Lustrous in the velvety moonlight of its own moon, Mahanabh had a pandemonium of welcome for *'Malesty'*, the New-God of the Vio-Crazy Colony *'Nebel Shift'*.

In order to be able to use the Mummy-Ointment easily on Malesty, he had been invited on Mahanabh by giving him the temptation of the *'Gardi Technology' (the science that made the Gardi soldiers immortal)* by *Lord de Ros*, according to whose plan if Paras was found right away, then extracting Paras' Daarck related memories through the *'Discovery Copperhorse Engine'* that Malesty was bringing with him in exchange for the Gardi Technology, and finding the location of the *'Mummy-Ointment'* and *'Transmission Germ'* that Daarck had hidden. Exchanging Malesty's body along with its aura... And after that both the colonies *'Nebel Shift'* holding two hundred and fifty grand planets and *'Cons Lydia'* were going to fall in his lap altogether. Ros wanted to finish off this deceit today itself even if it meant stopping Malesty for some more time.

"My intelligence wing and along with that my great Chairmen, will you be able to answer one question related to the investigation of the shameful failure of the

Kangra scam?" Lord de Ros was speaking earnestly in the massive courtyard of the castle made of the black stones on the peak of Mahanabh widely spread across thousands of acres. The jungles covered with trees spread over thousands of feet deep valleys could be seen from the summit. "Can you tell, what is the most powerful thing in this world?" He had asked looking towards the *'Catalytic Priests'* of Mahanabh temple expecting Ros' orders to determine the auspicious moment of death for all the commanders including Gosha who had failed to get Paras.

The expressions of dilemma that rose up to respond were identical on each face.

"Destiny, my Gardis, destiny… Destiny behaves as per its own will, does not discriminate between a dirty-sloppy man on the planet and the immortal owner of fifty such planets..." Ros got up and with him all others also got up. Caressing Gosha's hand held in his hands, *Ros* gestured the others not to straighten up. Gosha, being carried up towards the valley, was fluttering like a bird in the hands of a hunter.

Intending to win over Gosha's loyalty, Rihon got up patting his lusterless blonde hair displaying an expression of grief caused by failure on his face and looking with a glance appealing for forgiveness, he spoke in a humble voice, "My lord, Malesty's delegation should be arriving."

Ros checked his hand intending to open the belt on Gosha's neck half way after having changed his mind. This meeting seemed to be an unnecessary errand for the Catalytic Priests. "Go and don't come back without him." Ros retorted in response to Gosha's screams echoing from the emptiness of the deep valley.

*

"I was quite skeptical about whether we have really picked up that famous Diaboli…?" When Arina entered Ros' *'Delfian Chamber'*, *Beaumont' (A guard of Ros)*, was bent on the lady dressed in a great black coat and was piercing her with arrows of sarcasm.

"Malesty will leave Lydia Dyaan within a few hours. You have been turning over these *corpses (Paras-Susan's)* back and forth for the last three hours. Do you even know anything or are you also fooling us like the others?" Arina dressed in a dress made of pink leather asked her as asking with a spear on the thighs.

"I have already tried my best. Yet, let's try one more deadly method. As the Diaboli wearing a magician's gown sat in the circle made with candles, closed her eyes once again, Arina's attention fell on the screen hung on the wall as she raised both her hands in a bored pose and moved towards the left. Malesty emerged amidst the *'infantry'* that was marching in a row with a stick. Lip reading what Ros was saying as he stood in front of him, she murmured, "Welcome on Cons Lydia, Malesty the great."

Malesty's body structure was a little bigger than Ros but the internal body composition was exactly like him. Lavishly spreading laughter, Ros came forward and presented a *'Dancing Bouquet' (The dancing flowers of Ros' private garden)*. There was a furor of *'fireworks'* in the sky akin to what Lord de Ros had inside him. Giving an invitation akin to asking trouble to come and catch the throat, Ros had succeeded in postponing Malesty's visit to Mahanabh thrice after promising to provide him with the Gardi Technology. But this time Malesty had come forcefully. Four suited *'Win Makers' (Special force of the Nebel Shift)* started arranging the six feet long *'balt' (A holocryptic that kept the evil powers away)* having a python-like periphery, around Malesty's seat. Waves rose and vanished like a water-influx in balt's transparent body. The baton was encrypted with some ferocious animal as a symbol of his colony.

Within a short time, from the blood stream flowing from the corners of the Diaboli's eyes it could be perceived how much power she is exerting. She started speaking without opening the eyes, "These are the people, who are experts in the feats of how to escape from witchcraft. The abyss is giving it shelter." She was speaking in a witchy voice that was frightening. "My eyes cannot see him separately, as if his body is congruent with some concrete thing."

"And that girl Susan?" This straight forward question from Arina created such an effect on the layer of the Diaboli's face-flesh as if a person without any guts had seen a big disaster.

"Her delineation is worth an atrocity... My head has started reeling. After seeing that girl's corpse, my eyes will get burnt looking out for where she is. I can clearly feel that there is a constant conflict going on between her and thousands of souls confronting to get into her body."

Recollecting the failure of someone like the Diaboli Secret Society's chief *'Almuro'* in this matter, Arina thought it wise to avoid asking for more explanations and leave from there.

*

One and a half years later, in India's Mumbai City

On the stage of the Power Basilica of Picasso School of Art and Design, a *'lady hunter'* dressed in a blue suit was delivering his speech on the term starter subject- *'The Real World Vision'*.

"Now, as a final solution to remain infinitely happy, I have accepted this world as a business these days." With every single sentence uttered by the school superstar with a rock-like broad chest, the hall was reverberating with whistles. "Dion or Paras…" Upset with the thoughts jousting in the mind for boyfriend's selection, Susan got up from Dion's side and sat in the front row. Paras spoke further as he smiled at Susan, "An emotional investment will bring you on the road. There is no value at all for this conduct in this selfish engulfing world. In this world market, one and only one single currency is capable of keeping any kind of mourning anguish away and the single lettered name of this currency is *'P'*. P for Personality, P for Power, P for Position and P for …."

Along with the school crowd, even the row of teachers seated on their right side applauded to the rhythm of claps. Seated between two girls looking more beautiful with spectacles, Dion was admonishing someone through the phone. "Don't you get the matter in your brain in the first instance? His interesting speech should start exactly in between his nonsense lecture." Sitting in his back row on the right side with his fingers moving on the *'Memory Machine'* as if on a piano, Sebastian now moved them into his pocket and caught hold of a gun. *(Many other assistants of Dion and Elvis had changed their names here but they are being addressed with their old names so that there is no confusion)*

When Susan passed in close proximity to Paras to reach the mike, acting in front of her as if a rosy fragrance had come, Paras pressed his lip with his teeth.

"Ohhh…" The woeful exclamations of those *Majnus (Majnu – A legendary lover)* transformed into ghosts quite a long time back by that killer-woman standing near the mike, charged up the hall. The one created adhering to interest started with laughter displaying dimples in his cheeks ~ "I insist that the book of your life should always be written with a pencil. So that instead of tearing one entire page of regretful decisions of the same day…" The hearts won over by Paras' orator ship had just started gathering around the stage to bestow the legacy of love on Susan's name, when the mike suddenly became deaf as if it had got offended and the speakers of the convention hall automatically started uttering nonsense…

"I think when you jumped from the chopper by paragliding into the school-plaza to propose and landed with a bouquet on Dean's beloved Professor *'Kanan'* instead of Susan, that angry psycho scolded you with her oral lashes in front of the whole school, your heroic impression in Susan's heart and mind were burnt." Paras' dialogue with someone was now being broadcasted. The entire hall was shocked first. Paras looked up towards Dion, his smile that was on the verge of bursting into cynical laughter and the conference proceeded forward without considering the happiness in the pig temperament of the Dean who was the subject of the conversation.-

"Bloody mercenary, instead of taking the revenge of his cracked feelings on his eloped wife, he is going around taking it out on helpless, innocent students like me." When Paras' voice was heard, she put her hand on her right cheek and turned her face away from the Dean. Paras stopped punching the mike and started waving both his hands like a wiper to Dean trying to hint that it was not him. Roaming restlessly between the rows of chairs, as the Dean now got up aggressively in the intolerable sounds of whistling which could have revealed the gorgeous entry of some popular hero, panic stricken on seeing Susan laughing, Dion instructed to stop the broadcast in the phone.

"My voice, no… no…" Paras shouted but Dean's school proclaimed anger had flung him from the eleventh heaven. He ran behind Paras like an enraged bull.

Realizing that there won't be any opportunity to offer today's flower, Paras picked up the rose placed near his heart and swiftly inserting it in Susan's hand, he ran outside leaping and jumping over chairs as he appreciated the sloganeering. In order to see how far the Dean could run with animosity, the whole school toured the entire campus. Paras turned as he pushed back the gate guards intercepting his way with a robust hand and blowing a flying kiss in a supple manner to Susan, he disappeared behind the gate.

Wiping his face with his tie, the gasping Dean looked towards Dion and then towards Susan and said, "Who brings such outside loafers into this campus?" Before the lethal Dion could get down to despotism, Susan entangled her hand beside her potential lover and pulled him away from there.

*

That same evening, while strolling with his colleagues on the lake strip situated at a distance of two miles from the Picasso School, Elvis approached the suited man on the bench and starting bench, he said, "According to Luciano's intelligence, Just a few days ago, Paras' Aura was found matching in this area for three seconds by one of the Aura Monitors of the *'Devil Family'*,. Afterwards during our investigation in this vicinity, the name of the girl on whom Dion's heart has softened, is Susan. And co-incidentally, the name of one boy studying in the same college is also Paras. After five days of persuasion, the girl is now ready to get engaged with Dion. Every person who is interrogated about the past of Paras and Susan, of course with the thought-steal attached to their minds, it is observed that they were telling a lie. If these are the same people then they are very weird. Who will believe that they have kept the same names again? And there is no question of doubting Luciano's information." Elvis said taking a deep breath, "Yet that hoax might also be for misleading, his aura signal might have been given in an area where there are individuals by the names of Paras and Susan in order to crash-down the rotten base of our intentions which are already weak due to one and a half years of search in vain, so that we would be roaming here. And despite all this, if we have found them at all, this will be the first time that my luck would have rendered me with friendly treatment."

The daylight had still withered just a little when the lake strip awaiting its departure had sparkled up with brightness.

"It is true that the current aura medicine does not have any side effect but its effect wears off within a week. This is so easy," Dion said, "Kidnap both of them, within one week of stopping the supply of the aura medicine it will be known whether or not they are the real Paras and Susan.

"There is no need to wait even for a week." Elvis said, "Luciano has discovered a test kit from Colony Metal Casting. And it will be in our hands within a few hours. After that, it is not going to take us more than five minutes to examine if the aura medicine is present in their blood or not."

"And there are total six hundred thousand people bearing the name Paras or Susan in India. Are we going to go around kidnapping each one of them like this for the blood test?" Meriano said raising eyes with sternness.

“But out of these six hundred thousand people, how many of them have some mysterious men roaming around them all the time? Moreover, there is not a single firm evidence about their past.” Lessie said, “One woman shadows that girl Susan studying in the Picasso School continuously and cautiously.”

Helping an old man terrified by the conversation in some weird language, to get up from the bench, Elvis said, “I am not able to believe this, what are they doing here till now? Would their brains have decayed to such an extent that they would have continued to wait back here to welcome the Devil?”

“A welcome to destroy the Tunnel of Love…” Lessie spread her arms in a welcoming posture.

“There is some mystery.” Elvis opined, “Either this is a meander for those eleven Project Discs. Or otherwise this Picasso School is the only one of its kind among the entire six galaxies? As per the latest report of Lydia Dyaan, they have left Galaxy L3 and re-located to some other galaxy and why would they not do something like that when such superpowers are chasing them?”

As if love had suddenly spurted for Elvis, Lessie said, “Ohh.. The owner of one of those yearning hearts that have been waiting for the prophets who prophesize about the doomsday…”

“Absolutely.” A slight smile originated on Elvis’ face, “With the hope that this doomsday will bring an end to my burning heart… Anyway, it will make me very uneasy to perceive that girl whose name is Susan, tomorrow during the time she is getting engaged with Dion."

*

"Professor, now this school is not suitable for sincere students anymore." A girl wearing spectacles covering almost half her face had come during the following day's lunch break and was standing there with open doors on which the name plate displayed *Professor Viraj's* name.

The Professor looked up and gave a broad smile like a joker.

"An auction of girlfriends is being done in the campus." The girl said.

"Who is that mannerless brute?"

"Who else can it be except that maniac?" The girl said.

"That maniac did not even give me an invitation…."

"Oh sorry," Making a face to Professor Maskeeto who was making fun, she asked, "Where is Professor Viraj?"

"Twenty-five thousand for Sanam… Come on manful buddy. Twenty-five thousand one… two… and three… Sanam is Luis' sweetheart now onwards." Susan pushed *'Sanam'* towards a boy sitting with the *'Auction Coin'* raised. Looking at the girls standing in the shortest possible dresses that were next to bikinis in the auction organized by Susan's group in the plaza, it appeared less like a school and more like a fashion studio that designed summer attire for a country having a scarcity of cloth.

"And now we have up for grabs the school's 'hotest chic', 'rivalry winner' 'Yaana' due to whose hotness all the airconditioners of the classroom are perplexed."

"Contrary to that, I will rather charge money for her." One boy said putting the coin down. When the girl looking like a mobile tattoo studio took out her tongue in front of that rowdy looking boy, the silver earring embedded on the tongue shone up. Suddenly Susan's mischievous face became blurred as if it had been eclipsed. Paras was calling her from behind a tankard looking boy. "I shall be back in a minute." She said in a heavy and helpless tone as she gave the note to Tanisha and got up.

"I am fed up with your repeated nonsense." She said without eye contact with Paras who was waiting near the bicycle stand, "Will you quickly prattle what you want to jabber?" Sizable, extensive smilies were stuck on Paras' facebook as he enjoyed her restlessness. Susan's glance was on Dion who was standing with his leg resting on the wall of the *'Campus Service Center'*. "You please go away, Paras. I do not want to spoil my mood with any scuffle today."

"You don't feel anything for me?

"Yes, I do. Do you know what? Till the time you are with me it feels as if *'Life is like a third degree torture'*. His attention is still not there." She said looking towards Dion with anxiety.

"So what? Am I scared of him? Dion…" Paras shouted loudly and waved his hand but he was still engrossed in talking with someone.

"Looking at your theory P for Power factor you cannot overpower him."

"The talks for which a stage is not suitable are like this: All other *'P'* factors become inferior in front of *'P'* for *'Dominion'* of Love." Paras held her hand and surprisingly today Susan did not object.

Susan said, "I like you? No… There is something different also which I am unable to understand. In one instant I feel that I am infatuated to you and while that moment has not got over as yet, it is something like that you are my biggest enemy. And if you are getting destroyed then I am also willing to sacrifice so many months of my hard work."

"Your strange attitude has already destroyed me. Neither am I able to accompany someone else nor am I able to divert my attention from you."

"Dion has come here just a few days back, but I feel like this for you from the day I saw you in this school for the first time. I think I will go mad if I try to understand this feeling any further."

"I can get my mind to work like a slave except this one matter. My attraction towards you is gigantic. I am unable to control it. As if I knew this from quite a long time, I am aware that there is one such thing, that forces you to think about me like this, and once we get rid of it, we are *'Forever Followers'* of each other."

"You just forget me right away, Paras."

"Ask for something that is possible."

"Dion narrowed his eyes and stomping his feet as if another lion had come into the limits of one lion, he came towards the bicycle stand. But Lessie's voice that was heard on the road, stopped him, "Elvis is summoning you. Where do you keep on roaming…?" Susan waved her hand towards him.

"Everything will become clear once she actually gets engaged with you tomorrow. There is no need to do any quarrel now." Saying this, she pulled Dion outside as he was smiling and waving his hand in front of Susan.

"And now I am also not going to come to school." Susan said.

"Just once Susan… How did he learn that you have not been able to live your childhood like me?"

"No, never. You want to take me to a crook wandering on the roads..!"

"He will make everything all right forever. Just meet him once. He has said that he will commit suicide if he is unable to do it. And that too at a time when he is living a happy life."

"Not at all…" Susan turned her face.

*

Paras had just started his blue colored *'Ferrari Spider'* when Susan's friend Tanisha hurriedly said *'Hi'* to him. If it would have been someone else, Paras would have crushed that *'Hi'* and gone away.

"You are also looking happy today like your psycho friend?"

"You don't know the secret of that happiness? Ohh…" Tanisha said leaning her elbows on car's roof. "Susan is going to get engaged tomorrow." Paras jumped like the cap of a champagne bottle. "There is no need to ask with whom. Everyone is going to Goa today evening."

After remaining silent for five seconds, Paras asked – "Why? Is the ring ceremony in Goa?"

"No, for the party. But Akshay uncle said that he will not be able to believe until about an hour of the exchange of the rings that Susan is still firm on her decision. You know her very well. She keeps on changing so many colors that even the chameleon will be ashamed looking at her…"

"Yet this anxiety will not set me free. By the way which boyfriend is accompanying you?"

"That has not yet been decided. But probably the one who has been successful in getting my complete attention since the last month."

"Oh… It means that you are trying to say that a rose has grown on the stone?"

"After the *'Ferrari Ride'* escaped from near Tanisha who put her hands on both her hips and was about to abuse, he gave her a flying kiss in the rear-view mirror.

'That same night, Uttarakhand, Skeleton Lake'

"After such a long time, how did the Devil remember the serial numbers of the notes for the money we had given to the person who had come to give the sample of the corpse that had been used by the Diaboli?"

"Ssh.. ssh.. ssh.." Dervil gestured *Sierra (a member of the Devil family)* to keep quiet and entered into Terror-Street. Terror-Street that was based in the abyss of *'Skeleton Lake'* filled with bare skulls. The entrance view was such that the *'heart would say that it should never end'*. Sparks emerging from the flames of fire illuminating Terror-Street were getting attracted to the handsome *'Blue-Devil'* and vanishing. He was addressing a delegation of several young Satanics from Galaxy L6 amidst the Devilish evening melody echoing in the hall huge enough to accommodate innumerable elephants-

"As the dimension called time continues to age, the faith of all these worlds will continue to increase on the directives of the Satanics freed from the trivial restrictions of sins and virtues by evoking my powers. To the extent that the existence of religion will end completely. His voice was mysterious like Enigmatic Spell Erudition "No restrictions at all, no anxiety of the laws of *Karma (Deeds or Actions)* and no fear of punishment. After a slight interim silence he raised both hands to indicate the dismissal of the gathering.

When a *'carouse' (A congregation of food and drinks)* with riotous colors and music started in Terror-Street, the Devil took a bundle of notes from the hands of an unknown Satanic and came towards them. Before the Devil could demand, Sierra put a paper note on which the serial numbers were listed in his hands without any further delay.

"It is such a strange thing," Matching the numbers with the notes, the Devil said, "The bundles of notes in that mysterious woman's sack on that road of Kangra one and a half years ago, were the same that were given to that private detective. What was his name? Yes, Shashang. And that same private detective finds the corpse used in the ritual by the Diabolist consulted by Paras." He said throwing the chit of paper to one side, "He has discovered these bundles from the sack that is still hanging on one of the trees in the valley on the other side of the road at the venue where this whole fiasco took place."

"I am feeling dizzy with this type of talk." Standing a little away on the back side, Malachi softly said in Titus' ears and due to the Devil's presence, he prevented himself from pretending to feel dizzy and fall down.

Appreciating the Satanic who had discovered the bundles of notes with his glance like that of a reward donor, Dervil said, "However, his body language represented him in the category of an ordinary citizen of the toy planet." Dervil said as if he had struck a deal with Shashang yesterday only.

"But what would this man be doing in such a dense jungle?" Sierra asked.

Malachi said, "People of the ancient times used to hide treasures at such places. And people nowadays use it for hiding their crimes."

That terrain is probably hiding something even now." Dervil said, "We should go there once again, from where he had found that corpse. We should flip over the surrounding layers. By *'once again'*, I mean to say right away."

*

The dance frantics who were enticing the ordinary silent night in this Casino at Goa didn't even have any clue about how many *'aliens'* were dancing around them today.

Amidst the discotheque filled with Susan's admirers, Dion was making her dance like a voluptuous Barbie doll. Pointing towards Paras, dousing the searing of his heart by splashing the whisky's sting, near the display of alcohol, he asked, "Will he continuously roam after you like this..?"

"He will gradually understand this. By the way, Mr. Lucky, you could have been in each others' place."

Dion said, "If I would have been in his place, then would everyone be enjoying here like this?" Dancing next to Susan, *Tanisha* saw her laughing cruelly and getting confined in Dion's hug, as she escaped the jouncing feet and reached Paras.

"She doesn't even give you a damn and why do you injure your selfie and keep chasing her again and again? Why don't you put a full stop to it?" She said with bewilderment, "The school's *Cream of the crop* from good to the best is waiting for you in a queue, and you…"

Laughing a little wanly, Paras said, "You think that my callousness is so cheap that it is worth any one like this? My wrath will be for a very special girl…" Struck motionless in astonishment, Tanisha came back to her senses when Paras added, "And buddy, to tell you the truth, I am getting angry this time. What should I do? Kill Dion?

"Bloody imposter." Tanisha contorted her mouth and left him alone.

"Throat has dried up? You want to have a drink?" Dion asked.

"Yes, please."

As soon as Dion left, Susan's gaze started wandering towards the fair mocktail mixologist, but the seat in front of him was now vacant. "Hi Susan. Dance..?" Pushing aside the hand of the young boy, sniffing an inhaler like the victim of an epidemic of craving, inviting her to dance, Susan snatched his inhaler and placing the inhaler near the nose where an innocence always kept playing the most, she started sniffing the drugs from it and tried crushing the troublesome thoughts.

"To my right, pageboy hairstyle…" Dion gestured and Elvis seated on the last slot-machine found a middle aged woman on the Crepes table number five of the main gaming floor. "She is the same one who always keeps on shadowing Susan. And just now she spoke with a man of the same height and shape as Sebastian. It's unfortunate that their aura-print is not with us." When Dion uttered this sentence in the hands-free set, that woman dressed up in shape wear got up and went towards the crowd that had gathered near the *'Pachinko Machine'*.

"All this is beyond my understanding." Elvis said restlessly.

When Maya reached next to Sebastian who was roving his eyes there like a laser spread trap, he got up in an unexpected manner and went to sit next to Paras who was seated on a roulette machine.

Gulping down the remaining drink in one single swig, Paras turned towards Sebastian who had come and sat down next to him, "I also don't have any trust in particular. It's just that she should stay with me a little longer, and hence I tried to make her understand. But she just presumptuously said 'No' to come to any such crook. You also stop following me henceforth."

"Till now, we were in search of a Susan, who would get equally attracted towards you as well. But there seems to be some confusion. Why don't you hold her and give her a kiss. Maybe she might become yours forever…"

Paras looked towards Sebastian as if he was blowing a trumpet. "She is going to get engaged tomorrow. And can you see that boy in the front waiting for a new drink? I am thinking of killing him. And if you continue talking nonsense like this, your ghost will be giving company to his ghost in this casino and keep on boring him right from tomorrow."

"Paras, it is not reasonable to waste any more time now." Sebastian said quietly, "As the Billion-Couple created on Earth by Kundali is in its final stage, the continuous presence of its supporters and opponents have presently made the *'Orian Arm' (Solar System Area)*, a center for several interesting activities. And you will get to know about how dangerous this is for Daarck only after using this memory machine."

"As per what you are claiming, if the memories of past births of Susan and me are stored in the memory machine you have, why don't you use it on me alone and prove that you have something to validate your claim?"

"All this is very strange. And you will also not trust it so easily. A Satanic soul has been imprisoned with both of your souls. And most probably only due to that, whenever you kiss intimately and profoundly, the hold of the Satanic element seems to loosen a little on your minds and this is the only time when the memories from the Memory Machine can be pasted in your mind. This seems to be Susan's batch number, right?" Sabastian asked gesturing on that side when Paras placed chips of one million in the *'21'* number slot on the roulette table, but before something could come out of Paras' open jaw, saw Susan coming, Sebastian got up, turned and went near Maya.

"You should try your luck on some other number for winning." Susan said removing the chips from number 21.

"My joy of winning is only associated with this number."

"I have read somewhere that understanding reality is called real maturity. It is better for you to accept that Dion has been more successful in attracting me towards him rather than you."

"Changing the reality is what is called true maturity. And you would not have read this anywhere. Susan, this is haste."

"No further discussion on this subject, please. I just want get rid of this cruel confusion." When Susan said this, Paras' lips were going near her.

"Not here." Sebastian held back Maya's hand as she was taking out the Memory-Machine from the bag on the Pachinko Machine in the left corner.

Drawing in the same breath that was coming back after colliding with the changing color of Susan's cheeks from the touch of the whiffs of his breath, Paras said, "Ahh… this fragrance, is enough to make me your slave willingly. Getting separated from you is akin to getting separated from life. If you are not there then no bud will blossom in my deserted life even with the rain of *nectar (referred to as Amrut in the Indian mythology and believed to bestow immortality to the one who drinks it)*. No sooner had Paras' lips barely touched Susan's willing lips amidst uncontrollable heart beats then Paras' wrenched lips tasted the flavor of his own blood as Susan under dominance of some obsession, powerfully punched him.

Throwing away the drinks held in both his hands and clapping, Dion reached near them. "Try again…" He said laughing.

Wiping the blood from his lips and moving his fingers in his hair, Paras got up in front of Dion.

"He should not die." Hearing Elvis' advice in the bluetooth, Dion raised the gun pointed on his chest slightly higher. Elvis' gaze had fixed eagerly on the one who was thought to be Sebastian to see what he would do now, but he was still seated nonchalantly and cold bloodedly on his seat. Dion raised the gun point a little higher and fired on Paras' shoulder but to Elvis' sheer surprise, the presumed Sebastian was still looking calmly as he remained stable in his place. Amidst the stampede that had started with screams in the casino, Dion flung the bouncers intercepting him as if they were whits and reached near the door. But Susan's heart as she exerted force to slacken the tight grip of Dion's hand was reluctant to move away from Paras' side. As soon as Dion disappeared, Meriano jabbed a gun in Paras' back and took him outside.

The moment Elvis moved from there, Maya reached Sebastian as fast as if running behind a departing train, "What are you waiting for? They have kidnapped him for the investigation of the aura medicine…!"

"Cool down Maya." Sebastian said holding a packet of cigarettes in front of Maya, looking at him with a gaze declaring him useless, "Nurai is there. They have already monitored Paras' aura fifty times during the last five days. I don't suppose they will repeat the convention again after his blood test today."

"I did not understand your meaning."

"It means that Paras was devoid of the medicine today evening at eight thirty hours. And before Qadir could give him the new dose, Paras escaped from his hands. They have already monitored his aura-print several times. Now Elvis just wants to confirm if the aura medicine is still present in his blood or not."

"And what if they match his aura print once more?"

"We cannot get into direct encounter, Maya. Elvis himself is an Energy Warrior and although small, Luciano has an army of his own. Even if he is identified, they would not have any other way except to set him free to reach Susan, just like us… Maya, what are you looking at?" Sebastian laughed and asked.

Glaring at a young woman engrossed in kissing a boy following the latest fashion of grown beard and moustache like sheep, Maya said, "Will you give me the aura monitor for a minute?" It looked as if a race was going on amongst the horses in Maya's mind. Looking around when Sebastian inserted the aura monitor in her hand, Maya said monitoring her own aura after holding Sebastian's hand, "Oh God… Why did we not understand such a straight forward thing, when the bodies of two individuals are touching each other en masse, their aura-print assumes a strange structure. New and weird…"

"So what? We have already monitored them when both of them were separate from each other and also when they were not touching anyone."

But the smile on Maya's face continued. She said, "Paras did not want that Susan should become a victim of the side effects of the aura medicine. Had I told you that he had stealthily taken the blood sample of Dion's *Mashooqa (lady love)* Eliza on Koll's Asteroid?"

A winner's sparkle emanated on Sebastian's doused face. "Right, how can any aura-monitor match the print of the magnetic fluid flowing out of a body in which two souls are imprisoned together..!" He quickly connected the phone to Nurai. Such a song was playing there at the moment that everyone had been deployed in the style of dancing with a hubbub. "You will have to rush to Africa right away." He said snapping his throat and started walking outside to talk further.

*

That same night, Kangra Bypass Highway, 11:10 pm

"It is natural that after having found the corpse, whatever thing he had come to hide at this spot, he must have changed the thought of packing it in the tomb. This is just useless hard work." Sierra said as she put a *'Metal Detector Bubble Box' (Metal detectors of the size and shape of golf balls)* that had a circumference of a large suitcase down on the ground and pressed the protruding cleat on the box with her shoes. Just like countless mice would run on a rat-island, the bubbles identified with names R-One, R-Two, etc. started sliding in all directions.

Glaring at Malachi, who was frequently pushing the Contraption's antenna in and pulling it out for receiving signals of some bizarre object, Dervil finally said with a throat slitting glance, "Black-marketeers dealing in old scrap things will pay you a good amount for this type of gadgets."

"This is probably happening due to the rain water…" Mumbling vaguely, Malachi finally spoke in a loud voice, "Signals are being received from the side of route eleven." One bubble detector *'R-Double One'* is not ready to budge from a spot half a km. away from that location.

With Titus' first onslaught of the axe, the anxiety of mystery silently knocked on the mind of every Satanic who moved backwards. As the grave continued to become bigger, the surrounding air started filling up with the stench of decay. Extra hard work was not written in Titus' destiny…

"Carefully..!" Dervil had already seen one piece of cloth. Covering their noses with a handkerchief, the Satanics sat around the clumsy grave in a circle. Standing in a tight skirt, Sierra estimated the age of the child whose corpse it was to be not more than eleven years. When Dervil raised the face of the decayed corpse of the tender girl hidden being the single piece of cloth from shoulder to knee, it seemed as if a bone was getting detached from her neck.

Titus and *Moses* carefully picked up and took the corpse out. *(Moses – Another Devil family member)*

"Can this be Susan, then?" Dervil said, "Or maybe at that time Shashang might have come here to bury this corpse, and he could have found the corpse used by the Diaboli?"

"On the other hand, that old woman and that man Shashang might be involved in the business of girls' trafficking?" Malachi said.

"Whatever it is, there is no way now to determine if this is Susan or not." Titus said. *(The aura print that is frequently discussed here is related to the subtle body of the human being and not to the physical body. Subtle body – Second cover of the individual soul)*

"Three deep stabs with a knife have been done on this girl's back." Sierra murmured moving her fingers on the corpse's back. "The owner of this girl was a tormentor." She said pulling out a ring from the corpse's ear that was intact, "She must have experienced extreme thrill with the groans of pain when the whole ear of the girl would have been pressed and fit in this small ring."

"It is a matter of surprise," Moses said while taking a D.N.A. sample of the corpse, "Compared to the other organs, this ear has still not decayed that much."

Removing the top and bottom hangings in opposite directions of the ring, Sierra said, "There is a British seal on this. Special types of metals are added to this type of ornaments to prevent the effects of the environment on the body. In those days, showing such marked ornaments would affix a stamp of authenticity of the royal message."

"What would be the current time in the clock of the residents of Britain?" Gesturing Titus to get the flying machine, Dervil asked.

Mumbai, 1.15, Susan's house

"Sirrr… Master Dion's car is in the porch once again." The watchman informed over the intercom and closed the gate with the remote.

"So late in the night…?" Akshay said and rushed towards the door quickly replacing the receiver.

Sebastian's guess had fortunately turned out to be true in case of Paras. When the traces of aura medicine were not detected in his blood, the thought of monitoring his aura-print once again had not occurred to anyone from

Elvis' entire troupe. He had been released after a little callous beating.

Waiting for the door to open, Elvis said straitening his tie and hair- "No aura-monitor in the world would ever be wrong while it is functioning correctly but after examining Paras' blood, we have missed out on monitoring his aura once again. We will have to repeat this activity once again tomorrow."

Without moving from the doorway, Akshay turned back and told the butler loudly. "Dion the wise has arrived to cancel the engagement while there is still time." And said turning towards Dion, "If you have come to say no for tomorrow's engagement, I'm ready."

"Hee.. hee.. hee… I apologize for the cheekiness of waking up my future father-in-law from his dream."

"May we come in?" Elvis asked as if he was giving a threat in a soft voice. Left with no option, Akshay helplessly moved aside. Reaching the seating area, Dion said, "Sir, Mr. Liam is a *magnetic fluid repairer. (An aura physician, who investigates the luster of a human being and repairs it)* He will fix Susan's stubborn crying processes in a flick of a moment." Putting the briefcase on a cushioned sofa and taking out an aura monitor and blood test kit from it, Elvis watched Susan's pictures hung on the bungalow's walls with utmost concentration as if counting chickens. When he took out the *'aura-monitor'* and held it in front of Akshay, Dion turned and said, "I do not want that my engagement flashes in the national news highlights due to some new commotion by Susan."

Looking at Akshay, it appeared as if he is in a hesitation to determine Elvis' nationality from his appearance.

Dion said, "Now, there would be a Kirlian photography session and her blood samples will be taken. After that, she will have to go for a full body scan tomorrow. I will be back with Susan." Dion got up and quickly proceeded towards the stairs leading to the upper floor without waiting for Akshay to permit him.

"Dion, you will not like my raucous talk, but you know that Susan is still not sure about the relationship with you. If you really love her then you should persuade her not to do the engagement right now."

"Liam is present here at this time especially to fix her dilemma aggrieved mind." Saying this, Dion climbed the stairs with agility.

'Knock-knock.' Holding Dion's hand that was knocking on the cheek, Susan said, "You came so early…?"

"At least for this girl, no one can tell the truth that '*I have in me the strength to wait.*' Come down in five minutes, and no arguments at all, I will explain everything later."

Smiling like a baby princess, Susan came and sat beside Dion. She was still in her evening-suit. A sigh escaped Elvis' throat looking at the reflection of clean beauty emulating from her sleepy face surrounded by the elegance of disheveled hair.

"Then you feel that *'I'* am mad?" Susan, who was calm two seconds ago, roared like a lioness that has come out for hunting.

“Dion has brought him here.” Akshay said taking both hands behind.

“I will need less than half a minute’s time, Ms. Susan.” Elvis said with a hypnotic voice, holding a syringe to take the blood sample, “The world is at the feet of beautiful people but when made unhappy by kicking, the world does not even hesitate to boycott the beauty. As such, ego cannot be won over by beauty…”

After comparing the sophisticated talks of the youth, who appeared to be around twenty-two to twenty-five with his age for five seconds, Susan roared, “Dion, I am telling you right now, if I see even a single insolent guest in the engagement tomorrow, I will remove your ring at that very moment and throw it away.” She got up with the style of a dictator and marched towards the bedroom.

“I beg your pardon.” Akshay said, “Sometimes when she suddenly starts behaving like this in the midst of normal behavior, it appears as if this girl has some ghost barrier. In my last attempts, I had consulted a shadow expert. Poor fellow, he was just muttering the words of guarantee when suddenly- *‘this girl, certainly there is someone else also in her body’* - Susan burst out on him. Uuh..” Akshay let out sighs of repentance.

“Susan, come here.” Dion said in a submissive tone and got up taking the test kit from Elvis’ hand. He went near Susan who had stopped on the steps and forcefully took her blood sample.

“Since when has Susan been with you?” Elvis asked, during her blood examination.

"Since a long time…" Akshay Namkar said in brief. Elvis used the aura monitor on Susan after it was confirmed by the report that came after about three minutes that Susan was not taking any aura medicine. "This is not Susan." Elvis murmured in a dejected voice as he quickly gathered the things and put them in the bag.

In response to the congratulations regarding Susan's engagement given by Elvis at the time of leaving, Akshay made a face as if there had been an Income Tax raid.

In the night, 8:00, Imperial War Museum, London

The *'car'* that had descended from Dervil's aircraft was now running on Royston Road. Before *'Sierra'* could express further curiosity about the two-floor high city buses running under the brilliance of the Mercury Street lights, the car stopped a little further away from the staff entrance of the *'Imperial War Museum'*. Under the surveillance of the capacious C.C.T.V. network the door of the car could be seen opening and closing, but no one could be seen descending from the car. *'Moses'*, being invisible with the Thistle Quiet Crown, had entered from Gate Number Three and had now reached the *'Large Exhibition Gallery'*. The weapons used during the First and Second World War had been exhibited all around. Old warships were hanging from the hooks of the high ceiling with long chains. The daylight here was almost without any significance. Seeing a guard coming out from below the chamber on the right side bearing the *Coffee*

Shop board and patrolling near the *tank*, Moses thought, "I should find some better person than this one." He caught the funnel of an old two-wheeler cannon and pushing it slightly behind, he went ahead. It took three seconds for the thunderstruck guard seeing the self-moving cannon to get suspicious of a ghost.

Passing through the first world-war death gallery, Moses could see worms of botheration of shrewdness crawling on the face of the guard coming from the opposite end. When they passed close to each other, Moses instantly removed the *'thistle-cap'* and appeared.

"Hello…" Moses said in a soft tone.

The guard turned back and looked towards the one who said *'Hello'* and as if someone had hammered a peg in his chest he put his hand there.

"The thought is not good." Moses enunciated the thoughts of the guard, who was breathless with fright and was staring at the *'evacuation alarm'* button, in front of him. "Your assumption is not right, I am not a dacoit. No, not a thief, either. Uh.. Neither a smuggler of antique objects…"

"Oh my God," He spoke in a pure British accent and covered his forehead with his palm, "Here, can you read the headlines of my thoughts?"

Moses remained silent until his new thought could be experienced and said after that, "Right, I can help you get back your girlfriend, but before that, tell me where I will get the details of this?" Moses asked, showing the ring they had got from the girl's ears.

"Museum of Royal Content's current director, *'Professor Brett'* should be able to tell about this." The guard said looking at the ring meticulously.

"And where can he be found?"

"In our other branch *'Churchill War Room'* located in the South-east. Nowadays, the professor is writing a book, *'Turning Point of the Second World War'*. But even after reaching within three hours on a traffic free drive, you would be late.

"I will need only about ten minutes to reach the professor. You can fix a rendezvous with your girlfriend any time while this thing is hooked up behind the ear." Moses said, giving him a disposable *'Thought Steal'*.

8:30 PM. Churchill War Rooms, Kings Charles Street

"Professor it will be very helpful to me if you can give me some information regarding the owner of this ring."

After removing the reading spectacles and putting them on his desk, Professor *'Brett'* gazed at Moses standing far and gestured him to sit down.

"Is this the same desk on which the plan to destroy Hitler was prepared…?"

"Absolutely…" It appeared as if Brett had liked the dialogue. Before the professor, who had been seated alone for who knows how long, could involve him into a long discussion, Moses immediately came to the point, "This jewelry somewhat confuses in a way that although the design is Indian, it is marked with the seal of Britain's royal family."

"It has been said about such ornaments that many women of the royal-family, influenced by the ornaments of indian regal women had got them designed during their travel to India. after ten years of establishment of the *Museum of Royal Contents*, with the recommendation of the then Director, an auction was arranged for such things that were 'real' but there was no specific basis for the details of owners or any other information. This ring can be one of those."

"A bill would have been surely made for this." Moses said.

Brett kept the ring at one side and looked up.

"Professor, it is of utmost importance for me to reach the owner of this ring."

"Is this a question associated with national security?"

"No, with the security of the whole Galaxy."

"Means?" Brett asked and waited for a long time for Moses' response. Finally getting offended on Moses who evaded an explanation, he said, "You will have to submit an official permission paper to obtain the details of ownership of this item."

Moses took out his identity-card and put it on the desk. *'British Interpol. Special Agent'* had been written below one long code on the card. After matching Moses' face with the photograph in the card, the professor took out a small paper of the new password to log-in to the museum's computer.

"Bidders list of Auction 1961." Raising his face slightly higher to see from the spectacles, Brett mumbled, "But the second address of this British Indian is missing. He might have shifted to India later on. His name is Anuj Namkar." After three seconds, Brett was dictating him his Liverpool address.

"Thank you, Professor. And good luck for your book."

*

Today's special day was eagerly waiting for Paras to get up from the auto-*hypnosis (deep sleep)*. Because finally, one unexpected visit that was going to start from today, was going to lead him to his real identity. But he was unable to escape immediately from the blurred memories of some mysterious past life to preserve today's valuable moments. The person whom Earth Eleven's chairman Antonio was addressing as Daarck said, "The intentions of the Master Galaxy is one supreme mystery and one day it will eradicate all these galaxies. Anyways, presently I have come to explain about how to recover from the Pure Energy invented by us." When Daarck, who resembled a model of a magnet-man extended his hand for giving a briefcase, an uproar as if many prophets were calling Paras, went in his ear and collided with his dormant consciousness, "Paaaaaaa…ras..." He opened his eyes and jumped up in the bed as if he had encountered an electric shock… "Oh, damn it…" Paras clutched his head looking at the alarm that had finally accepted defeat.

"Forget it, you still need some more sleep. You can go with a bouquet to congratulate Susan regarding her engagement even in the evening…!" Calming his criticizing mind, he rushed to the bathroom. Spreading toothpaste on the brush, he connected the phone to the driver, "I am coming down within five minutes. The car's engine should be on and the door should be open."

*

Paras thrust today's rose in the plaster of his left hand that had resulted from Elvis' beating. Passing slowly through the plethora of cars, his car came and stood in front of Akshay Namkar's *'Wigwam'*. "Entry of the Anti-Hero has been done." Meriano, who was standing in the porch, told Dion in the wireless in ear.

"If he gets in then you get out. But in absolute silence… The atmosphere should not be spoiled."

The *'alien'*, fed up with Dion, stood intercepting the way of Paras who had become a *'hellien'* and was approaching the porch. "Go away from here before Meriano gives a kiss of death…" He said in a soft voice.

"Dion's intolerable bloke… Don't make the mistake of interfering today." Paras expressed his deadly notion and shoved him with his normal hand. "I am coming outside." Dion said but at the same time, a spotless moon was seen rising on the red carpet that was spread out on the flamboyant stairs. "Let's conclude this first…" Dion said swiftly handing over the *'ring ceremony tray'* to a lady from Susan's maternal side.

Paras took out the gun and pressed it in Meriano's abdomen. "Let me go in quietly."

"Let him come in." Dion, who was listening to the altercation on the phone, fearing a feud, finally left his obstinacy.

One would assure beauty more than this would never exist in this world or any other world once he watches today's decked up Susan standing next to Dion. Nor such a volcano of beauty would have ever erupted in the past also. The future and the past had become impatient to relentlessly drink the juice of this beauty as if shoving the present aside, but even the one watching this ultimate height of beauty would not know when and how much flowed out from their eyes. When Dion was inserting the ring on her ring-finger, Paras rushed and stood in front of them by pushing the applauding guests.

Susan's accelerated heartbeats instantly gave her an inkling of this presence. Susan abruptly pulled out Dion's ring that he had slid half way up the finger. Bewilderment gave one tight slap on cheerful Dion's exuberant face.

"Sorry Dion, I can't do this." Susan spoke in a melted voice and it took Dion only one second to find Paras.

It was difficult to say whether the claps of Akshay Namkar trying to stop himself from looking happy, were to welcome Susan's decision or to get the attention of the guests. "Please stop looking at my daughter in such a strange manner, before she changes her decision once again…"

But Dion had become violent. “After today, I will never let you get confused…” He pushed Susan to one side and proceeded towards Paras in a dangerous manner.

“I am Professor Palash… remember…? One minute, I want to tell you one important thing.”

“Not now.” Easing off his hand from the grip of a stranger who was trying to pull him by holding his wrist, when Paras came to Susan and gave her the rose, pouncing upon Paras’s neck from behind and hurling him to one side, Dion roared, “It is the limit of these worms and spiders.”

Catching Akshay who had come to Paras’ aid by his neck and dragging him, Dion said, “Now I am fed up of putting up an act of gentleness.” He took out a gun, and aimed at the plumb center between Paras’ eyes, but before the trigger could be pressed, looking at Dervil who had come and stood in the doorway nodding his head in refusal, the frightened Dion threw the gun to one side.

“Mister Akshay Namkar… such a corner of the bungalow, where we can leisurely discuss about this ring…” When *‘Dervil’* blinked his eyelashes towards Akshay who had been seized amidst the closed group of Satanics, the fear of old disasters knocked in his eyes.

“People are not telling the truth that the mettle of the spying industry in India is getting suffocated.” Malachi said scrutinizing Akshay’s flashing bedroom on the second floor, “The meeting in Simla can be said to be a little short to remember my face.”

Gripping Akshay's neck with madness, Dervil said, "I am not aware what must be your role in this dangerous drama but alas, you have become part of such a conspiracy which is formed against the *'Lord of Lords' (The Devil)*." When Sierra freed Akshay from Dervil's ironic claw and gestured Malachi to copy his memories, glaring at Malachi who was connecting the Memory Thief with Akshay's head, Paras muttered- "One unit of this gang of lunatics confronted me yesterday also. This has been meted out by them only." When Paras raised his plastered hand and showed it, watching his hot-shot personality, Sierra snapped her fingers and gestured him to get out.

"What is all this Dad..? Anxious Susan's naughty looking nose had now become a dance floor for her anger to dance on.

"I don't know but are you asking me..? Our guests are not going to get bored to praise your spectacular performance below for days."

Moses moved forward and injected the point of the device to investigate the presence of any kind of foreign body in the anatomy, in Susan's thumb. "No metal at all. Not even a liquid clot to interfere the aura flow." After the first phase was completed according to expectation, anxiously and fearfully, Moses took Susan's blood sample.

"Start talking about this quickly." Dervil put a ring in Akshay's hand.

"I had got this ring from my father in inheritance. But I have nothing to do with the matter about which you are talking."

Akshay got up and opening the wardrobe, he took out a small *'Cactus Koch'*. He unfolded a bundle of papers from it and handed some photographs to Dervil. In the photograph, the overwhelming craziness of the blood soaked woman, who had been tied to the bed, to break forth was captivating. "Actually, my wife was a sick woman. When kept away from the intoxication of distortion, she would become adamant on killing herself and whoever was there in front of her. We did not have any child for years and then one day she mentally decided something and told me, *'I am ready to adopt a child.'* The beginning was intolerable for me but frightened with the thought of my wife's last rites, I learnt to live in my own world. We would go to far away regions, tempt those who were needy. Even at that time in Kangra, we repeated the same story. We would seize two, four or five year old children of some people. By the time the children would become eleven or twelve years old, my wife's mind would be satiated playing torturous games with them, and finally she would kill them."

"I had found the corpse *'described in your advertisement'* while I was disposing one such corpse."

"Then how does Susan get saved…?" Dervil asked.

"Susan's matter was somewhat different. Right from childhood, she was ferocious, obstinate and powerful. At the age of twelve, she snatched the chopper with which my wife rushed to kill her and cut off my wife's throat.

The task for which I could not gather courage for years, she insouciantly executed it in a minute. At that time, I had got my wife to Kangra to get her a new toy where we had never been earlier. That lady was our quarter's servant. And greedy as well…!"

Keeping a very serious countenance, Sierra was nodding her head in denial in front of Dervil to say that this is not the real Susan. While all these talks were going on, she and Malachi had together completed the investigation of Susan's *blood (For checking the presence of the aura medicine)* and had monitored her aura print also.

Dervil was now despondent in an unusual way with this failure. He asked Akshay Namkar, "And from where did you get the inspiration to name her Susan?"

"A tag had been embedded on that girl. As if she had been kidnapped from a big stock of children… Actually that lady had a pair. Including one boy.. I did not develop any interest in keeping him. As such, I did not even want to keep Susan, looking at her innocence of the girl whose corpse I had buried, I had decided that it was enough, not any more. But looking at Susan I had developed a strange affection."

Gesturing to wind up everything in a disappointed manner, Dervil said, "It is not impossible that the woman would have kidnapped the children from some other place. Yet the circumstances indicate that this should be Susan whereas the evidences indicate that this is not Susan. There is only one meaning to this that the Gardis would have reached Kangra prior to us. This entire phantasmagoria is created by Ros. He is playing games with us."

"Do her real parents still have hope? Have they sent you? Are you her father?" Akshay added looking towards Dervil, "How insignificant is my question. Who else would be searching for a few days old girl from such a long time?"

"Her *'salaried'* parents had been set free from this troublesome world on that same day, but as you have not remembered, this matter is associated with the *'Excellency of Darkness'*, hence maybe your days of happiness are over. But just a minute, you were there in front of me in Simla on that night, to give the sample of that corpse… How did you reach Kangra before us?

"I have my own chopper." Akshay Namkar said shrugging his shoulders.

*

'Kundali' is engrossed in walking briskly in the courtyard of the aviary of *Fight Club of Earth Renovate's* headquarters located in Central Mumbai. Wishing the evening's seven o'clock traffic to increase even more and the screeching of the wheeled creatures to dominate his worry, Kundali had just changed the side of the stroll path, when he jumped up and trembled as if a brake had suddenly been applied to a car running at a fast speed. *'Simbal'*, the Chairman of Colony *Glee Metal Casting,* had come and stood in front of him as if he had originated from air. Brown hair swayed around the shoulders of Simbal who was dressed in a sky colored overcoat. Pushing the cap

made from the skeleton of the eagle's face slightly back, he said, "I have not popped up here to give *reassurance (consolation)* for your failure." His upturned snout brought the reminiscence of a balloon that was on the verge of exploding.

Before the mystery of the Satanic like costume he had worn could be asked, he started, "Only one year for the success of the first Billion Couple and the second one is going around hiding its face in uncertainty even after one and a half year…? Even the three minds of his Excellency, Lon are worried about this matter. Kundali you must understand this matter, for this *Majmoon (The issue related to whether the Master Galaxy will throw out the Vio-Crazy New-Gods for getting the inhabitants of the toy planet to rebel by remaining childless)* the foundation of *Off-Idiotic's* victory now depends on the success of the Billion Couple on the Earth which is the last Billion Couple to be filled up very soon. That is on you."

"My Master," Kundali said criticizing the helpers of his failure- "Although anger does exist in the inhabitants of Earth, it is not enough to sacrifice for the revolt of acquiring a desired life. These are exhausted people. A furor has risen up within them to enjoy as much happiness as possible by using the limited vitality and entertainment resources that they have. A saying is in vogue there, *'A lion will remain hungry but will not eat grass.'* They frequently keep saying this, but these helpless people are enduring poverty due to lack of fighting spirit for implementing it…"

"There is no need to get totally disappointed." Kundali saw *Simbal's* abating smile. "The discretion that stops them from revolting says that it is better to enjoy whatever is available rather than wandering in search of unguaranteed things. And in the whole world if any language has been made to silence this reasoning, then it is the language of miracle."

"But we are also unable to open the chest of miracles in front of the common people due to the fear of the *Master Galaxy*."

"It should never appear that the Billion Couple is a conspiracy." Simbal said in a cautioning tone. After remaining silent for a few moments, he spoke, "We should go for a *'small entertaining visit'* on this road overflowing with cars in front of us."

Kundali looked at him with doubtful eyes and said yes.

Looking at the bizarre appearance of Simbal who was walking on the footpath, the people passing from there were forgetting that they were getting late to reach their destination. Coming near the *'fountain circle'* that divided the triangle, Simbal took out a steel-camera from the coat and opened its cap. Before Kundali who was becoming an interrogator could open his mouth, noticing a car crossing the bridge and coming there, Simbal asked, "Whether there will be an air bag in this car or not?"

"The possibility of this luxurious car being without an air-bag....." Before the sentence could be completed with the word *not*, Simbal held the camera in front of the metallic colored car coming at the speed of fifty and clicked it, and as if the car's engine was melted by giving thousands of Fahrenheit of heat, it appeared to be embedded in the ground for a moment, and in the next instant, doing furlong dance of flips, it went and fell on the *'old Bentley'* that was parked below the official advertisement of *'Go Slow'*.

"In your *'Public Meeting'* that is going to be conducted after fifty minutes, the crowd of hundreds of thousands of people will not be seeing the cameramen covering this kind of a miracle of yours but a Kundali tossing up and throwing the car with his eyes. Understood?"

"Means that when one of the photographers standing beside me on the stage is doing such a plight of the car with this camera, I will have to veer it into a miracle done through the smack of my eyes, right?"

"Yes and one specific matter of precaution," Cutting the airbag that had squeezed the driver with a knife, amidst the shrilling alarm of the car, Simbal said, "The Devil will never wish that the verdict of the Billion Couple would go against the Vio-Crazy group. You should not come out from the protective encirclement of the holy things that keep the Devil at bay under any circumstances. The lurid personalities of the Master Galaxy themselves are also afraid of this great power generating unholy confusion."

Their return journey had now reached a point from where the central gate could be seen.

"Why…!" Kundali stopped, expressing a big surprise in front of Simbal who was throwing the camera in the dustbin.

"This camera that is based on the mysterious technique of emitting rays rendering anything motionless by reaching the nucleus of its basic molecules through its reflection can be used only once." Simbal said taking out a new camera from the overcoat and giving it to him, his legs were now hanging in the air. He put a hand on Kundali's shoulders, "I am disclosing to you today the solution to the mysterious question which the New-Gods of the entire L3 are groping for. So you can trust that ultimately, all this is being done for the benefit of people. Metal Casting's New-God *'Lon'* who is renowned as the God of Benevolence is the one who has entrusted Daarck with this assignment to eliminate the Vio-Crazy group from Galaxy L3."

*

"Kundali's assembly is just about to begin there and what has come over you to play this game of hotel now?" Luciano said getting upset, because this was the third time that Elvis who was following Sebastian and Maya had called him up and changed the dinner location. It was seven forty-five. Sebastian and Maya were finally giving an order to a waiter in the reception lounge of a hotel located at a distance of approximately ten kilometers from Susan's house. After Dervil's unexpected arrival in the morning, Nurai had knocked Paras unconscious and kidnapped him from Susan's bungalow. He had pulled him into the shower-room and stuffed two revert-pills together as well as one aura medicine in his mouth. He had continuously kept Paras unconscious, even in the airbus during the trip to Africa.

"My son, you will not even have any inkling about how weird the new mystery that has come out of Devil's mind captivating my peace and happiness is." Luciano said coming and sitting on the chair in the front.

"Ssh.. ssh.. ssh…" Elvis gestured him to remain silent and engaging a Bluetooth dot in his ear, he pointed the *'microphone laser beam'* coming out of the cell phone in the direction of Sebastian's table that was twenty feet away. But the conversation broadcasted from there was going on in a private language. Although excessive use of the revert-pill was dangerous to health, Elvis' team had changed their appearance once again. After Dervil moved away from Akshay's bungalow, Elvis was as such convinced that this was indeed not Susan but along with that a suspicion had also aroused in his mind that Akshay and his daughter had something to do with the real Susan and Paras.

Looking at the *'laser spot'* colliding with the flower pot lying on his table, as Sebastian put his phone aside, Elvis turned towards Luciano and raised his eyebrows in front of him. Looking around him after taking a sip of Sangrita, Luciano said, "There can be only one reward for the dangerous role that I have played between Lord de Ros, Daarck and the Devil in all these acts of the Mission Walk of Life, the throne of Mahanabh."

"I am going inside now." When Nurai said after investigating Susan's house all around, Sebastian heard the sound of a taxi's door opening in the phone. "I cannot tolerate this weird gypsy any more now." Nurai was speaking swiftly, "If he was not ready to allow the installation of Hindi in his mind, what was the need to break the *Language Installation Bag.*"

"And why did he do that..!" Sebastian asked.

"Would there be any other fear apart from magic in his mind? He thought that I was doing magic on him with the Language Installation Bag." Saying this, Nurai put the phone aside and Meriano, hiding on the terrace of the bungalow beside Susan's house, connected the phone to Elvis and started giving the commentary- "There is some movement here. A seven feet tall gypsy similar to a Caribbean practitioner of sorcery and one man with a normal physique have got down from a taxi and are entering Susan's bungalow. There is a long plastic bag in the gypsy's hand, probably there is a corpse or maybe a person knocked off unconscious in that. They have also not worn a thistle cap."

"Had Susan called up someone?" Elvis asked.

"No, but after today morning's mess was over, Akshay had called up some *exorcism* company. Maybe these are the same people." *(Exorcist – An enchanter knowing the techniques of alchemy to remove an evil spirit from some person or place.)*

These words of Meriano opened the doors of Elvis' mind. Amongst the few old and new sentences rambling in his mind that started organizing themselves in a sequence, the first sentence spoken by Akshay was-

"Sometimes it appears as if this girl has been possessed by some evil spirit." The second sentence uttered by Lessie in a worried tone one and a half years ago was- "The sample found from the Diaboli's site was a mixture of blood of three people."

When Elvis ran out colliding with the waiter standing with the menu card, Sebastian and Maya who were sitting far away were more surprised than Luciano. "Let the happenings inside go on, whatever it be, just ensure that no one comes out of the bungalow." Saying this, he gestured Luciano to follow.

Glaring at each other Maya and Sebastian opened their bags and started running swiftly taking out *'Microphone Guns'* as they saw Elvis running. Maya aimed the gun on Elvis' car parked below the hotel's portico but not even a single window was open. When Elvis opened the door, the microphone pin fired by Sebastian went whistling slowly near his ear and got stuck to the front seat.

"Bandra West." Elvis said as he struck the microphone pin with his mobile.

*

"No, no, wait a bit, I had just inquired." Having a one sided conversation with the seven feet tall *'gypsy'* who was putting the plastic bag on the sofa, when Akshay remembered that the gypsy did not understand his language, he cleared his throat and ran to Nurai.

"Due to your interception in Kangra, our whole plan got ruined, you sleazy person." Pushing Akshay's chest with his arm and hurling him in the couch, Nurai was stomping his feet while walking to express his anger. "Do you want those hateful morning guests to pop-up again in your house?" Nurai said with threatening eyes as he picked up the phone from the table beside the couch, "Your's and Susan's mobile, landline, all phones are in cloning with them. This time, they will come and once again while they are searching for your daughter, they will not make the mistake of thinking that it is not her and believe me, after that you will not die, but will pray for death to come every day. If you want to save yourself, do as I say quickly."

"Susan… Susa…" Before Akshay could yell once again, the *Voodooist* gypsy, hanging his *'single breasted suit'* on the *'coat rack'*, put a finger on his lips in a dangerous manner. *(Voodoo – A black magic of the African people)* The gypsy took out a Barbie-pink colored powder box and started circumambulating the entire seating area of the living room from one end of the staircase to another. He had drawn a thin line with the powder. After that, he took out a gift-box wrapped in shining wrapping paper and kept it on the sofa. Looking around for something, the gypsy finally got the telephone table-stand and placed it inside the circle, after which he took out a black claylike substance and spread it on the table. He gestured Akshay to give water. Akshay had expected the gypsy to moisten the clay and make toys from the sludge for black magic, but leaving the sludge just like that, he arranged some nasty pictures, one each in all four directions of the living area. Now Nurai and he hid behind the staircase and signaled Akshay to bring Susan.

Knocking on the door of the room in which Susan, aggrieved with the treatment she had meted out to Dion, had locked herself up, Akshay said in a loving voice, "Dion has come downstairs. He is not upset with your behavior yesterday, rather he is asking for forgiveness. I am telling the truth. Why don't you come and see it yourself?"

Slowly opening the door, Susan came near the staircase and suddenly turning her head, she glared at Akshay with deadly eyes…!

Chewing his lower lip in fright, Akshay said, "He was right here, where did he go? Probably he is outside. See he has also brought a gift for you." Seeing the box lying on the sofa, Susan started getting down slowly and gradually. With every step she took, Akshay's heartbeats, as he glared at the material arranged by the gypsy, were getting thunderous but even now, Susan's eyes were riveted on the gift-box only. Susan's favourite song was now playing on full volume on Akshay's mobile so that the gypsy's elephant footfall would not reach the ears of Susan opening the ribbon of the box after placing it on the sofa's handle. Susan looked towards Akshay and he gave her a formal smile but the gypsy had stopped there. Slowly turning back, he completed the circle that had been left incomplete near the staircase.

Before the concept of the gift with the paper napkin from the box could become clear, the gypsy who had come and stood behind caught a strand of her hair and lifted it upwards. But before the scissors could be used, an animosity had descended in *Eliza's* haunted eyes through the warning given by Susan's sensors. As if watching a dream, Akshay saw the huge gypsy falling down and clashing onto the *'Mask Piece'* of the pierage hurled by the punch hit by the delicately shaped Susan. In a flurry, the gypsy tied the strands of hair left in his fist with the *'voodoo doll'*. The gypsy wiped the blood on his lacerated cheek with the toothed mask that was lying at the side and tried to get up but till then Susan came close to him again. "Oh sorry… by me, this…" Susan, who had once again become dominant on Eliza, gave a hand to the gypsy. Catching hold of Susan's hand and getting up, the limping gypsy chose to reach the sofa via the route passing near the telephone table spread with the sludge. As soon as he reached there, he poured the glass filled with foul smelling *'voodoo syrup'* on Susan's face. This was enough to arouse Eliza concealed within Susan. Looking at the *'outraged'* Susan once again hurling the seven feet tall gypsy like a child, standing outside the circle, Akshay inherently decided. "Now onwards, even loving conversations with Susan should be from far only."

Eliza was now on the outer level and taking advantage of this opportunity, the gypsy pierced the crocodile's tooth worn in his thumb, into the shoulder of the *'voodoo doll'*. Already frightened looking at the blood spurting out from Susan's shoulder and dripping down to her palm, Akshay got even more frightened when he saw the ghostly spirit running beside him. But *'Eliza'*, who was crossing the *'gypsy borderline'*, turned back in the direction of the gypsy on realizing that Susan's body was being left behind. When the atrocious gypsy started a battle with the witch using his total strength, Akshay felt that Susan will not survive today. Before Eliza could again immerse deep into the soul, the gypsy having a palm, three times as huge as Susan's, clenched her delicate neck and dragged her towards the telephone table. The gypsy uprooted the nail of her little finger with which she was trying to rupture his eyes and Akshay frightened with the outcry rising up in the living room, started pumping his abating heart with his palm as a support. The gypsy threw Susan's face in the sludge and started kneading it with disgrace. As soon as the arrogant Eliza, distraught with this insult of the gypsy's not accepting defeat in this trial of strength, left Susan's body, the gypsy instantly threw a garland of something that looked like shells in Susan's neck and at the same time as if Eliza had become a sweet little girl, the bungalow's harmonic doorbell echoed one after the other... *'Let me take you inside', 'Let me take you inside...'*

"Aw shucks, our ghosts have unshackled..." Nurai spoke and Akshay, craving for some normal person for quite some time, ran towards the door... "Fool, your death is knocking at that door..." Nurai said screaming and Akshay glaring at Elvis' stretched face in the peephole, now ran towards the window.

"I will kill you Yaara.. Kill Viter. Uh.. Uh.." Amidst Eliza's frightening screams as she bent from the waist and condemned, Nurai said to the gypsy in Portuguese, "She will have to be silenced somehow. Soon.. soon.. soon.." When Nurai shook the gypsy lost in thought, he said slowly, "A body will be required to bind this tempestuous spirit." When the gypsy responded in Portuguese, Susan's doggy entered into this spookiness from Akshay's bedroom.

"Police...? That too so soon? Who would have called?" Akshay moved the curtain and glanced in the direction of the roaring sirens. Looking at the convoy of police vans, it appeared that they had believed Sebastian's marauding talk. A shoot-out had started outside between Luciano's army and the local police that had come only to be martyred. Susan, who was standing with her temporal lobes held with both her hands, finally looked up towards Nurai and started moving backwards...

"No Susan, these are your enemies." Nurai said as if he was almost shouting, "Dion also." He ran behind her and injecting a syringe filled up with the aura medicine in Susan's neck as she was about to open the door, he picked her up from the waist. Lifting Susan punting her feet in the air as he proceeded towards the staircase, the door had weakened to bear barely three to four blows. As it is he was having difficulty in dragging the hefty Susan on the stairs and in the meanwhile, his nose was crushed by the smack of Susan's elbow. Susan released herself from Nurai's grip and ran towards the door again.

"Go to hell..." Saying this, Nurai ran towards the third floor staircase with the gypsy, who stood holding Paras closed in a plastic bag. "I had thought that your hired soldiers would have been given the payment...!" Nurai roared at Sebastian in the phone while he opened the chain of the plastic bag and pulled Paras out in the last room on the third floor.

"You are not paying attention, those forlorns have reached for their last battle, and along with them Maya and me as well." Nurai ears pricked up, the noises of the shoot-out that was going on outside had now doubled. He stopped patting Paras' cheek and finally poured the glass of water lying on the dressing table on his face. Startled, Paras opened his eyes. Acting as if he was feeling giddy even now, he groped all around the room and reaching the door, he showed his third finger to the man who had yesterday knocked him off unconscious in this same bungalow and locked the door from outside. He saw the gang coming up and getting smaller as they distributed in every bedroom on the staircases that were made like the Snakes and Ladders game and changing the direction, he ran towards the fourth floor.

"Hi Susan. What is going on here, dear?" Seeing Dion, Susan's doggy ran towards him like a cheetah, but before it could reach there, Akshay picked it up in the middle itself. Elvis told Susan who was quietly glaring at him amidst the barking noises, "Alas, you have forgotten your best friend. Your illness must be really dangerous."

Susan said, pulling the aura medicine syringe that was still hanging on her neck even now, "If that is really the case, then let me go for the sake of our old friendship."

"This doggy wants to change its owner." Smiling in front of the doggy biting Akshay's hand, Elvis responded to Susan- "If the keys to the door of my personal heaven would not have been with you. Kidnap her." Elvis ordered but Luciano was thinking about something else, "Just a minute," going near Susan and widening her eyes, Luciano mumbled- "This idea of penetrating two souls in one body to cock a snook at the aura monitor is not one of the master pieces of his mind. Daarck had mentioned about this tactic in front of me at one point of time. Diabolis of big means on the Master Galaxy can do like this."

After rubbing his cheek for three seconds with the palm Luciano made a numerical table on a paper and giving it to Susan, he said, "Make a replica of the same numerical table on this page." And there was a blast within the spicy tempered Susan who was not accustomed to listening to such an approach but before Luciano could be burnt with it, Susan remembered that, "After he gets convinced, probably they also will go away like the people who had come yesterday."

"We will keep this for some other time, it is getting late for us to go out. As it is now, Susan is not like she was before." Akshay looked at the watch with consternation.

After Susan drew an exactly similar numerical table within sixteen seconds, Luciano continued to watch that paper up to six seconds without blinking his eyelashes. "This girl is staying all alone in her body." He said.

"Catch up her, Meriano." Elvis said and added, "We can benevolently try other ways again. Is it necessary to do all this now?"

"There is no other accurate way in this world for this task." Luciano spoke, "The victim frees herself from the possessing spirit and that too with absolute ease. There is a language of its own in numerology. Knowlegeable people can arrange numbers in an appropriate order and make sentences. Can make a conversation… Can generate an effect like spells with the combination of specific numbers by going further into the depths… Before a body holding two or more spirits could complete this *'numerical table'* made with such spells, *'The Invading'* spirit has to leave that body and run away."

One of the bullets from the battle that was going on outside had torn *Mirashi's (An agent of Elvis)* skull apart and gone out through it, as he was investigating Susan's blood. The battery of his gizmo belt that was draining down had finally betrayed him. Several hired soldiers of Sebastian who were confronting with Polonium guns had now encroached inside. Wiping her face smeared with drops of blood, Susan moved back a few steps and directly ran towards the stairs. Shredding Sebastian's soldiers into fragments with the attack of Pure Energy, Meriano, Elvis and Luciano ran behind Susan. Passing from near the firing going on in the corridor of the room in which Nurai and the gypsy were hiding, Susan reached the fourth floor. She closed the door of the room from inside and ran towards the window.

"Paras…! What are you doing here?" Peeping out from the window, she had seen Paras slowly slipping towards the pipe on the narrow parapet. "How did you reach here?"

"Oh, I have not gone from here at all." Saying this, he extended his hand towards Susan. "You were leaving me alone here and running away." Saying this, when Susan started imitating Paras as she descended down with the help of the pipe, standing on the other side of the road, Maya and Sebastian started aiming at Elvis, Meriano and Luciano who had broken the door and come to the window. "Ah.. I didn't even know that you were here and that you are still firm on your decision to get separated from Dion."

"I don't know why but my choice's welkin seems to be absolutely clear to me now."

After running continuously for four minutes in a manner that would astonish even an athletic runner, they had found a *baxis (bike taxi)* on a crowded street. After a reckless trip of approximately eleven kilometers, they had alighted seeing a big convoy of the police corps. When Susan was quickly removing her wrist watch and giving it to the driver, a person riding on a motorbike, passed through Paras' sight. In the very next instant, Paras turned his head there and riveted his eyes on him. He was the same individual, who wanted to talk with him by introducing himself as *'Professor Palash'* at the time of Susan's engagement.

"Your personality is like a steroid. Energy is felt immediately on meeting." Paras said matching the rhythm with Susan's quick steps. Without bothering about the thumping heart, he caught her hand but to his bewilderment, it was still oblivious that this strong response given by Susan was now really authentic.

"I am the one who is in need of steroids now. Who knows when all this will move out from my mind… I am not going to go back to that house ever again."

"You want to smoke a cigarette?" Paras asked.

"Actually there is a need of drugs to forget this gruesome experience, yet for the time being get me a cigarette." That parlor on the right side from where a few beginners drawing in puffs were staring at Susan was still far.

After Paras got her a lighted cigarette, Susan gave such an addictive smile which one would be addicted to look at frequently, and said showing a big hoarding on the end of the opposite ground in which *'Kundali'* was holding the boxing gloves which was the symbol icon of *'Fight Club of Earth Renovate'*, and hinting towards the heavenly empire with his index finger, "You must be knowing about this enemy of child specialists and child content manufacturing companies, this virus of rebellion is going to do vasectomy of billions of his followers without surgery today."

"He Is doing a good job." Paras said, "There was a necessity of some *'smart donkey'* like this to kick the individual plaintiffs troubling the earth with an increased population." There was a gathering of government management personnel, broadcasting vans of media people, generator trucks and *jamming trucks* upto quite a distance in front of the entrance of the ground where Kundali was giving the speech. *(Jamming trucks – Devices that bust the remotes for bomb blasts)*

"I feel that it is useless to go to the Police Station. There is a Public Relation Office of the army in Colaba. They are the only ones who can save us from these aliens now."

"That is if we reach there, unscathed..." Paras held Susan's hand and pulled her towards the crowd that had gathered near the very huge gate of the ground, noticing that Nurai who was riding the bike and Elvis' deadly gang that was getting down from the row of cars behind him had seen them.

If this would have been some ordinary convention of this toy planet, then they would have directly pounced upon them even at the expense of eliminating it but Elvis knew that along with the numerous Chairmen and soldiers of both *'Vio-Crazy'* and *'Off-Idiotic'* groups, the *'Devil Family'* themselves will also be present here.

Keeping an eye in the direction of the neck, Paras and Susan pushed aside the crowd and entered inside. On the path leading to the stage that was exactly in the middle of the ground, a truck was deployed for the feat that had to be shown by Kundali and on both sides of that road, hundreds of thousands of *'fight club followers'*, eager to fly away to heaven with every single sentence of Kundali were flapping their wings. A close-up broadcast of Kundali was going on now, in all the big screens that were set up on the edges of the ground.

"Ohh Devil..." Elvis lost his senses when he entered the ground. He said making a rascal-like face, "If they take the revert-pill here then it's over... If you do not want to be the unfortunates associated with the longest scrutiny of the world then be quick." In order to be quick, he outspread both his hands and put them on the backs of two agents standing on his left and right and spreading out on all four sides they ran like hunting dogs.

After hiding in front of a weird group of people with a little more height than normal, Paras bent towards Susan's ear and said, "It is difficult to believe that all this is really happening. Are we seeing some kind of a dream?" After susan glaring at him with questioning eyes, Paras slanted his glance and hinting behind, he said, "The language that the people standing behind are speaking, I have heard it several times in my countless dreams." He now turned his ears there to carefully listen to this discussion-

"There is nothing to worry about. Such an incident against the Vio-Crazy New-God that the king of kings *'Lord de Ros'* will not like and that too openly on a planet of his very own Cons Lydia… Even if *'Lon'* and his Chairman *'Simbal'* take pleasure in exerting their power for this dreamy success. Some of our *Gardi soldiers (Ros' army)* are staying in a guest house near this place. It is fine if Simbal's *'Warlords' (Lon's army)* catch them and experience contentment before they shower rocket launchers in this ground from there, no one can even guess the actual arrangements made to blow up Kundali."

"And what is that...? Another person asked.

"With reference to the security, there are many who think about the things associated with the stage, but anyone who would doubt on the material from which the stage is made of would not be found. Exactly after four and a half minutes, as a result of the short circuit that is going to happen with the *'high current'* flow, the stage made from explosive material on which Kundali is standing will be blown into fragments." Paras intended to turn back to appreciate this idea, but Susan held his hand and pulled him in the front. "No… My observation sense tells me that the future of this event is not right." Saying this, he would have taken Susan about ten steps towards the right when Susan clung like a statue as if there was a cobra in front of her. They had been saved by inches from colliding with Lessie and Elvis who were standing in the front. They slowly moved backwards but the people standing there shoved them and pushed them further.

"Isn't killing one Kundali similar to billions of elephants coming together to squeeze one ant for the mammoth structured *'Vio-Crazy'* Group that rules half the galaxy..!"

Lighting the darkness of the questioning star that had broken from Lessie's conceptual celestial sphere, Elvis spoke, "True, but not when *'Off-Idiotic'*, a group equally and probably a little more powerful than that is protecting that Kundali. This is a question associated with their being or not being there. If the *'Idiotics'* prove any straight or crooked attempts of the Vio-Crazys done to make this Billion Couple of Kunali unsuccessful, in the *'Joint Colony Organization'*, then it is feared that possibly the *'Master Galaxy'* will issue an order to remove every single New-God of the Vio-Crazys and therefore those ill fated ones have been forced to adopt trivial paltry gimmicks. Kundali who is standing wearing the Advanced Gizmo Belt amidst the trunks of *Aakrids*

(Aakrid - A pious fish making the devilish powers unsuccessful), innumerable Warlords and paintings that keep the Devil away, currently holds as much importance as a New-God." When Elvis completed the topic, Susan and Paras who had been standing at the back had become successful in making place to slip away from the left side.

"What happened…? Your observation sense had forgotten to put on the spectacles…?" Susan asked because colliding with the crowd, Paras was pulling Susan and taking her aside in such a way, as if a fire had erupted behind in the ground.

"This stage is going to blast within a short time. I do not want that we also should get crushed and die along with thousands of people in the stampede that is going to take place after that. There is a VIP entrance behind the stage. We can get out from that side."

When they came and stopped in the front, towards the left side of the stage, in the Northeast corner, Susan asked, "You heard all this in the conversation of the alien clan?" But Paras had become engrossed in looking at Kundali.

"We intellectual creatures, who give the name of compromise to the thing that squeezes the throat of living life according to our yearnings, for whom we are mediators to bring them into this world, until we cannot give them a guarantee of a satisfactory life, we do not have any right to get them face to face with this world till then…" Kundali's passion generated a sharper effect than the biggest rockstar of Earth. He said further, "Throughout the world, millions of Fight Club warriors fighting for *'Earth Renovate'* will today take the pledge to remain childless until this Earth does not become heaven." Kundali spoke, hinting towards the very big sand watch that had been erected at the right corner of the ground, "In the effect after the governance period of terror, an unimaginable truth will be manifested in front of more than seven hundred billion inhabitants of the Earth, sorrows, deficiencies, diseases, suffering, poverty… all these things will be remembered like the previously forgotten eras by modern inventions. Thinking about the previous life filled with uncertainties, you will be surprised…" Kundali had stopped looking at a disabled boy of about fifteen years, frantically trying to climb on the stage with a garland of roses. Kundali gestured the guards who were checking the boy to move away and the great attempt of the boy who was climbing with the help of the cane, as per the instruction of its owner, his stick carried out the insolence of slipping from the sixth step. Despite falling, his morale had not reduced. Cleaning the blood from his forehead, when he started climbing again, the *'crowd's hero'* Kundali finally took pity on him and started descending down amidst Lon's special force. Throwing away the stick and standing on his one and only leg who cursing his destiny, as soon as the boy donned the garland on *'Kundali'* it signaled the beginning of his *'defeat'*.

Kundali looked into the boy's eyes and at that very instant, he could feel all the remaining voices out there disappearing. He surrendered himself to the tempest pulling him into the empire of world conquering devilish hypnosis.

Kundali who had come to his senses with a shock as if he had been awakened by jabbing a trident, now climbed the stairs with a haughty style as if he thought of himself as the Devil, and went near the mike.

"Devil eye…?" Simbal mumbled. He saw Kundali's eyes in the live screen, which was now not Kundali's. He ran towards the stage on the empty path amidst the ground rocking with the new antics of the new Kundali and the racket.

"Success is very near, just across this star…" He started speaking pointing his finger towards the sky. "These despaired colonies are on the end of this rope." He started self-annihilation. "Oh you fools… You are being cheated by imbibing in your limited minds that the world is bothersome like this. Continuing firing in the same irascible irritation, he mumbled, "The fact is unbelievable. It's intolerable. There is someone, who is addicted to watch real life tragedy dramas and those despaired ones are the emperors of the *'Vio-Crazy'* colonies. Oh trivial people living in the panache of thinking yourselves to be of supreme importance, these powers have billions and trillions of toys like you… *'They'* are not willing to free your minds at any cost…"

"Kundali has gone mad." *Dustin's* thrill that had reached the limits did cheers with *Ajar's* guffaw. *(Dustin – A Chairman of Malesty, the New-God of Vio-Crazy Colony, Nebel Shift. Ajar – A Chairman of Lord de Ros.)*

"Phrenetics of wisdom, you feel that all this that is coming out of my mouth are not divine-sentences…? Then see the motion pictures of a Billion Couple done on a similar planet *Opti-L.*" Rummaging his pockets in the fervor of devilish hypnosis, Kundali took out his cellphone. "Stooooop..." Simbal screamed in the conference call but the Warlords arranged near Kundali were silent…! Whiteness had eveloped the screen. Simbal who had flown and risen upwards with the thought of going upto the stage, saw the Warlords standing on the target of the *Castifo (A high speed laser gun of the Gardi-Force).* "Believe me, the entire Earth is bound in the trap of the desires of these New-Gods."

"Kudali has gone mad."

"Simbal took flight in an attempt to recover from the failure standing on the verge of victory, but the neuron chip fit in Kundali's brain had matched the broadcast of restricted data and given an order to activate the bomb. Kundali heard the bell rung by death delivery in the dome behind his eyes. His Devil eye continued to become bigger in a spirit-obsessed manner and finally just like a bomb exploding in a football, his brain was blown into fragments. Exactly at that moment a horrifying explosion on the stage also accompanied him as if it was binding together with him.

In between the crowd petrified with the belief of a terrorist attack, Paras' attempt to start running with Susan lifted like a flower had become unfortunate in such a way that he had gone out colliding hard with Meriano's right shoulder.

"He is here. Near the host entrance." This S.O.G. language of Meriano as he roared in as loud a voice as possible against the uproar of one hundred thousand people coming out safely from the ground and the screams of the people getting crushed under their feet, also fell nearby on the ears of Dervil who was just preparing to fly. Meriano was willing to leave Susan's leg that had come in his hand only after getting hit with Paras' brutal punch.

"Maximum worms should be crushed in the stampede." *Ajar* said scolding the Gardis so that *'Simbal'* standing in front could hear, "The Fight Club's name will be taken and open confession will be done that now, with full potential, we will become instrumental in bringing new people in this world." A little further, Sebastian who was preparing to fly had stopped. With a thought sprouting up in his brilliant mind he slipped towards the Gardi soldiers standing at the very end. *'Dustin'* also added a note in the paranoid sarcasm of the celebrating Vio-Crazys. He said giving a bitter threat to *'Simbal'* like a charlatan- "We will make such a plight of Lon who is out to auction our freedom that it will keep reminding the world not to interfere in anyone's matter for eternity.

Simbal thought it best to go away from there before he himself became instrumental in igniting the small spark for the Armageddon for which Galaxy L3 had been waiting. Sebastian said in the ears of a Gardi soldier after he flew away, "I am thinking what will happen to you when His Excellency *'Lord de Ros'* gets to know that when the whole Devil Family was ready to get hold of that boy Paras out there, all of you were standing here doing mockery and jeering?" Saying this, before the Gardi would do some movement, he flew away like a rocket.

Maya and Nurai were also running a little further with their fists clenched along with Paras and Susan who had come out of the host entrance and were now running on the main road. Nurai pulled out a driver who was putting the meter down and hurled him onto the road, and in that period the passengers sitting in the taxi showed their hand indicating peace to Maya and jumped out on their own. The way a falcon bird dives in the air to pounce upon its prey, Dervil who was flying with the human wings mounted on his back, came down and caught hold of Susan's hand but at the same time the taxi that Nurai was driving negligently collided with him and hurled him away. After Maya seated beside the driver's seat turned behind and opened the door, Paras and Susan had jumped inside, but now Elvis and Lessie were flying right beside the door on both sides of the taxi. Elvis punched and breaking the glass, when he leaped upto the waist in the taxi to kidnap Susan, he saw the nozzle of Maya's Polonium gun rising up in a dangerous manner. Nurai was racing the taxi as much as possible from here to there in a snake's gait. Maya rapidly showered bullets on Elvis' skull and Paras opened the door of the taxi with one jerk and bumped it into *'Lessie'* who was flying outside. Tumbling down on the road, Lessie went and collided at the uttermost edge of the footpath. A sequence of accidents had been created amongst several vehicles that were applying brakes to save her. In this much time the trouble had now increased by hundred times. A peculiar tug of war had started amongst the Gardi soldiers, the Satanics and Elvis' agents who had encircled the taxi from the top-bottom, on all four sides as well as front-behind and were flying around in every place. Deployed in the ground again, Dervil broke the glass and catching hold of Paras' collar, he pulled him out half way through. Susan had exerted abundant force and held onto Paras from the other end. His shoes were just about to slip out of her hands when Dervil colliding perilously with the street light pole slumped down. "Let someone dare to take you away now." Susan said winking.

The temperature of the old Fiat taxi had risen up. Sirens were echoing on all four sides of the road. There were noises of explosions and far away from all this, a beggar-like man was also following this running procession on a motor bike. People walking on the footpath were running inside the shops to save themselves from the dangerous attacks of the bullets and the lasers that were shooting past as a result of the Gardi soldiers and Satanics flying like war crafts doing acrobatics to knock down one another. Accidents were creating world records on the road.

"I am twenty meters away on the back side, khaki colored BMW. I am changing the route." Sebastian said quickly, "Taking the right turn from ahead, at this speed, you will be at Juhu Beach within six minutes." The airbus is there in the sea in front of Platinum Cafe." Maya looked back, she found Sebastian's BMW. She and Nurai had just taken a breath of relief when suddenly pure energy like the white tusk of an elephant attacked the car, flinging and overturning it several times in the air before it finally collided with a truck. Even the thought of what would be Sebastian's condition in the car that was totally smashed to a pulp was very frightening. It was as if the whole world had become motionless for a few moments.

Looking at a city-bus coming like an arrogant bull from the opposite side, Dervil who was flying above the taxi gave a forceful kick in Elvis' back. Elvis penetrated through the glass beside the driver with both his hands forward in the style of Superman and folding them into fists, he broke the glass at the back and came out. As if something had occurred, Nurai suddenly turned the taxi towards the left side into the basement of the brightly sparkling shopping mall. Since the passage to enter the basement was narrow, many winged Gardi soldiers collided with the Satanics and caught fire. Nurai directly boarded the taxi into the big lift used for taking goods and material, in which several workers were arranging cartons. Quickly pressing the fourteenth floor button, Nurai took out the revert-medicine syringes from the bag. During the time Nurai was administering the medicine to Paras and Susan, Maya injected the syringes in her own and Nurai's skin. After reaching the last floor, he again took the lift down.

As they crossed the garments piled in the open cupboards on the sixth floor, each one of them swiftly picked up clothes that seemed suitable. They rushed into the changing room removing the tags from the clothes to avoid the ringing of the alarm at the time of leaving the mall. Nurai quickly emptied the bag after changing the clothes. As he threw off the old bag in the trash basket and stuffed the memory machine and other things into the new bag, meanwhile the revert-vaccine had done its work. All four of them separated after deciding to meet on the service road behind the mall. Amidst the mayhem aroused due to the entry of several aliens laden with weird instruments on their back, Elvis made a sully face looking at Susan who had transformed had into an awful and ugly woman as she passed from his side. She got into the lift ensuring that fear similar to that of other people who were running could be seen on her face.

Boarding the car picked up from near the gate of the *'Cat Breeding Training Center'* on the service road behind the mall, they now arrived in front of the Juhu Beach, Platinum Café. The shock of Sebastian's death was reflecting in Nurai's voice. He said, "This is your last chance to return to your real identity. Believe it or leave it. But now that Sebastian is not there anymore, we are automatically being released from this assignment."

"You are getting scared as if you are the Chief of this country's secret service and this machine will steal the confidential information from your mind." Raising the Memory machine, when Maya, told Susan in a spicy tone, an insolent person knocked so loudly on the glass beside the driving seat that Nurai got enraged.

A beggar who looked like he had not bathed for ages was peeping inside with his cheek stuck to the glass.

"Broker of the asses..." Mumbling, as Nurai quickly lowered the glass, the beggar instantly thrust the plate filled with coins inside. Smiling as generally insane do without any reason, he extended the plate towards Paras seated in the back seat. If he would start nodding his head, the Mumbai Municipality would have to be busy for two full days to remove the filth that would come out of his tresses.

"Go away, run..." When Nurai reviled him in a voice like water falling in boiling oil, he ran away spreading the coins from the plate in the taxi with a shivering hand as if he had got a current.

"I have seen such a Nobel Prize winner beggar for the first time." Paras said.

Despite having explained twice about the use of applying this medicine on ourselves if the previous appearance cannot be availed back within a few hours, Susan said still glaring abusively at Maya, "I do not want to listen to any nonsense, they also had a similar thing. It is difficult for me to tolerate a new supernatural event now."

"The machine with which your screening was done was an aura monitor." Nurai started explaining as he gestured with both his hands busy, "It identifies the framework of the non-terrestrial microwave of a person that you refer to with names like aura, luster, nimbus, magnetic fluid, etc. and matches it with the data stored in it. "The enemies are equipped with the aura print records of your previous birth. The new birth cannot change this thing. And this is a Memory machine. Filled with the memories of your births prior to this..."

"But what has this got to do with using it during the time of kissing?" Susan asked as she recollected the news *'Beware of Live Sex Maniacs'* read on the net and visualized it in front of her eyes.

"There is no need to fulfill the condition of kissing for the trial run of the *'memory machine'* on any ordinary person. However, no one knows the real reason. Probably the wrinkles generated with a bountiful kiss, relax the grip of the evil spirit imprisoned with your souls through the chemical spread into the internal parts of your mind and after that, maybe this memory can be pasted…!"

"You both are in need of help and I have a psychiatrist's number…" Susan said and before she could speak further, Paras caught her hand and blinked his eyelids signaling her to agree.

"It's alright." She spoke rapidly, "If I can remember my pre-natal with one kiss, then I am ready." Turning towards Paras with a blush of consent on her face, she continued, "I'll have to agree, these people are countless and you are just three, yet victory can be achieved even with minor comforts."

Nurai pressed the trigger of the Memory machine in the very next instant as Paras starting devouring Susan's luscious and soft lips, which would even make the butter envious by believing itself to be torpid if applied over them, but at the same moment… each one of them shook up hearing the noise of the glass being reverberated with such strength, that it would again not break and still break.

The beggar was once again standing in a pre-accustomed style with his cheek stuck to the glass.

"From now on Mumbai will have one beggar less to earn virtue." Saying this, Nurai moved the curtain over the glass and aimed a pistol in front of the beggar. The beggar, smiling in front of the pistol being aimed by Nurai as if he was scaring him with a toy, raised his left hand. Before he could pull the pin of the hand-grenade that was swinging in his hand like a keychain, Paras pulled Susan from her neck and directly jumped outside, but before the alarm could ring in the minds of Nurai and Maya, who had become lethargic with the life passing in a dilemma for the last one week, the *Messengers of Death* had clenched them in their embrace.

*

After Paras emptied the entire magazine of the Polonium gun picked up from Maya's tattered and battered corpse on the beggar, throwing the gun on his crushed face, they had run towards the taxi stand.

From the time they had taken a taxi from Juhu, neither of them had uttered a single word. Finally, breaking the silence, Paras spoke up suddenly, "One minute, stop a little… in the side, yes here…!" He had told the driver as if he had changed his mind that was racing with the taxi as it sped towards the airport.

The taxi had come to a halt a little further than a medium sized jewelry shop. Continuing to look towards Susan's neck, Paras said, "I have never believed in talks like re-birth, yet I don't think that they were telling a lie."

"Paras, what will we do when the effect of this appearance changing medicine will be over?" Removing and handing over the diamond earrings and chain, Susan said in English, "I do not see any such place on this Earth, from where these shrewd aliens would not find us." Susan said, as she watched the stirring movement in the flesh of her cheeks in the taxi's rear-view mirror, "We don't even have the *aura medicine*."

Paras spoke, "For the time being, we can only do this much, go as far away from this place as possible. To such a destination where arrangements for a fake passport can be made."

Watching Paras until he got down from the taxi and entered the jewelry shop, she glanced on the road. She got a feeling as if Mumbai's roads shining in the yellow lights were bidding farewell to her forever. As if her heart was telling her that now she would never be returning here during her entire life. Her thoughts were interrupted by the withering siren of a beach emergency ambulance that passed nearby and stood ahead. The back door of the ambulance opened and frightened, she directly ran towards the jewelry shop with a face like a corpse as if she had witnessed the suspense of a horror climax.

As she reached the ornament store, realizing it fruitless to enquire for the back door, she picked up a manifest from the counter and hid her face behind it. Showing the beggar with a torn and broken body moving forward on the road to Paras as he came closer with the bundles of rupees, she reminded him, "You had crushed his entire face…"

"Looking at our enemies it feels as if we must have been some stalwart personalities and the repentance of not being able to live these personalities again will never stop chasing us." When Paras said this as he led her behind the crowd of customers, the beggar looked around on the road and went to their taxi. Supporting his hand on his tummy, he communicated with the driver. The driver was telling him something by gesturing towards the jewelry shop. As Paras pulled the phone from the counter and dialed an emergency number, he stopped on seeing that the beggar was taking out money from the gown and showing it to the driver. "What is he doing?" Paras mumbled and kept the phone back.

As the beggar disappeared, walking in the direction from which the taxi had come, Paras gestured Susan to come out.

"What was that beggar asking?"

"Nothing sir, he was weird. Whether the taxi is engaged or not? I said that the passenger is in the shop, then he misunderstood as if I am making an excuse believing that he did not have money. I feel…"

"If we may consider one of the instances from these two merciless incidents, would the beggar have forgotten to get the bomb, the first time?" Susan asked stuffing some bundles of notes in her jeans, "He came back again when Nurai's talk had finished. I think that the microphone along with the coins spread from his plate must have confirmed the target first."

"I feel that two groups that can benefit with our lives and deaths have still not come out in the open."

*

After one hour

The Devil had now prepared so many *(approximately sixty thousand)* energy warriors that he was in a position to eliminate *Lord de Ros'* Colony *Cons Lydia's* special army Gardi-Force, easily. Ros was given a three-hour ultimatum by the Devil. Rihon and his companions with whose souls a part of the Devil family's head *Robrelco Fero's* soul was imprisoned should be handed over to the Devil or be prepared for Cons Lydia's destruction. An environment of war had been set. The preparations of both the parties were at their peak. With the indirect support of *Off-Idiotics*, the rival group of the Vio-Crazys, the Devil family had now acquired such a big batch of modern armament equipments that they were in a position to turn Cons Lydia to ashes twice. And apart from Ros, the remaining ten among these eleven chosen New-Gods present here, against whom the Mission *'Walk of Life'* conspiracy had been planned, had such a delusion that this meeting has been organized by host Ros with the intention to avoid war, or to get their abundant support for Cons Lydia if it becomes mandatory.

In these eleven New-Gods' council organized on the asteroid shaded with deep brown colored high mountains and the trees challenging them where oblivious to the existence of day, only the darkness of the night persisted permanently, such an incident was about to happen today, to describe which the historian of the Vio-Crazy group was going to leave in search of several new words that could give justice to the word adventure. The conflict of turbulent rains and atrocious winds had uprooted and thrown off many trees. In a *'Natural Chamber'* on the highest mountain of this floating island of space, Ros came and stopped exactly in between the ten New-Gods seated in an oval shape. Casually arranging the distinct trilby which he was famous for wearing, he spoke, "Even the Devil sometimes take the help of dreams to experience pleasure. After finding the solution to defeat one Gardi-Force with Daarck's support, he now feels that the Devil's *arti (a worship ritual in the Hindu religion)* is being done on *Mahanabh* instead of Ros."

Every New-God had worn black gloves in the hand, a black suit and a trilby-cap.

"Then what will be the benefit of participation in this war?" Nebel Shift's shrewd New-God, *Malesty* asked. "A share in countless Devilish asteroids after victory..?" He observed that Ros was asking for help, but there were undertones of formality in his voice instead of urging.

"The benefit is the preservation of your existence." Ros spoke looking towards Malesty, "Its fine that the tradition of helping is just a delusion in our Vio-Crazy group. I know that. If a New-God's colony is being destroyed, then our companions are eager to assist the enemy. But presently, the enemy of each one of us is the same." Before Ros could speak further, the door of the chamber tall enough for a *mahavat (the one who rides an elephant)* riding an elephant to get up in order to open it, could be seen opening. Ros' Chairman *Ajar* had presented with *Dominic* and *Sierra. (Sierra – A member of the Devil family. Dominic – A Gardi soldier spying on the Devil family for Ros)*

After completing the inspection of the chamber immediately on entering, Sierra asked directly- "What do we have to take back, war or Rihon…?" She showed Ros *'The Menithus' (A document that bound the Master Galaxy to inevitably mediate throughout a three year term following the agreement)* held in her right hand. Which revealed that according to the agreement executed between the Devil family and Ros, if *'Ros'* would hand over Rihon, then up to three years after that neither the *'Devil Family'* nor *'Ros'*, amongst the two of them can initiate a war under any circumstances and it was binding on the Master Galaxy itself to intervene in case of a situation of infringement of the agreement.

"It is your Rihon who has done the foolishness." Malesty said, "Robrelco Fero is a thing to be killed through betrayal. Not openly at all."

This surprise was intolerable for the remaining ten New-Gods present there, each of their Chairmen, *Levi (Antonio's loyalist)* and Antonio, and oh for *'Rihon'* himself also, "When there is a question of preserving the ownership of Cons Lydia would Ros even think before happily handing over not just one but one hundred thousand Chairmen like Rihon to the Devil…? But ultimately, what must be the mystery associated with Robrelco Fero, for the solution of which, the Devil was willing to even forget Cons Lydia. And Lord de Ros was even willing to lose Cons Lydia so that the secret hidden in Robrelco Fero's mind does not reach up to the Devil…!"

Turning towards Levi and Antonio, Ros said making one last attempt, "Do you want that all the fifty planets of the colony that gave you the gift of heavenly life for centuries should now become a dreadful market for the Satanics to do black-magic?"

"Not at all," Levi responded, "Without further botheration Rihon's ownership license should be allocated to the Devil."

"Together with Daarck, you offered this colony at the feet of the Devil. But there is still one chance to rectify the mistake. Along with the Pure Energy Warriors, Daarck must have also made an invention to survive their attack."

"That is quite likely, boss… But when there is a question of *Cons Lydia's* protection, shall we even think twice before sacrificing ourselves?" Antonio said sarcastically.

Laughing wanly, Ros turned his gaze and spoke looking towards the council, "Some of these *'New-Gods'* are devoid of the faith even now that something like Mission *'Walk of Life'* exists. The Billion Couple was a cheap strategy to remove the Vio-Crazys. Otherwise today, the Devil is the owner of those eleven project discs containing the hidden secret of destruction of each of our special forces, prepared in collaboration by *'Daarck'* and our own traitorous *'Chairmen'*. In the form of a solution for the destruction of each of your armies, armed forces are being prepared on Galaxy L1 through the remaining ten project discs. And when they will be ready, we will not have the opportunity to get rid of the Devil even the unison of all of us. Believe me, Ros will not be the only one, who will be suffering in a foul smelling prison cell of his own colony's planet. The only difference is that *'Cons Lydia'* is the first choice of the Devil."

"Sahebaan…!"(Lord) Sierra said after looking every 'New-God' in the eyes one after another, "This infantile narration of Lord de Ros is nothing special than blank verses associated with rumors. If the Devil is really the owner of those eleven project discs today, then the termite has not yet started eating the brain considered to be the *'World's Best Conspirator'* that he would choose Cons Lydia which is considered to be the shoddiest of the eleven colonies, on priority…!"

For the first time in Ros' lifetime of thousands of years, someone had dared to look directly into his eyes and tell *'Cons Lydia'* wan. As a revenge for this intolerable insult, he only needed to raise his hand from where he was seated and in the next instant, it would be impossible to even get ashes of the remnants of Sierra's reminiscence. But instead of that, he raised his hand and said, "Kindly instruct each of your Chairmen to leave us alone for some time. Ajar! You also go out."

After the last Chairman went outside and closed the door behind him, Malesty spoke, "Anyways, whatever it is, the puzzle as to who this *'Daarck'* is, where has he come from and what his intention is, has really become problematic for all of us. In order to uproot us he has made use of the *'Devil Family'*, agencies of our colonies and our own *'Chairmen'* against us. Rejoicing in the panache of being God, we cannot take him lightly anymore, at least from now onwards."

As if Ros did not find the discussion about Daarck particularly interesting, he neglected Malesty's talk and chattered, "Then shall I presume that not even a single *'New-God'* will be supporting me on Mahanabh in this *'warfare'* against the Devil...?" Whether Ros interpreted the silence as a mute disapproval or whatever, but after gesturing to *'Gosha'*, he got a violin and put it in Ros' hand. Ros said in a voice as if he was feeling powerful, "I am ready to hand over these five loyalists of mine, Rihon, Ekaksh, Antosa, Damitri and Leonid, to the Devil."

Sierra handed over both the copies of the Menithus Agreement to Gosha, but before Gosha could pass it over to Ros, giving the violin with such a tenderness that was similar to the undertones of meekness mixing in the voice of a competent *Sultan (A ruler of an Islamic country)* after his delusion of competency is shattered, Ros spoke, "Will you not present that tune in service to your master for the last time?"

"My lord...!! Mercy almighty, mercy..." The narrative of which would compel even the *'Holyman of Letters'* to search for new words, Rihon's gang trembling with such fright started struggling at *Ros'* feet. They spoke up in one note, "The whimsical dreams of becoming New-God took away the sacrifice of our intellect."

"And the entire strategy of imprisoning His Excellency was of this insidious Rihon alone." Antosa said rubbing his nose. Before more of their prattling could spoil the ploy, Ros put a finger on his nose and looking with eyes telling them to shut up, he said, "I am forgiving each one of you. And probably the divine tones of this heavenly tune might even rescue you from the Devilish punishment? I am confident, the tune that has won over the heart of your *'Lord de Ros'*, is also capable of making these great New-Gods slaves."

Rihon's eyes shone up. All his fear disappeared within an instant. Ros' ploy was atrocious. After imprisoning all these New-Gods within a short time with the Tie-in tune, Ros was going to make their Chairmen helpless in joining in this war against the Devil by blaming the fierce Satanic Sierra for kidnapping them with magic, Ros was. And after that, the Devil Family was going to grapple how to save themselves from the armies of these eleven colonies coming cumulatively. Not only that, but when the time would come, when the Rebuilt tune, Mummy-ointment and Transformation Germ would be in his possession, Ros would relieve these eleven New-Gods from the souls of their employees and would change their bodies along with the aura with his loyalists and those loyalists will once again transfer those colonies in Ros' name. In this way, he was going to become the owner of the eleven colonies at once.

"Oh! This man has turned out to be superior to the Devil himself." Rihon thought, "And Robrelco Fero who is bound with me will also stay with him." Taking the violin from Ros who was gesturing with his eyes to be quick, he put it on the chest with a trembling hand.

The Gardi soldiers who came surrounding Sierra and Dominic, had quietly gone near the New-Gods and deployed themselves towards the right side of each one of them. There was a difference of approximately half a second between the beginning of the Tie-in tune and the start of the melting of the bodies of all ten *'New-Gods'*. Suddenly as some invisible element connecting the atoms of their physical bodies became invisible with the assault of sound waves of the tune, their bodies separated and started flowing towards the Gardis standing on the edge of the *'magic place'* on the right, after which they started getting imprisoned with their souls. Standing dumbfounded, Sierra now leaped up to stop Rihon as he burnished the violin like a madman but amidst her *'heart stopping surprise'* Dominic caught her hand right in between and hurled her towards one side.

The tenure of great Malesty's living existence is now getting finished." Going and standing in front of Malesty who had melted upto the waist, Ros now said with authoritative humility giving rest to the cruel laughter dancing on his face, "Very soon the administration of *'Nebel Shift'* will be done through Ros in a *better* way than this *God*." Putting a hand on his chest, he bowed his head in front of Malesty. Going forward upto the *'New-Gods'* who were getting imprisoned with the souls of the Gardi soldiers due to the violin's wrath stinging waves, he said, "Forget the illusory antagonism against the will of nature and make the end easy."

When even the scary faces of all the *'New-Gods'* who were fluttering their lips to finally scream looking at Ros' monstrous face that was lit up with a cynical laughter filled with cruelty, disdain and the flag of victory flying on it vanished in the air, Ros instantly told Rihon in bailing words, "Dominic will take you safely down on Mahanabh." About to open the door, Dominic held the hand of Rihon who was glaring doubtfully and told Sierra who was getting up with the support of a wall, "An easy bet to survive, leave quietly. The Chairmen of the New-Gods standing outside are not going to trust a Satanic like you and doubt on *'Lord de Ros'* for whatever has happened here."

Glaring at *'Ros'* with eyes as if a dog had eaten dogs, when Sierra remained silent and nodded submissively, Dominic knocked on the door and moved back by a few steps. As colony Run-Cap's Chairman *'Painter'* having uncouth features put up an act of being sad looking at Rihon leaving with Dominic and Sierra, Gosha's horrible scream was heard from inside.

'Malachi' (A member of the Devil Family), sitting amidst the Energy Warriors with one leg over the other, saw *'Dominic'* and *'Sierra'* speedily running with Rihon's congregation towards the shuttle and without moving his glance from the Gardi-Force, he started rolling towards the *"i4"57"* shuttle in a defending position.

Before the Chairmen of the imprisoned New-Gods could reach inside, all the Gardi soldiers had become unconscious following their owner Ros. Staring sometimes at one and the only door of the chamber and sometimes at the walls as if they had swallowed their owners, all the ten Chairmen were looking at *'Ros'* regaining his senses as if they were seeing magic. "He was not Dominic, but the Devil himself." Ros spoke with a suffocated voice like a cold blooded person, "All of our eleven colonies have to announce a war against the *Devil* together without wasting even a minute in tawdry arguments."

"Not before a thorough investigation." Painter said looking at Ros with a doubtful gaze. He went on nodding his head in negation. He spoke again like a lonely bugle's melody, "Galaxy L3 would not have seen such an incident of the simultaneous disappearance of ten immortal *'New-Gods'* that during ages and even the biggest fool in this world will not make the mistake of holding the Devil responsible for this before an investigation."

A *'Chairman'* slapping him on his wrist in a supporting tune was speaking normally in *remote-sympathy (through telepathy)* with his Army-Chief on his colony, but presently, he thumped his leg on the floor and said loudly looking at Ros, "It appears so strange that the Devil kidnapped such New-Gods who did not have any concern and kept the ploy reserved for the main enemy. Within a short time all my *'Blue Cape' (Special Army)* will gather here. I want to see this entire mountain scattered by every single inch.

*

Without even taking the trouble to see whether his loyal *'Pilot'* was taking the shuttle on the way to *'Mahanabh'* or not, staring like a child looking at an ice-cream towards Sierra who was again glaring like a deadly cat, Dominic said, "The discussions that will continue to raise an interest for months must have already started, that the *'Devil'* who had come in *Dominic's* appearance made use of the pocket to kidnap the ten *'New-Gods'* and these colonies will not even give the *'Devil'* an opportunity to fall on his knees. Engaging the shuttle on auto-pilot, the *'ruins loving person'* came out of the cockpit and stood in front of Dominic looking at his palm, even then his nonsense continued, "Undoubtedly my opinion will affect the decision that is going be taken regarding your life on Mahanabh, but after your existence has completed my slavery. Your beauty has driven me crazy from the first day itself."

"Dominic feels that he spied on the Devil for *'Ros'* as a *'Devilist'*, but his own hallucination betrayed my loyal Dominic." Watching with courage shattering eyes, the Blue-Devil made an effort to utter one more sentence, "If it is Dominic's behest, then can this shuttle fly towards *Pendigyura* instead of Mahanabh?" *(Pendigyura – A Devilish Planet)*

*

In order to be safe from the airport cameras, they had descended at five fifty-five in the morning in the *'Barak'* river of Silchar in East India through a private jet. Finally after enquiring here and there for quite some time, an owner of a guest house in a dirty locality towards the west had disregarded their identity cards and had allotted a small room for them on the fourth floor. After resting till late afternoon, Paras caught Susan's shoulder and shook her quite gently. Desirous of Paras' caressing strokes for opening her eyes, Susan quickly jumped up in bed and pounced to grab the bottle when a forceful slop of water hit on her face, but till then Paras had already reached the door.

"Until I get some stuff and come back, consider that there is no door at all in this room." Standing with his head tucked in between the door, Paras threw the bottle of water on the bed and closed the door.

Peeping outside, Susan flicked her disheveled hair and said rubbing her kohl lined eyes, "One pair of jeans for me and… Not one, bring three jeans and some t-shirts."

"Any other type of clothes apart from that?"

Picking up a sandal from the shoe-rack lying at the side, she showed it to Paras.

After twenty minutes, Paras returned with big plastic bags which he handed over in the hands of the lady consumer staring at him with astonishment and opening the venue catalog, he spoke, "Get ready in ten minutes. We will have to go missing from *'Silchar'* also before those born without the benefit of the priest reach here."

"I am feeling a strange thrill thinking that I know you as backward-born even amidst this creepy ambience." Murmuring words like this, as Susan started changing her clothes behind Paras' back, he switched off the TV that was going on in front of him and concentrated on the TV.

*

Due to the fear of their trail being followed, they had decided to stay away from Silchar's taxi cab and reach

'Tjol' that was one hundred and seventy-two kms. away by obtaining a lift in the foreign vehicles. They were sitting beside the driver in a truck carrying motor-bikes. Due to the blockade ahead, their truck had not moved even an inch since the last fifteen minutes. Towards the right side of the highway, near the board on which *'Peep-Peep Don't Sleep'* was written, a taxi came and stood in such a way as if it intended to back out and escape from the Mizoram Police. Guessing the fair-madam to be scared of the police, the driver said, "This is a combined routine checkup of the Wildlife Crime Control Bureau and the Mizoram Police. Since there is less vigilance for smuggling of international wildlife products, the *'Mizoram Border'* has currently become a favorite corridor for the smugglers."

Finally from the time they left Silchar, *Mizoram's* rain that Susan had been anxiously waiting for had now started showering attractively and generously. She put her hand out of the window and shook hands with the first rain of the season. Getting down from the truck amidst the rumbling of the quarrelsome clouds that were re-tuning the mood, Paras could hear words left behind by the driver like *'Smuggling for making medicines from the bones of the tiger, etc.'* After opening an umbrella against dark clouds, he slowly, gradually moved forward enjoying the feel of Susan's showering in the soul.

That taxi driver who instigated doubt had now opened the boot and stood in front of the inspector in a stance asking- What is it? As Paras identified his truck's horn in the voices of horns and looked back, Susan was calling him to receive her with the umbrella. Wiping the spray of rain from his face, as he looked with curiosity on the back seat of the taxi, he felt as if the man sitting there used the goggles worn on his head to hide his face. The boot was still open. Turning behind, when Paras reached near his seat, he was peeping out with his head from the window on the other side and was searching for Paras.

"Excuse me. Excuse me…" When Paras called out loud to the man who was pretending to hear less he made a face like an employee of a Government institution's enquiry counter and said, "Yes…?"

"I think this is our third meeting…"

"I do not think so." He said.

After taking out a mobile without a sim-card and gesturing him to wait for one minute, Paras immediately told him, "Oh yes.. Right, Picasso School..!"

"No, no no..!"

"Ah… then?"

"Act of God" Paras reminded.

"Oh, yes. Remembered... Those portraits were incomparable. Amidst your impressive sketchbook impression, it is indeed a little difficult to remember your face." Saying this an unfriendly tone, he again turned his head in the other direction saying farewell.

"But your inflexibility filled visit has not let me forget this face even today, Professor. At that time I felt you were inclined to tell me that you were willing to postpone the program of your special friend, famous painter

Devdan's painting exhibition if the date was not convenient for me."

"In your sketchbook's art, I felt new shelters created for my departed friend's lonely art. I felt that you should not miss out on some of those specific paintings of Devdan. Anyways, I have one possession of yours…" The professor said quickly but stopped as he saw the approaching policeman.

"This is not strange..? The value of those four paintings of Devdan is many times more in comparison to his reputation? By the way so far, at this time, alone here?" Paras asked with the intention of silencing the Professor's reticence.

"Ah… traveling. Inspirational traveling… What else would artists want except inspiration, right, isn't it?"

"That's right. The coy, high-inspiration at the balcony of the artist's heart opens the lambrequin and performs the *mooh dikhai ceremony (An Indian wedding ritual)* either when he is alone or else just when he is experiencing the unification of the soul with someone. But those paintings should have been sold by now?" Paras asked, but the driver had started the car and without the formality of bidding farewell, the Professor also closed the glass and became engrossed in his portfolio.

Expelling the effects of the strange behavior, Paras again walked towards his paradise.

"With whom were you talking?" Susan asked.

"Visual Art's famous Professor Palash. Do you know him?"

"No!"

Before Susan could ask more questions in her melodious voice, Paras gestured her to remain quiet. He did not want to lose control over the steering feeling himself preposterous comparing a dismal life to be finished on the highway in comparison to a fascinating and happy life with his charismatic fairy.

Nested in the far away mountain ranges and valleys, the spectacle of *Ijol's* elegance that was like a *'Queen of Heaven'*, attracted them amidst the apparition of the upcoming *'new'* yet *'familiar'* life. "You did not give a lift to anyone today." Explaining that, Paras took out two notes of five hundred and give them to the driver.

Fifteen minutes had passed since they had acquired shelter in a room on the terrace of a three storied government school from where the landscape of *Ijol Five Star* that had come up on a high hill on the city's border just six months back was visible. Noticing a figure seated on a picnic chair in the balcony of the Presidential Suite on the eleventh floor of a hotel that was a little far and staring towards their room, Susan asked, "What's next? Till when do we have to keep on running like this?"

"It seems that 'Actually life is a purposeless celebration', But the secret to understanding the true meaning of life is very deep," The knocks fell on the door exactly when Paras was completing the sentence with "It is also fun to keep on running if no one is chasing."

Professor Palash's driver was standing flaunting a sluggish laugh. "Room number eleven zero six. Professor is waiting. He wants to give you one special thing of yours that he has and go away from here as soon as possible. It will be easy to go up to the Professor's room as a group conducting research on *'Global Warming'* that has come from New York is waiting there in the reception area to check-in." Saying this, he put a leather bag in Paras' hand and went away.

When taking out the fake beard-moustache and a white colored wig for Susan, Paras said, "How the Professor who suddenly met us here in East India, had some days back pestered us by persisting to see the exhibition of Devdan's portraits, and how pursuing me, he had come right up to your bungalow at the time of your engagement." making a face as if she was told to bring out Cryptex's secret document in two minutes, Susan said, "This is also related to those people. And it is necessary to reach up to its facts to come out of it. Maybe the key to the sensational thrilling truth is hidden in these paintings?"

*

In the range of the *Orion Greasepan (West from the Solar System. An air highway going via the 'outer arm' upto a toy planet of Ros)*, after *Gostel's* aircraft synergized with Ros' space craft as it matched and locked the speed, route and distance of both the shuttles, coming out of the forearm of the *'vehicles'* flying side by side at a speed of one million and six hundred thousand kms. per hour, passing through the connected canal bridge, *Gostel* entered Ros' shuttle and immediately on giving rest to the soles of his feet, he said with some disappointment-

"In these minutes now, I spoke with Gosha who was making me restless that I had carried the VIP account's form of the *'Hell Hall'* with a lot of enthusiasm along with Lord de Ros' invitation. *(Gostel – The owner of a private jail 'Hell Hall' on Galaxy L1 that gave an offer to take care of powerful prisoners of a big stature)*

Ros said, "I can understand that the presence of a prisoner of Director *'Apotheosis'* himself is a matter of so much pride for the owner of Hell Hall, yet..."

He said nodding his head, "No, it is not at all a work of prestige to scrape the reasoning for taking out information of *Anjeolmac* which is not at all available with their prisoner who has come in *Hell Hall's* custody after the interrogation of Apotheosis' chairman *'Solon'* and his supreme council got a rap of failure. Ah... Everyone knows it." He closed one of his eyes and nodded his head in resentment. "Well, you will not believe it," The chamber was totally empty except him and Ros, yet he bent forward and said slowly, "Getting your invitation was so thrilling..." *(Anjeolmac- A 'Mithalia' named woman associated with 'Daarck' and Mission 'Walk of Life' in a very mysterious manner had acquired the secret of the death of both the Directors of the Master Galaxy, Prestige and Apotheosis, and had hidden it in Anjeolmac. More information of this matter has been given in the following chapters.)*

Ros' face with reduced distance of the eyebrows turned towards Gostel.

Kicking aside the surrounding thoughts, Gostel spoke, "Yes, these were the words of Director 'Prestige' himself, he said that the support on which the wobbling steps of the Vio-Crazy Group on Galaxy L3 are currently sustaining, if there is one such cane, then it is one and only 'Lord de Ros' who has proved the Devilish foxes to be stupid. *Prestige* admired you open heartedly for imprisoning all the ten New-Gods and creating a threat on the existence of the Devil Family." *(Director 'Prestige'- Owner of the other half Master Galaxy and Galaxy L4 to L6)*

A smile shone on Ros' face.

"But it is quite difficult to understand this." Gostel said, "If there is something the Devil gets pleasure from, then it is destruction, cruelty and spooky pleasure derived from tormenting people. And you Vio-Crazys are the creators of all these things. But yet the inclination of *father of lies (Devil)* to join in the insurgent group of Mission *'Walk of Life'* for establishment of benevolent New-Gods in your place has currently become a top class thrilling mystery as of now.."

Ros spoke, "Whosoever has spread this news, that person is at least not a friend of the experts encouraging or spreading false information in this world of conspiracies. Shall we march towards our useful *'blob'* of selfishness…?" Ros said, gesturing with a brandishing hand and taking a few mummy-apples from the dish, he went behind the sofa.

Gostel said, "It's quite evident that the owner of a wealthy colony like *'Cons Lydia'* would have absolutely no interest in the petty profits of Galaxy L1's private jail. And comprehensively, in such a situation when all the services of *'Hell Hall'* are available within the amount that does not even come in the measure of insignificance for *Ros*."

"And with that, Gostel's interest in opening another modern branch of Hell Hall updated by experts on Galaxy L3 is very obvious." Ros said.

"That is alright, but after the advent of Apotheosis' prisoner, it has become difficult for me to remember how many offers I have received for selling *'Hell Hall'*. Ros, I will not sell my world under any circumstances."

"You are not exactly able to gather what I mean to say. What are your thoughts about the apportionment of Hell Hall's ownership?" When Ros said raising his hands and tweaking the flesh of his body, their indirect glances taking stock of each other's need jostled for half a second. Giving a strange smile, Ros said further, "There is only one condition, the matter regarding my high stature prisoners, means the matter of those ten New-Gods… being imprisoned there and this deal between us about my partnership in Hell Hall should remain a secret for a just a few months. Otherwise, I don't have any interest in taking out Anjeolmac's information from Apotheosis' prisoner and becoming the owner of half the Master Galaxy, right now."

*

When Paras pushed the Filmfare's trophy shaped handle of the door waiting to open with their hands, the Professor who was seated stiffly like a ghost on the drawing room's sofa, got up quietly and making a drink, came back and sat on the same seat.

"May I have it?" Paras asked gesturing towards the bar.

"Of course, why not."

Making a drink for Susan and himself Paras came and sat in front of the Professor.

"I coercively risked it at the time of the engagement of this Polish colleague of yours even though I was aware that direct contact with you means death. I tried to talk to you but the atmosphere had become impenetrable. Coincidentally, at that time, I had the GPS locator for my dog's belt with me and I slipped that in your pocket. When I came back again in the evening this girl's house was converted into a battlefield. I have been continuously following you, from the time I saw both of you running away from there." Taking off his glance from Susan, the Professor said gesturing towards the four paintings hanging on the line tied from one end to the other in the room, "For you, my friend *'Devdan'* had a lethal message which took sacrifice of his rhythmic life." There was exasperation in Palash's voice. Paras thought that the Professor who reached the shelved desk would take out a gun from the drawer and shoot him on pretext of his dear friend's death, but the Professor got a long piece of the frame of the painting and putting it in his hand, said, "Six months ago, from today, when several aliens chasing you on Mumbai's streets yesterday came, my late friend Devdan and me were in an exhibition in Mumbai. Whether he got a premonition or might have seen weird faces roaming around, or whatever, but he quickly came to me and gesturing towards these four paintings, he said, "How can a mortal man work like someone's message box? That too, at a time when he couldn't even hand over that priceless heritage to someone else…" In some weird and hard to understand talks, he gently gestured with his eyes towards every painting one after another and said, "In order to identify the secret hinting script of the portrait, attention should be paid to several such events that do not match with the whole painting." After that, he smiled farewell in front of me and opening the bottom part of the lighter, he ingested cyanide. Catching the falling Devdan in his arms, the alien told his companion in English, "This was Eddie's last source." Using electric torches on each of these paintings, they investigated them up to the last layer of the picture-panes right in front of all of us, but there was no script or hinting symbols, neither was there any map."

"Looking at people failing to match their pace with Devdan's high intellect, I always thought that he was among wrong people, but he actually turned out to be of another world. After a long time when I decided to reframe these ominous canvases and sell them, I found your name and address below one of the frames."

Reading the *'Bension House'* address and his name written with a brush below the piece of the simply sculpted frame with a silver coating, Paras passed the piece to Susan for her perusal.

"After remaining confused for a long time whether I should let this task, of the one who separated me from Devdan, happen or not, I felt that his martyrdom should not be wasted. I am only doing this for *Devdan.*" Saying this, the Professor went away.

*

Restlessness had deprived Susan of the delicious dinner ordered in the room. Lost in thoughts, Paras was still quite far from the dessert. A torrent of rain on the window and the doorbell chimed one more time, but the waiter was standing with the coffee. Susan put down the coffee and moving the curtains, when she came and stood on the balcony, in order to impress her, the rain with the wind's help, started pouring down in different styles. Perhaps the rain was also in love with her.

"If you were to stand in front wearing this dress, then the re-diagnostics of those secret hints will become impossible even for *Devdan.*" As Paras said looking at Susan who was standing with her hand on her waist in a pink colored *'side tie halter'*, the doorbell rang once again and this time it was Professor *'Palash'* himself standing with a magnifying glass in hand.

"This side here," Taking the magnifier and reaching the first painting, the Professor said, "Two different groups of children deriving pleasure by catching tender frog babies and killing them while these soldiers are standing far and watching them. The soldiers have worn the uniform of the British army, but their *casques galeas of bronze (helmets)* are like the ones worn by the ancient Roman soldiers. In each of these if there is something weird, then it is this man"- The Professor held the magnifier in front of a small figure near the warriors and said, "All the characters in these pictures are engrossed with each of their own groups except for this man." A man standing with a Sorabji like hat was looking towards the corner of the lane. "That message is just hidden in such weird things within each of these four paintings."

"This is a task that will go on for months even for an expert." Paras spoke in disappointment.

The Professor said opening the wrapper of a chewing gum, "I will have to leave now." He handed over the magnifying glass to Paras.

After staring in his eyes for a few moments, Paras spoke, "Thanks for everything Professor. Do you know someone who makes fake passports?"

"I met an employee of Air-India at the reception. He is staying in this hotel only. I will talk to him before leaving. Best of luck..." And the Professor actually left them and went away.

Despite revolving around the paintings until late in the night, this knowledge admiring troupe made of two people was unable to bring any specific result apart from the copy of an insect getting entangled in a spider's net. Getting bored Susan had finally come into the balcony. Lying on the relax chair, when she was watching the houses spread on the mountains, there was a scintillation in her mind just like lava bursting in the chest of the ocean. Shaking Paras who had struck a rapport with the bed, when she woke him up as if there was an earthquake and it was necessary to run down, they came and stood in front of the first portrait.

With the glass, she magnified the hat of that man standing secluded and said, "I have seen this hat many times. My grandfather was a fan of London's famous prop-comedian and magician *'Tommy Cooper'*. A set of his TV series cassettes is still lying in the wardrobe. In most of his shows, he has worn exactly the same hat. And he is staring... On the corner of the lane." Taking the magnifier from Susan's hand, Paras magnified the signboard hanging at the corner of the lane. "This is actually a picture of the railway-engine." Saying this, he started the *boom-box (computer)*.

"Britain is the one and only similarity between the railway-engine and the analysis of *'Tommy Cooper'*. The birth of both *'George Stephenson'* famous as the Father of the Railway who made use of the first steam engine and *'Tommy Cooper'* was in London apart from which a hard coffee will be required to investigate other matters unrelated to the painting."

During the time Susan was ordering coffee on the intercom, Paras who went and stood in front of the second portrait, was noting down a number from his mobile dictionary onto a paper. Dialing a number in the hotel's landline, Paras said, "Professor *'Malan'* is an expert of ancient signs and now he is not even there in Mumbai."

Quickly finishing the formal talks, Paras said, "Sir, some archaic symbols are blocking the way towards the multi-objective life." After a desirable response, he pressed the button of the remote that would pursue Malan's mind, "Which country's army has chosen to keep a shooting-board as a symbol on a *torpedo*?" *(Torpedo – A naval destruction water missile)*

The response received after a silence of a few moments lit a smile on Paras' countenance. Malan said, "After the second world war Britain's army applied *'Ingram'* like insignia similar to fighter jet on the naval weapons also."

"And another symbol is- An eagle spreading golden wings and looking towards the right side." Paras asked.

Refreshing the speech delivered just two hours back, Professor Malan said instantly, "The use of an *'acquila'* or eagle standing in this stance was done during the Fascism period in ancient Rome."

Thanking with heart-felt words, Paras kept the phone.

Curling the strand of hair hanging on Susan's face with his first finger, Paras said, "If the first portrait indicates a country, then the content of this portrait must be hinting towards some place located in Britain."

"And this pyramid?" Susan asked putting her ring-finger on the pyramid portrayed on the road behind the sailor. "Cestius pyramid of Rome and that too in Britain...? The indication of *'Acquila'* or eagle and this pyramid is actually towards Rome."

"One minute," Paras tore some pages of the notebook and asked her to get the bottle of oil from the dressing table. Preparing butter-papers as he arranged the pages from the sailor standing near the British torpedo to the *'territory'* of small plants made on all four sides of the pyramid, Susan said, "Maybe some institution starting from Rome's name in Britain?"

After marking every plant of grass on the paper and drawing a continuous line on those points, Paras searched the map of London in the computer. To their surprise, the map was an exact copy of the map made on the paper. "Your catalyst-pages are always around the winning plot." Paras said grinning, "But not an institution, a venue starting with the name of Rome in London. An attempt has been made to explain the same thing even in the first portrait. A British uniform and soldiers wearing Roman helmets…"

After a minute of wearing Google gloves and starting boxing with the questions, Susan said, "This is possible…!"

"It's amazing, a straight forward but a shrewd move. A lethal message with Devdan is an address. East London based *'Roman Road of London'*. We have with us a country, a city and a locality…!"

"And where we have to go in that locality is hidden in one of these two paintings."

"Then the next destination of these vagabonds is London."

*

Half the night had passed away. The atmosphere was refreshing. After completing the necessary procedure for the passport in room number five hundred and six and coming back, they kept two more empty cups on the coffee table and settled in front of the third painting. Putting out the lights except the light hanging on the ceiling above the painting they started focusing on the picture-dance.

The creation dialogue of this portrait was somewhat like the unique scenes of the sexual intercourse being done by people who looked like creatures of some extinct civilization of the cosmos towards one side of which in the right corner a temptation was being given by several rowdy looking boys to the owner of a drama company to give the fake beards and moustaches to them. A boy looking like a team leader was offering a guitar to the shopkeeper. And was pursuing him to give the *'wig'* in exchange of that. It was possible to give a bag full of wigs in exchange of the expensive guitar, yet the shopkeeper was strictly scolding them to go away from there.

"This style of Devdan displaying a person's intentions on his face for every face would put him in the category of an aboriginal painter, isn't it…?" Susan said, "This immature age and an expensive guitar, probably some boy has robbed his family."

Following the habit of mind bracing professionals to light a cigarette at every talk, they kept on wrestling with the third portrait for a long time. But unable to understand anything despite that, when they finally got fed up and went to the fourth picture for the next clue of the address and stood in front of it, the doorbell rang once again.

Susan had returned taking the transaction entry of the money deposited by her friend in one branch of Ijol Five Star located in Mumbai. When she came inside, Paras who was taking out chilled beer bottles from the fridge spread both his hands in front of her hinting to have solved the mystery and said, "RG Timewarne International." A supplier of wig making tools and wigs... Unit Eleven, E4, Roman Road, London... He pulled Susan's hand and took her near the fourth painting. Strands of hair growing over the toes, is very weird. This might be happening with inhabitants of other planets." Two skinheads standing far and watching old people cutting the strands of hair coming out of their toes in the portrait had been painted.

"But what must be the mystery of this third drawing with the guitar..?" Susan asked.

"It's clear, the owner of RG Timewarne who offers private locker facility in the pretense of the business of wigs will hand over our valuable things in exchange of this painting of the guitar shaped like a key."

*

Filling up the arrival card given with a smile by the immigration officer of Heathrow Airport, when Paras looked at Air-India's officer Abhay forcibly pulling Susan who was standing sixty feet away towards him, he instantly pulled his hand back.

Looking at Abhay who had helped them in getting emergency viza from the Super Priority Service, Paras laughed in such a way as if he was giving him permission to tease.

When Abhay entangled his hand in Susan's waist as she stood with her head turned around, swallowing the abuse that had come upto her lips, she said, "A time comes when a woman enjoys the thrill of being with some other man in the presence of her boyfriend, but my relations with Paras have not become so old and boring as yet."

"Wow… finally after three decades, I did find the woman having the overwhelming *'sex sense'* I desired. Baby, we should go to purchase some toys for tonight's fun. What do you say?"

"Of course…! Standing with the support of a stick in a white silk saree, Susan said pressing her fake nose.

Hearing a response which was not difficult to understand to be a false promise, he said giving her a threat, "The London police would not have any specific interest in listening to the arguments of an Indian girl and her courier boy boyfriend."

"I have about three days of work in London." Standing blocking Abhay's path as he was proceeding towards the authority, Paras said, "Meanwhile I won't be able to roam around taking her with me, if you don't mind, can you give her company?"

Hiding his excitement, Abhay shook his head.

*

When they took a taxi from Heathrow Airport for *Roman road Market*, it was three in the afternoon as per the clock hung on the gate of Terminal Five. *Ornella Venoni's* album *'La Punta Mento'* was intoxicating the senses on the radio.

"Right now, I am about to reach Unit Eleven. And although not for dinner, I will surely meet you for coffee in the evening." Abhay disconnected the phone and gestured the driver towards a building on the right side. A hoarding starting from the roof and extending up to the ground floor had been installed on the corner of the five storied building in front of which the taxi came and stood. Different types of wigs had been displayed near the shining words of RG Timewarne International. The glass of the right side door had been covered with some *Rudeness Hat Group's* flag.

Seeing a shop dedicated to unique things found from the ocean on the opposite side of the road, Susan said, "By the time you finish the work, meanwhile can Abhay and me go there and come back?" She had guessed that if she would not dispose of this trouble forced on them soon, then certainly something adverse will happen.

Before Paras could give a response, Abhay said, "Then in India, drug smuggling in the pretence of wig-business? Or diamond smuggling? Taking out Devdan's painting from the bag hanging on his shoulder Paras caught the hand of the mumbling Abhay and directly entered into the front office.

As Paras showed the painting in response to the office-assistant's question of- Whom do you want to see? He communicated into the intercom.

The second round of inspection of the office cabin was about to get over, when opening the door slowly, an old man of about sixty-five years having *'Uncle Rich'* type of thick moustaches entered. It was not difficult to guess from his courteous etiquettes that he was the one who had established *'Rudeness Hat Grop'*. Paras handed over the painting to the old man like a spy striking a deal where only code words would prevail instead of verbal communication. His heart started Bungy Jumping as the veteran eyes of the old man shone up. The old man returned the painting after starting the computer with the big screen and turned towards them in a minute. The painting in the screen was not exactly the same, but in the portrait prepared with the primary outline, the moustaches of the man refusing to take the guitar was exactly similar to that of the man seated in the front.

"Devdan was the most unique man among those I have met in my life. At the time of giving me this rough drawing in Los Angeles, he had said, "To my nature generally having an allergy of people, you are one of those rare people whom I like. I shall definitely try to see you once again."

"But a very big risk has been incorporated in these type of arrangements made to reach up to the things. Just suppose that other companies related to this business also have opened in this area, then…?" Susan said raising her eyebrows.

"There is going to be no harm in that." Alistair replied, "Maybe last, but you were to come here, right?" He said and got up. Locking the cabin, he gestured towards the retail area and said, "The person whose name is Paras, he is the only one who can come with me."

Susan pulled the blue colored layered skirt coming out of the old woman's sari to the extent that of having to fold the hands in order to prevent more pulling and sat near Abhay as she took a cold drink from the plate and stared at the back of Paras moving forward with Alistair till it disappeared.

Passing through the residential gardens behind the showroom, before Paras could enter the living room, a girl coming out from there and running screaming 'Donnez Moi' behind a boy who was fleeing, bumped into him. "She is my grand-daughter." Alistair said about the little *'fairy'*, "Whenever she comes to stay here from Paris, I can easily defeat my debility during those days."

"It is adequate to remove the belief that only the *'biometric lockers'* of reputed banks can keep the things safe." Alistair said taking him to the end of the room being used as a library, "The generous words of Devdan's offer to upgrade my locker facilities were somewhat like this, 'I can give you the *technology* is even beyond the imagination of any country."

"Then... You now have the world's latest locker facility?" Paras' illusion of that path leading to a hidden Darlington-hall was broken exactly when Alistair put on the switch after descending two floors.

"My response that had come out from a high-handed nature was that if you do not have faith on RG Timewarne, then I do not have the time to waste in the discussions about the terms of the contract. Till then my brother and I had not yet jointly established the *Rudeness Hat Group*." He said laughing and moving the iron shelves, he inserted the key in the seven feet high rusted safe and stood there. Imagining the safe moving to one side to open the path of a mysterious vault behind the walls, Paras awoke with an acute tweaking noise. The door asking for oiling in the language of such weird sounds since who knows how many years, opened two inches and got exhausted.

Opening a thick layered aluminum box from the safe, Alistair took out a token from that and reading the number he handed over the box to Paras.

"This might be the one and only locker facility in the world where there is no pair of the key at all with several customers like me." Paras said putting the box on a table lying in the middle of a big rectangular room and opening it, "As such this was the foolishness of the most unique man you met in your life. Forgive me but such blind faith?"

"Yes, it is like this over here. Naturally intellect will believe this to be foolishness but overriding your accusations, the credit of our clan's lineage providing services for the last three hundred and fifty years has remained untarnished till date. If I tell you that among the chosen few people in the world who know about the locker facility of this lineage, the former President of Russia also had made use of RG Timewarne's locker facility, then probably it will be easy for you to confine in us. Here heirlooms are handed over from generations to generations."

The thing that was kept at the very top inside the locker box was an exact copy of the thing seen on the seashore in Nurai's hand. Licking his lips with his tongue, Paras took out the *'Memory Machine'* and put it in the bag. Below that some *'thistle caps'* had been put. Paras closed the locker after taking out the files stuffed to the brim below two Chile wood boxes of six by six inches placed after the thistle caps. Different types of wigs had been arranged on the wig-block in the open cupboards of this multi-purpose godown. Paras finally proceeded towards the staircase as he did not find it appropriate to express his desire to click some snaps by wearing these wigs to *'Alistair'*.

"There is still something left for you." Paras stopped as he heard Alistair's voice with less power. He was pushing a nine feet high container on a wheel-frame from the opposite corner of the godown and coming towards this side. Pushing aside the moustaches that were annoying the upper lip, Alistair lit a *'Monte Cristo'* and held the pack in front of Paras.

"Now, what is this nuisance?" Paras surmised as he saw the machinery in the container huge enough to assemble some monstrous robot.

"A super car…?"

Paras asked Alistair who was helping in predicting, "Can we use your guest-house for some time?"

After he conceded past a long consideration of about fifteen seconds, they decided to transfer the container in the guestroom and went out.

*

The RG Timewarne premises were almost as long as half a cricket-ground. The guests roaming in the rear garden of the bungalow were busy guessing the exorbitant amount that must have been charged for the locker services provided.

Susan who had jumped up like a kangaroo on seeing the Memory Machine once again, asked for Abhay's desire also in a heart-winning voice as she connected the phone to the kitchen and ordered a *'burger'*. The hands of the clock that had reached to show five P.M. in the evening were making the approach affirmative for those who were fond of the pleasures of the night. "Will the battery of this be functioning after so much time or not?" Susan asked and pulled out a file from the bag. "Wow… how nicely someone has written *'SP'* inside the heart in angelic letters." Reading an envelope that had come out of the file, Susan said waving a plastic bag in the air, "There are someone's blood samples in this."

After seeing the password in the hand-written user manual and typing it, Paras said handing over the Memory Machine to Abhay, "This must not move away from our faces even for a second for exactly one and a half minute."

"What is this exceptional thing?" Abhay saw the user manual and mumbled as he turned the Memory Machine upside down, "The mind can experience a confusion-like condition for a few minutes while the old process is setting up amidst the new memory clots…." Pulling the user manual from his hand, when Paras threw it in the club room and said, 'During the time you will be holding this we will be kissing', He leaped once and sat stiffly.

"I am not going to fill up anything new in the brain on an empty stomach." Saying this as Susan went to relax on the swinging chair, Paras yanked her hand and pulling her closer, he directly put his lips on her lips. Susan's lips slowly, gradually continued to succumb to the lips enjoying fierce monopoly on her plump lips. After their experienced personalities passing amidst the *'revelation'* of the new world assimilated all the memories of the previous birth from childhood to death, giving an immortal tradition's smile, Susan said looking with a love bombing glance- "I wish I also had four *'hearts'* like a *'hangfish'*... after giving one to you, one to Elvis and one to Dion, there would still be one left with me."

"Before that I would devour you raw just like that" Saying this, Paras who was searching the bag, took out the tool box and added, "What is the advantage of these things that upset the mind." He hurled the Memory Machine in the corner and pulling Abhay's hand, he directly ran up to the terrace. Alistair's servants had already delivered the container on the terrace.

When Susan finished her burger and glass of wine and leisurely reached the terrace, Paras had finished the last stage of the three-seated space-shuttle assembly and was starting the engine.

"These women are so strange, aren't they?" Abhay said, "If you deal with them politely, then they will neglect you considering you to be ordinary. If you handle them with a hard-attitude then considering you to be egoistic, they will not even wait to say goodbye." Checking the parking brake, Paras looked at Susan fixing a stamp on Abhay's last time, and with that, Susan pulled him with the smile's cord and took him down.

As Paras went down after making arrangements to receive pirated signals of the Canadian satellite for the

GPS navigation system of the space shuttle, Abhay had worn a school-girl dress and preparing for the role-play session, he placed a whip in Susan's hand. Giving a devilish smile, Paras dragged a chair and sat in a corner. Moving closer to Abhay seated on the bed, Susan was looking at him with eyes that were dripping with sweetness. With a delight to see the thing hidden behind her back, Abhay bent his head towards the left, but by then she had come and stood in front of him. Bringing one hand forward, she waved her fingers a few times in front of Abhay's eyes as if she was selecting A. B. C. D. and quickly thrust the rod held behind the back in his right eye.

"Shit…" Paras pushed aside Susan who was uttering exclamations of repentance for the misfire of missing the target of the eye and piercing at the side of the nose, and squeezed Abhay's neck. Before the windpipe that was being pulverized could secede, the repeatedly ringing doorbell gave a knock of intervention.

"On the terrace…" Running to peep through the key hole, Susan heard Paras' scream that was like a blast of a petrol-station. Paras looked in the window adjacent to the door, Alistair was staring at the dying Abhay with such perplexity which was akin to the little bit of perplexity that difficulties could generate on the face of the elderly.

When they passed from the open bedroom door on the upper floor the mystery of Alistair's unexpected visit was revealed, the television that was displaying their photographs was saying that "Who can imagine the faces of these two innocents as deadly terrorists…!"

*

North India, Antonio's Castle

They had landed the small space shuttle about a mile away from the main peak on which Antonio's castle was located. The silence spread in the castle and its surrounding mountain range including the entire jungle was revealing the intention of the Gardis to easily trap the prey. Through the violent mentality throbbing inside them, they had already known that even now that part of the Devil-Family's leader *Robrelco Fero's* soul was bound with their souls like a hanging sword of death. They had no other option except to reach Benedict whose name was mentioned by Antonio on that night. He was the only one who could relieve them from Robrelco Fero's menace.

"It's strange," Paras said looking at the clock, "Finally when the time had come to lose this *'Eden' (Heavenly Garden)*, even that night making forcible changes in the destiny had reached exactly up to this time only." Following him and proceeding on the lake's coast, Susan glanced far into the demon's forehead like peak of *'gloomshadow'* where she, Paras and Elvis used to spend this part of the time in few new conversations every day. Putting down the *'scorpion box'* on the lake's bank after reaching a little further and opening it, when Paras' glance fixed on his reflection in the water, the lake-water offended by the old buddies, carried him away into the act of reincarnation. They glanced at the flowers of the coast and felt that they were saying, "For whom should we blossom now…"

Burying the dead past with the feel of fresh energy surging forth, Paras started the remote monitor and he pulled out the antenna by turning the box filled with about two dozen artificial scorpions upside down. Through the sensors attached on their back when the crawling scorpions sensed *'human magnetic waves'* and started running to find the hidden Gardis, he quickly dialed a number in Abhay's cell phone. "Identification number *6951556* Agent *'Sami'* S.A.M.Y. The fraud of March 1967 perpetration is modified and is going to be applied once again on a high-level contract. Bond Spit Exhibition… These aircrafts will be flying over North East 34° N, 77°E to 78°E in the next thirty minutes. They can be seen with the Orchid Ray."

He told Susan who was widening her eyes, "I had made the security arrangements for this tour of Antonio Castle from Dion's asteroid itself. *'Kongka La Darra'* that has been declared as a *'No Man's Land'* is considered to be a landing field for aliens. The agents of both the countries, India and China, keep on patrolling in this area. The Chinese Commanders had done a strange caper during the *'boundary'* controversy that happened in 1967. They prepared a dish shaped aircraft that is generally shown to be used by aliens in the films and sent it inside the Indian boundary. When the Indian commanders were careless in welcoming the aliens, they captured three outposts of their country. The aircrafts of the Indian Air-force still offended with this will be hovering over the sky within a few minutes. And I hope that they will be able to offer combat to the Gardi airships that is sufficient enough for us to safely get out of here."

Susan pulled her face behind with interest.

On the other side of the mountain where there was Antonio's bed-chamber, a water stream had now sprouted out from the mountain's sides. One of the two Gardi's who were enjoying the hot water of the swimming pool near the water stream told his companion, "These brave *youngsters (Paras-Susan)* have taught someone like *'Lord de Ros'* a good lesson even though they do not have any special powers…"

"Ouch…" His companion suddenly screamed.

"What is stinging you now…? It is not a water snake, is it….?" Before the Gardi who had recoiled on seeing foam on the lips of his partner as he exerted pressure to get up, could jump out of the pond, the sixth scorpion monitored by Paras had stung him.

Despite the *'thistle cap'* that made one invisible was useless in front of the Gardis' *'Kirlian Glass'* they had worn it. And had now started climbing towards the hidden chamber in the western part of the castle in which the Book of Bell's trouble had been thrust down their neck. They found it easy to climb as the mountainous rocks were totally rough. However, the bawling winds were sometimes pushing them to the other side.

Standing in front of the safe in the chamber where their souls had been honored with the monstrous gift, Paras said, "We have fifteen minutes to get out safely from here." And he entered the password in the toe of the monstrous claw carved on the safe. Lighting the torch of the mobile he peeped into the safe. Apart from a book having a black colored front cover, years old air and the torch light, it was absolutely empty. After opening that black colored book the form of realization of the surprise was completely new. Seeing the pictures of countless owls on the very first page of this uncompleted book leading towards the devilish path, Susan said, "As the owl has the characteristic of turning its neck round up to 180 degrees, the *'Howlet Scripture'* refers to the owl as an eight-directional penetrator. It can see in the night, and it is worth noting that devilishness is primarily practiced at night. According to the bird omen scripture, an owl is a nocturnal creature having supernatural powers. Maybe some mysterious use of the owl is done in the ritual of acquiring special powers." Saying this, she held her dress flying with the gust of wind and closing the book, she started descending down behind Paras.

*

"Did you hear something? It looks like the airships of the Indian army are nearby." They had now come down and stood on that place in the ground, from where the Devil had kidnapped Antonio. "You unnecessarily raised this commotion. No one here would have any expectation of our arrival. Apart from a few scattered Gardis there is no one else here. They would certainly not consider us to be so stupid to make the mistake of coming here again and they would catch us easily."

Paras said rubbing his right ear, "Just suppose you have very little time left. Just a few seconds... And when you have a lot of things left to talk about, what would you do then?" They looked at each other and as if singing the National Anthem, they uttered in a one toned chorus… "You send them to such a person who can finish your half conversation."

Opening the *Book of Bell's* chest brought from the debris lying a little far away from the place to get down into the lake and keeping it horizontally at one place, Paras said, "After being caught in the Devil's arms, the three things towards which Antonio had gestured, one of them which is this, was right here. You were standing here next to me. And Elvis, approximately twenty feet away, towards the right... Antonio had also gestured towards Elvis."

"But that is not particularly important," Susan said, "Luciano had come here that night. Antonio might have seen Luciano who was hiding in the jungle behind Elvis."

"His first sign was towards this chest and second towards the sky. Or else towards these trees…" Paras said, starting to expel the wells of reminiscence. "There is something written on the chest in Chinese letters and there is also a symbol of the *Swastika (an auspicious Indian symbol)* on the inside portion.

"Whatever it is…" Susan said without getting into the bog of arguments, "But it is necessary to remain alive to understand his sign language and I don't think that we should wait here even for one more minute." As she finished, a powerful flash of light and blast happened in the sky above them. Before the war craft of the Indian Air-force could complete its surveillance round, the missile of the Gardi-soldiers fired from the ground had scattered it into such pieces that they would have to be searched with the help of a magnifying glass.

A storm of wild winds cheering the rod of the Gardis had come into existence. The Indian war crafts had started showering storm shadow rocket-bombs on the main castle at the top, a place from where several Gardi-Soldiers had flown towards the foothills. Susan who was being pulled half on her own and half by Paras, said shouting in the ears of her ruthless squire, "The abodes where the age of floating paper-boats has passed by are no less than any kith and kin." She turned round and watched the small world that made her heart dance being destroyed with a last bow. Paras was just making her run away from one more world that was on the verge of destruction. "This is only the first time that the Indian army has been so lucky to achieve success in the imaginary war against the aliens." Mumbling, Paras shoved her into the open door of the cockpit from a three feet distance and jumped into the shuttle, with that the shuttle standing ready in an auto-pilot mode became invisible in the blink of an eyelid.

*

In the journey started for an unknown destination when they would have hardly moved ahead enough so that their breathing could become normal, making a commotion in the massive mind of the intelligent Google, Susan said, "Out of the total forty-six Japanese alphabets not even a single one is ready to match the three letters carved on this *Book of Bell's* box." 七十八

"Then look at Chinese. Hongkong, Singapore, Malaysia, Myanmar, the letters of the language of some country will match, right." Paras quickly said looking at the decreasing fuel level, "Did you match with the Japanese digits or only with the alphabets?"

Scrutinizing of the first line of the Chinese alphabet, Susan said, "I'll check the Chinese words first."

"First match them with the Japanese digits." Paras said, "The fuel now gives consent for a maximum of about three hours of celestial excursion."

"There is no need for you to be very happy." Susan said, the *totapandit's (the parrot cognoscente)* predictions also come true sometimes. 七十八, these three digits carved on the box is a Japanese number *718*."

"Postal codes 718. City tram number 718… An organization manufacturing puzzle video games based in phase 718 and a *law* firm bearing the name Erection 718..." Susan said, troubling Google so much that it would have to take a leave, "There are millions of venues associated with the number 718 in Japan. And apart from that, the sacred symbol of Swastik that has been carved on the inner side of the chest has been incessantly used since the fifth centenary before Christ throughout the world."

When Paras put the shuttle on auto pilot in the direction of Japan, Susan said snatching his respite again, "Apart from Japan, the meaning of these words is 718 in the languages of China and Hongkong also." There was a smile on her lips that was teasing Paras.

Remembering the phase of his career as a Direction Instructor thousands of feet below on the Asian Pacific dwarf islands, when a grin of contrasting helplessness formed on Paras' pink cheeks on seeing the glittering lights of a light house, Susan said showing the *'Prayer Wheel'* carved at a distance of three inches from the carving of 718 on the chest, "During one memorable journey with Antonio when I was turning this type of a *'Prayer Wheel'* with a playful mentality in the courtyard of the World Heritage Site *'Mahabodhi Temple'*, one guide came to me and explained that these type of Prayer-Wheels are used for acquiring wisdom and purification of misdeeds. Protective energy is believed to be manifested with the spells written on the clock-wise moving Prayer Wheel. When he was explaining it appeared to the boys standing nearby as if haunted walls of the classroom could be seen rising up on all four sides."

"Where does your topic lead to?" Paras asked with disconcertment.

"Just up to the exit door of this labyrinth..." Susan said, "I mean to say that the fabrication of this chest is like the ones used in a religious institution. It will be more beneficial if we associate the number 718 to a religious sect instead of tram number, city-code, car number, house number and start the search." Saying this, Susan started the iBook again. After the result of place starting with 718 presented itself as a huge net, Susan searched for *'A place founded in the year 718 in Japan'*.

"Hoshi Ryokan established in the year 718. The one and only inn of the world functioning since the longest time… At that time in Japanese history, a great teacher of Buddhism saw a dream of some miraculous site and therapeutic warm water springs had been discovered from that site. That inn had been built on the same site. But this world's oldest hotel that has been recorded in the Guinness Book of World Records is being run by one single family for more than twelve hundred years."

"That's interesting." Paras said and raising the cheap space shuttle to the ultimate speed, he started gathering important things. Watching him with doubtful eyes, Susan asked, "Should I wear a parachute?"

"No, one is enough." Saying this, he put the diamond pouch giving exemption from the trouble of currency conversion in his pant's pocket and started searching the map for such locations where the shuttle could be hidden in the *Ishikawa Province.*

*

Komatsu City in Japan

"What happened baby…? Pouring a torrent of hot water on Susan's face, when Paras broke her sluggishness, she was preparing to drown in the ocean of the Komatsu city beach through her dream once again.

Before their desire to take the shuttle up to *'Shibayama Lake'* by four o'clock in the morning could be fulfilled, the hopeless shuttle had conked off and directly dived into the ocean of the *'Kwesaiy National Park'*. After being consigned to the watery grave, their space shuttle that had transformed into a *'water scooter'*, had started pulling them into the depths of the ocean once again like a deceitful fish before it could deliver the questers to the shore. After the other end of an important file had worked like a straw for the drowning Susan, the resentment of it getting spoilt had gone away. As a result of fatigue and sleeplessness, they had kept snoring up to seven in the evening in a room of Hoshi Ryokan. On asking the manager about the chest, he had said that *'Kenzou'*, an old employee of the hotel would know about it. They had decided to relieve their fatigue in the natural hot water pools that were in the hotel itself until Kenzou's arrival. Although the *'evening'* taking on the form of the Japanese night and awakening aspirations of vagrancy, beckoned to come close when they stepped out of Ryokan's natural swimming pool, it was not possible for them to leave the hotel as Kenzou had already arrived.

Gesturing Paras to meet near the passage-way's tree as he went towards the men's locker, Susan removed the swimming cap and went into the changing room. The candle lit corridor ranging from the swimming pool to the bar lounge was equipped with every quality to give a pleasantly moist awareness of strolling on the pathways of the heart decorated with amour. The *tavern in-charge (bar boy)* who was serving just one *'alcoholic medicine'* for all types of pains, gestured from far that Kenzou was on his way. They went and sat at the bar table. The first sip of the first drink had not yet gone below the dry throat when gesturing towards Kenzou who was dragging his broken leg and coming towards them, the bar boy spoke- "There is not a slightest change in his years old belief.

Kenzou believes that he is presently in this condition due to stealing the chest of a good man which is now with you."

"This chest..?" Paras almost stood up.

"It will be much better if you listen to his submission about the captivating story which no one here is ignorant about from him only." Saying this, the bar boy lit the Marlboro that was dangling between Paras' lips.

"Whatever I think about does not go right." The seventy year old Kenzou who was still mumbling in his self-owned world, ignored Paras' extended hand and picking up the *Book of Bell's* chest from the table, he directly started cross checking. Speaking about the traditional Japanese music with a modern touch reverberating in the bar lounge, Susan said, "Impossible to discern, yet it is fun, isn't it?"

Slightly bending his head in front of her, Paras said to the bar attendant, "Shall we do one thing? Let's delay the appointment with the owner a little." And giving relief to the neck from the loop of the tie, he started listening to Kenzou's weird talks.

"A delegation of *Examine Cease'* a rapidly flourishing cult during that period stayed in this inn on that day. Each one of them had the same kind of chests like this. On that day almost half the inn was jam-packed with mysterious people who did not look like residents of Earth. When he came, his son was also there with him, handsome…"

"Who..? Who had come then?" Susan asked.

"Levi, Levi was the name of that silky-coat. As it is, the camp of his companions was here right from morning. That big gentleman gave me his child and lots of *'yen'* and told me to make an excuse of being ill and stay in my quarter looking after that boy. I had just got up to implement the greedy thought of getting tips from other guests and locking up the boy in the room when he knocked on my door again and trapped me in the greed of the enormous sin of stealing this chest."

"Ssssh…" A Turkish engrossed in the music meditation nearby, gave an angry stare looking at Kenzou's waiter's dress.

"How far is your quarter?" Paras asked.

"It can be reached within two minutes." Kenzou said.

Paras got up putting the total along with the tip on the counter and so did Susan with reluctance.

"None of the supporters of that new cult staying here were present in their rooms as if there was a passion to have meals together at one time only and it became easy for me to steal that chest. At least at that time for sure…" He shook his head to and fro with regret. "I picked up a similar chest. I emptied it and brought it to my room. Probably, this one only! No, but at that time such carving on the chest…"

"What..? Wrinkles appeared on Paras' forehead.

Suddenly as if a reunion had happened, Kenzou kept staring at the *'718'* and *'Prayer Wheel'* that had been carved on the box with amazement. "This is the same chest! This is that chest for sure…!" His fingers were going to the ear lobes again and again while speaking.

"In which way..?" Susan asked.

"I'll show once we reach the room. After some time of my stealing the chest and bringing it, Levi came to my quarter and what was the name of that book..? I am unable to recollect even after sqeezing the brain…?"

"Book of Bell..?" Paras reminded him.

Looking at Paras with shining eyes, Kenzou said affirmatively, "Levi must have stolen that book and had just kept it in this box when their commander reached here fuming with rage. He absolutely did not look Asian, yet he talked with me in Japanese Half of his weird chattering was hollow as if termites had nibbled it. Smoothing his blonde hair, he said to Levi who was bearing an attitude of looking normal, "During decades of service, against whose loyalty not a single thought has come to poison the ears of even one of us five Presidents, that *'Levi'*, himself did this…!"

"What was Levi's response? And that handsome boy? Did the commander take him also?" Paras asked.

"No, the boy had been moved to another quarter even before he came. Levi spoke in a proud voice that- *If I would not have stolen and hid the 'Book of Bell' here then the Devil would now have been sitting idle turning its pages. My attendant has matched Dervil's aura here just some time back.* But it did not appear that the commander was very convinced."

Opening the lock of the quarter which Susan was waiting to be opened for the last three minutes, the mumbling *'Kenzou'* entered inside on back foot, "Since the whole life of my father was dedicated to this place, I was the one to be selected without any doubt for the service of such important guests." Saying this, Kenzou gestured towards the opposite wall.

Seeing exactly the same kind of Japanese digits on the opposite wall as those carved on the chest, Paras slid into the past. After some strange President left Susan and him with Antonio, Levi, Antonio's loyalist had come and taken him away. Paras' memory that was passing through scenes of him wandering through several mysterious places with Levi during those childhood days finally stabilized in the time that Levi had come with him to this hotel.

"I am hungry." When Kenzou with the stolen chest was hanging the lock beside the door, Paras seated with his elbow resting on the handle of the armchair said gesturing.

"I'll get something." Kenzou said as he wrapped up the chest in a cloth and went away locking the door once again.

Getting up after about two minutes or so, Paras moved the curtain aside and glancing outside, he opened the cloth and took out the chest to see what Kenzou had got. Pulling out a sharp needle file like thing from the tool box hanging on the opposite wall, he started carving the *'718'* and Prayer Wheel shape drawn in the old plank hung on the wall, on the chest.

"You are also quite weird." After coming back to the room, when Paras narrated his anecdotes that gave inspiration to epic dramas, Susan said, "Leaving aside

'Hoshi Ryokon' that was written on the plank, you were only able to think of carving 718 and the Prayer Wheel."

*

They had continued to show the chest and interrogate Ryokon's employees, owners and several men in the surrounding area till late night on that day and the receding afternoon of the next day, but they did not have any clue of the person whom Antonio wanted them to approach. The person towards whom Kenzou had directed them to avail more information had now left Ryokon's employment and was working on a fishing ship. As the ship was not going to come to the shore in a short while, they chartered a boat and sailing along the coast, they reached that *'Classic fishing tall ship'* in the East Ishikawa Bay.

Paras showed the chest to that man and kept it on one side he took the basket from his hand with the intention of helping him and emptied the fishes in the barrack. That old man having a wrinkled but strong physique straightened his back and said- "Alongwith Kenzou, I had also been appointed for the service of those forty *magis (mysterious men)* who were staying in Ryokon that day. I do not know much, but the person who had come to meet one of them that day lives here a little far in Awazoo itself. His name is Anazim. See him, he might know something about this."

The evening had to compulsorily wane away. After anchoring the boat, they went and sat in a grass cottage a little away from the coast. As a Japanese who rented *'Beach Game'* toys kept his trolley aside and came to sit in front of them, Paras picked up a cup of ice-tea from the tray and suddenly asked him, "Are there any trees having specific types of characteristics around here?"

"The vendor gulped the *'tea'* with three times the speed and prepared to escape from there as if he had seen a terrorist, the old owner of the restaurant running in the cottage played the role of an interpreter and interpreted Paras' question in Japanese. The uncouth looking old man shocked them by speaking in English.

Lolling her leg below the bench, Susan sipped ice-tea and twirling her tongue on cold lips, she said, "If the Book of Bell was to kill us it would have occurred long back. And now it is not necessary to be a genius to decide that instead of roaming on Antonio's gestures, gather the remaining wealth on *'Opdrazen'* and live a comfortable life on a faraway planet. I am getting an intense inclination to become a part of a new world again for quite a long time."

Paras gave a *'yen'* to the old man who observing the smoke of his cigarette attentively and said looking towards Susan, "That night was full of fog. Many Chairmen of Colony *'Metal Casting'* have the characteristic of making their body transparent. It is possible that Antonio might have gestured towards some Chairman hanging there in the air like a goblin?"

"Smoking tree…" The old owner of the cottage suddenly spoke up.

"What?" Paras asked.

"A tree having such a characteristic is present here in Awazoo also."

"Means..?"

"Sometimes smoke comes out spontaneously from the shades of the tree. And that too, in the style of smoking… Although there are smoking trees in other countries also but a person named Anazim who lives a little far away, has a smoking tree in the backyard of his house which is totally different." Susan looked towards Paras and she felt as if he will get up and hug the old man. But instead of that he thanked the old man and gave him enough *'yen'* to enjoy retirement for a month and gestured the man horse standing far with a *'pulled buggy'* to come closer.

*

That night after showing the chest Anazim's servant had insolently expelled them from there saying that it was impossible to meet him for such unnecessary inquiry. Anazim, who resided six kms. West from Hoshi-Ryokon, was not particularly fond of the smell of other two-legged creatures. He was one of those people about whom a presumption had to be made after listening to rumors.

After meticulously observing that isolated house surrounded by mountains on the new morning, they had spent hours till the afternoon in the preparation that its owner Anazim would happily give the newcomers permission to enter. In the evening, when Susan came out dressed in a fully backless, prom party dress, caressing her silky body with his eyes, Paras said, "Does any man have the daring to even give a fake rejection to this flawless beauty."

After crossing the bridge constructed by pilfering some part of the sky above the vibrant springs, Susan said, "This area surrounded by mountains is an excellent block house to hide secret activities, isn't it?" She said but some thoughts were passing between the present and Paras. Passing below the coffee, yellow and dark green colored trees, Paras put a finger on the nose and gestured to keep on walking quietly. Turning back, Susan saw that far away the glasses of the windows of *'Hoshi Ryokon'* had now shone up. The possibility of electronic eyes and ears hidden on the trees of the jungle, forced them to keep on listening to the music of the night creatures on the road ahead.

They stood near the gate and spent nearly ten seconds staring at that house which looked like a collection of ruins. They viewed the smoking tree having a paw shaped trunk again in the light of the bright searchlights, about twenty feet away towards the right, after entering the gate. The sound of the gate opening of the gate was hoarse enough to burn the hearts of those who hesitate to go to the disagreeable site and start the conversation. The veils of the strong trees grown on the arch of the mountain at a distance of about eleven feet towards the left of the house were looming on the roof as if claiming to own them.

They pulled the *header* of the doorbell decorated in the old style and stood in front of the entrance with folded hands. A slow sound of bells chimed inside.

The splendor packed view inside was in rigid contrast to the ship-wreck like view outside. A servant came out from the rear room and quickly removed the pin from a gramophone disk chanting spells like the Caribbean black magic.

"I am sorry for the trouble." Susan said, but obviously, on seeing Susan, Anazim had indeed been troubled. With a Malaysian traditional type simple *kurta pyjama (an apparel worn by people in certain parts of Asia)*, his waist to thigh portion was wrapped in excess clothing. "I am from the *National Association for Motifs Research of Tree* organization." Moving her glance from the *Castifo (A high speed laser gun of the Gardi Force)* kept in a corner, Susan extended her hand. "My crew is currently staying in *'Ryokon'* with a hope to get at least one week's permission for research on the smoking tree that is in your ownership."

"If your task is done by uprooting the smoking tree and taking it then it's a *yes* from me." Left with no choice, Anazim who generally used the language of expressions had to take the recourse of words.

"We will manage with a permission of about three days also." Paras said.

Consequently, Anazim looked at his servant and turned to go inside whereas the servant, who could have shown even a professional killer to be kind, raised his hand with sternness and showed the door. "Hoshi Ryokan. Room number 35. In case some pleasing thought becomes a patron, then I am available..." As Susan walking on back-foot threw a mouth grenade of greed on Anazim's back, the door hit on their face.

After they came and sat at the bar restaurant in a mentality suitable to rush for alcohol, Susan said, "He was a Gardi-Soldier. Didn't you see? Apart from him, whom would Antonio want to send to? He must be Benedict and might be known by the name of Anazim here."

Paras said, "Coming out in the open before knowing what exactly is going on there will be an invitation to death. It is also possible that the Gardi's to whom Lord de Ros provided the scent of Antonio's group and released them, might have seized this station of Antonio and may be waiting for one after other of their comrades. Without determining whether enemy or friend, this can prove to be suicide."

"And if he turns out to be an enemy…?

"That is the difficulty. The neck can easily be sliced down by opening the neck belt, but how would that happen?"

"There is a way." Susan said, "A little risky but accurate."

"Do you think that stripping off your clothes will make his neck belt obstinate enough to be opened up..?"

"What is going on?" The bar attendant who had come behind the counter formed a crack in their concentration.

"Why are people scared to go to Anazim?" Susan asked him.

"The fright of being deprived of life… You must have heard about the use of unmarried girls in black magic, but this devious person is so strange that he does not leave even the pregnant women. Especially women having pregnancy of a few days…

"Maybe he likes the extra flesh of the pregnant women." Without paying attention to the talks of one of his companions who was eager to tease him, the bar-boy was about to speak further but as they turned back to find out the reason for his wilted face, Anazim's butler was gesturing Susan to come near.

"Only you and your companion…" The butler said.

"Sure, we will come by tomorrow afternoon. Give him the message of thanks."

"You should not go there." The barboy expressed concern.

In response, Susan gave a smile that was given to a lucky few and got up.

*

The possibility of a boxing scene being added to today's drama, Susan's attention had been drawn towards the choice of tight purple skirt and air force blue colored top. However, she did not have any idea that she is giving Anazim an advantage by the colors that make a person more aggressive. Paras was dressed in his daily custom suit. Right from the time they left the inn, Anazim's servants who had besieged and followed them like wolves from a little distance had now disappeared.

Anazim intending to show that powerful personalities did not need the support of insignificant things to impress women was present to welcome Susan in yesterday's dress only.

"This side, our arrangement has been made in a special *Groom-room*." Anazim drew them inside.

Pretending that she had not understood the significance of his double speaking glances, Susan said, "Lab setup will reach in about an hour." And taking out a butcher's knife hidden in a sealed plastic wrapper from the purse that looked like a hand-fan she started fanning herself. "You took unnecessary trouble. Forget the metal detector, no one here is bothered even to search with an empty hand." She mumbled in a slow voice.

"After spending *'patience'* that has to be spent during the whole life for something favorite, it becomes impossible to keep patience for anything else." Saying this, Anazim pulled Susan's hand and made her sit beside him.

"This one thought of yours is certainly one that will accomplish friendship between us." Paras said.

Playing with Susan's ear on the sofa, Anazim said, "One whose identity is absent in the cross reference list of the *'World Fact Book'* of the *'C.I.A.'*, can be easily found in Anazim's records. Two birds that flew away from Mumbai, at this end in Japan…?"

"You have caught us." Thinking, whose door of death the closing door of the room would open, Paras spoke, "Some cunning people are chasing us. While searching for a shelter for just a few days, our eyes had been drawn to this deserted house." His gaze went towards the corner where the Gardi had put the Castifo gun.

Anazim stopped caressing Susan's thighs with his fingers and getting up, tied Paras' hands behind the same chair that he was sitting on and came near Susan. Taking away his glance falling frequently on her varnish-thighs towards Paras, he said, "Why is your partner not making any protest?"

"That partner is just a gift given at the time of difficulty."

"Oh, you spilled all my *interest*" Anazim said as he started the LCD hung on the wall of the display table and dialed a six-digit number with the remote. The entire flooring of the bedroom started slipping down like a lift. Anazim kept the remote aside and took off his clothes. Paras' neck rose up, a similar flooring from the bottom of the adjacent bedroom was coming out and taking its place. Raising the knees resting on both sides of Anazim's broad chest as he lay upright pressing the springs of the bed, the big cat caught the chopper and said as she started meddling with its skin-tight wrapper, "Open this belt of the top dog from the neck…"

"Gnaw…" Susan put up an interesting act of preparing to bite his entire body, reckless with the lust and opening the door of life-loss, the out of control Anazim opened the belt from his neck and hurled it at one side. Susan turned her neck and gestured Paras struggling to release himself from the rope, she opened the chopper behind Anazim's head. Putting the chopper on his throat, Susan made eye contact with him, "Where is Benedict?" The colors of Anazim's iris changed. His hand waved in the air, hurling Susan, he directly leaped towards the Castifo gun that was lying in the corner. His hefty athletic nude physique was enough to pummel the courage of the competitors. Paras who had intervened in the duel between the most beautiful girl on Earth and an attacking *'Gardi'*, sunk his teeth in Anazim's shoulder By the strength of the lion but it was useless… Before his chunk of flesh could be spit out, the feinting Gardi became intact once again and was running towards the Castifo gun.

Anazim's hands rose up but before the Castifo held in them could ring the tinkle of Susan's death trance, Paras attacked by poniard with such *'Titanic'* strength that even *Susan* herself started trembling out of fear. Anazim's hurled head fell upside down in a *Shirsasana (headstand)* pose and blinked the eyes three times. "My salute to the Romance Captain" Saying this, kicking his head as if playing the Fifa final games, Paras said to Susan, "Your little risky idea would have grabbed our lives."

Saving her leg from the puddle of blood and opening the door, when Susan winked and said "Hello brothers" twenty-five of Anazim's stout hooligans, standing with electric weapons of *Glee Metal Casting's* workmanship in the underground world, turned in one single direction and kept staring at Susan's long and polished legs. Balancing the faltering of the haphazard combat, Paras had held Anazim's cut head in one hand and the Castifo in the other hand. "Antonio has returned once again." He started hitting an arrow in the dark, with a throbbing heart, "Loyalty or body, you have five seconds to decide which one of the two to exchange."

Anazim's commander immediately started observing the monitor displaying the outer part of the house. Kenzou dressed in a Japanese traditional outfit had come with his comrades in time. Hiding their faces from the camera near the smoking-tree, they stood together in a circle. "Antonio is waiting for someone." Paras said. But the commander was not ready to budge from the side of the monitor.

"What are you staring at?" Susan asked sliding close to the commander, "Where is Benedict? Take us to him soon."

"Here." The commander said and placed a finger at a place in the electric-diagram affixed on the wall of the entry canal where they were standing and gestured them to follow. They were now six hundred feet below the ground.

During the quick journey of four minutes after coming out of the entry canal, they travelled through several machines taking out the used Oxygen, staff apartments, meeting rooms on the third floor of the storage, restaurants and power generation rooms. Finally after passing the corridor leading to a glass cage hanging from the ceiling at one place, a person was seen clenched in iron bonds. A Trogolodyte like superhuman was in intense contemplation in a glass cage. At one corner, a five feet tall wooden box was kept. All the things decided to be enough for the necessity of his life were accommodated in that space only.

Holding his hand in front of the overhead light troubling him, he stared at Susan in a way to identify the visitors. Paras instantly snapped his fingers and gestured to switch off the light, he ordered the commander to take his comrades and go away from there.

"You are Benedict?" Paras asked.

"Yes dear *Black Horse.*" *(A nickname of Daarck)*

"Why didn't you come to receive us that night?" Paras asked as he snatched off his *communication stoppage cap* and started opening his remaining bonds. *(Communication stoppage cap- A cap stopping the messages being sent to someone through thought)*

"I was just coming. But Anazim, a loyalist of one time and the whole and sole of this underground world, imprisoned me with deceit on that same night and seized this entire site."

"Anyways," Paras spoke, "We are desirous of a permanent *Sunday* from the Book of Bell and the entire Galaxy Mafia Club that is chasing it, as well as from the Antonio Group. Release us from Robrelco Fero's soul as soon as possible."

Benedict called a guard upstairs by snapping his fingers and said as he turned towards Paras, "I'll meet you in the dinner room within ten minutes. I'll have to make several phone calls in order to get information of the current situation."

*

The sound of pouring alcohol in a silver goblet was heard up to six seconds, then Benedict spoke, "Anazim never missed to drink this favorite brand of mine once a day, sitting in front of me." Every sip of the *'Paramount Lady'* going down Benedict's throat was bringing forth an exclamation of contentment.

Paras gulped down the drink that contained the soaked flowers in the goblet same as the Chinese generally do to add aroma to their tea and as he was fighting against oppressive hunger, pounced onto the gourmet dishes of Romanesco, Samphire and Durian. Keeping his glance fixed on Susan drinking the delicious juice of the Kiwano Melon, Ben spoke leisurely making use of the teeth, "Did Antonio give you Filipa's message?"

"No he could not deliver it." Paras retorted.

"The President who brought you and Susan had delivered Filipa's message that- "If this world has to survive then *'Daarck'* should never come back. If he comes back than the life on all these Vio-Crazy colonies will be hundred times more ruthless and fraught with hardship than it is today. My love towards Daarck has bound me to make arrangements of his rebirth, but the use of the *'Discovery Copper Horse Engine'* should not be applied on him at all." As Ben emptied the glass and getting up, he gestured them to follow, Paras spoke, "It does not necessarily happen that you always remain as you are. Without knowing the mystery of why Susan alias Filipa did that betrayal with me, there is now no meaning to this life for me."

Benedict spoke, "The question why Filipa did something like this with her lover, and what Daarck really wanted may be necessary for you? But this question concerning just two people does not essentially hold any significance. There is only one question that holds significance, whether we shall be successful in giving the gift of a beautiful life forever and ever to the billions and trillions of humans residing on several planets of the eleven Vio-Crazy colonies? Just imagine about such Messiahs who have come with the mission of transforming not just one society, one country or one planet but the entire world into heaven. Only this question is of importance and against this, the personal difficulties of each one of us does not hold any significance."

After walking for about three minutes, the view of the *'Deathless Lab'* in which this trio had entered was very strange. In a big hall, several pregnant women on a bed stand had been connected with a six feet tall computer-panel lying nearby through the medium of syringes injected in the portion of their abdomen and head. Taking the last sip from the bottle of Paramount Lady, Ben spoke, "We have succeeded in forming the spells of the Tie-in tune, the Re-built tune and the spells of the Contrus Affair through the study of the programming languages of the bodies connected to these most neoteric computers of the universe that dragged the format of the human body onto the screen, which is programmed in such a manner that even a scraggy pathogen visible through a microscope can lead to its death and by the strike of sound waves of these things the physical body can be separated, such a separated body can be sent back into the same person's soul and such a soul can also be imprisoned with the soul of another person. The study of the way in which the sentimental robot named man has been programmed, can be done during his embryonic journey in the period when his body is being formed. Since the elements which the human body is made of are infinite, in a way man also is infinite. And if you can re-program the body in the beneficial form of this reality, then it can perform miracles according to your imagination."

"Master-stroke…" The words slid and came out from Susan's tongue as she was seeing the complexity of the unique alphabets and symbols being noted in thousands with the gradual growth of the embryo on the screen.

Benedict said, as he closed the power supply of the computer panel, "After re-programming the *'data structure set'*, it is installed in any one of the billions of electrons, neutrons or positrons in the body. Now even if such a body is tied with a bomb and blasted off, the setup file present in the molecule will auto-run and co-ordinate with the infinite molecules to create a new body which is same as the creation of the first human in which no man or woman were needed. Ofcourse by plugging-in his soul with the same molecule… The connection of these two things is in fact the biggest miracle. It's most recent achievement will be to make the desired changes in the body by re-programming directly through the thoughts of the mind without the help of machines."

"All this is remarkable." Hiding the envy, Paras said, "Means, that opening the top drawers of the brain and bringing out ideas of such weapons and fulfilling them. Magnificent…."

"Daarck never disclosed the secret about His agents supplying *'intelligence'* to let alone Antonio, not even to his special *Filipa*." Extending a packet of triple strong cigars *'Straight Jacket'* towards Paras, Benedict said, "We should leave now. We are already late because of Filipa's betrayal. We should now go to Metal Casting and make use of the Discovery Copper Horse on you as soon as possible, so that those Project Discs can be acquired from Susan alias Filipa."

"But what about the task of removing Robrelco Fero from our souls?" Susan asked as she wore the *'Gizmo-Belt'* that Benedict had taken out from the table of valuable things and given to her. *(Gizmo-Belt – An electronic armor)*

"That will now have to be done by us in front of Devil's eyes. The fact that Robrelco Fero has not yet killed you proves that you are Daarck and she is Filipa." Saying this, Benedict locked the studio with the card and pressing the indoor-station-black box after asking whether the shuttle was ready or not, he said, "The Devil is meeting us in Rome after one hour."

*

A City of Southeast Europe, 'Rome'

Benedict's small space vehicle buried in invisibility slowly appeared at the edge of a dark lane. Susan and Paras gradually moved forward behind Benedict who had opened the door very slowly and got down. As they reached a cottage bookshop situated at the junction of three roads, a little further and stopped there, Ben said glaring at a tall hoarding on the road, "It appears that he has not come yet."

"I don't understand one thing." Susan asked, "If you were imprisoned there in Japan, then was your meeting in Romania with Dustin a rumor?" Susan's bright eyes suddenly fixed on a house's window at the opposite side of the road. Moving aside the vines hanging on the window, a scary, witch-like woman was staring at her.

"Anazim must have arranged that meeting. Using my name…" As Ben said this, a Limousine was seen below the Moghul doorway on the right side of the road The Limo came and stood below the *'Evil Piazza'* panel inlaid near the shining wall-lamp on the wall of the opposite house. The road ready to go to sleep was offended by some dangerous visitors. Malachi got down wearing a shining black jacket and stood with civility after opening the door. Paras looked up as he shook the shoulder of Benedict glaring at the hoardings once again. As the face soaked in perspiration in the hoarding confirmed the identity of the one who got down from the Limo to be the *'Lord of Darkness'* himself and not any duplicate, *'Ben'* went ahead, bowed his head and honored him with a black-rose.

Satan's fluffy face was scrutinizing Paras and Susan with distrust. Standing beside the King of Evil looking at them with hollow eyes, Susan sensed the effect of the qualities of this great power awarding favorite things in the snap of a finger, cascading on her.

The staircase passing through the tireless candles building small and big tents of light and bubbles of glass filled with scorpions, ended on the third floor and that witch was seen in a narrow doorway welcoming *'Beelzebub'* by giving him a black rose. She said, "Welcome to the Hellhound, providing the sweetness of luxury to the bad luck." They arrived in the middle of the big hall decorated with scarce things of the magicians of necromancy. Benedict made haste to finish the ritual to release Paras' and Susan's souls from Robrelco Fero as per the plan of a short visit, but when the Devil raised his hand and told him to keep patience, he spoke rapidly, "The Re-built tune is with Paras, that is Daarck. And that will be handed over to the Devil Family only after we get the planets of our share."

"The demand of *'Kpenika Lady' (a kind of cat)* in the Sibilina world is always full of covetousness, yet this is for my Lord." Saying this, the witch extended her hand forward. To love whom one would have to become a Devil, fondling such a *'lanigerous'* dangerous cat like something that has been fortunately found, the *'Devil'* snatched it from the witch's hand. After slapping Sierra's hand holding a gift, when the *'witch'* pointed a finger towards *'Susan'*, the Devil nodded his head in refusal and gestured to Benedict. Paras held Susan's hand as she stared unblinkingly at the witch and took her on the *'magic plate'*, while the power of the spells that Benedict started chanting appeared to be giving orders to release Robrelco Fero's spirit in a unique language used in the world of ghosts. A bizarre fracas, such that even a corpse would get up and run, started out there. The cyclone of red light emitted out of Paras' and Susan's bodies transformed into the angry eyes glaring like the fire of hell and was gradually absorbed into invisibility.

The Devil said, "*Lon* has given an appointment that is six hours later, for the use of Discovery Copperhorse on his space vehicle *Daddy's Woolybear.*" Paras looked towards Susan in an indicative way, as if he wanted to say that

"Even death received from you is acceptable to me. Provided you give it to me because you loved me and not because of the greediness of the Project Discs."

The Devil said, "There are only the Devil Family, Lon and the Antonio Group in the competition. After the use of the Discovery Copper Horse on this girl Filipa, the Project Discs hidden by her, it means that those eleven colonies will now be distributed in three portions only."

"Not three, four." Everyone turned their heads in the direction of a known voice, which had come from the side of the door. Luciano was standing there with Elvis. "What have you got with you Luciano?" The Devil asked.

"Daarck's real dark secret…" As per habit he came in with agility and putting the hologram on the table, he spoke further, "Who was Daarck? A soldier of Apotheosis himself or his Chairman *Solon's..*? Or else sent by the Vio-Crazy group leader Kaylos or otherwise a midshipman sent by Lon? The speculations about Daarck are infinite. But infidels of the power seat! Sit tight, I am pulling down the underwear of this great mystery this very second." Saying this, Luciano put on the holograph. *(Solon – A Chairman of Director Apotheosis)*

Solon, sitting in front of *Daarck* explaining the strategy in the video, was seen in a big dilemma. Daarck said, "As per my opinion *Walk of Life* will be the correct name for this mission to take humans on a real life jaunt. There are several benefits, of the co-partnership of the Devil-Family responsible for impiety, in this strategy. Apart from making use of the Devilish powers to mesmerize the Chairmen hesitating to associate with this, the huge Devilish community prevalent in Galaxy L3 can be used as soldiers. We will get the help of Robrelco Fero an expert in science and the facility to prepare armies on countless Devilish asteroids…"

"Is Daarck not forgetting that we have come together for establishing good governance…?" Solon said straining his eyebrows.

Presenting *Devilet Again* against the expected question from him, Daarck retorted, "As soon as the Project Discs are ready, I will get the eleven Chairmen helping in this mission to say goodbye to their lives and the Devil will be imprisoned with Devilet. No colony will come in anyone's control except Lon and Solon."

"A defeat of even as much as the point of a needle cannot be seen in your preparation, Daarck. But you don't even have a conception, Lon," As if he had got a shock, 'Solon' spoke suddenly turning towards 'Lon', "On which scale does the conspiracy for making arrangements of a life for the creatures residing on the planets of the Vio-Crazy colonies to enjoy the highest level of happiness, affect Director Apotheosis' policy. Under any circumstances, even if he wants, he cannot tolerate this kind of interference done in the world management. The stiletto will be seen under our sleeves at some point of time and there will be no scope of forgiveness."

"Which is that policy of our Director? What do you mean to say by even if he wants? By any chance you are not trying to say that in this world-management going on in the universe, there is someone superior to *Apostheosis* also! To whom he is answerable?" Lon asked but *'Solon'* turned his face away with embarrassment and ignoring his original question, he said, "Ultimately this mess of Walk of Life is for the selfish and jealous humans only, no…?" Are they really worth that heavenly life? You ask yourself."

"I had never expected that Solon who made me a fanatic for the establishment of heavenly governance on all the planets in the entire universe would utter these words sometime." With an unwelcome glance to Daarck who was prying on all four sides in the room like a partridge, *'Lon'* spoke further. "Now there is no question of taking it back. Because this question is not just of the quality of the life of billions and trillions of humans living on the seven thousand toy planets of the two hundred colonies of the Vio-Crazy community only, but if we calculate the age-limit of the creatures of hundred, two hundred or planets like *'Replica'*, then it is the question of the happy life of an equal number of billions and trillions of new borns after a term of two hundred and fifty years and of an equivalent number of lives that would be coming after a new term. If this always keeps on happening, then why should such a change, that would become convenient to humans not be done…?"

"I am ready." Solon said, "Yet I do not think that even if we fall from the top to the bottom, we will be successful in becoming the pioneer of this great transformation. That's because at least for the next 600 years to come, Apotheosis will have to maintain the *'Demand Strategy'* of the tragic, cruel and painful dramas created by people living in sorrow and hardship. Yet I have come to know a mysterious thing regarding the behavior of the ultimate power. And I am supporting you in this insanity of yours as a small hope has sprung up that we will just do this and probably they will agree to this change."

"Demand Strategy…?" After *'Solon'* remained silent about the question asked against such a sentence for which there would be repentence after speaking, *'Lon'* said adding weight to the words, "This risk now needs to be taken for the *'happiness'* of countless *'performers' (human)* passing on the '*hippodrome' (a huge theater)* of Galaxy L3."

"Yet I cannot give any direct help in this." Looking with eyes full of vigor, *'Solon'* said, "If my Lord Apotheosis gets to know about it, then death… And after going into the new life, I would be found again and once more a struggling life and a painful death… This would continue until my punishment will not be completed as per his calculation."

"And me too…" *Lon* who had shaken up said putting on a fake mask of fitness, "I never want to be instrumental in the disastrous war of the Idiotics against the Vio-Crazys. Whatever Daarck has to do, he has to do it on Daarck's own might. He can increase his fees by ten times if he wants to."

"Oh my Devil…" Luciano closed the holograph and Sierra spoke up. "Demand Strategy…! Yes, Apotheosis will have to maintain this Demand Strategy for the next 600 years." This conversation clearly indicates that there is a very big mystery hidden behind the world management that is there in our universe. An ultimate mystery… About which not even one of the New-Gods from the many colonies is aware till date. Not even someone like *'Lon'* who is the leader of the entire Off-Idiotic group."

"This Chairman, *'Solon'* of Apotheosis is gesturing towards something very big mystery." Dervil said.

"Yes and like Lon even he also wants that the Vio-Crazy group should be wiped out." Sierra said, "Because he is aware of that last mystery. He said Apotheosis cannot do it even if he wants to. The one whom we have believed to be the owner of three galaxies and half the Master Galaxy and the *'God'* of even the New-Gods, there is someone more powerful than that Apotheosis also. To whom he is accountable. And who wants that along with goodness, there should also be an existence of evil in the other side, equally powerful. When the ultimate power itself is protecting evil, these helpless ones like Lon and Solon are in the indecision on how to wipe it off."

"Great…., this mystery that has unfolded itself for us today is such that calls for a celebration." Saying this, the Devil raised his neck to ask a Satanic, who had appeared like the rain in summer, what news he had got, but before he could say something, the Dervil asked, "From where did you get this tape, Luciano?"

"As such Daarck is originally an inhabitant of the Master Galaxy." Luciano said, "But in order to give an outcome to Walk of Life, he had been replaced with the owner of the intelligence agency I was associated with by giving all the things including the appearance, tongue print, finger print, iris identity, etc. Daarck was now my new owner. And during one of his espionage, I had found this recording. Daarck had discovered a special *'Spy Camera Set'* for this meeting with Lon and Solon. Through this spy camera that could be affixed inside the eyes, the opposite person's recording can be recorded with his aura-print in the chip fixed in a specific part of the brain. After killing the Chairmen with the killer painting, when these eleven colonies are won over, after imprisoning the Devil with Devilet Again after that and then black-mailing even Lon and Solon with this recording, Daarck alone was going to become the owner of those eleven colonies. But alas, I now want Colony *'Nebel Shift'* in exchange of this tape."

"And also this girl…" Gesturing towards Susan, Elvis completed Luciano's sentence. Blinking his eyes in front of Paras who showed Elvis a fist, Devil reached close to Elvis and said slowly in his ears, "Once the Project Discs and the Re-built tune come in hand this scorpion-herb Paras will be of no use to us. And after that you can take that girl."

"But the recording that you have got does not appear to have the aura-print capturing characteristic." Sierra said.

"Am I a fool to come here with the original recording?" Luciano said, "One of the two tapes made with both the eyes is still with Daarck."

"OK let's suppose we believe you but those like Lon, Solon are not so foolish that they would come to such a meeting without even taking the medicine that could change their actual aura-print. Then this recording is useless." Sierra said.

"*Daarck*, who made the tape of Apotheosis' Chairman himself, would not be so foolish that he would have expected them to come without taking the aura medicine. Anyways, whatever it is, it can be said whether Daarck's alchemy has been successful or not only after checking the real tape." Saying this, the Devil looked at the Satanic who had come to give the news.

As if he did not want to be instrumental in giving this news, he spoke with fear, "There is a bad news. Ros has convinced several traitorious Chairmen of the eleven New-Gods whom he had imprisoned to join him in the war against the Devil-Family. This means that the armies of eleven colonies can get together and attack us any minute now. Ros has given them the temptation to make them the New-Gods of their colonies after this war. If they do not agree then Ros will release their New-Gods. And in that situation, they will not get anything in their hands." As if accepting defeat before the Satanic's lips could close, Benedict said, "I do not see a to counteract to this step of Ros anywhere. If this happens then there will be no trace of even a single Devilish asteroid. And also of the energy warriors…"

"Then do we have any policy left with us now?" Sierra asked.

"There is only one way to recover from this situation now." Dervil spoke. "Lon takes his ally colonies and associates with us in this war."

"If Lon directly wanted to do war then why would he do conspiracies like *Walk of Life* and *Billion Couple*?" Benedict asked. "According to rule any colony of the Idiotic against even one colony of the Vio-Crazy group, means both of the entire groups against each other. Does anyone even have an idea, how terrible the war of all the colonies of both the groups of Galaxy L3 will be?"

Listening to Benedict's talks, the Devil said smiling in a mysterious way in front of him, "I am confident that Lon will certainly give us support with all his might in this war."

Sierra said in a grim voice, "It is probably impossible to stop the initiation of such an Armageddon which is difficult to end. The buzzing of cataclysm is getting bigger." Even after so much effort of Lon, '*Walk of Life*' has failed for the time being and also the Billion Couple. Now the chances are that aggravated Lon would now be ready for the direct war with the Vio-Crazy. Ten minutes have passed since the Billion Couple has started there. Moses claims that 'Solon' gestured the guard standing at the gate of the Billion Couple and he allowed a person to enter without giving him the medicine to counteract the effects of the revert vaccine. I think he should be that same beggar-like man destroying everyone associated with Walk of Life in a covert way. And he is there only to wipe out 'Lon'. We should reach there immediately. If Lon goes then we will also be finished. It appears that Solon has got frightened after the death of Daarck and Filipa. It appears that he is the one who has hired that agent, wandering in a beggar-like outfit. And he is now getting everyone associated with this eliminated in order to eradicate the proof of his involvement in Walk of Life. (*In order to prevent anyone from changing their appearance with the revert vaccine and entering the Billion Couple, entry into the convention was being given only after giving the medicine to wipe out the effect of that vaccine.*)

*

That which was given the appellation of Billion Couple, the auspiciousness for which place to conduct it on would be seen before every big convention of such a *'Joint Institutional Organization'*. After seeing the auspiciousness, it had come forth that the results of the decisions taken in this time's convention would prove to be the least pernicious if held in the middle of the sea of *Climate Canopy*, a planet of Cons Lydia. Huge wooden-cottages without roof were hurriedly constructed in the stormy sea. The New-Gods of the Vio-Crazy and Off-Idiotic groups had deployed themselves with the large convoy of their bodyguards far apart but opposite each other. *'Solon'* was seated leisurely on the judge's chair in a proud posture. He was currently looking like half-man half-God from the Greek story.

"It has now been undisputedly proved that the Billion Couple of the Earth was not just an outcome some capricious revolutionary's mind but a pre-planned conspiracy to remove the New-God of that planet 'Earth' by proving him to be extremely cruel in the eyes of Apotheosis." Solon said further after the screams of the Vio-Crazy New-Gods calmed down, "The blast happened in Kundali's mind after taking the restricted activity up to the enigma decryption (A secret code with a puzzle) proves the Billion Couple to be clearly 'counterfeit'. I really pity the conditions imposed by Master Galaxy on the culprits trying out the Billion techniques. After Solon said this much, his companion put a letter of judgement for the petition of mercy filed by Colony Studium's New-God Alkemy in his hand.

Dervil and Sierra, who had arranged themselves on the left and right of Lon were floundering on all four sides so that the beggar's falcon bird that secretly destroyed the enemies could not come anywhere around him. Benedict, Malachi, Luciano, Elvis and all of the other Satanics were patrolling all around this massive wooden castle with the photo of that man given by Moses. On the cottages wobbling with the whacking of the turbulent waves of the sea, Ros' bodyguard Beaumont who was standing behind him said, "I can bet, they cannot find another place better than this to commit suicide." Saying this, he gestured his companion Donny towards an island that looked like a speckle far away in the sea and asked, "Do you know swimming?"

Seated on the topmost position of this assembly of New-Gods that had assembled amidst black clouds, turbulent winds and torrents of whipping rain, Solon removed the *'Eye Crown'* from his head and said quickly, "The reasons for escape presented by Alkemy are considered to be baseless." With Solon***zx***'s dignified voice, even the rain that was raising turbulence got drenched in sweat. "Alkemy's three hours to hand over the charge of Colony Studium to Master Galaxy, starts now." Saying this he set his watch to zero. *(Eye Crown- A crown embedded with cameras in all directions. That gives the facility to see in all directions as a result of being connected with the brain by thin needles.)*

As soon as Solon's words finished, an open cart on which the prisoner was taken to the neck chopping block in times of French power revolution, was requisitioned. When Solon's guards forcefully cast the New-God *'Alkemy'*, who was jumping like a goat in the hands of the butcher, into the cart, the Idiotics seated in the direction of the island screamed as they hurled shoes on him. Pulling the mike-pin from his chest, *'Alkemy'* said in a cool voice, "With the creation of a new history, *'Alkemy'* is presenting the invitation of a grand goodbye party to the both groups, Vio-Crazy and Idiotic New-Gods on my Colony *'Studium'*. Friends, let's meet in thirty minutes."

Every Vio-Crazy New-God favoring Alkemy gave Apotheosis a warning of war by hitting their claws on the chest in a dreadful way. This was the first time in centuries, when Apotheosis had shown the audacity of uprooting and throwing off a New-God himself. "This Apotheosis is weird." Due to the brisk strokes of wind that were blowing off the words, Susan murmured taking her lips near Paras' head. "If the New-Gods want, then they can exterminate numerous planets in their mutual war, yet there is no mediation by Apotheosis. Make use of the *group of gypsies (common people)* as you wish, yet no hesitation. Only that the existence of the colonies in front of the citizens of their toy-planets should be invisible like the *'walnut-crack'*.. And with the mistake in doing that the New-God is uprooted and thrown off…! How strange is this..!" Listening to the complaint trobling the innocent face of the little angel, Paras' face chortled up in mirth. He said, "Don't know what the wounded ego of a great New-God will make him do. Someone's well-being is at stake today."

As if they were standing in the auction of heaven-ticket, the Vio-Crazy New-Gods now got up from their domes and came in the middle. They re-sounded the sky with exclamations like, *'The helpless Lon and his Billion Couple'*. Lon also got up and coming in front of them, he raised his hands in a challenging pose and spoke, "Oh you fools, man is not of some trivial existence. He is omnipotent and we New-Gods are present in this universe to make him realize this possibility hidden within him." Solon also got up and started walking towards Lon.

"No… No.. no.. no…! The creations of frivolous and ordinary humans are being preordained for us New-Gods to just play favorite games only." The Vio-Crazys spoke up in one voice. Before *Lon* who was standing in front of them could respond, it appeared as if suddenly a ghost had run and passed through the middle of his transparent body, and amidst Lon's amazement, his body suddenly started possessing a physical appearance. The Satanics became alert. With Sierra's order given in the micro-walky talky, everyone ran in the direction where in 'Lon' was standing, but Lon had become so excited that without paying attention he continued speaking, "With this attitude of yours, there will be an existence of only one group in the future, the *Off Idiotic Group's.*" As if the flock of the big winged sea bird "Albatross' had got a premonition of fresh meat, flocks had started hovering over the assembly and from that flock suddenly the falcon bird dived towards Lon like a rocket, but when it was about an inch away from his chest, Dervil's bullet shredded it into fragments. Before Lon could understand anything, a person tore open and jumped up on the wooden flooring on which he was standing. By the time Dervil and Moses who were standing the nearest to 'Lon' started running towards him, the New-Gods of both the groups along with each of their commanders-in-chief had now started brawling with hands and feet.

"Getaway, Lon…" Lon's Chairman *'Simbal'* screamed and jumped on Lon, he pushed him far. But he had failed to save himself from the beggar's sharp *cutless whip*. The sharp whip had completed its journey from his head to his foot. The cottages of the wobbling castle started getting demolished one after another and immersing in the watery grave. Lon could be seen getting up as if a big statue was being raised up with big ropes to install it. When he went and bent near Simbal's corpse that had been divided into two parts, every Satanic along with Lon's bodyguards leaped onto the beggar who was coming towards Lon. But before their hope to catch the beggar could be fulfilled, in order to see the weird incident that happened Gosha along with all of Ros' Presidents forgot fighting and watched it shockingly. Lord de Ros' animal that would not do the indolence of even moving without getting his signal, suddenly leaped and swallowed up half the beggar. When Paras, the only one to see the mesmerizing weapon of Solon's eyes hitting Ros' animal pushed aside the crowd and came ahead, the entire wreath of the wobbling castle fell into the watery grave in one stroke.

"Ah… Apotheosis have mercy.. You are fine Lon, isn't it?" Solon, who had reached nearby, said. He was standing floating in the air like Lon and several others. Looking at the New-Gods' bodyguards who were fighting in the water even now, he spoke, "Uhh.. These *'cake fighters'… 'Solon'* flew gesturing Lon to come towards his aircraft in the sky above and so did Lon after tearing apart that animal of Ros.

Moving aside the corpses of the guards of the New-Gods floating in the water to make way, Ros' bodyguard Beaumont said, "I do not like to get soaked in this way at all."

"Me too..." Said the foolish Donny who was swimming beside him and pulled up the one whose head he had squeezed and kept submerged in the water. "Oh.. Forgive me, my Lord." When Lord de Ros' asserting face came out, they turned back with alacrity and started swimming in the opposite direction from the island.

"I do not know anyone else here who has the power to subdue that beast-like creature of Ros." Glaring at Simbal with a fierce look, Lon said further, "That beggar-like person was your agent only. You were the one who killed him so that it could not be proved that you yourself had sent him to kill me."

"Lon, refrain from staying engrossed in this petty little talk. Don't jab the shafts of doubt to Solon who helped you at the cost of hell punishment by pledging his own soul. Anyways, if you feel that the Galaxy L-1 syndicate will not be angered if I reach late, then you are wrong."

"Don't worry Solon, I have forgotten Walk of Life. Now you also uproot and throw off that danger notice hung in your mind, in which it has been written that 'Walk of Life' is your baby. Nobody will be able to prove our involvement in this."

*

On the Principal Thoroughfare Route between West and East Africa

"What are we currently doing here in Africa at the time of crisis?" when Paras asked this, Benedict finally turned the tram running on the highway piercing through the endless fields that seemed endless, towards the Motel at the right hand side. Paras said, "Is the food available here tempting to this extent?" But Ben was not in a talkative mood now. He just kept quiet. "Which of the specialty of Kpenika Lady tempted the Devil to come all the way to Rome?" Susan pulling up the jeans with difficulty on her plump thighs with a hairpin pressed between her lips on the back seat asked in a voice lifting up the anchor of Benedict's silence.

Parking in a disorderly manner, Ben finally spoke up, "Many secret powers are engaged in this universe to show every man in the world his real face in the all powerful form. Of all these mysterious powers that do not get any spare time from the Herculean task of finishing the Devil, there are several such powers that cannot be recognized by the Devil. In comparison to the common cat that usually has thirty-two nerves in the ear, this rare cat, Kpenika Lady having only 'twenty-one' nerves immediately cautions the Devil about the presence of such powers by its capability to hear the world's most mysterious sounds." Saying this, he shook hands with the manager who had come near. In the century where reluctance is declared for spending about thirty minutes without getting abundant entertainment, an extremely hungry nomad had barged all the way into the guest-booth. Benedict told the bearer to give him food.

Susan spoke, "I have seen, many Gardis coming to meet Antonio had kept such strange cats as pets."

Benedict said, "Yes… A separate scripture can be created about its mysteries." he gestured to manager and an attendant brought a gas cylinder from the kitchen as if he was carrying a paper flower and put it.

Keeping the cylinder inside and putting the tram on '*aircraft*' mode Benedict spoke, "In ancient Egypt, the goddess of psychic or supernatural powers, and at one time even worshipped as God, '*Apotheosis*' himself has confirmed that cat to have 'nine' lives." The tram transformed into an aircraft once again after which he landed it on the deck of the specially designed speedy ship with three masts standing on the shores of the Atlantic Ocean. After a safe landing, he took out the gas cylinder and pressed the dust-cap on the top. As if the top part was a lid, the cylinder opened up in two parts from the middle. Opening the lid of the jar that had come out of it, Ben mumbled, "This is one thing that can make Ros victorious even before the war." He alternately jabbed injections on Paras' and Susan's arms. "This vaccine that is ready to go into the market as a successful medicine against death due to lightning, increases the amount of the body's resistance against an attack of pure energy by many times."

"Up to hundred percent?" Paras asked, wrapping a bandage on Susan's hand.

"Yes, so much that it makes the body capable of being a conductor of thousands of mA voltage and delivers the lighting upto the gravity-mid-point in the body via an undiscovered way. Our army, pure energy warriors cannot do any harm to us now."

"Means every strike of a Pure Energy Warrior will keep on making us more powerful instead of killing us?"

"Absolutely..." Ben quickly started climbing towards the S. Station room that was on the upper floor of the airship.

"And what will be our condition after the contact of two opposite charges...?" When Susan, who always thought in the opposite direction, asked this, they had settled down in front of the station room's camera.

"The elements of our body including water are good constituents for conducting electricity. Yet, this vaccine transforms every cell into an energy-carrier. But alas, the effect of this vaccine does not last for more than two days and over-doze is risky." Before the camera's click could ensue, Benedict's phone rang. "This was Dervil's call. He said, "Ros has changed the venue of the meeting. Ros now wants to meet in Alkemy's party on Studium. He said that if we are not there within twenty minutes then this deal to return Antonio and Levi in exchange of his spy Dominic can be postponed."

*

Disconnecting the call, Dervil opened the loudly squeaking door. As if the cloud of sweat had burst, when Glen's face smiled forcefully from behind the specks of sweat, Dervil pulled him and took him into Terror Street.

"An extinguished aura, changed useless DNA, missing brain, half leftover heart.... There is no solution now to acquire his real identity." Checking the thumb of the leg of the beggar's corpse, was lying in the frozen locker, Glen's impetuous sentences were akin to an appeal to quickly be rescued from here.

"It is binding for us to know his real identity, Glen." Standing in a piteous state like a baby bird that could not fly, Glen turned his attention to the *Devil* as he heard this. "Even if you do not give a result that is based on the *Absolute Truth*, I will not do any harm to you, Glen." Becoming a little relaxed with these sweet words of the Devil, Glen opened his suitcase and taking out a device like a *'small-hand-pasta'* machine having a needle below it, he kept it on the beggar's stomach. He stopped at the specific changes observed in the lines similar to heartbeats on the screen. After about seventy seconds of beginning to turn the handle of the device, Glen again reached near the thumb of the corpse's left leg and started pressing the thumb. Finally he took out a cutter from the bag and cutting off the thumb, he pulled out a chip as small as the eye of *Madam Berthe's* mouse lemur from the flesh below the thumb and inserted it in the device. He spoke after some time, "Channel S. prepares a totally new *'Universal Identity Token'* every year for the agents of a high stature doing espionage work on the world panel. Through such a token present in the form of this skin-chip, he can confidentially travel, do financial transactions and communicate in any planet of any colony. There are only three such machines in the world that can read this chip. This is one of them. This chip has to say that he is Solon***zx***'s special secret agent *Keskin.*"

"Solon has betrayed his special friend, Lon. And this much proof is enough in order to rouse Lon's anger and instigate him to burn the pyre of Ros and the eleven colonies of his comrades through that anger." Saying this, Sierra took the chip and that small device and kept it in a bag.

*

When Susan stepped out of the S. Station established on the terrace of two hundred and fifty storied tall building in one of the cities of *'Infiltam'* expecting to see a grand farewell ceremony of New-God *'Alkemy'* who had been uprooted and thrown off, she felt as if the entire universe was whirling. The holocaust of images of mass destruction was still squandering more and more cinders all around as if the humongous havoc of the city was not enough to douse the fire of Alkemy's revenge. *(Infiltam – A vast country of planet Opdrazen of Alkemy's Colony Studium)*

They sat in a small shuttle waiting near S. Station and reached the *Titanium Flooring* erected a little away in half a square km. It had been arranged in the sky above the city in such a way that one could precisely enjoy watching the city being ruined. Upset with the machines that kept it suspended in the air, the *'Titanium Flooring'* was wavering from here to there. Most of the Idiotic New-Gods had already left. Spread all around with the huge convoys of their own armies, the Vio-Crazy New-Gods were enjoying the fun of the annihilation of destruction. Standing in front of almost five hundred Energy Warriors, when the Devil sent off *Lord de Ros'* special secret agent Dominic, *Ros* who was standing about fifty feet away exactly opposite pushed Antonio and Levi towards the Devil from there. When they reached close to one another, they checked each other's aura through the aura-identifying machine and confirmed that they were actually Dominic, Levi and Antonio. The guests were now waiting with interest for the beginning of the turbulent hustle and bustle between the huge *'Devil Family'* mafia gang of Galaxy L3 and Ros' Gardi soldiers. More than three hundred aircrafts of the Energy Warriors and the Gardi soldiers stood barricading in the sky above the flooring.

"So these ungrateful *'Chairmen'* are swaying in the intoxicating dream of becoming *New-Gods*…!" The Devil spoke looking at the Chairmen standing abreast Lord de Ros, "Fools, Ros will never let you become New-Gods.

After using you in this war against the Devil Family, his strategy is to usurp all ten of your colonies by exchanging all ten of your imprisoned New-Gods with the bodies of his loyalists using the Mummy Ointment. And after that consider yourself fortunate even if *'hell'* comes in your fate."

"Hahaha… Ros said laughing, "Friends, it appears that the Devil is getting scared of the war!"

"Frrright...! Hmm, the infinite armies of all your eleven colonies put together, and the countless Energy Warriors fighting against them… Lon's infinite Warlords giving them support. The entire planetary area getting inundated with the carcasses, ghosts and ship wrecks, Ahh... Swear on the God of Devastation, what else can be more captivating than that?" As Devil gave a squelching response to Ros with his unique smile, Alkemy's special war-ship *'Bir-Sinif'* was seen coming. Looking like a high magnitude hell-messenger, *Alkemy* came out of the airship and rode towards them on a *'fly-bike'*. He tied the floor on which they were standing behind his airship and took them towards a new area of the city. One thousand and five hundred feet below the flooring, a modern looking city representing a *'brand of futurism'* had accepted defeat against the sudden alien attack. Citizens raising turmoil with the intention of escaping as far as possible, the soldiers of Infiltam army counter attacking Alkemy's war-crafts with supersonic missiles and the uproar arising from the echoing Emergency Alert System sirens from all directions were reaching up to the ears of Susan, the bearer of a kind conscience and were transforming into one word only *'helplessness'*.

Benedict said sighing, "Something is about to happen which is similar to support wars that would bring a result even worse than the situation of women selling their bodies for a one-time meal."

Today being merry-making in Infiltam, all the citizens were dressed in an attire accepting the elementary responsibility of bewitching. Acid rain that could melt even metal was showered on the citizens forcefully gathered in the ground situated right in the center of the city through a cargo plane. Going in front of the *'Devil'* who was enjoying silently, Susan said looking with eyes signifying her readiness to fall on the knees, "Before Alkemy's ruined oath proceeds further, if he can be stopped…?"

The Devil told Susan who was talking directly to him for the first time, "When you are telling even a small lie, you are voting for the Devilish power that is there in this world. What can you give me in this deal that will make me weak by stopping the great man Alkemy?" Susan closed her eyes but the view was not going to transition itself.

The new afflicting-presentations of *'Alkemy'* who had awarded eight medals to the Vio-Crazy group were ready. Citizens kept ready with tied hands and feet were thrown down from the terrace of the tall buildings. This was the end of the world for them. The painful screams were such fierce that it seemed as if the sky wanted to accommodate them and escape. The dams on all the rivers of the great country *'Infiltam'* having a massive geographic area had been broken. "Long live Alkemy, live…" The guests were screaming to provoke Alkemy. Fed-up with the small scale destruction, Alkemy had now given an indication of a large nuclear explosion with the purpose of total devastation. But the other *'New-Gods'* provoking his brutishness in the loudspeaker had not run throwing the mikes and trotted in the direction of their own shuttles to escape because the siren of the nuclear explosion had started…

Amidst the murkiness that was rising up to meet the sky, the unfortunate ones who had missed out on seeing the three luminous lines of light coming towards the *'flooring'* were stuck there even now in the manner that could make the donkey feel intelligent. Director *'Apotheosis'* of the Master Galaxy, the personal appearance of whom the *'New-Gods'* of Lon's level would strive for, had come there himself.

"Honestly, Alkemy! Your audacity is liable to make me flatter you like a slave till the end of my life." Ahh… His melodious chattering was enough to instigate all the musical instruments of the world to renounce in exchange of listening to one sentence. "If you would have done this while holding the New-God's position, then it would have been alright. But when I have removed you, then this deed of yours gives me a direct challenge." Everyone including the New-Gods stood with heads bowing down like *'obligatorily purchased slaves'* in front of him. The imagination of each one of them including the New-Gods that Apotheosis would have a monstrous personality, had now dumbfounded them. Because *'Apotheosis'*, having a face like a teenager over which innocence had not yet stopped reveling, did not even have any kind of a clothing-dash around him. Alkemy's biggest trouble was to miss out on the opportunity to commit suicide. But now it was too late. Apotheosis moved away from him and went to Susan. Susan felt as if the drums of her heartbeats will tear open the walls of her heart.

Beaumont said to Donny standing on Ros' right side, "Who is that idiot declaring this child to be an emperor of three galaxies including half the *Master-Galaxy*?" Moving around Susan with slow steps amidst the crowd of Satanics leisurely smelling the scent of her aura liquid, Apotheosis finally proceeded towards Paras.

Ros looked back and raised his eyebrows, yet Donny said to Beaumont, "One day the person who has the courage to make the secret of this *'King of the Universe'* available as cheap as the chickpea seller, might also be Aptheosis himself."

"Means?"

"It means that, didn't you notice that before Apotheosis popped-up, no one has even sensed when, from where, how the Devil disappeared. Actually, the Devil himself is Apotheosis…." Ssh.. ssh.. ssh…. Ros raised his eyebrows and Donny kept quiet.

Both the girls who had come with Apotheosis were dressed in gorgeous garments styled like South Sumatra's traditional wedding clothes. Looking like crooked coquettes, both the girls were wandering all around smelling the aura scent of every individual along with that of Apotheosis.

"Idiot… Look at his ear." When Apotheosis, who had stepped forward and stood facing Paras took out the packet of cigarettes from Paras' pocket, Susan gestured to him with the eyes.

"What is it?" As Paras still puffing the cigarette asked uneasily with his eyes, Susan pressed her earrings and gestured towards Apotheosis. In the third second after having looked towards the key hanging in the form of an earring on Apotheosis' ear, Paras remembered which charismatic personality he was standing in front of. Quavering, he instantly threw off the cigarette and taking out the lighter with a trembling hand, he lit the cigarette for Apotheosis.

Throwing of the remaining cigarettes and playing with the empty box, he walked towards Alkemy. Continuing to watch Susan jealously glaring at the girls who had come with him as if she was seeing a *sauten (another lady in the life of one's partner)* with a slanted gaze, Apotheosis went near Alkemy's nose and started rubbing fingers filled with affection on his eyebrows.

In the beginning phase of a second… He made Alkemy as small as a peanut with the use of some private monopoly science and trapping him in the box of cigarette, he immediately stomped his right foot on the flooring in the middle fraction of the second and in the last fraction of the same second he picked up Susan standing among the Satanics and flew off. Susan could be seen being dragged behind a brilliant lightning that took place in the sky in the very next instant.

Of the guests falling down with the fragments of the Titanium Floor, Paras was the first one to fly with the help of wings and before he could experience more helplessness, astonishingly, Susan was seen falling down. Before Paras flying towards Susan could save her from crashing down, Lord de Ros rushing to capture Levi bumped into him with a bang. When Susan's wings suddenly started working again, death and the statue of Infiltam's garden were about three inches away from her.

"Why is he capturing Levi once again?" Sierra mumbled, staring with narrowed eyes. Her eyes suddenly shone up. "Ohh Devil... Why did this not occur to us earlier..!" Saying this she flew towards Dominic who was about to get into the shuttle. "They are going to the *Raag* Lake." She screamed to Dervil while catching Dominic from the neck.

"Now what is this Raag Lake?" Paras asked, flying behind Antonio"

"There are rumors that out of the two sides participating in the war, whoever gives the sacrifice of a big spy from the rival side in this Raag Lake earlier than his opponent, the Goddess of War becomes benignant on him. His victory almost becomes inevitable."

"Run... Be quick you war-vandals... I will pull apart the skin of each one of you if the Gardis reach the Raag Lake first." Dervil roared in an authoritative voice and a competition to reach Raag Lake first, started in the sky between the shuttles of the Satanics and Lord de Ros. The shuttles of the Satanics and the Gardis were flying side by side on the elevated celestial highway. Looking at the speed at which they were firing *'air to air'* hell-fire, it was as if a miraculous fate would be required for even one of the *'aircrafts'* to reach the destination. Finally, following *Benedict's* objection Dervil retreated and changed his path.

*

The *'Highland Mountain'* having height equal to three times the Himalayas was located on an aerial island two hundred thousand miles away from Infiltam. Today after a long time, the *'Raag Lake'* encompassed in the lap of Highland's topmost peak had started spreading vocal melody to welcome some new guests. The shuttles of both the sides landed quietly without making any kind of noise or clamor on the small snow-covered mountain ranges surrounding the Raag Lake on all four sides. That was because no one intended to invite the wrath of the War-Goddess by conducting violence in this area. From the parked shuttles, the Satanics and Ros' Gardis flew towards the shores fluttering their wings like a torrent of frogs. Far away, in between such a war-weapon restricted Raag Lake where a sculpture showing a sword to the sky was emerging, massive boats with oars were plunged down in that lake. The competition to reach up to the sword for giving the sacrifice started before those boats could utter the warning of sinking as a result of taking more weight than their capacity. The boats of the Satanics and the Gardis were sailing exactly side by side in a row. How can it be that seeing Ros himself propelling the oars, Dervil would not pick up and throw one of the Satanics to one side and start attacking the water with the oars as if it was Ros' head. Colliding with rocks hidden behind the moist fog of the lake, several boats were turning upside down.

"For a moment I felt as if I would never see you again..!" Paras said looking into Susan's eyes. They had to travel up to the Raag Lake in different shuttles. Now they had finally got an opportunity to talk after settling down in one of the several boats of the Satanics with Antonio and Benedict. "But how did you escape from his hands?"

"That bastard Apotheosis pulled out my Gizmo-Belt and threw me down."

Paras retorted, "I don't understand what mysteries are involved in the life of the incomparable woman sitting in front of me that the supreme dictator of the corporeal world would be inspired to do such a deed?"

"Ssh.. ssh.. ssh…" Susan put a finger on her lips and gestured towards the cyclical waves rising up towards the western coast, from where the sobs of the '*war-maiden*' could be heard now. The estimate of the hint of the gruesomeness of the war given by the Raag lake that could be assessed from the tranquility spread despite the presence of many cruel and wild personalities, breaking that silence and propelling the oars with ease, Paras said speaking loudly, "What kind of a sorrowful voice collection is this that shreds the heart into bits? The night is just about to arrive, and the bell of the music school of some ingenious daemons under the sea has not rung yet or what?"

"You cannot see more misfortune than this anywhere else." In the chill, enough to convert the man into an ice statue, *Antonio's* trembling lips said, "Raag Lake is the soul of two such unfortunate lovers who were separated through deception by some barbaric forces. This incident happened long back in the century of fighting with stony uncouth weapons. After creating a delusion making both of them experience the most deadly feelıng like *'He does not love you'* and *'She does not love you'* through deceit. And after that, using the force of destruction rising from their broken hearts..." Before Antonio's monologue could continue, the melody of the holy-mourning was heard again from the lake...

Listen O sailor... When the love brought melody from their Soul, heavens did my slavery....

When it made my Soul colorless from the colors of its love... All the heavens in the universe by doing ruined, Could not make me laugh for a moment...

Kill my waiting O sailor... The waiting does not kill O sailor... kill the waiting O sailor..."

The sword now being close in the lake where the sacrifice had to be given, accompanying the zigzag track of the mountains and expanding to an unknown destination in the world, Ros spoke with the intention of distracting the attention of the Satanics, "Luciano, would you open a ticket window to publish the name of that treacherous inside enemy or what? The one who delivered the Tie-in Tune to me so that Antonio could not imprison me at that time…"

"Forgive me but I cannot say that Lord de Ros is a liar." Luciano spoke. "Yes it was Daarck himself who ordered that I surreptitiously deliver the Tie-in Tune to Ros."

"Hahaha.. And when the helpless Antonio who had come to imprison me, returned with empty hands, *'Daarck'* must have taken off the burden from his chest with an aggrieved heart."

"But why?" Antonio almost screamed.

"Only Daarck would know that. My position did not permit me to question Daarck." As Luciano spoke, Ros swiftly turned his head and hitting *'Dervil'* on the nose with the oar, he caught *'Levi'* and plunged into the water with a swoop. The sculpture with the stone hand was about one floor tall. Dragging Levi, Ros started climbing to reach up to the sword that was at the top of the sculpture. Since any kind of devices were prohibited, it was not even possible to make use of wings. The very powerful Dervil caught Dominic's neck and jumped into the water, but he was very late as compared to Ros. With Sierra's orders, many Satanics shirking with fear emptied all their pure energy on Ros and Dervil got an opportunity to go ahead. When Ros' body dispersed like a swarm of bees with the strike of Pure Energy started binding together again, the rhythmically rising intolerable lake water slowly rippled up and swallowing the two rule breaking Satanics in its depths forever, it again started narrating short poems at the speed of a blast in tears.

Standing in the style of a weight lifter with Dominic lifted in his hand Dervil finally pushed him down upto the sword's knob at the blow of the hammer. As soon as the drops of the struggling Dominic's blood met it, the periphery of the water ripples of the lake from which the screams of a witch with jingling bangles started coming out, kept on infinitely increasing louder and louder.

"Our defeat in this war is certain… Ros is useless…" As the reproach by the Chairmen of Ros' ally colonies started pouring in the doubt of the outcome of defeat, Ros bellowed like a flash of lightning to shut the mouths of those reproofs: "Utter nonsense… Ridiculous beliefs… Ros has followed this absurd legend only to please his comrades. If Cons Lydia would be fighting alone in this great-war, then I would have gone ahead and handed over my spy Dominic to the Devil myself." His loud voice failed to hide the trembling arising from fear. "Fierce intentions win wars, my friends! Not the blessings of some sad-singers who have become a lake."

"Why don't you trust the wretched Ros..?" Dervil spoke copying Ros' voice exactly like a lyre bird.

Enduring the trenchant defeat, Ros turned the boat and his face towards the shore, yet the verbal-slap of Dervil swirling near the sword, reached his cheeks- "Consider this war with the leadership of a boar gone from your hands."

*

They had already reached *Daddy's Woolybear* the biggest space-craft of Galaxy L3 to use the Discovery Copperhorse on Paras and Susan. Paras and Susan were getting more and more restless to the point of intolerance, as the moment of cracking the secret of why Filipa would have assassinated Daarck, came closer and closer. "Why don't we go there flying?" Paras asked while coming out from the S. Station and walking towards the railway leading to Lon's office, and taking him near the left side elevation, Ben gestured towards the open sky.

"Ohh…" All the air-routes were jam-packed with flying saucers, private jeplins and the Woolybear residents flying with wings. "Today a festival is being celebrated on Woolybear." Benedict spoke.

Reluctantly getting into the train to Lon's office, Susan said, "Antonio, now when that secret that Daarck was going to imprison the Devil with Devilet and was also going to kill you is not a secret any more, then what about our safety after we hnd over the Re-built Tune and the Project Discs? And especially what about Filipa's that is my safety?"

Antonio looked at Susan with a serious countenance but did not say anything.

After the independent-computer-operated train running amidst the decorated high-rise buildings, slowly started gaining speed, Paras said, "I have a suggestion." But before he could speak further, Susan drew his attention towards the train's window. After seeing several illuminated advertisements of Wanted *'Boy Friend' 'Girl*

Friend' shining outside the restaurants and malls, when he said very gently glaring at the compartment's ceiling, Antonio said, "Don't worry. The transponder signal conveys the location of every single moment of Woolybear's guests up to the *'Defense Booths'* but never any conversations taking place between them."

"I'll clarify that Susan and I want *Colony Runcap.*" *(A Vio-Crazy Colony located in the Gamma area of Galaxy L3)* He said, "We should now proceed further only after executing the Menithus Agreement related to that matter of which colony will come in whose share."

"It will be done in that way only." Benedict replied in brief.

As the train again entered the area with modern buildings like that of the next-generation, an announcement was made for their station. Getting down behind Benedict, Paras asked, "Shall we win this war because we succeeded in Raag Lake, even if Lon refuses to support us?"

Looking in the front in a strange way, Ben retorted, "If I would try to explain in which way these mysterious powers function your mind be blown away like vapor. Anyways, the Raag Lake problem has actually been resolved. I am worried about the Hoodoo-Eye."

"Hoodoo-Eye?"

"Yes it is an unlucky eye. The glance of which falling on the rival army, renders that army useless. And right at this moment, *'Almuro'* the Chief of the Secret Society has reached Mahanabh to strike a deal of the Hoodoo-Eye. This deal should not materialize."

*

Mahanabh Mountain

"You will not even have an idea of when this great-war demanding a great effort was won. Guarantee…" Taking the rolled 'Menithus' from the manager on his left, the Secret Society Chief 'Almuro' opened it and laughing, he gave the 'Lazo' and Menithus Agreement to Ros. {*Lazo - A pen that keeps the live aura-identity of the signee connected during the signing with the Menithus office of the Master Galaxy through the S. Station medium.*}

As Ros continued to read the details described in the Menithus his eyes widened. Finally, *Ros* who was seated on a throne like the diamond embedded royal seat constructed by Samrat Ashok in the third Centenary Before Christ, loosely threw the glass of *Shorba (Meat juice)* on Almuro's face. "Five of my precious planets in exchange of one Hoodoo-Eye..? Fool, have you realized now how under graded your weightage is…? Right now my Gardis don't even have the time required to push someone out. Get out from here."

Grasping Almuro's arm as he was about to respond to Ros, Arina pushed him out and said- "Even a single word will allure your own premature death."

As Almuro looked down and went out quietly, Ros spoke, "Such farces of circumstances have now started, those who did not have the courage to breathe aloud in the presence of Lord de Ros, they are now raising their heads and negotiating the quantity..! Come with me." Ros got up like an arrogant mountain and with him, even the *'Chairmen'* of the remaining ten colonies who were conceiving the dream of becoming New-Gods.

When they reached amidst the self-motivated walls that identified the requirement and accordingly unfolded the protective spells on its surface, *'Painter'* the Chairman of Colony Runcap ejaculated, "Awesome. A lot has been heard about this..!"

"Yes, this is it, invaluable walls having *invisible crayons (colorful sticks).*" Ros said.

"How weirdly Apotheosis was staring at that girl Susan, isn't it?" Arina said avoiding the instinctive female envy from her voice.

Ros responded enthusiastically in an enhanced voice as if the trend of discussion had diverted in a favorite direction- "Probably Apotheosis must have observed in that girl Susan, some resemblance to the characteristics of that fugitive woman, whom he was madly searching for quite a long time." Huge staircases of brown stones left them after taking them to the Western doorway and they had started a journey on foot to reach the formal S. Station constructed on another peak across the valley. As they just moved a little further, the soft voice of the light-lady originating from Mahanabh's local area network was heard- "Cocksure confirmation"

"Before Lon could decide whether to give support to the Devil Family or not, we would have demolished a large part of the Devil's asteroids and Energy Warriors." Ros said and turning towards the light-lady, he asked, "Capacity?" *(Ros' meaning was how much power from the total power of the armies of their eleven colonies put together)*

"Twenty-two percent…"

"Weapon delivery system..?"

"Win Maker and Fifty Carats" *(Win Maker – Colony Nebel Shift's army. Fifty Carats- Colony Run-Cap's army.)*

"Contact timing?" *(Within how much time will it reach the targets that have to be destroyed?)*

"Local time 1.49 minutes… From target Zero One to Zero Twenty-one. Total twenty-one on *Pendigyura* asteroid... *(Pendigyura – A devilish asteroid)*

"Lead?" *(How much additional counts of Win-Makers and Fifty-Carats against Devil's Energy Warriors)*

"Thirty-five percent..."

Finally Ros signaled clearance and with that, the light-lady started a video broadcast out there yelling, "Activate mission *'Candy-dead' (sweet death)*". In the video, *'fifty thousand'* light-years away from the Solar system, on Division HNR, the senior commander of Colony Runcap's army base S. Station number five was showing the green flag to proceed with the attack. War-crafts were arranging themselves in Colony Runcap's army base S. Stations having the capacity to send thousands of jumbo aircrafts together at once anywhere in the world. Hundreds of thousands of *Fifty Carats'* soldiers were arranging themselves with the emergency of fire-fighters on the conveyor belt to reach this huge S. Station. Finally

Ros gave a voice command to shut the video as he turned towards Gosha and spoke, "Gosha, I don't want that even a single Satanic civilian should be spared. And there should be least possible damage of valuable Satanic planets."

"Who is the woman whom like Apotheosis is searching?" Before Arina could succeed in starting the previous round of discussion, *Dustin* the Chairman of Nebel Shift who was walking behind the crowd, ran and came forward. He said, "We will get a running commentary of what the Satanics are doing on Lon's Woolybear within a short time. From an old spy of Malesty.. Who is spying on Lon..."

Ros dismissed the envy of Nebel Shift's New-God Malesty's espionage network thinking that he himself would become the owner of all ten colonies including *'Nebel Shift'* within a few days.

"Who went missing and made Apotheosis mad?" Arina asked again.

Ros spoke, "Gosha, call back *Caprio's* bagman. He shall be landed on a formal S. Station. *(Caprio – Dealer of weapons)* And turning his head towards Arina, he said, "Yes that *'sweet lass' (young woman)*, who as an ambulation of love put her ear on Apotheosis' heart and heard all the secrets of his inner-self. That young lady whose audacity called both top personalities Director Apotheosis and Director Prestige, who were like great comrades, together and threateningly ordered both to accept her dual *'love'* or kill her. She had compared forgetting the *'love'* of even one from amongst both the *contrasting* personalities to a lion-deer friendship for her. And for the first time that most beautiful woman in the universe, persuaded both the Directors together and in a way acquired the authority of the entire *Master Galaxy*."

"How much age of this story? Did that troublesome girl deceive our Director Apotheosis and go to Director Prestige's account or what? What is the mystery of the key hanging in Apotheosis' ear?"

Taking into consideration the deadly patience of the listeners, Ros now started speaking quickly along with his quick steps, "This was that non-trivial mishap as a result of which both the Directors together put a restriction on women's *'Chairwomanship'*. I was also there in that *'Manner of Governing' (Manner of Governing – A treat given every three years by the Director for the 'New-Gods' and Chairmen of all the colonies within their limits)* The party was almost over. Most of the *'New-Gods'* had already left. Some of us extremely intoxicated ones were fooling around with a Bimbo tail piece when suddenly subject to the temptation that could not be killed even with strangulation, Director Prestige came there. He had come there pursuing this elite woman *'Mithalia'* with the sprint of the *'Sport Spring Interactive Carnival'*. On any other occasion where a lethal conflict would start, the authority of even a small move was now in the hands of that ravishing beauty Mithalia. The mystery whether this incident was a pre-planned conspiracy or a quirk of fate was an ode will be known when the girl would come in their hands again. But the real ploy started now, after making our Director love-struck with her captivating eyes…

For a few days, she would stay with Prestige and for some days with Apotheosis. The Directors were helpless in front of such behavior of Mithalia due to her beauty. After some time, both the Directors got an envelope as soon as they opened their eyes one morning. There was this key in the envelope that is currently hanging on the Director's ear. A key, who revealing the secret of death of the opponent. A similar key is also there with 'Prestige'. It was written in that letter that- "I can no longer tolerate the loathsome prose which my splendid beauty and even greater than that my 'personality' creates for me, after the ebbing of this 'tweeny-love'. After one of you is proved to be the 'best' through destiny, I will get freedom from this binary-love and one of you will get the entire Master-Galaxy."

"But what such challenge was given to both the Directors in that letter…?" Arina asked, picking up her *'Belly-Misty' sisters (twin cats)* walking at the risky edge, in both her hands.

"The challenge was to deliver the key to *'Anjeolmac'* hidden on one of the thousands of our planets shared by both the Directors. The name of that planet also was given. Where, the secret of death of both the Directors was hidden. Anjeolmac, where this mischievous girl had hidden both the *Directors'* acquired secret of death and proved herself to be the best. *(Anjeolmac – The key melts after inserting that metallic key developed with a specific pattern in the key-hole. And after that, a disposable messaging box delivering the information upto the brain through the medium of the eyes.)*

"Both the Directors now have to reach *'Anjeolmac'* before their opponent to be safe from death, and three prizes in his sack- total submission of that amazing woman, the remaining three galaxies and an immortal life."

"What was the reason with the Directors to believe that woman Mithalia's tale to be true?" Dustin asked when the Station Chief opened the gate.

"Several such facts about the secrets of Apotheosis' and Prestige's powers had been written in the envelope by Mithalia that there was no question of not believing the rest of the topics of that woman. Some crazy *'New-Gods'* on Galaxy L-1 hired outstanding *'Swagmen'* in the world and participated in the race to acquire this Anjeolmac. Hahaha.. Does the world actually give birth to such crazy people and experience blessedness." When Ros finished talking, Caprio's bagman had opened the suitcase and started the projector.

"Show us some such thing that will shorten the life of the accursed war." Ros said, prying at the man who had accompanied the bagman with x-ray eyes.

Gesturing towards the video projected in the front, the bagman said, "This is IBCM-48, the latest weapon having the capacity to do a small super-nova sized blast. The ultra-modern orbital bombardment system… Hundred percent failureless radar protecting fixture... Autonomous guidance system… Easy launch platform…"

"May I smoke?" Before the bagman could start a slide of new weapons in the projector, his weird companion asked showing a cigarette to Ros.

"Yes." Ros had given a monosyllabic response and diverted his attention, but Arina kept watching the robot-human-bomber made of explosive bones and flesh lighting a cigarette between his lips.

"Eeeee….." Noticing that fire turning to ashes within a second, running from one end of the cigarette to the other, the screaming Arena directly leaped behind Ros' huge body. After the blast, the star filled sky could now be seen in place of the five feet strong walls of the S. Station's Alcove House.

As if haunted by the two Chairmen having made the mistake of believing Mahanabh to be safe and who were now roaming spirits without the Gizmo-Belt, Arina's cell phone that was smeared with ashes rang up, "It's Benedict…" Arina gave the phone to *'Ros'* with a frightened face.

"Accept the first compliments of war, my Lord..! Hello..? Hahaha…." Giving the phone back to Paras, Benedict extended his hand towards the W*arlord* who had come to take them. *(Warlord- The special army of Glee Metal Casting's New-God Lon)*

*

"Forgive me, I am a little late. This way please." Paras felt a little ashamed looking at the Warlord who had come to receive them at the railway station. He had worn exactly the same kind of suit as Paras. Amongst the small crowd quickly proceeding towards Lon's office behind Paras, Susan said, "Isn't it an overconfidence of our great host Lon? All nuclear commands, space-aerospace commands, defense air-force commands, control stations of the light globes as well as the residences of many Chairmen in one single craft…?"

"Despite that, we are worried." The Warlord spoke. "Why have we been still deprived of the challenge of demolishing a lonely shuttle floating in the sky and winning over *Glee Metal Casting*…!" Listening to his proud voice, Susan walking behind his back laughed and winked at Paras. A fragrant drizzle of ice was showering on all four sides. All the bars located on the ground floors of the crowded buildings were jam-packed. A calm music was flowing out from the speakers placed at frequent on the road. Their desire to *'walk'* along the edge of the footpath to extend a little more immediately came to an end with a turn.

As they reached a chamber on the one hundredth and forty-sixth floor, Dervil was giving a bouquet to Lon who had arrived a few seconds earlier.

"Shall we start?" With a slanted glance towards the Devil, Lon raised a hand in the direction of the Discovery Copperhorse Engine that was lying in a corner. His overcoat was gliding like the waves of the ocean. Paras and Susan were seated on the seat of that Copperhorse Engine that looked like a very big Mimeograph machine, but before the operator could thrust needles in their throats, Lon spoke up. "*Ruhan*, I am afraid this machine will make the folly of supplying an automatically modified content to the code structure. I think that the Copperhorse Engine moved on *number two (the previous version)* is drawing special attention for credibility. *(Ruhan – A Chairman of Lon)*

"That's better." Saying this, Ruhan made them stand up and without waiting, started a flag-march behind Lon.

"Lon, even after crashing the codes securing the hidden information of Daarck's mind, you are to get the confidential memories of Daarck that you want to know of, in the form of a private language only." The clapper in between the Devil's lips started ringing bells of the words. "Then this machine is just right."

Lon did not respond and got into the lift. After coming down, they entered a bar having a *Bull's Head* title on the opposite side of the building. Getting attracted to the scent of chilled wine that was more attractive than the thrilling past to be acquired after a few minutes, Paras pretended to feel giddy and seated himself on the counter.

"Are you fine?" Antonio asked.

"Yes.. But I think I will not be able to stand." Sitting catching hold of his temple, Paras picked up three glasses of wine from the tray that was getting ready and emptied them.

"What the hell are you doing? You are supposed to stay away from these things until the Discovery Copperhorse is applied." Ben said and holding his hand, pushed him behind the queue that had gone quite ahead.

"What shall I do, stress is strangling my throat."

As the back door of the bar opened up to a big garden, the sound of a *drone* bringing the *'Copperhorse Engine'* could be heard from the nearby sky. *(Drone- A small aircraft without a pilot)* Paras and Susan were attached with the chip-in connection to the plate of the Copperhorse Engine like an indivisible part of the drone. After that, a big urn of glass was overlaid on them. Instantly memories of every single minute of the last two births started transferring from the human souls like billions of infinite memory accumulators in their current mind. And with that a race also started between every heartbeat of those standing there. Looking at their faces, it was difficult to ascertain in which of the two states they were in, whether consciousness or a dream.

† This was now Daarck. The way the newly acquired identity during the years spent with a lost memory have no importance whatsoever when the memory returns, similarly Paras and his entire life performance got submerged in Daarck. Instantly the appearance of the shine that was there in his eyes, changed. The facial expressions transformed. Styles changed. First of all he looked at the Devil. After that towards 'Lon' and finally groping to find Susan in Filipa's face, even this much purring of Daarck was done with difficulty. "For what Filipa….?"

Divided in a deadly confusion similar to a do or die situation, Filipa spoke, "Background of unimagnizable mysteries, in which even evil is included, there was only one way take 'Daarck' who had such a past, far away... the path of death. Dark-magic had already captivated my heart at first sight itself. But I had complete trust that my affection towards him that limited the world could not even take pleasure in the sacrifice of one of his dangerous wishes. It is not easy to change someone's basic nature. And that of a Satanic like you… Unachievable… If I would have wished, I could have waited till your rebirth, but I accompanied even in death."

Even though Daarck's name opening the list of betrayers was pricking him like thorns, Antonio bloomed by the mysteries opening like petals of flowers from Filipa alias Susan, said, "But for what did you do all this, Filipa…?"

The kind woman was missing. This new incarnation of headiness, arrogance and if required, one that went down to the point of violence for a desired thing, said removing the overcoat and taking it in her hand, "Daarck, you are not going to be able to easily remember that evening of that turning point. I surreptitiously reached our Canopy's resort to give the good news that my tour of *Zestlit* has been postponed by one night. I open the door with my key and enter to see that your God *'Devil'* has come to meet you. On hearing for what horrible vested selfishness you and the Devil created the Walk of Life by beguiling Lon, Solon and all eleven Chairmen, the floor slips beneath my feet. It was good that you had taught me that private language being used between you and the Devil, otherwise what would have happened to those billions of helpless humans, for saving whose lives Walk of Life has been created." The Devil's eyes were now communicating disapproval to *'Daarck'* but Filipa's speech had grasped the focus of attention of the others.

"What kind of a vested selfishness Filipa?" Lon asked.

"Ah… Lon!" Daarck spoke, "Filipa has made a mistake in understanding. She has perceived a completely different meaning about the plan to avail the help of the Devil Family. Stop it Filipa." Saying this Daarck slipped close to her and going near her ear, said, "I will tell you everything truly but don't say this now. Everything will be ruined."

"When the 'Messiah' who had set out to make Galaxy L3 heaven suddenly takes the form of a Satanic, then you cannot blame that girl for doing this, the girl who trusted that Messiah with her heart and was congruent with his soul." Filipa said.

"Enough… this is too much now." The Devil spoke, "Someone stop the nonsense of this amusement bullet of men, or else the sleep of the real Devil will be broken."

"Or maybe you are a spy of the eleven *'New-Gods'* against whom the Walk of Life conspiracy had been done? Whose mission to take the Project-discs and eliminate *'Daarck'* becomes successful..." Dervil roared.

"Antonio your daughter actually turned out to be your father. Haha.." Sierra spoke up.

*

At the same time on the Devilish asteroid 'Pendigyura 06'

A strange person was hurriedly moving ahead on the way to S. Station number T-7 of Pendigyura 06 by pushing aside a crowd of ghost-seekers roaming on the street with discipline as if they were the students of some mysterious Voodoo school. There are no tall buildings on the street. The lanes are narrow. The shops don't open on the street. The face of most of the market's crowd is covered behind a black veil. Every Satanic spends the time spared from the rapid completion of daily transactions of employment in the secret activities to achieve new powers and immortal life. No one is even willing to make the necessary communication.

The second lieutenant of this army base S. Station number seven that had the capacity to send the aircrafts, energy warriors and all the material of war arranged in the three kilometer sized huge hall together on any Galaxy in the world at one go, opened the pack of cards and gaily settled down in front of the search-light in-charge on the tall entrance booth of the courtyard. "The new information of our spies is interesting." He said.

The in-charge looked up with sparkling eyes.

"Lord de Ros has executed a Menithus Agreement. According to which there is a possibility that this war can at least be postponed for the next ten years. If the Devil brings to Ros the *'Re-build Tune'* and *'Transmission Germ'*, then in return for that Ros will not attack even a single Devilish asteroid. *(The two things with which Ros was in a position to awaken the ten New-Gods he had imprisoned and giving an aura identical to them to his loyalists, it was possible for him to acquire those ten colonies all together at one go)*

"I am not ready to believe that this chaos will now go into standby mode…" When the in-charge said this, that strange man had reached there.

"Hey.. Hey.. What are you doing up here? How did you come..?" The lieutenant rushed towards him like an angry bull. "Do you have the clearance to come on this level?"

In response, he smiled at the *'Lieutenant'* and leaped into the internal part of the yard from the three hundred feet high booth, "This is a *Fifty Carat.*" *(An army soldier of the Runcap Colony having the characteristic of transforming into a body of glass)* As the lieutenant said this in the walky-talky, all the radio signals of Pendigyura had been jumbled up by the chemical blast. His body getting shattered into pieces with the bullets pouring from all four sides and the attack of pure energy was getting connected again within a short time. His glass body had to suffer the acute pain of the re-generating sessions six times as his glass body scattered during the successful entry of the ten- digit code on the key-pad near the nuclear resistant door of the army S. Station as wide as a massive ocean bed located across the sector.

As soon as the half km. long gate of the station opened, the Satanic Warriors fired a net to catch this weird thing that could not be killed but alas before getting caught, that Fifty Carat soldier had seen the view of the missile coming from the east direction with a sparkle like a *'Little Ghost Nebula' (An atmospheric luminous group roaming in the sky)* and blowing up the station.

*

"What is the actual matter, Filipa?" Lon, Antonio and Benedict spoke up in one voice.

Staring in Daarck's eyes with a glance asking for guarantee to become good person, Filipa finally said in the sixth second, "The actual thing is that I am a culprit of you all. My misunderstanding of considering Daarck to be a real Satanic paralyzed *Walk of Life*."

"Where are the other ten Project Discs, Filipa?" Dervil proceeded further.

"I will give those Project Discs only to Lon. But only after being totally assured that he is not doing all this for his internal selfishness under cover of bringing divine governance." Standing near Elvis, *Filipa's* bloody speech is setting fire even in this extremely cold night of *Trubolt (A weather of Woolybear)*.

"It is now a very far away matter that Filipa gives the Discs and accordingly we prepare armies with ten types of different characteristics and win over those ten colonies." The Devil looked towards Lon and said in a stony voice, "Right now there is only one question as to how to stop Ros who is ready with all eleven colonies together to attack my *'Energy Warriors'*. If he attacks, then Daarck's entire project of Energy Warriors will be ruined."

"It will not happen it's happened." Sierra spoke up. "All finished…." In a mourning style she put her Tolmy on holograph mode and published the video that had come from Pendigyura. This video recorded just an instant before the contact with Pendigyura twenty was lost was making the heart a flambeau. "The armies of Ros' allied colonies have attacked our twenty-two asteroids at a time. This is a hundred percent one sided riot." She said, "And the lead is thirty-five percent. That too, when the Energy Warriors have not been programmed to fight against *'Fifty Carats'* and *'Win Maker'* soldiers… This attack is with the total 22 percent capacity of their entire eleven colonies. It's strange, they had the codes of the total 165 army S. Stations of all the twenty-two Pendigyura asteroids that changed every hour."

"What is strange in that?" Lon said. "There will not be a shortage of traitorous Satanics on Pendigyura who would take the decision of leaving a sinking ship while there is time to escape."

"They have blown off all those S. Stations altogether." Sierra spoke, "It is not possible for even a single Energy Warrior to escape from even one Pendigyura now. They don't have any other way but to face the ocean like massive army and wait to get wiped out. Within the next fourteen minutes, the combined Fifty-Carat and Win-Maker armies would have reached on eleven out of twenty-two asteroids and on the other ten asteroids within the other sixty minutes. There is just one Pendigyura 022 where they can reach in five hours and thirty-two minutes. On which totally forty percent of our Energy Warriors are present." Sierra said glaring at Lon with eyes whether they will get some help or not but Lon's reply of the silence was, "What can be done, you have ended up messing around with such competent people." *(In order to attack in the situation of war, colonies have kept Dummy S. Stations ready around every planets of each of the other colonies so that they can be reached after an air travel of two, four or ten hours. It was going to take five hours and thirty-two minutes for the Win-Maker and Fifty-Carat armies that have descended on the S. Station constructed near Pendigyura 022 to take the war-craft and reach there.)*

"At a distance of five hours from Pendigyura 022 there is an Idiotic Colony *'Antpatic'*, which can give clearance to Lon's Colony Metal Casting's army. In this way, we are in a position to reach Pendigyura thirty minutes earlier than them. This is the one and only way to save almost half of our Energy Warriors." Malachi said wrestling with the keyboard.

"We just can't reach at all." Sierra spoke, "This is One Seventy degrees North, *Bog Down (The area of the Marshland of small asteroids)* Wayland Outer Rim. Even if we calculate the minimum possible time lost by Lon's army in departing from here and descending on Antpatic, we will be thirty minutes late to see the ashes flying on *022*."

"One minute, one minute." Malachi spoke again. "They use Hydrogen Bromide old model war-crafts and their speed is 1.7 million kms per hour. Calculation of the *Galaxy field rotation (Just like the Earth the time difference of two different locations in the Galaxy that rotates on its axis)* and if we add the high-speed of the *Metal Casting's* airship, then we have additional ninety minutes."

"Means the matter can be resolved." Dervil said.

The *Devil* who looked in a compos mentis like even now success cannot evade me, said to Lon. "If you want to take your ally colonies and join with the Devil Family in this war, we are in a position to defeat these eleven colonies easily. After giving one of the eleven colonies to Antonio's group, one to Luciano and one to Daarck, there are still eight of them left. It is not bad to start the heavenly governance with four Vio-Crazy colonies. If the prayers of billions of humans of nearly three hundred planets of these four colonies put together are granted…."

"Huh.... Have you taken the trouble of coming this far to waste Lon's valuable time..?" Lon spoke. "Is Lon mad, make use of such Maneuver? The Devil has forgotten that when any Idiotic Colony will attack any of the Vio-Crazy colonies, the entire Vio-Crazy group is bound to help that victimized colony, such an unalterable contract has been done between them."

Scratching his cheek with a pointed nail, when the Devil finally spoke, *'Kpenica Lady'* who was ambling near Lon's feet became steady and raised her head in an alert stance-
"And if I get the *'Menithus'* signed by Vio-Crazy group leader *'Kaylos'*, in which it is written that not even a single other Vio-Crazy colony will give support to Ros and his ally colonies in this war, no matter how may Idiotic colonies get together and attack them?"

"The preparation of Lon and his ally colonies for war is such that the celestial-body of any corner of Galaxy-L3 would be demolished hundred percent with its content in the fifth hour. But such a *'Menithus Agreement'* signed by Kaylos is nothing more than an imaginative jaunt."

"It is my responsibility to get that. You just be ready with your allies on that planet of *'Antpatic'* that is near Pendigyura. Daarck is coming with me. Dervil, hand over that Orked roll to Daarck. We will send you a copy as soon as Kaylos signs on that Menithus. In this way, before Ros' army reaches, you will be present for the confrontation on Pendigyura 022."

"I do not know how you would get Kaylos' signature on such an agreement, but that's fine," Lon spoke glaring at Daarck with a gaze asking whether his part of the promise to imprison the Devil was intact or not, "I have a condition, on the colonies coming in each of your share when the *'peep-noise' (The trouble borne by common residents)* exceeds beyond level-two, those colonies will be automatically under the accreditment of Colony Metal Casting."

"Agreed." The Devil said without delaying even for a second and gestured Daarck to come towards the shuttle.

Looking at Daarck with spear jabbing eyes, Filipa spoke up, "It is advisable that someone should accompany these two ends of one grave instead of sending them absolutely alone." Pulling Daarck to one side as he was getting the Vio-Crazy leader *Kaylos'* location from Malachi on the ladders of the shuttle, Filipa said warning him with her eyes, "Daarck, I am expecting that I would not have to kill you once again."

Gaping into the eyes of Filipa who looked like a marble cake, Daarck spoke, "I'll return very soon to devour you. Anyways give me one chance. I'll make everything right."

"There is no such problem that can deprive your face of laughter, right. If you do that, then this time I will really eliminate Daarck forever. Remember that." She slipped a microphone in Daarck's pocket while hugging him in such a way that no one could see it.

"Who knows if Daarck's and Devil's conversation that made you take that silly horrifying decision, following which you killed me, might be displaying the half truth of using evil for good governance?"

"I think that there is no scope for that. But I wish with all my heart that it would be like that only."

"One minute Daarck." Before the door of the shuttle could close, Antonio who looked extremely-insane even now said, "You cannot go without clarifying why you delivered the Tie-in Tune to Ros."

"One clarification from Lon." Lon spoke up before Daarck could respond, "Although not with the capability of the army made with the Walk of Life's disc, but we can injure the special gene-contexture cell of the *'Fifty Carat'* and *'Win Maker'* soldiers and stopping their re-generation, we can make them lifeless only for a few hours."

"That's enough." Responding to Lon, Daarck raised his head towards Antonio and said, "If I would not have delivered the Tie-in Tune to Ros, then would we have taken the trouble to prepare an outstanding spell book like Contras-Affair? *(Since Daarck had delivered the Tie-in Tune to Ros earlier only, Ros had re-programmed his body. And when Ros could not be imprisoned when Antonio tried to imprison him with the Tie-in Tune on Mahanabh, they had finally prepared the spell-book named Contras Affair, through which the Book of Bell was created.)*

Filipa watched Daarck's shuttle until it disappeared and after that she turned her head in the direction of Luciano's mumbling as he was going far and telling Elvis that, "You must have now learnt what can be the outcome of keeping a foolish woman with you and trusting her."

*

Universe Island Galaxy L3. On Vio-Crazy group leader Kaylos' Colony Codeman Time's toy planet Delphi79's country Onmil's capital Metralic located on 240 degrees New-Outer Southern Constellation.

Instantly after the spies on Lon's space-craft Woolybear had given the news, Ros had sent across a team of Win-Maker's soldiers on *'Metralic'* to stop Devil and Daarck. The Win-Makers, who had been posted in a fighting position outside this one and only S. Station that was six miles away from the area the Vio-Crazy group's leader and New-God of Colony *'Codeman Time' 'Kaylos'* was currently in, were waiting eagerly for Devil's and Daarck's shuttle to come out of the Station. As this was a toy-planet, only those shuttles having the characteristic to transform into a *tram (lengthy van)* were given permission to land on this S. Station situated on the sixtieth floor of a building. The Win-Makers' Commander was continuously in contact with Ros via phone.

"It is impossible that Kaylos will sign on such a Menithus." Ros said, "But this is Devil and if they would succeed in acquiring such a Menithus Agreement, then Lon and his ally colonies together will shred us into pieces. I am not bothered at all about how many points of Nebel-Shift are reduced by the blatant chaos created by the Win-Makers to stop the Devil on Delphi79. If required, grab the nuclear site of *'Metralic'* and topple the entire Delphi79 from its axis, but under any circumstances after Daarck and Devil come face to face with *'Kaylos'* there is no need for you to come back."

"This is an obligation of Kaylos. Otherwise for the purpose of Kaylos' security, no one gets clearance on Delphi79 during his presence on Onmil." The Win-Maker's Commander had just said this when a *'MES' (Satanic aircraft)* was seen transforming into a lengthy van and coming out of the building. Daarck was driving it. As soon as the shuttle that was on the target of approximately more than hundred shotguns, sub-machineguns, and automatic sniper rifles crossed the border of the S. Station and came out, the Win-Maker soldiers waiting readily rapidly fired rocket launchers from both sides of the road. But the Devil's speed was many times more than that. His body had transformed into a grey colored fog wrapped around all four sides of the van. As and when the rockets burst into the fog like lightening sparkling in the crux of the cloud, a dim light similar to glimmering embers shone up. As an unprecedented political event was to take place today on Metralic, a hoard of Police vehicles was aligned on all four sides. And these vehicles of the local police also had now started following the Win-Makers showering gunpowder on Daarck's van. The Devil transformed into a foggy monster leaped from the van's bonnet and reached the fire-truck running about ten feet ahead.

"I'm a goner…" Before he could feel the satisfaction of seeing the fire-truck lifted by the Devil, colliding with the Win-Makers shuttle chasing them, Daarck spoke up on hearing the warning tone of his Gizmo-belt that had got spoilt.

Leaping and jumping like kangaroos on cars running in six lanes, the 'Win-Makers' were chasing Daarck's van that was pervading the things coming in front and speeding in the direction of the Northern Suburb. When the Win-Makers lifted a running tram with two hundred Metralic residents on the left side of the road from the tracks and threw it on Daarck's van, luckily for him a tunnel was starting on the right side. Daarck, who had entered the tunnel by turning the steering ninety degrees right and immediately left with a jerk, had ended up crushing a bike rider. Now looking at the miraculous view of the foggy monster fighting with the Win-Makers stuck to the tunnel's ceiling and were running topsy-turvy, a series of accidents had taken place in the tunnel. As Daarck came out safely from that canal with motor-cars running on all four sides right-left, up-down like a motor-drome, the rotocraft-squad of the emergency response team in the sky had doubled. The stampede of the Metralic residents was at its peak on this sovereign path leading to the President House which was converted in to a stage for deadly melodramatics like the police bullets that were being thrown back after pressing the Win-Makers bodies like chunks of flesh like rubber and the foggy monster wrapping himself on all four sides of the van and swallowing heaps of ammunition, etc. An isolated bullet penetrated Daarck's neck. Pressing a hand on the stream of blood spurting out from his neck, Daarck took out his head from the window and craned his neck towards the sky that had taken on a strange appearance. Suddenly a shower of Holy-fish had started pouring down from the sky. (*Holy-fish – A pious fish that weakens the Devil and his powers*) Due to the rapidly banging fishes, the front glass was almost on the verge of breaking.

Seeing the lightning striking around Daarck's van from the sky that had covered with horrifying clouds the Win-Maker's Commander roared aloud, "The lightning never chases anyone in this style… who is this new enemy of the Devil who has suddenly emerged on the scene? It is beyond the capacity of Ros." The acute inclination of both the lightning and Holly fish striking from endless monstrous clouds towards the van was fix the Devil's defeat, provided if an upheaval would stop the pouring of lightning and Holy-fishes. When a powerful thrust of the Win-Makers' shuttle hit the rear portion of the van, it crashed down on the footpath stumbling with a cyclonic detour.. The Devil though weak had coiled himself around the blood smeared body of Daarck to protect, was struggling with his full power not to get detached from his body. The Win-Makers swiping up the bullets hitting them from the brusque firing of the Metralic Homeland-Security like a dust from their body, had reached the van, caught the toppled van from both sides and pulling it from the opposite sides, they tore open it. But before they could lift up Daarck trapped between the seat and the steering, the Devil gathered his entire power and in one last leap hurled Daarck fifty feet away from there.

Before getting lost in a deep darkness, Daarck saw beggars merrily picking up *'Holy-fish'* from Metralic's streets and immediately his eyes shut off.

"Exactly at the same time, 1.9 million kms South from 'Casiopia' on Diaboli Secret Society's chief Almuro's rocky asteroid located in the central area of the contingent of big planets." (Casiopia – A constellation near the North celestial polestar)

"The importance of acquiring the *'Hoodoo-Eye'* from Almuro is not at all less than acquiring the Menithus Agreement from Kaylos." When Antonio spoke, far away a figure was seen near the two trees that had grown in the style of gate-keepers on both sides of the door. The dim light of the hurricane lamps hung on the trees could be seen even from far away because of the livid moonlight. Almuro-devotee, who was standing in the traditional gown of the Diabolis, took Dervil, Filipa and Antonio inside.

When they reached between the door to the inside room some *witch-doctors (Those who treat people who have been possessed by a witch*) who had worn fruit garlands, passed close to them in the narrow door. A modern pomp had now started in this multi-level apartment. A voice that had come from the left side drew the attention of Filipa who was studying the lifestyle of this strange species- "Damage is done." Saying this, a spike faced ugly woman who was seated below the scary lady's portrait gesturing towards her left shoulder in the *'Combat Room'* location of the activities associated with the family had gestured an old man sitting in front of her to relax and go back.

"The watchman of our graveyard has come to dispose his late brother's son to his father who had made his own son a 'Necrofelic'." (*A person who has a sexual attraction towards corpses*) Their guide calmed down Filipa's curiosity. After passing a small row of chambers dim-lit like a club, finally, they sighted 'Almuro' seated leisurely on the couch in the hall covered with velvet and linen. Before Filipa's guess about the woman, looking as if she was accepting the invitation of middle age, seated at ease in the gorgeous gown approximately ten feet towards the right as *'The honor to be present in this crucial meeting might be in terms of being Almuro's wife.'* could extend, Almuro spoke, "Apology for simultaneous murders of four Diabolis together there's just no question of that. In exchange of any amount whatsoever." (*Here Almuro was referring to the murder of those Diabolis through whom Paras and Susan had got the ritual done. & whom Dervil had killed in Kangra.)*

"There is always a price, Mr. Almuro, which finally compels everyone to say *yes*." Antonio said.

"You really want to know the price for the entire five planets of Cons Lydia?"

"This meeting is ending like a victim of premature death." Dervil said and jumped from the sofa like it has caught fire as he listened to the Almuro's demand. A humped Diaboli, descended from the staircase swaying with sharp clattering on the left side and entered the hall, spoke in a hoarse voice, "Then *'Walk of Life'* that is suffering the retribution of Dervil's crime will now be in existence for just two to four minutes."

"Metralic's news channels are witnessing that. Why don't you see it with your own eyes?" Saying this, Almuro started the television. The Devil who was on the verge of finish, was fumbling to drag Daarck and take him far away. "And if you have a desire for a jargon then I think you do not have much time..!"

Looking at that woman offering a bowl of a dish made of supple human ears with disgust, the Dervil's stiff neck became a little pliable. He spoke. "Very good, then this is done. Out of the Colonies allotted to the Devil Family's share, I am bestowing a gift of five planets to Almuro. Bring the Menithus. And please stop this now."

The hunchback came down pushing a cannibal like man with him. He tossed a key towards Almuro. Pushing aside the wild tresses of the cannibal, when Almuro opened his skull with the key and took out a larger than normal sized glass bottle that was filled with eye, Antonio spoke up, "Oh, is this explicitly the same…?"

"Hundred percent original." Speaking in a proprietary manner, Almuro covered the sinister 'Hoodoo-Eye' in the glass bottle with a black cloth, and said, "A lot of bloodshed has taken place to acquire this Hoodoo-Eye." Accompanying them to the lift, Almuro now said grimly, "But be careful, the glance of this Hoodoo-Eye that is oblivious to the difference of enemy and friend should always be in the direction of the rival force, otherwise…"

"What is this thing, Actually?" Filipa asked, with the chime of a sweet tune like an advertisement chant of a free thing, amidst lousy noises.

"The eye of an impaired chef of the great *Solom*'s army." How could Almuro miss the opportunity to impress the beauty, who could perform an organic diabolism on the heart? He said enthusiastically, "The chef had a very atrocious desire to become a soldier. But it was not possible due to his physical deformities. During the period of his long life he watched warriors come and go with this burning desire. And finally one day he fell in the cauldron and died. After the peculiarity of this eye that it casts drastic evil glance on the rival army and determines their defeat came to the fore, bigger wars than those Solom's army might have fought during their lifespan took place in order to acquire this."

In the lift opening up in front of the unbelievable scene taking place in *Ẍ Blest (Holy Place)* the scared Filipa moved behind by two steps and collided with Dervil…! Exactly in the middle of this very long hall of violet color that could enlighten the melancholy mood, emissary of the heaven like priests were engrossed in worshipping

'Grubby Deity' with sacred material. The priests were epitomizing the hurricane incarnation and chanting the spells. The Grubby Deity, who had been *imprisoned* in a cone shaped bamboo cage as if skulls had been embedded, was screaming in pain. "The weaknesses those are required for victory are not only of the opponents." Flaunting his *grey-matter (Intellectual capability)*, *Almuro* said, speedily raising steps towards the cage.

The facial expressions of the nude *'Grubby Deity'* who looked like a spokesman of a ghost assembly was like a superman using powers beyond his capacity without bothering about the ripping veins of his brain. Filipa who was vacillating as a result of the shame coming from the distraction of his bulky thighs and arms packed with flesh, turned her head towards the right and asked, "But how can a Grubby Deity be imprisoned and made to arbitrarily do what you want?"

Almuro spoke, "The Devil is only famous in this world. Otherwise many other evil powers are also existent on this world's screen. This is just one, otherwise the Secret Society has a long list of such Grubby Deities who can be pleased by worshipping them with bones, flesh and filth of pus, whose worship if done with sacred material like holy deities in a ceremonious way are provoked to the extent of becoming your slaves. During those few minutes unable to tolerate this sacred ceremony, the corrupt, lecherous deities are ready to follow orders with mechanical-allegiance devoid of any ifs and buts."

"But how do they get trapped?" Dervil asked. Respect could now be seen cropping up in his eyes towards Almuro.

"By all odds, through the daemonic rituals learnt by risking the life for invoke them." Almuro said and as if he did not want to miss out on the opportunity to display miraculous powers, he severed the bonds of the cage with a visual stroke. The suffering *'Grubby Deity'* went out of the window that had been left open from the beginning by the hunchback and flew away.

*

As if Planet Delphi79 had got bored with its celestial sphere and escaped at the speed of *'light'*, suddenly the rain of Holy-Fish and the black clouds had disappeared into thin air. Before Daarck, connecting the stinging line of breath with the disjointed breath, could pass away with Ros' revenge, the Devil made him recover within a few seconds and wiped out the cluster of bullets being fired in front of his face. The Devil, who had luckily got up after being injured with arrows, attacked the Win Makers with his full capacity. After wrapping up all the Win Maker soldiers together in his foggy body and sucking up their life, he caught the tail of the aircrafts hovering in the sky and destroyed them by colliding them against each other. When that scene of the crowd escaping from the shower of dregs and sullage of the burning shuttles, cleared from the sky, both that foggy monster and the mysterious van driver had disappeared from there.

*

When Daarck's glance fell on a TV-reporter on the right side as he passed from the crowd to go near *'Kaylos' (Vio-Crazy Group's Leader)* who was standing on the stage towards the other side of the high security zone in *Papazi Palace Square (A ground that was in front of Onmil's Presidential House),* the eyes that were staring at him looked very familiar. Despite the dangerous crisis of time, Daarck could not stop himself. He went to the girl and taking out her *'Custodian Helmet'*, he said, "Have we met before?"

"I have just come to apologize, Daarck."

"Mithalia..." Daarck's eyes and voice had burst forth. Due to speaking out very loud, the people standing around had started glaring at them. After holding Mithalia's arm and taking her far from there, he spoke, "What is all this, Mithalia? The secret of the death of both the Directors has been hidden in Anjeolmac... What's all this that is going on? These things were not there in our plan as such...!"

"It's not ours but my plan Daarck." She held both shoulders of Daarck and said in a soft voice. "Why are you roaming around with the flag to change all these worlds? Whatever is there, everything is right in its place."

"Ohh.... So you are now speaking the language of the New-Gods and Apotheosis. Why not, if you are able to get along with the Director himself and rule over the Master Galaxy as well as the other Galaxies, then what interest would you possibly have in the welfare of the people?"

"Let the people go to hell." Mithalia said, "And to hell with your mission. The world is filled with selfish people. They deserve that only. Of these two, not even one Director is going to be able to reach Anjeolmac. They know that. And hence both of them have started their efforts to eliminate each other. One day one of them will be successful. After that, I along with the surviving Director will rule over all the six galaxies and the Master Galaxy."

"Mithalia come to your senses. We are approaching success. You cannot spoil everything like this. See everything is ready. The Mummy-Ointment, Transmission-Germ, Tie-in and Re-built Tunes as well as the chip with Robrelco Fero…"

"Chip..? Which chip?" Mithalia's eyes narrowed.

Excitedly fumbling to explain her, Daarck changed the topic and said, "I promise you, there will be no harm done to Apotheosis. Or if you say, then to Prestige.. If you want you yourself can be the Director. But after exchanging your body with Apotheosis by the Mummy Ointment, you will get an entry into the owner family and after that the last task of mine that remains, just do that for me, Mithalia. After that, you can go your way and me, mine."

"How can I trust that you will finally not betray me as well?"

"The universally-wanted Mithalia, to understand whose betrayal even the six brains of both the Directors put together are experiencing helplessness, what capacity do I possibly have to betray her."

"I cannot do that." Mithalia said.

"You can fool the world, but not Daarck. And it will not take me much time to deliver the fact that there is no secret whatsoever of the death of even one of the Directors in Anjeolmac, to both Prestige and Apotheosis.

"Hmm... You are telling the truth. I had several secrets about the powers of both the Directors. Those secrets were enough to make them believe that I knew the secret of how to kill them. But anyways, I'll think about whether to do that final work of yours or not. From now on we will not come in each other's way."

"Anyways, despite that, I have liked this Anjeolmac work of yours. At least in this way you will reduce one enemy of mine. May I ask where you have hidden Anjeolmac?"

"Yes, why not… It is on Earth. Locked in the twenty-sixth step of the tallest pyramid of Giza.. Exactly in the central portion towards the South.. And I have faith that you will not dare to mess around with it at all."

"Absolutely not.. But why did you come to the fore again?"

"I have not even become so stone-hearted that I would not realize that I owe you an apology. I have been loitering around during the period that started from the moment Daarck stepped onto Galaxy L3. Around.. Always.. In order to get an insight into Daarck's conspiracies.. Actually you should have thought about this before including me in this plan and sending me to beguile the Directors that the attraction of the extremely Godly Directors was capable of smothering anyone's intentions. Those worlds themselves are like that. Beyond the imagination.. Whose allurement you cannot kill.. Now I have become one of that world, Daarck. It is now impossible for me to be a part of all these trivial worlds. I had come to meet you for the last time and bid farewell, but…"

"Where had you got stuck, Daarck?" The Devil who had moved ahead with the crowd had come back to take him. Daarck's heart skipped a beat. When he turned his head from the Devil's side and looked again in Mithalia's direction, she had disappeared.

Crossing the ground that was totally jam-packed with a suffocating crowd, when they reached close to the security-ribbon in front of the stage, Daarck's chest experienced a shiver. He took out the mobile. It was a message from Sierra: "How far has your task reached? After thirty minutes, the life of four million Energy-Warriors on *Pendigyura 022* will have become a thing of the past."

Sending an *'Almost done'* reply to Sierra, Daarck glanced towards Kaylos' innumerable bodyguards. A large part of the guards here were the *signature-band* in the garb of the Metralic Police. *(Signature-band– The special force of Kaylos' colony Codeman-Time.)*

Gesturing the guards who were stopping Daarck and the Devil to let them come on stage, Kaylos once again started talking like an implacable orator. He had worn a garment like that of the Arabic dynasty *'Abbasid*

Caliphate'. "An assurance given by the President holds the value of an oath." He spoke, "The privatization of the Government will get much better results. Trust me, this change will certainly make Onmil's jurisdictional structure much stronger than the existing system." The Devil went near the mike and caught Kaylos' hand, and pushing him far from there, he spoke, "The speech of our President comes to an end here." There was a severe drop in the temperature as Onmil's thirty-five hours long drawn out night had reached its prime. And this being even more dangerous than the Win-Makers shivering, Daarck walked quickly towards the Presidential House door behind Kaylos. Before entering inside when he turned back to see, the banners had started getting hurled in the ground.

Kaylos, who had been quietly glaring at them until the conference room door closed, finally spoke in the style of an instigated dinosaur, "What is this violation of peace rampant on the streets of my toy planet? The crossing had not at all been opened for this. I have three minutes. Tell me what is that offer that can benefit me?"

"The work of haste is mine, Kaylos." The Devil said giving a hollow smile like that of an old man. "But what interest could the most powerful New-God of the Vio-Crazy group possibly have in becoming the President of a toy planet?"

Kaylos spoke, "In this way I can be in direct contact with the common people and directly drive them. Politeness, culture and science.. The fun that is there in first taking the toy-society to the topmost height of progress and ruining them after that, its pleasure is something entirely different. The fun of spoiling tiptop, organized things is quite different… The contribution of the ruin creators in this creation is not a thing to be overlooked. In order to destroy the world of a planet, there is only a need to produce two to four whimsical idiots, who would change its history, geography, maps, just about everything."

"Really they have chosen the best person to grace the position of a Vio-Crazy group leader in an excellent way." Daarck said, "But in this time's election there is not even a single reason for which the Vio-Crazy *'commission'* will vote for Kaylos as their leader one more time." Saying this, he give a Menithus in Kaylos' hand.

"Except if Kaylos carries out the feat of getting those ten New-Gods imprisoned by *'Lord de Ros'* in the Devil's name released and gets back their colonies for them." The Devil said further speaking in an exquisite voice, "Yes, we will do that exploit, and attribute it to your name and you will be the Vio-Crazy group leader once again. But in return, you will have to sign on this Menithus."

When Kaylos raised his face with a tensed-brow from the Menithus handed over to him by Daarck, seeing the Devil who was seated on the opposite end of the rectangular table, suddenly seated next to him, he spoke with a shivering voice, "Apologies for the slip of tongue of the Dominion of Hell… But by signing on this written Menithus that none of the remaining Vio-Crazy colonies will help those eleven Vio-Crazy colonies in this war I should slay Kaylos…"

"We should be talking this on the way to the S. Station." Daarck said looking at the time and got up with fright.

"Goras... Without looking towards his *'Chairman'* standing far on the left side, Kaylos gestured to him with snapping fingers.

When they came out, the driver of the air-tram was waiting on the porch steps readily with the door open. The navigation lights of the helicopters based in the Papazi Palace's sky were fixed on the air-tram. The demonstrators opposing the privatization of the government had raised turbulence all around. On whichever part of their body the *'vacuum bomb'* of the Metralic Police would hit and get stuck, the skin of that portion would dangle like a wilted flower. The fleet of additional Win-Makers had reached there but they were only watching Daarck and the Devil with helplessness as Kaylos was with them. Extending a *Lazo (a pen)* towards Kaylos in their *'air-tram'* running surrounded by the phrenetic battalion of the Win-Makers that was similar to the *'Macedonian Army'* of Sikander the Great, Daarck said, "There is another Menithus below. Our confidence that after reading it there will be an alteration in your thoughts will not prove to be sleazy."

"Hmm... The Devil always has a new ploy ready for deception, isn't it?" After reading the second Menithus, Kaylos said, "Apart from the *'New-God Transaction'* named book in which twenty thousand years earlier, a *'New-God'* of L-3 paid the price of breaking the *'Menithus Agreement'* by losing his colony along with a painful death, there is no mention of any kind of shrewd solution of the

Menithus. According to me it is difficult to find even such a single fool in this world, who will believe such a story of yours, that you will instantly returning the colonies that have been won to their original owners after having won this war full of casualties. Yet I am ready to sign on this Menithus. Not with the intention to emerge as the biggest fool, but out of curiosity. To see how someone can break the uncompromising Menithus and fool the *Master Galaxy*.... Because I do not think, you will give back even single planet after winning the war." *(Even such conditions had been included in the agreement that until the New-Gods imprisoned by Ros could not be found, their Chairmen only would govern the colonies. The right of the Devil Family would not be on even one particle of sand. And in order to fight against those eleven colonies of Ros in this war the Devil can take help of just eleven Idiotic colonies.)*

The conferment of mutually mysterious smiles was going on between Daarck and the Devil when suddenly the *'Devil'* saw Daarck's face that was like a ruler who had got his dominion plundered. "What is it?" The Devil asked.

"Before the gale of aspirations could avail victory, the waters of negligence drowned it. We are defeated. Ros has blown off the S. Station itself. Now the nearest station from here is at a distance of twenty hours." He had said looking at the frequent failure of Kaylos while connecting the *'Lazo'* with the S. Station.

"I know it." Kaylos spoke, "Ros will pay a huge price for this audacity, but don't worry, we will be able to connect the Lazo with my backtrack *'S. Station'* that is at a distance of six minutes from here." Kaylos who was entering the clearance code in the Lazo said in a voice as if he had stopped the trigger from changing the position, "*Meri man (Driver)* take the tram upto East-bar's new S. Station for our guests." In a style as if the express-way of happiness had been opened up, Kaylos signed on such a *'Menithus Agreement'* wherein not even a single colony from the remaining ones would give support to Ros. Taking the Lazo from Kaylos, the Devil told Daarck in a private language, "I am aware of the inherent nature of the real *'Satanics'* who trick even their God into a conspiracy for their own selfishness, yet with what efforts can I possibly stop myself from getting upset for your deceit of hiding the Re-built Tune and the bunker that was in Japan?"

Responding with a forced smile, Daarck turned his face.

† Although Daarck had sent a copy of this Menithus Agreement on time to the Idiotic United Kingdom leader Lon who was ready with an army on one of *Antpatic's* planet, before the rescue squad's reflection could penetrate the pupils of the vehemently great *'Pendigyura 022'* known as the nation of *Devilish Temples*, the souls of millions of *'Energy Warriors'* who had been attacked by the Win-Makers and Fifty Carats had bid adieu to the world with waving their souls.

*

"Today on the fifth day of this '*melodious- commemoration of war*' flaming with the pyres of the hearts of billions of residents of thousands of toy planets, one hundred thousand megaton Species-destructive nuclear explosives have been used in the war that has erupted simultaneously on five thousand six hundred locations by virtue of the total 'one-six-five' home planets and '2000' asteroids of the twenty colonies (Ros' eleven and Lon's nine put together) of both the parties. Total 650 million warriors have already received medals of martyrdom. 187.5 million trillion gallons sweet water…. Quick Site 26 onto the main screen…" The reporter removed the mike and said quickly, but before the main screen could broadcast the missile that was creating turbulence in the sky of Site 26 even for a second, its fiery chariot had singed one more lake. "Along with the indexation of this 260th river of Nebel Shift's Black-Island, explosives sapping an aggregate of 187.7 million trillion gallons of sweet water till now, have been used. With the over-doze of the medicines that were slapping the cheeks of the need of food-supply, soldiers falling victim to hallucinations and losing their skills…"

At a distance of sixty miles from the one and only vestigial eastern shore of Pendigyura 022, in the *'war safety box'* established on a little oval stone the *'reporter'* who looked like a character from the Victorian novel suddenly stopped reporting and taking the water bottle to her lips, she put it back in her purse like an invaluable thing.

In the bunker made with ten meter strong transparent walls adjacent to the buzzing temporary headquarter of Galaxy L3's popular news channel 'Eye-opener', the musicians of the Diaboli 'Death-band' were playing the musical instruments in a high tempo like maniacs. Their aim was to transport the martyred souls to the door of the seventh heaven through their mysterious music.

Although a large part of the speakers that were airing their music in the every nook and corner broadcasted in front of them on Pendigyura 022 which looked like a gigantic corpse of a whale on which vultures were hovering had been destroyed like the drone-cameras that were covering every corner of the 'Eye-opener'. Despite that, their enthusiasm was enough to tempt the souls of the dead to take part in the war again without bothering about the painful death.

As several ally colonies of Lon had denied to associate in this war both the parties were now equal to each other in terms of strength. Since hope as little as a straw was not there to commit for anyone, both the parties had now turned towards taking support of conspiracies.

The Sixth Night of War. On Mahanabh Asteroid

Coming to stand beside Ros who was standing on the last rock of the valley-mouth that was such that the gaze would ask for respite to reach the bottom, Gosha said, "If the *goblin-spirit* that is available only with Director Prestige in the whole universe could be acquired and proof of the meeting Mission *'Walk of Life'* between Lon, Solon and Daarck could be accessed, then we are in a position to present it in front of Apotheosis and easily invite Lon's annihilation. And in this way this war will end with ease in our favor within a few minutes." *(Goblin-Spirit – A three-D time camera having the capacity to make a video of the events that have taken place in the past. That also has the characteristic to capture a video along with the aura print of the people present in the incident.)*

"Then for whom are we waiting for?" Ros said stretching his hand and touching the sky, because a black cloud that had come so near that it could be touched by stretching a hand, had engulfed the entire Mahanabh mountain within it.

"Yes, Prestige's Chairman will inform whether to give us that camera or not within three hundred seconds. Is this some kind of a new weapon of Lon?" Gosha asked looking towards the terrible cloud.

"Cannot understand what this thing is. An unknown frequency has started encircling Mahanabh's Celestial body, and now it is proceeding towards *Palmfit (Mahanabh's sun)*."

The rock on which Ros was standing, Apotheosis was ascending up exactly from the bottom of that valley. Apotheosis had been attracted to come here as the communication radar on the Master Galaxy had recorded the use of the *'Anjeolmac'* word ten times in the last couple of days and nights on Mahanabh,. Descending from his transparent airbus like a blue snow-ball nebula, he now started the journey on foot with his Chairman Solon towards *'Jakhebaaz' (Treasury with Ros' secret possessions)*.

Apotheosis spoke, "Solon, you should have heard the innocent jokes of that shrewd woman Mithalia. When her sweet words would be pouring in the ears, there was a feeling as if butterflies were sipping nectar from the flowers. I am scared that when she meets me again, I should not be proved to be a coward? My soul-energy will not severe the relation with my hands raised to strangle the neck of that unimaginable pleasure (Mithalia), isn't it?"

"That immanent spiritual teacher who groomed Mithalia is certainly an exceptional mind."

"Whoever may be the *King-Bolt (Main Conspirator)*, he is a product of the Master Galaxy. One who has everlasting trust in himself." Saying this in a strong voice, when *'Apotheosis'* who was exasperated with the climb now prepared to directly leap up to the thousands of feet high peak, suddenly the whole of Mahanabh trembled with an overwhelming jolt.

"What is this thing?" Solon asked in a frightened voice.

Looking towards that monstrous cloud covering Mahanabh's sun, inspired by the potent-transcendence Apotheosis said, "The ruin of all twenty-two Pendigyura together has indeed antagonized the Lord of the Satanics." When he said that, with the gravity field created by *Palmfit's* electrons which had kept the Mahanabh asteroid's electrons attracted being defeated by a billion times strong electromagnetic force, first a voice like the tearing of rope that kept a big container hanging was heard and instantly slipping from the hold of its sun's gravity field, Mahanabh was hurled in space. Seeing this Devilish power that released the whole asteroid from the hold of its gravitation and throw it in infinite sky, a shiver of fright passed through Solon's entire body.

When that black cloud spread over thousands of miles shrinked and took the form of the Devil, the smiling

Apotheosis flattering that only the Devil can do something like this in the Universe, was seen in a superfast reaction chasing Mahanabh that had cascaded with a centrifugal force as he deprived Ros of his laughter.

"Prestige's Chairmen have agreed to give the Goblin-Spirit camera." Standing holding on tightly to the things on the hurtling Mahanabh, Gosha said shouting in Ros' ear, "Now there's only a difference of those minutes left until the Striado-Unit gives the location of that meeting of Lon, Solon, Daarck, between 'success' and us. There is one and only condition of *Prestige's Chairmen* is that after victory the main aim of our eleven colonies will be to search for Anjeolmac through which the death of Apotheosis is possible. (*Striado-Unit – A department remaining continuously connected with the aura of non-residents entering Director Apotheosis' portion of the Master Galaxy and making a root record of every location he visits in the Master Galaxy*)

Chasing Mahanabh which had been hurled upto fifty miles away from its sun, Apotheosis sunk into Mahanabh's ground upto its silver like waist the way a spear is pierced on the fish's back. Instantly Mahanabh experienced Apotheosis' consciousness upto its extreme end and started running back towards its permanent location. Ros bend, kneels down and gently presses his ear on the ground of Mahanabh that had become a constituent of Apotheosis' body. Throb throb.. Throb throb… But before the life of Ros' happiness could increase as he stood up with a joyous leap, the Devil was on Mahanabh once again. Spinning the monstrous iron sphere hanging at the end of the long chain in his hand round and round, he thrust it with a bang on Mahanabh's chest. Just like a great mine gets blasted with a dynamite, at the time of Mahanabh's breaking with each assault of the iron sphere, *Apotheosis'* originating screams were echoing across the cosmos. But before Ros' favorite *'Mahanabh'* could be doomed, the highly-capable *'Apotheosis'* put it back on its *rotation-field (orbital level)* with such ease as if he had gone out for a *'space adventure'* and came out. And sent across a glance with a deadly challenge in the Devil's direction... But before that glance could reach there, *Bilzebub (Satan)* had disappeared in the blink of an eyelid.

*

In the 'Fusion Empire' area of 'Links Bearer' (One of Lon's home planet that was three times bigger in size than the Earth), a planet on the Glee Metal Casting Colony, from where it would take a journey to the Galactic Core (The central part of Galaxy L3) to come to an end after thirty thousand light-years

Preparing to take part in the war from the edge of the *nine hundred meters tall (Thirty meters taller than Burj Khalifa)* battle-station located in a majestic cross town of Links Bearer, Lon cast a blank glance towards the infinite sky in front of him and delicately blinked his eyelids on his eyes which were enduring the reflection of thousands of yards of the sky pervaded with billions of Vio-Crazy war-crafts. This scene of the sky filled with war-crafts of Lord de Ros' ally colonies' armies *'Fifty Carats'* and *'Chargeman'*

(Chargeman- An army of Lord de Ros' ally organization 'Evil Stock') and against them Lon and his ally colonies looked as if *Links Bearer's* sky had been filled with all the birds of Galaxy L3. Taking off his gaze from this *air-crew cluster (A cluster of war-crafts)* that looked less different from the thousand storey tall buildings squandering to collide opposite each other, *'Lon'* turned towards the New-Gods of his ally colonies *'Liquor Mine'* and *'Adopt Baby'* and said, "I request you to give me support for just three more days."

Pushing out the words attempting to jump out from the tip of his tongue, *Litharm*, the New-God of *Liquor Mine* finally said, "Our power is not for giving support to Lon's racial-estrangement with the Vio-Crazys. Just six hours and after that, both of our colonies will move away from this war. Before the realization of being a New-God gets converted into being a hired soldier, while fighting for Lon." Saying this Litharm and Colony Adopt-Baby's New-God *'Abzman'* flew away from there. Exactly at the same time the Vio-Crazy aircrafts having started isolating Lon's *'Antiniuc robot vehicles'* and destroying them, Lon transformed into a *sharp-edged flying saucer* and flew towards the war zone. *(Only Lon had that technique available on Galaxy L3 wherein he was able to make changes to the structure of his body molecules and transform it into a strong metal.)* Looking at Lon who was pouring havoc at the speed of 65 thousand kms per hour on the Vio-Crazy war-crafts, it appeared that he alone will lock up this *'Automic Café'*. (*Antiniuc robot vehicles – Robots that fired a special kind of open air S-ray [salvage beam] and made the nuclear blast unsuccessful by extinguishing the energy being released in the form of thermal radiation through the separation of the center of the atomic-spore.)*

Flapping the wings supported on the backbone, Dervil, Antonio, Daarck and all others reached close to Lon. When Lon stopped fighting and came back to his original form, Antonio spoke, "You will have to convince Litharm and Abzman, Lon. At any cost. Otherwise we have had it."

Before Lon could respond, Sierra who had come akin to a sudden bolt of lightning, said, "There is a bad news." Her face was tarnished with the lines displaying big difficulties. "A delegation of Ros is currently standing on Apotheosis' threshold. They are demanding to cancel the Menithus done by Kaylos. They asked for permission and who knows why *'Apotheosis'* agreed to meet these trivial conventional literi."

Lon, who was filled with anger, spoke, "Yes why not, looking at the suffering that the Devil has given Apotheosis on Mahanabh, he will not take even a second to cancel Kaylos' Menithus in apathy of the Devil, and in about the next three hours we will see all the colonies of the Vio-Crazys standing against us."

"There is only one way now to survive from the destruction…!" The wilting faces had to turn towards Antonio. "Apotheosis is not present there. If we find all of those ten New-Gods who have been imprisoned by *Lord de Ros*, in the hours before he reaches the Master Galaxy and cancels this Menithus, then this war ends with our victory."

"Impossible…" Daarck spoke up. "Even if those few hours extend throughout the life, it is impossible to find those ten New-Gods hidden by *Ros* in this Universe. Do you think that Ros would have even let his other brain know about their location?"

"Would this information be of any use to find them?" Dervil spoke suddenly, "*Shifa*, the foolish boy of *Gostel* the owner of the private jail *Hell-Hall* on Galaxy L1 had come to meet *Nebel Shift's* Chairman Dustin today. Our intelligence was present there at the time of that meeting. Dustin wants the help of few scientists of Hell-Hall to unlock the memory-spot of one of his prisoners. And this meeting had been organized for that only. The drugged tongued *Shifa* said by mistake that- "You called me all the way here for such a small thing…! Even your ally *Lord de Ros* will give you permission…." As if cursing himself for the stupidity, he quickly picked up the *sombrero (a hat)* from the table and ran off from there. *(Nebel Shift – One of Ros' ally colonies)*

"It Means that Ros has struck a partnership in Hell-Hall so that those ten New-Gods captivated can be kept there in a totally safe way." Lon said, "That's alright. A prisoner of *Solon (Apotheosis' Chairman)* is over there. I will tell him and make arrangements to enter Hell-Hall. Daarck you get ready to leave." Saying this, Lon took him far in the sky. Keeping a hand on Daarck's shoulder, he said, "I am more worried about the recent widely-discussed rumor, in which it is said that for the Devil it is necessary to release those actual New-Gods who have been imprisoned by Ros and return their colonies to them after the war in order to complete his Ultimate Mission. But if that is true then even after wringing my brain I am unable to get an answer anywhere about what benefit will the Devil ultimately get by doing this. Hence the time has now come to imprison the Devil. You will have to do it as per the promise. Tell your source to take *Devilet (The book that could imprison the Devil)* and reach Woolybear right away. You take the Devil from Hell-Hall and come there directly. We will finish it off right there. As it is there is no requirement of him in this war now."

Scratching his temple with the first finger of his right hand, Daarck spoke, "Note down this number. It is *nine, zero, three, six*."

"Whom shall I find here?" Lon asked.

"This is the number of one of my spies who is hidden in the guise of Ros' Catalytic priest on Mahanabh. He is safeguarding *'Devilet Again'*. By dialing this number he will bring Devilet and reach anywhere you say."

*

Towards Five Miles North from Mahanabh.

About to traverse the stream of the old city populated in the foothills, Ros stopped with a shout that had come from behind. A Gardi soldier had caught a Catalytic priest and got him there. The Gardi spoke. "He was running through the bottom line of the dry canyon, my Lord."

"Our highly-religious personality and such behavior..? Leave him." Ros said giving a fake rebuke to the Gardi soldier. In the moonlight coming from the side of the dome of the four-faceted palace, the Gardi pushed the *priest* slightly forward so that *Lord de Ros* could see him properly.

"Why…?" Ros looked towards the priest and asked.

The priest whose face was like a scary dream, spoke. "Terrible misfortunes are making my mind rumble day and night. Mahanabh is not safe anymore."

"Only for you or for all of us…? And what are you taking in this sack of yours?" Saying this, *Ros* signaled to the Gardi.

Checking the priest's sack, the Gardi spoke. "There is nothing ambiguous in the personal stuff, my Lord. There is only this one *Lexicaptive (Priest's book)*"

"Bring the Lexicaptive here." Ros ordered.

"According to the rule, no one can scrutinize this scripture against the wishes of the priest. Not even a *New-God*." The priest spoke.

"To hell with the rule… I am the owner. You just get it." Ros spoke but at the same time when Arina who had come back gestured that they were getting late to reach Hell-Hall, Ros said, "Keep him locked up in a cell. I'll come back and take his decision."

*

∞ *'Calmork' a harmony planet on Apotheosis' portion of the Master Galaxy* ∞

(A home planet is referred to as a harmony planet on the Master Galaxy)

Gosha had got permission to stay on the Master Galaxy for three hours. A President of *Deivinthyoti (A Chairman of Director 'Prestige'. Meaning of the name – Crown of the Deity)*, had got the Goblin Spirit camera and come with him. Travelling in the train speeding on the sixth floor of the ten storey highway, they were proceeding towards the location of Lon, Solon and Daarck's meeting given by the Striado-Unit. Shaking with anxiety, panic, disappointment and curiosity, Gosha knew that once this tape proving that Lon and Solon were the founders of Walk of Life came in his hands, this war was going to be finished with their victory in its next minute. He picked up the cup from the tray and giving a creamy smile to the train hostess with tresses like an ostrich's crest, he turned his face towards the window. The disappointed Gosha who had been expecting to see an *'Electronic Haven' (Modern Heaven)* on some planet of the Master Galaxy gestured towards the monster-sized creatures sitting far in the fields and asked, "What is this thing?"

Yakshek spoke, "They are called Azmetly. A large part of them live peacefully, but not all. The residents of Calmork who are infected with a particular disease are admonished to this field. For some strange reasons the bodies of these discarders follow the gigantic development. They have become more disappointed as it is not possible for them to come to the city and create turbulence due to the construction of a wall."

"Can These creatures be used very effectively in the army?" Several Azmetlies were sitting staring at the ground in a profound mourning adumbration in front of small hills, garbage dumps and old buildings. Although they were seated they were looking as tall as two storeys.

"Not at all, Azmetlies would never do anything that would benefit others. They have taught everyone to expect bitterness from them for what has happened with them." When Yakshek responded the train had reached and stopped at their station.

After bidding adieu to the taxi taken from the terminal in the area named *'Casino Square'*, taking out the route-map and zooming it, Yakshek started identifying the sign-boards of the *'dolly-shops'* that were there on both sides. Walking behind him, Gosha was coming propelling the Goblin-Spirit camera in a *'Wheel Barrow'* on the streets overflowing with *joyous* and *disappointed* gamblers. *(Wheel Barrow- A kind of trolley)*

"That location is still about ten stores ahead." Yakshek said and added, "After this, Daarck's Employment Security Contract will be for *Prestige*."

"To search Anjeolmac…?"

"Yes, but before handing over that assignment, a research report is being prepared on Daarck. It has been heard that he has prepared the *'Transformation Germ'*. Just a little suffering and the exact aura of two individuals is switched for a few hours."

"Impossible." Gosha spoke. "If at all this happens, a chaotic confusion will occur in our world which basically functions on aura-identity. He is an expert Satanic, Mr. President. And Satanics are masters in just one trick, convincing the other persons that they have an imaginative thing."

"If he has really not discovered the Transformation-Germ then why would they sign a contract with Kaylos in which it is written that after this war their colonies will be returned from our end to the New-Gods having the original aura?"

Gosha shrugged his shoulders. The footfall of darkness was closer, and as if he did not want to get into further discussion, he turned his face towards the side of the modern gambling dens illuminated in the heavenly light spread there. After going a little ahead, he turned the trolley towards the big *'store'* that Yakshek had shown saying- "Here it is."

*

In the Hell-Hall constructed on 'Lieuma' Asteroid of Colony 'Rub-Crisis' on Galaxy L1

"Mr. Daarck, it seems that you have Never heard about the one and only of its kind Hell-Hall situated in the local group (*local group- the area that includes all the six galaxies*)." The security-chief of Hell-Hall who had a *sadomasochism*

(*A person who gains sexual pleasure from cruelty*) like face standing amidst his own '*defense-scope*', said raising his palm towards the right, where 'Hell-Hall' fabricated with a highly costly material developed for gravity-resistance by the Master Galaxy was hanging six hundred feet high in the sky. Huge anchors had kept the two hundred and fifty storeyed Hell-Hall bound with the ground. (Fabricated with such a metal that on which there would be no effect of gravity)

Apotheosis' Chairman Solon had got them here under the pretext of investigating the security of this private jail by making an excuse that Apotheosis' prisoner was not safe in Hell-Hall. It was very important for the Devil to find those ten New-Gods whom Ros had imprisoned before Gosha acquired the video of Daarck, Lon and Solon's meeting by any means. Otherwise it was certain that Ros would force Lon to get out of this war through that video. If such a situation arises then once again he will have to confront Ros and his ally colonies all alone.

"Your doubt is like a concern about a knot on the bone." The security chief said moving his glance on Daarck, Filipa, Antonio, Dervil, Benedict everyone, "The blueprint of our Hell-Hall's structure having global clients is not available anywhere in the world. Yet just suppose that you acquired it. Even the owner of that prisoner is ignorant of the information regarding which floor, which street, which barrack number his prisoner is in. Yet suppose you have the prisoner's location and after clearing the voice match, fifteen digit password and aura-identity security you even hacked a computer in the panel room which is impossible to hack for operate the lift, opening in the living room of the prisoner barrack…"

It was clear that the matter had become intolerable for the chief that Solon would get Apotheosis' well known prisoner who had been the reason for gaining quite a considerable publicity for 'Hell-Hall', discharged on instigation from someone like this Daarck. When the chief spoke further continuing with arrogance, gathering the panels within itself, Hell-Hall's bottom door opened. Going through the door their small visitor-vehicle now entered the huge reception area.

Before the security chief's comprehensive learning session could conclude, Filipa said in a peppery voice, "Means, if we want to abduct ten prisoners from Hell-Hall now, it is impossible as per your opinion..?"

"What..?" When the chief asked, *Gostel (The owner of Hell-Hall)* was seen rushing. He was surrounded by his special-protection-group. He spoke as soon as he reached, "The entire Hell-Hall is equipped with a *centrally magnetic fluid receiver. (A network that opens the doors after identifying the aura-print of a person)* The security level is immediately damaged with an un-authorized entry in any corner of Hell-Hall. And with that every safety door gets locked automatically. Things like Thought Steal, Memory Machine, are the boons of this bank of ours only."

"Mr. Gostel," Solon spoke in a tensed tone. "There is information that the wind fowling security alarm of your unique jail had rung aloud just a few minutes before we reached here?

"Ah! That was just the over-reaction of the system. The alarm went off due to some minor pollution in the oxygen contact of Sensors Lonizing. Nothing can be detected, you see." The chief said wiping off cold sweat from the face. *(In the system that the chief was talking about, a siren would automatically go off as soon as any kind of harmful gas is detected in the air coming in or going out of the prisoners' barracks.)*

"How can you say that the alarm would not have buzzed when the Devil would have taken on an aerial form and entered inside from the roof here? Reaching up to your barracks, the Devil has come out safely after making magic-plates around several prisoners with an invisible ink." When Daarck said this, they had now reached near the 'gas-main box' *(the machine for flowing of air)* on Hell-Hall's roof.

"What magic plate..?" When Gostel asked, Daarck made a slight gesture with his head and ninety weaponless 'Warlords' and an equal number of 'Liquor Mine' soldiers cordoned the entire roof of Hell-Hall having a one mile circumference by moving back.

Finally getting fed up as he was unable to understand what all was going on, Solon said in a concluding voice, "It is not right for you to get offended when the question is of the safe custody of the prisoner of Apotheosis, the owner of all of us. Hell-Hall should remain safe at least until our prisoner is there."

"I do not know what material the Devil is made of, Mr. Solon. But it is impossible for any type of inflammable-poisonous gas to cross this gas-main box and go ahead. Only the air that passes the purification test by hundred percent can go ahead from the filter chamber that is sixty meters below the box-cabin. With that I should remind you that almost half the prisoners including Mr. Solon's prisoner in Hell-Hall are *'inhabitants of nose-free planets'. (Creatures of nose-free planets have a body system that is free of respiratory needs).*

"Will get to know right away whether your arrogance will perish or not." Saying this, Daarck put the stick on the violin's wires with the style of an expert violinist. Antonio and Dervil placed a two mouthed rubber vacuum on the mouth of the air-cabin, so that the tune of the violin could reach up to the barracks of the prisoners and the melting bodies of the prisoners could come out from there through the air. Holding the violin on the orifice of the rubber vacuum with mike, and as Daarck started playing the tune, everyone including Gostel slipped closer to watch this weird act.

"With the touch of the liberating melodies of the Re-built Tune, I am re-awakening those New-Gods who have been imprisoned with the souls of my Gardis. Oh... Colonies... The eleven great colonies in the ownership of Lord de Ros..." Before Ros' daydream could proceed further, shaking him Arina woke him up and said, "But this is the Tie-in Tune…."

The period of *tunnel storm (The five hour treatment through a machine to take out the information hidden in the mind and spiral of the prisoners)* being on, the one thousand and five hundred prisoners who were tied to the 'forbid-chair', together turned their face towards the tune flowing out from the ventilation. Except Ros' ten prisoners who watched their bodies disappearing and passing through the air-way of the barrack through their melting organs and getting imprisoned with the souls of the Satanics standing on the roof.

The shuttles of Ros' ally colony Nebel-Shift from all the directions and planted them floating atop Hell-Hall's roof in siege. The door of a big shuttle inscribed with Hell-Hall Hoodlum was seen opening and Lord de Ros, Arina, *Ajar* and all others came flying and stood in front of Daarck. *(Ajar – A Chairman of Ros)*

Daarck, who was standing stifling his laughter, finally spoke, "Anyways, striking a partnership in Hell-Hall and sending the news to us that those ten New-Gods have been hidden here, this plan of yours to acquire the Re-built Tune when we come here to liberate them was really worthy of praise. But ultimately it was against the Satanics, Ros."

"Ha... Ha Hahaha...." The laughter of Daarck, Filipa, Malachi, Dervil, Antonio and the whole congregation kept on echoing until Ros, fuming with shattered aspirations did not attack them.

*

Yakshek opened the route-map for the last time and confirmed, it felt that they were at the right place. This was the same small restaurant where Lon and Solon had handed over the Walk of Life assignment to Daarck. When they met the restaurant's owner, she said that, "In the old times, we used that portion opening up in the rear street for special customers. But for quite some time we have converted that room into a store-house." She sighed and added, "This place was not lucky to enjoy the grace of mysterious clients forever. But I cannot vacate my store-room for any such experiment and please excuse me now, as you also appear to be people who value time." When the girl kept on looking into Yakshek's eyes for one long moment, Yakshek, who looked extraordinarily young caressed the strange pupils hanging on her eyes as if he was doing magic and gestured with his ring-finger in front of that young restaurant owner. In the very next instant she not only gave permission to remove the things of the storage and empty the room but also started removing the things herself with the servants with such ease as if she was giving it to her lover.

Yakshek, the owner of an effective personality, unloaded the Goblin-spirit camera from the trolley in sync with Gosha and putting it near the door of the store, stood staring at the intoxicating girl assisting in vacating the room. The girl's fair legs were covered up to her knees with boots. She had worn a deep blue colored skirt about six inches above that. The tresses were colored and the pupils were of an entirely different shape instead of round. When the man standing at the counter caught him staring at the girl, Yakshek gestured him to make two glasses of drinks and turned his face in the other direction. By the time the *'mixer'* plucked the flowers from the counter and prepared *healthy* and *yummy* drinks with special type of fresh, fragrant flowers, the room had been vacated. They took the camera inside and closed the room.

"Can this camera also send any person or thing into the past..?" Overflowing with joy, Gosha asked Yakshek who has pulled the partitions from both sides of the seven feet tall *'Goblin Spirit'* camera and making the space inside the room air-tight.

"No, absolutely not… This is not a *time machine*. It's only a three-D time camera. That too, only having the capability to peep into the past…" After fabricating a box to make as much portion of the store-house air-tight with the partitions pulled out from the Goblin-Spirit, *'Yakshek'* settled down in front of the camera screen. Entering the present date and the date on the day of Lon-Solon and Daarck's meeting, he pressed the button labeled VISIT and stood by waiting.

"With which technique does this amazing camera function?" Gosha asked Yakshek who was waiting with his hands clutched near the thighs.

"Time, which is the thing that comes into existence in the form of the result of events, is an imaginative thing, Monsieur Gosha. That cannot have any independent existence." Yakshek's response was in a peaceful dialect. "If it is necessary to give witness about the *'matter of fact'* of time, then at the maximum it can be called space. That provides space for the events to take place."

Noticing himself being stopped from speaking further, *Gosha* followed Yakshek's gaze.

Lon was now seen entering this room on the screen of the Goblin camera. After the Warlord who had come with him checked every single corner of the room with the *'Bludiation Wave-Fire Torch'*, Lon came and sat on the deep brown colored wood seat. Taking the memory-stick held by Gosha and installing it below the screen, *Yakshek* said, "Since appearance conversion is common in our world, until we made this camera with the aura-print matching feature, this camera was useless for legal use till that point of time." After about six seconds of the start of matching Lon's aura that was scattered in the room, a punch of 'unsuitable' flashed in the corner of the screen with a tro.. tro. tro. alert. When Gosha let out a terrible sigh of relief, Yakshek said, "I was telling you right from the beginning that no one will come in such a meeting without taking the aura modifying medicine. You cannot prove that this is Lon."

After one more minute passed, Solon entered the room arranging properly the *'star stand hat'* on his head.

Affectionately shaking hands with Lon, he went and sat on the palm shaped sofa in the front and said, "I quickly have to discuss about two to three issues with you. Before that weird *Daarck* arrives."

"Yes, you said the truth. I have not liked him. There is no harm in waiting a little if we can hire some other agency." When Lon said this, Yakshek pushed some more buttons below the screen. Even Solon's aura-print matching reports that had previously been saved in Goblin Spirit turned out to be negative. Both of them knew within their hearts that no one would have forgotten to take the *'aura-interfere-medicine'* for this type of meeting, yet Gosha kept on pushing the re-match button again and again…

Although the disappointment was not unimagnizable, it was hard to tolerate. When nearly three more minutes had passed *Daarck* entered in his original appearance that was there at that point of time. Despite being on this verge of defeat, a sigh escaped from Gosha's throat. "His eyes… Ahh… Hideaway for the mysteries of the whole world…"

Giving an enchanting heavenly smile as always, *Daarck* shook his left hand with Lon on the right and his right hand with Solon on the left side. As if scalded, both the VIPs rubbed their palm and glancing slightly on that side, they went and sat in their place. After removing the shining gloves from his hands, Daarck spoke as he settled in front of them, "My Lords…"

After thanking the glamour-girl and coming out of the restaurant, Gosha connected a call to Lord de Ros.

*

After Ros squeezed Daarck's throat and hurled him across, a fierce battle had started in the one mile periphery of Hell-Hall's roof. Solon who understood everything late had attempted to escape from there. Lon's army Warlords and the Liquor Mine soldiers were on one side, whereas Ros' ally colony Nebel-Shift's Win-Makers were on the other. And apart from that, the host Hell-Hall's spider-shaped robots were now lifting these hateful guests and throwing them off from the roof. The dual specialty of the Warlords had got them the top position due to their special characteristic that their height was one and a half times more compared to others, but at the end it became the smallest. After every attack of the Win-Makers, the upper layer of their body would get scattered and a small sized Warlord would come out from the chrysalis and start fighting again with the same agility. But the best performance of the *Liquor-Mine* warriors fighting after having consumed the *war-drug* was remarkable in this fierce battle. Because of the war-drug that excited the insight, their body made any attack from any side useless at a lightning speed. When this scuffling conflict became Stubborn, a Gardi soldier flying out from the airbus, stationed in sky, came and stood near Ros.

"Gosha." He said giving the phone.

"Destiny is not in our favor this time also…" Gosha said in a voice as if deep clouds of mourning had emerged, "The aura of not even one of them could be matched."

"Hum." Before Ros could respond with another word to this news that was the opposite of the good news he had expected to hear, Daarck came and stood in front of him. The tired soldiers had stopped fighting and had moved to one side now.

"Let's come straight to the point." Daarck spoke. "It is clear that we are never going to find those 10 New-Gods you have hidden. And at the same time, it is also clear that you are never going to be able to extract the Re-built Tune and Transmission-Germ information from my mind. Yet consider that somehow you acquire the Re-built and Transmission Germ. And after releasing the New-Gods you even became the owner of the eleven colonies. Yet, we will seize those eleven colonies of which you would have become a new owner, through the army prepared with the Project discs in just about six years. You cannot doubt that we do what we say, Ros. You will not be the owner of anything except the sighs of repentance. Reaching the destination apart from my proposal, your hands will be seen praying to a God without ears to get back *'Lydia Dyaan'* It is better to save the ownership of Cons Lydia than to become the prisoner of Mahanabh prison and keep praying for the end of immortal life." When Daarck turned and looked behind, standing in the crowd of Satanics, Filipa looked towards him and complacently gave him a smile of disgust. Taking Ros a little further, he spoke, "Ros, you are the only one who knows which fairy thing the Devil is going to acquire by returning their colonies to those New-Gods. I am giving you an offer on behalf of the Devil, hand over the imprisoned New-Gods to us and one New-God will be in your ownership. You know how he will be in your ownership. Permanently. And that too of your choice. I don't think you are so foolish to spurn this offer of becoming a partner in this fantastic concept."

Shuddering from Daarck's conclusive confrontation, bending his face in agreement Ros came closer like a namby-pamby and said, "Alright, where should I come with that New Gods?"

Looking into Ros' eyes and widening his lips, Daarck said, "I'll let you know the location in twenty minutes." And as if he had remembered something, he suddenly turned behind. His eyes were looking for Filipa in the crowd. "Oh shit. Swine, catch her…" Daarck screamed and with that, Malachi ran clenching his fists and stopping for a moment after reaching the edge of the roof, he directly leaped from the two hundred and fifty storied Hell-Hall.

After reaching below in Hell-Hall's Plaza, Filipa had literally run towards the S. Station two hundred meters away exactly in front to reach. Entering the S. Station, she quickly opened the purse hanging on her waist and taking out the travel-card, she gave it to the station in-charge. Rapidly connecting the phone to *Ruhan (A Chairman of Lon),* she glanced at the glass wall; Malachi was marching to reach like a cyclone. And a little behind him, a group of Satanics as well…

"It is necessary that I meet Lon right away." Filipa said quickly.

"I apologize, Ms. Filipa. Because as per Lon's orders, even Apotheosis himself will not be allowed to meet him in case he were to come right now."

"If you can ask Lon in this very second, then ask…" Filipa said talking intensely in a cutting-edge manner, "If you do not want Walk of Life to be eclipsed by Daarck's deceit, then he should spare some time for this *Protective Angel of the Truth less Infant." (Spurious Infant- Lon. Protective Angel- Filipa)*

As if Lon also had heard these words, the moment they were over, an address-code of an asteroid that changes after every visit flashed on Filipa's mobile screen.

Malachi who had entered the S. Station was only half a second late for the green signal that closed Filipa's door.

"The priest's lamenting has become intolerable…!" Gosha had come to give this news to Ros seated in a garden-pavilion on a rocky summit.

Putting both fingers at the edge of the forehead and gradually absorbing his defeat, Ros raised his head and looked at Gosha, Gosha moved a couple of steps back seeing his eyes that looked as if a fire had erupted in this deep darkness.

Bending his head he said with a lady-like suppleness, "The priest admonished to release him right away else to curse that…." Gosha lost the courage to speak the following words looked up and screaming Ouch.. Ouch.. Ouch.., he wobbled as he moved backwards even more. But till then Ros came closer to him had thrust the index finger in his right eye and had pulled it out.

Pressing his hand on the hanging blood and flesh, he sobbed waiting for Ros' order.

"Go and drag him here." Taking small bites of the eye-ball and relishing it, Ros again went and sat on the *'Throne'*.

As Gosha presented the priest, Ros got up and came down once again. "Who are you? A spy of Lon, Daarck or else a coward…" Said Ros and slapped him on his chest. He went to the priest who was knocked down on his back and scratching his cheek with the first finger, said, "Monkey! Did someone tell you that the war has ended. And with that end there is no wisdom in somersaulting on *'Cons Lydia'* which has become even more prosperous than before.

Dragging himself towards his book flung far off, the priest turned his head and said in a thorny voice, "Evil element, the time of your wilting has started like a plucked flower…"

Ros kicked him on his back and picking up the book, he said, "Son of a worm, what ultimately do you keep filled up in this book that cannot find single *success* for your Lord?" When Ros went to open the *'Lexicaptive'* having pages as strong as if made with four layers of the rhinoceros' skin, the priest shrieked reproachfully, "Fool, how much more powerful do you intend to make your misfortune by looking at the *Lexicaptive* against a priest's will."

The antagonized Ros raised his foot to trample the priest, but that leg remained suspended in the air with Arina's yell. Arina said, "Is this the damage, done due to disregard of the Raag Lake, not enough?"

Ros' courage betrayed him. As Ros threw the book on the priest's face and went off, the priest ran off in full speed in his opposite direction.

*

Looking at the asteroid on which Filipa had reached, she thought that she had dialed the wrong address-code by mistake. The arrival camera that had thrown her outside was set up on barren land and was hanging on a stand without walls and a roof like an orphan. The territory was absolutely barren except few igloos made up of stones on the right side. As Filipa went to the rear portion of the camera thinking where could be the location of this asteroid on Galaxy L3 and what Lon would be preparing to do at such a strange location, her glance fell on something that could be called a bike to quite an extent. The bike that had auto-started as soon as the hand was placed on the steering, sped at the speed of a bullet on the one and only aisle and Filipa's mind ran even faster than that...

"Daarck's doll, you look here. Somewhere this caper of yours to expose Daarck is not against his feeling towards Mithalia, is it? Saying everything in two words 'Throb.. Throb..' made her realize that Daarck could not be a bad person for sure… Yet the mind was not ready to believe. She now started looking here and there to escape from this terrible dilemma. Some human beasts as if infected with a weird virus, were staring at her from a skeleton like building that looked as left over after bearing the brunt of a bomb shower. "You are an expert at deceit, swindling and manipulation of fraud, but now you cannot shake me." When the *smart* Filipa hurled the heart-enticing Filipa in the thoughts arena, realizing that an exquisite category '*wood* cottage' was getting bigger, she reduced the speed of the bike to a very slow speed.

Lon came and stood on the step of the porch waving a painting brush over the frame made up of wooden chips. "The great Lon is also interested in painting!" Parking the bike on the stand, Filipa said looking at the laughing faces on the right wall of the cottage made by Lon.

"Daarck is coming here with the Devil in a little while. These faces are made for the test to ascertain whether we have imprisoned the real Devil or not. The Devil does not have an aura to test easily the real or fake."

After continuing to be slapped on the face for several moments by the angry breeze, Filipa said, "I had thought Lon that it is almost next to impossible to deceive your skill to verify someone's truth. But I have not liked your work as an investigator in Daarck's matter."

"Ohh…" Taking her inside, Lon exclaimed artificially.

"Daarck's work concludes here, Lon." Vapor emanated from Filipa's lips whose face invited questions. "Take him out of this project right away. Imprison him if possible. Otherwise you will repent throughout your life." She said garnering her hand in the jacket, "The creation of *'Walk of Life'* was done to imprison those ten New-Gods and to return their colonies to them after installing a particular type of chip in their body and they have used you for that."

"Alright, but what will happen by doing that?" Maybe after fitting that chip those New-Gods will function like robots for Devil and Daarck?" When Lon asked while hanging a painting on the wall behind a bowl filled with light, Filipa said, "A noble person like you is totally out of league with the demonical theology, Lon. You cannot even imagine what kind of things those evil hearted people Daarck and Devil think of."

Lon spoke with sarcasm, "Oh.. a fairy, who denied to give the Project Discs till Lon's intention became clear, how did she suddenly get so much trust on me? Anyways, now when you trust me, you must have come with those Project Discs, right? Ruhan, take those Project Discs from Filipa and conserve them, and now if you demur in believing the tale of this Vishkanya (Poison girl) who has come to rescue us from some unknown calamity and once again sinking *'Walk of Life'* which has now reached the shores, then you will be even bigger enemy of mine than those like Ros and Malesty." Seeing Filipa sighing, Lon now said with a serious countenance, "If you would not have killed Daarck and mislaid the Project Discs then Daarck was to come directly to me with those Discs, after that meeting. Thanks to you that I am not the owner of these eleven colonies. And again thanks to you, so many Idiotic soldiers have died in this war. After even intense investigation which failed to cause the premature retirement of the best of the spies, I could not obtain even an excerpt of who you are and where you have come from.

Filipa thought, "The mysterious truth that I am about to reveal, how much value will that truth hold in the eyes of this person? Will he ever believe me? Maybe he might, yet will he be able to do any harm to Daarck or the Devil? Who knows if he also is not in affiliation with the Devil?" Yet she continued to scrutinize with indirect-signs, what reaction would Lon gave on this matter. Shoving aside the enemies of ardency, she said firmly, "Anyways, considering the status of your trust, I will be able to give you only a small portion of the truth now."

"Yes, yes. I am eager." Nodding his head, Lon now watched her attentively. Finally even this restlessness was not able to do anything more specific than adding a special feature of beauty in her appearance.

"The chip I am telling you about, after failure of its initial version, the Devil entered Robrelco Fero's body with his entire power and invented an amazing 'chip' through his mind. One that was made of human tissue…"

"I know. A chip that changes the aura & cannot be detected in the body." Lon said.

Filipa now found it useless to speak further. She said, "Let it be. I only want to tell you that from here onwards whatever has to be done, meaning that remove the presence of Daarck in taking delivery of those ten New-Gods after six hours from Ros and getting the souls of your loyalists to enter into their bodies, etc. Daarck has already given you the Re-built Tune, Mummy-Ointment and Transmission-Germ. So now you don't need Daarck at all. If he really wanted to imprison the Devil then the priest would have got *Devilet-Again* from Mahanabh and reached you by now. But he would never do that, right."

Before Filipa could finish talking, knocks were heard on the door as if a detonator had come and stood there.

The injured *priest* who had traveled with hardship was unable to reach even up to the lounge. He reclined on the wall right next to the door and fell down. Giving the priest a large glass of alcohol to drink, *Ruhan* stared at him with mercy that one would feel on the condition of low standard loyalists.

Filipa once again felt a strong urge to tell everything. She suddenly spoke up, "Listen Lon, in the end, they were to return the colonies to their real New-Gods only, then in this entire plan of theirs, the *aura-transplant* was not going to be required even in the dreams."

"So?"

"Lon! Now you listen to this entire ingenious truth and just die… Actually the real objective of that chip…"

"Quieeet…. The whole world in his hands. Understood…?

HU AA O Uh…. As if playing in a horror suspense climax, the music passed through one ear of Filipa and moving in every single corner of her skull went out of her other ear. As if an invisible ghost had come near her and softly mumbled in her ears, for a moment she just got rooted to the same spot where she was standing. A shiver of fright ran across every part of her body at the speed of lightning. She turned with a jolt and looked behind from the window, but it was totally empty. She ran and opening the door, she encircled the entire cottage and came and stood at the same place.

"Someone was there?" Ruhan, who had followed, asked looking all around.

"No one." The lost Filipa responded and mumbled in her mind, "Except for the wind carrying Mithalia's fragrance." She did not feel that apart from these two fools she had seen since she came on this weird asteroid, anyone else would also be aware of the address-code of this place. And she would not mistake Mithalia's feel even if she were lifeless. When her mind was focused on striving to figure out the meaning of Mithalia's words, Lon was speaking with Daarck on the phone.

"Let's leave Woolybear aside. Ruhan and me have made the arrangements right here. You manipulate the Devil and… Oh what did I say..! You bring him right here…. The priest has also reached with *Devilet-Again*."

"Evil-God (Devil) cannot come now." Daarck said clearing his throat.

"But why…?" Lon was shocked.

"He said that he was absolutely not in the mood to travel right now. There is also no likelihood seen that his mind will change in some time."

"The Devil is saying no to come here, Ruhan!" As Lon removed the phone and spoke, Filipa grabbed the phone from his hand and said, "In your efforts to bring him here there must have been as much obstinacy as required to convince one to buy an expensive conditioner, right?" Saying this, she gave back the phone.

"But I have convinced him to meet for as many minutes as required to get our work done." Daarck said, "In order to imprison him, you have to get *Devilet-Again* and come on Minikin-06. I am sending the address-code."

*

Daarck kept the phone and moved close to 'Kpenica Lady' with a cage filled with mice. *(Kpenica Lady- A cat that recorded and immediately warned the Devil of the presence of forces having the intention to harm him)* After maneuvering the cat and locking it in the cage he came out. The spell of darkness had spread almost an hour earlier on the subdivision of the Devilish planet 'Minikin 06' located on latitude 40, Galaxy-L3 West. Daarck went to the well in the cottage courtyard, bent to his waist and gesturing by putting a finger on his lips to Kpenica Lady, he hung the cage on the inside wall of the well. As he turned listening to the sound of someone's slow steps, he saw Luciano coming with a disconsolate countenance.

"Luciano, on account of your friendship with Gosha, you must be aware by now that Lord de Ros has made an unsuccessful attempt with Prestige's Goblin Spirit camera. That tape is useless. It does not prove Lon and Solon to be present in it. Anyways, now you don't have anything to barter against a share in the colonies. Yet, at one point of time you were my employee. Keeping your services in mind, I can make arrange a nice prosperous asteroid for you. Go with Malachi and hand over that tape to him right away."

Luciano nodded his head in agreement and without uttering even a single word he went towards Malachi.

Daarck returned to Terror-Street, he shoved some more logs in the fire-place and went to Rihon and his companions standing on the Re-build Tune's magic-plate with violin. Since Terror-Street was the private property of the Master of Betrayal (Devil), it was categorically special. A slight stench, like passing through a factory manufacturing leather products, was spread in there. After settling Rihon, Antosa, Damitri, Leonid and Ekaksh properly on the magic plate, he said, "The recent years have been unlucky for you. But now your right to freedom is established. Pushing Rihon inside with the violin stick, who was standing slightly outside on the Re-built Plate, Daarck looked into the deep eyes of the *Chief Misguide (Devil)* and said, "I am surprised that even the cunning minds are proved to be ineffective against the easy mystery of the Re-built Tune, *Re-built Tune* is just the Tie-in Tune played reversely from the end to the beginning."

Rihon understood that as the secret of the 'Re-built' revealed to them, these were now the last moments of them all. As if practicing for years, Daarck started playing the 'Re-built Tune' rhythmically. Although the *SARGAM (tune)* was melodious but was frightening. The layers of Robrelco Fero's soul coming out from their bodies united and stood in the form of a ferocious physical body with an eye scintillated flash. The drops of sweat trickling from the tip of Rihon's and his companions' noses were getting freezed into ice particles before touching the ground.

The entire *'Deviltry Theatre'* echoed with the horrifying screams of "Pardon … Pardon." Daarck slipped towards the door pressing his temple due to the noise.

After raising his eyebrow in front of Rihon and giving him a stinging look, Robrelco Fero spoke, "Forgiveness is just there in my dictionary... But to keep on reminding me that mankind is not at all worthy of it. And yes, Daarck's talk of freedom is not true..!" Daarck looked at this Huge-Demon in shock, because when he said this, Robrelco Fero was still restrained in bonds. Although his gender was dormant, the size inevitably appealed to attract the attention. He spoke further, "The real bonds are to start now. A powerful rotation of the souls of *all five of you (In the whole world the procedure to unite the souls of five people and create a super-powerful demon was* only *acquired by Robrelco Fero)* will start indefinitely working for me in the form of my 'bonded-servant' from this very moment." Saying this, as he wrung the necks of Damitri, Leonid, Ekaksh and Antosa one by one, and gestured Rihon standing far away with his index finger to come closer. This behavior was more painful than death for the Chairman of Earth Eleven who had thousands of Gardis on a stand to serve him. but realizing that reluctance would make death more painful, he slowly, gradually slipped closer to Robrelco Fero like a strict Headmaster's puppy-dog.

As if some group of the youngsters of a country governed by hypocrites who made the night vibrant with alcohol, youth and all types of intoxicating things and then get dressed up in neat and clean clothes the next day to formulate rules that would molest the independence in the name of culture for the rest of the countrymen, would be bustling in the intensity of a Rave Party and suddenly a stampede starts with the shout of raid…, similarly Daarck who had become alert as a result of someone having forgotten to descend slowly, took the chisel hanging on the wall and chopped off Rihon's head in one stroke. Fortunately, Rihon's head rolling in the style of a rugby-ball fell upturned as it hit the feet of Lon who had entered the door.

"Hey…" Lon confronted Robrelco Fero who had put all the corpses on his shoulder and reached the rear door, yet he just stood there showing his back.

The Devil said, "This is just the perpetual evening worship taking place on Terror-Street after giving sacrifice. You just go on, Satanic." The Devil ordered and *Robrelco Fero* went off banging the door behind him.

"Has some Dracula-Party just ended here?" Filipa, straightening Rihon's chopped head, asked without taking off her glance from Daarck's labyrinth-like eyes.

"Filipa!" Come here. The time is less. I will have to return soon." Lon opened the bag and put a painting with a smiling face in Filipa's hand. After that, taking out a heavy book from the bag and extending it towards *Daarck*, he said, "Here is your informer's Lexicaptive." He started watching the painting with slanted eyes. Seeing painful signs starting to emerge on the image's face, he instantly moved his glance to the small aura-capturing-device embedded in the ring, the report was blank and the Devil standing in front of him was real.

A squabble of cock fight had now erupted between the couple that always kept on fighting there. "You want to see, right… See, who was the betrayer…?" Saying this, Daarck picked up the shiny blond tresses of Rihon and held his blood dripping head in front of Filipa's face. When the nauseated Filipa turned off in the other direction, Daarck hurled the head outside the door. Hinting Filipa to remain calm, Lon gestured Daarck to be prepared and turned towards the Devil. With an intention to keep him embrangled in discussion, he spoke, "But I do not understand why Ros agreed to give those imprisoned New-Gods to us before Apotheosis would give a decision on Kaylos' Menithus?"

The Devil said in a slightly frightened voice, "Even if Apotheosis cancels this Menithus, what could be the other output than a great war between all the colonies of both your groups? Ros has now realized that in such a war there is no possibility for anyone else apart from *Caprio,* the dealer of weapons and S. Channel *Megacorp* to get an advantage in such a war. Then why not end this matter right here by taking several planets of these ten colonies."

With a glance asking Daarck, "What games are you still playing even though the opportunity has established itself correctly?" Lon said, shouting at him as he whisked the roll of the Menithus Agreement in the air, "Out of total ten colonies, one part of four colonies in my share, one part of four to the Devil Family and the other remaining two colonies will come in Antonio's and Daarck's share. Of course, the planets to be given to Ros will also be from amongst those two colonies only." Saying this, he glanced towards Daarck. Standing behind the Devil, Daarck was turning the pages of *Devilet-Again* in a hurry. While trying to find the end of the crystal chain carving that had spurted on the page by the magnifying glass, Daarck had just started feeling the need of an infinite life, realizing that everything going on is quite weird, the Devil turned his head and directly jumped to snatch the book from Daarck's hand, but before '*Devilet-Again*' could fall in his hands, the style in which the Messenger of Death throws a trap for sinners, similarly Daarck threw the edge of the crystal chain that had come out from the book on the Devil's neck and started gasping at a turbulent pace as if he was meeting his breath that had been in waiting for centuries.

A mysterious power had sucked the element of life from the depths of the *Evil-father's (Devil's)* soul. An ambience, as if the whole world was preparing to go to the region of eternal happiness by sit in the spiritual aircraft, had permeated there. As soon as the entire consciousness of the Devil left him, pulling the magnifier from Daarck's hand, Lon leaped towards the most horrifying corpse in the world. Selecting one bead from the countless small transparent beads of the chain that had encircled the Devil, he placed the magnifier on that and as if hit by a current he was thrown back along with Filipa who was peeping the chain from his right shoulder.

Inside the bead, an innocent, glass-like, transparent-bodied and sad *holy-doll* was seated in a sorrowful condition with her head leaning on the crystal wall. *(Holy-doll – The holy goddesses making the Devil inactive along with his entire power)* Lon instantly checked the other beads. In several places, on the connecting point of the beads, two holy-dolls were gossiping in their own prison with an *'Oh God this is strange'* expression. The eyes of many were desolate whereas some gave proof of having just passed through a holocaust of tears. Lon spoke, "Is the creator of *Devilet-Again*, not even the father of the Devil...? Who knows how many eras these pious souls have spent quietly crying in such a tragic imprisonment...?"

Lon desired to break the chain right away, "But surely after few days." Saying this he pacified his mind.

Getting a ragged coffer from the rear side of Terror-Street, Daarck kept it down and picking up the Devil who was wrapped in the trap from head to toe, he assigned him to the coffin. Holding the coffer's handle and picking it up, Lon turned towards Filipa. A passionate but veiled happiness of a dream about to be fulfilled was reflecting in his laughter. Lon said, "No one is going to get any share, Filipa. *Glee Metal Casting* will have control over all these ten colonies. The armies of these ten Vio-Crazy colonies will unite together and win the rest of the Vio-Crazy colonies one after another. Consider these last days to be a warm-up in front of this great-war that is going to start to capture the entire Vio-Crazy group. Galaxy-L3 will only be able to enjoy the relief of an un-soldiered time only after the merger of the whole Vio-Crazy community with the Idiotics." Saying this, he shook the coffer to and fro, but the coffer was only as heavy as his individual weight. Shocked, he opened the cover. On seeing the Devil lying just like that, he closed it again and looking at Daarck, he asked, "How long will it take for him to die…?"

"What...?" Daarck's voice was one to switch-off the heart. He spoke. "Right from the beginning when we have talked about *Devilet-Again,* its meaning was that I will be giving you a small part of *Devilet-Again.* It is true that *spells* and *rituals* for the Devil's destruction are given in *Devilet-Again,* but it is impossible to get that entire scripture. And you are assuming that the entire *Devilet-Again* will fall in your hands and this world should be released of its own existence along with evil…? Mr. Lon, the Devil is an essential base for the worldly creation and its maintenance. You cannot pull him out and bring the world to an end. The ones who rot in this world, also rarely have such a desire.

"Forgive me Daarck. I doubted you." Saying this, Filipa bowed at Daarck's feet.

"O... Filipa, get up... I have never loved you in a way that it would reduce even with your big mistakes." Although Daarck had expected such dramatic scenes to be enacted by Filipa, but looking at filipa's eye, who had bathing with tears, the antenna of his ingenious mind were spread out a little.

Crying with her head on Daarck's thighs, Filipa swiftly got up. Wiped her cheeks... And going to Lon, she said. "My travel card is empty. Since I have to go far, can I get a card on loan?"

"The time has come to return home, Filipa." Accompanying them up to the door and putting a special travel-card to take them out from Minikin-06 in Lon's hand, Daarck said, "But will my heart remain cheerful on the Master Galaxy, Filipa?"

"Yes sure. Before you complete the packing, I will have come back to you." As if the root of the conflict had gone into the grave, spreading a fiery smile, as soon as Filipa put her hand on Lon's shoulder, Lon, waiting restlessly, took the Devil and Filipa and flew away with them.

After Lon and Filipa disappeared on the aerial path taking them towards the Dummy S. Station of Minikin-06, Daarck got down into the courtyard. Pulling the torches burning on the right wall, he went near the well and got *'Kpenica Lady'* inside once again. In the dim light of Terror-Street, Robrelco Fero had opened his small lag-bag and was loading *'micro-chips'* in many tido-guns.

"The time has come *Rob." (Robrelco Fero)* Daarck said flicking his hand and looking at the watch, "The time, for which the melee of the Walk of Life is raised. Ros will take those ten New-Gods from Mahanabh and will leave to come here in the next sixty seconds. Are the chips ready?"

"Yes, it is absolutely ready." Robrelco Fero's high tone came "I cannot see the success of this plan any further now, but Ros will have to be sent the address-code of the station towards the West. Your wretched Filipa planted a mini-timer-bomb outside the station while leaving. She blew of the S. Station itself, thinking that we should remain trapped right here."

"It does not make any difference. But anyways, the address-code she dialed in the Station was to go to which location?"

"On the toy planet Earth of Lord de Ros… The code is of some S. Station near some Egypt city out there…"

Listening to this, Daarck's cerebral hemisphere got sparked. "How would Filapa have known that Anjeolmac is in a pyramid?" Daarck was just thinking about it when suddenly the scene passed from his mind's screen, in which while they were going to Kaylos' place from Lon's space vehicle Woolybear, Filipa had forcefully hugged him. *'How easily she had slipped the microphone in his pocket.'*

Daarck instantly connected the call to Ros and said, "We cannot do all this on Minikin anymore."

"Then?" Ros asked.

"In minimum how many minutes can you meet with those ten New-Gods in the Nile River region, near the Kahira Pyramid located in the South-West on your planet Earth?"

"Within ten minutes at the most."

"And block all the S. Stations of Earth this very second."

"There is no sense in doing that. There are a plethora of Dummy S. Stations on the Earth." Saying this Ros kept the phone and turning towards the Chairmen of his ally colonies, he spoke, "Congratulations, Prestige's Chairman *'Deivintyoti'* has agreed to the deal of weapons awarding victory within hours instead of days. He is meeting us in Egypt within twenty minutes."

*

Egypt's Capital Cairo

"I am willing to bet, Benedict, that Filipa's heart is not going to agree to break Daarck's head..." Dragging behind Filipa as she ran towards the *'Great Pyramid of Khufu'* with the bait of a competitive sprinter holding a big hammer, Antonio said to Benedict, who was walking on his right side. Finally getting fed up, Benedict asked,

"Filipa, ultimately what is the matter?" All three of them had worn the thistle-quiet cap that made them invisible.

"That Anjeolmac hidden in the Pyramid is the ultimate way to stop Daarck and the Devil. If Daarck does not agree, then I will take this Anjeolmac to Apotheosis and expose his entire plot. Although I am aware that if I do this I will lose Daarck forever, but as it is a question of the lives of billions of human beings, I will do it."

"Please speak something that would make at least some sort of sense." When Benedict said this, they had now entered the VIP area of the Khufu Pyramid campus crossing the Open-air theatre that was jam-packed with guests who had gathered to enjoy the light show a little away from the pyramid. Walking swiftly looking at the incessant scene opposite her, Filipa suddenly stopped balancing herself as if there was a fall ahead. Looking at the hustle and bustle of a band performing with big violins and saxophones, feats of jugglers taking out fire from their mouth and amidst endless cocktails, political leaders from across the world, countless guards, clusters of journalists in the campus of the Khufu Pyramid, she said, "Oh no... Damn it. All these fucking had to take place here at this moment only...!"

"Today is the night of thirty-first December. The night of New Year celebrations for the inhabitants of Earth..." Saying this, Antonio pointed his finger towards a very big count-down watch in the front that was busy wrestling with the thirty minutes standing between the residents of the earth and their new year, trying to pull the attention to itself.

"As of now, there are few minutes left for the extermination of the world. Anyways let it be." Filipa said, "Daarck was the one who sent Mithalia to Apotheosis. The place where he wanted to bring about a revolution was not only Galaxy-L3 but every planet of all the colonies of all the six galaxies. And to do this it was necessary to uproot and throw off the main foundations of authority. And the ultimate base of all this authority is with Apotheosis and Prestige. Daarck had sent Mithalia to the Directors by deceiving her that if the secret of their powers could be found out and could be taken in control, then the desired change could be brought about immediately and permanently. Anyways, even I am not fully aware of the final facts of what all is going on. Yet I have certainly known that Daarck's strategy of establishing good governance by eliminating Apotheosis, Prestige and the Vio-Crazy New-Gods of all the galaxies was only an excuse. An excuse for him and the Devil to do as per their whims."

"What arbitrariness?" Antonio asked picking up a piece of fish roasted with herbs from a counter on the right side. But before Filipa could respond, Benedict said extending the phone towards Filipa, "*Dustin* is on the line." *(Dustin – A Chairman of Colony Nebel-Shift whose New-God Malesty had been imprisoned by Ros)*

"Lord de Ros is fooling you." Swiftly moving away from the three tourists who had stopped on hearing the voices coming out from the invisibility near the meat roasting stick in the desert banquet, Filipa said further, "He has struck a deal of the New-Gods of all of your ten colonies with Daarck, the Devil's loyalist right in front of me in Hell-Hall. They will give them back their colonies within a short time. Can you imagine what will happen to your ten treacherous Chairmen after that?"

"Tell us more, girl..." Saying this, Dustin, who was hopefully moving ahead with Ros' caravan from the South of Menkaure Pyramid, put a smile on his face and placing his hand on Painter's shoulder, he suddenly reduced his pace. (Painter- Chairman of the Run-Cap Colony)

Filipa said, "If you can coax Ros and take him to your Colony Nebel-Shift right now, then... Just a minute..." After listening to the chorus lines of Michael Jackson's song, *'We are the world. We are the children. We are the ones, who make a brighter day...'* that was echoing in the Pyramid region in the phone, Filipa removed the phone and quickly spoke up, "Now you gone, Dustin."

"A small troupe of *Win-Makers (Dustin's army)* is worried as they are not getting a clearance from the South Pole S. Station, Ros." Dustin had stopped. And, about twenty steps ahead, so had Ros.

Standing in front of one of the world's heritage site, the Mortuary Temple of Khafre in Egypt, Ros, generously praising it, now turned towards Dustin and said, "Oh!... My recent New-God Dustin needs to be explained that because of this deal of ours being with *Apotheosis'* tough enemy *Prestige's* Chairman, it is imminent to block all the Stations on Earth. But don't worry, the security arrangements are adequate. Approximately ten thousand

Gardi soldiers are present around us right now." Saying this, Ros laughed in a loud voice.

Seeing Arina coming towards him with a supple gait, Dustin realized that it was too late now. Arina who had come closer snatched the phone from his hand, and when looking at this extreme pertness, Painter asked, "What is going on here?" Asking this, Arina slapped Painter with a whack. Listening to the resounding laughter echoing from the invisibility of Ros' caravan, a stampede had taken place among the tourists who had come to visit the Mortuary Temple.

Running staggeringly in the golden sand towards the Pyramid that was still standing two hundred meters away, Filipa connected a call to Lon and hissed, "Lon, you fool, Galaxy-L3 will always remember you and not Daarck as the real *Devil's advocate* for shoving them towards destruction."

"What has happened again, Filipa?" Lon asked in a cool voice.

"After having spent countless prayers of billions of sorrowful people, you have just purchased a zero, you bloody fool." *(The meaning of what Filipa was saying was that- You have not been able to give any benefit to sad people through the 'Walk of Life' that had been created from the cries of countless suffering people). Ros* who had promised to come with those ten New-Gods to meet you on *Myunar (A home planet of Lon)* after six hours has reached Egypt with them. That deal is going to take place right now with Daarck... Now come here and see their spooky game yourself."

Jumping as if Filipa's phone had twitched him, *Lon* said in a voice as if pleading for his protection from destruction, "Ruhan, I feel that we have taken Filipa's tale in very lightly due to her past misdeeds... Get the Dragon War-craft ready."

A live broadcast of the light show bringing to life the tale of *Misr (Egypt)* was in progress on the *'Khufu Pyramid'* from where Filipa had to reach to break the stone and take out Anjeolmac. Since the Thistle-cap was incapable of keeping them invisible amidst the laser-beams being cast on the Pyramid from a distance, exactly at the place where their pace slowed down a little, Filipa suddenly jumped and stood in that direction as a familiar voice hit her ears amidst the voice of the *'Sphoenix'* that was narrating the culture of Misr.

"OK! Let them come, we will see." Daarck said, "But Ros or even one of his Gardi-soldier should not approach anywhere around the Khufu Pyramid." Coming out from the *'Live Cooking Stations'* serving a delightful variety of delicacies, Daarck's gaze fell on Filipa *(Since he was wearing the Kirlian Glass that had the capability of seeing a person who had become invisible with a Thistle-cap)* and removing the phone from his ear, he snarled,

"Don't be mad, Filipa."

"Don't be monster, Daarck..."

"Just stand right there, and I will reveal even the ultimate secret to you right now..."

"And Antonio, it is not that this rook Daarck is going to fail in trapping us once again." Saying this, Before Filipa slowly moving farther from Daarck with backward steps could turn to escape, she collided with the back of an Egyptian who was gulping down alcohol." Before the surprise of the man wiping the drink from his face and groping to see what had collided could reduce, Daarck's collision threw him on his friends standing in front of him. "Go to hell, you primeval insane..." Saying this, Daarck ran behind Filipa.

"It's *Filipa* or *Fero...?*" Before he could regain his composure as he surmised in Arabic, *Antonio's* third collision threw him directly on his head.

Although she had worn an uncomfortable dress, Filipa's running was praise worthy. Running about six steps behind Filipa sprinting zigzag from among the party animals drowned in the emulation of displaying their best personality, as Daarck snatched an ice-cream candy from the hands of a tall girl and threw it between Filipa's legs, she slipped and dropped directly in Daarck's arms. While dangling in his hands, she raised a hammer and hit it on Daarck's nose. Daarck, who had leaped behind was hurled on Antonio and directly fell with him on an air-filled Santa Claus. because of the band serving music for the moon light party, frightened with the paranormal activity of soaring candy, falling guests and breaking counters, had suddenly stopped, the sweet exclamations of the 'children party unit' that was readily waiting there for new kinds of competitions like 'Beautiful Baby on Earth', looking at the Santa Claus from whom the air was coming out, the sounds of their claps echoed in all four directions.

Seeing a radiant shadow like a spirit exactly in the middle of the Khufu-Pyramid frequently changing its appearance with the purple, yellow, pink and green lights, Filipa realized that Daarck's informer had reached there before her. She started taking big leaps to climb the high steps, but before she could leave the third step, her collar was in Daarck's fist and The forceful jolt with which she resisted and stopped herself from falling backwards, ripped off a strap of her expensive dress with a rriiipppp... sound from head to toe. As Antonio caught hold of Daarck's other hand and flung him down, Daarck crashed with a bang on the dinner table of an American Ambassador's family. When they fiercely got up as if a rocket-launcher had fallen, a stampede finally took place with the fright of a terrorist attack in the party that resembled a *worldly heaven* a few minutes back.

As Daarck's informer had worn a Thistle-cap, his body appeared like a spirit amidst the laser-beam of the light show on the Pyramid. When he barbarically started hammering, Filipa was still about twenty steps below him. The Egyptians were experiencing the hammer blows falling on one of the blocks of the Seventh Wonder of the World's two million stones, hitting their hearts. After taking the Presidents, Secretaries and Political personalities of different countries into a protective encirclement, when a group of surplus guards ran towards the Pyramid to catch this spirit, a womanly spirit fuming with anger was seen running behind this turbulent ghost escaping with Anjeolmac that was taken out by breaking the stone. It appeared as if a quarrel had transpired between a demonic-couple having the specialty to give birth to ghosts for performing negative activities."

The focus of the laser-beam was exactly following these two spirits now. When one from the pair of girls recording a video of this ghostly event out there just like everyone else on the sands below, shouted and told her companion that *'It appears that Cleopatra's animosity filled spirit is behind Antony (A Roman General),'* at that time Daarck caught Antonio's face in his palm to pull out his Kirlian-glasses as he was scuffling with Daarck on the starting step of the Pyramid, but since the Thistle-cap of his trembling face fell in his hand every phone-camera now turned in that direction to make the video of this creature that had manifested from the country of demons. As Antonio continued to glare at the crowd screaming and shouting as they came closer on seeing his fight against some invisible thing, the Gardis started a shoot-out on *Antonio.* But fortunately, the battery of his Gizmo was still alive.

Since Anjeolmac had come in his informer's hand, Daarck took the path towards the Nile River instead of chasing Filipa. A guard of an *'Egyptian Thunderbolt Force'* picked up the Kirlian glasses of Antonio lying there withered in the sand. After he straightened the bent shaft and put on the glasses, he saw a scene of two weird armies standing opposite each other far away in the desert. When he ran to his commander to show this illusory sight, the commander insidiously gave him an intense shock with an *Electric Shock Device* in his waist and threw him down. *(Through, one of Lord de Ros' Gardi soldiers present in the Government of every country on each of his planets.)*

† "The Ultimate Mission – Stage of the Devil" †

In the stretch of the Nile River, Lord de Ros and Robrelco Fero had arranged themselves opposite each other with their respective battalions, Gardi-force and Energy-Warriors. Far away in the Pyramid's premises, where the eupnoea of the party had become normal again, Daarck patted the shoulder of Robrelco Fero as he watched the digits of *'2020'* on the verge of being burnt to ashes and placed the stick on the violin. Along with his nine Satanics, standing ready with the same type of *'Chip-in guns'* as his, Robrelco Fero now settled himself behind Ros' ten Gardis with whose souls those ten New-Gods were imprisoned.

Daarck started playing the Re-built Tune but as if the present was not willing to accept the responsibility of this event, Lon who had popped-up like a disaster, hurled far away with Daarck. Despite these horrible days of war having passed, Lon had turned up with the most modern war-craft of Metal Casting that was eager yet to prove its Deadly Performance. Once the 'Dragon war-craft' with nuclear supply stuffed in its belly enough to destroy three Earths like this, swallowed its tail and coiled itself up three hundred meters above this gathering, Lon's Chairman Ruhan flew out from it and came down.

"Four seconds are more than enough for my war-craft to clear off this sludge of yours." Lon said alternately moving his deadly gaze on everyone. "But before a new *red-carpet* to be spread I am really willing to give even half of *'Metal Casting'* to know what is the secret of this disgusting game of yours. For what Daarck..! Ultimately for what..?" *(Red-carpet – To fill the ground with blood)*

"For this..." When the Devil, the master of this ceremony pulled a Chip-in gun from the hands of one Gardi and waved it in front of Lon, Lon's eyeballs almost reached the point of falling down.

"Hahaha..." Raising his head like a wolf and laughing, Daarck said, "Wick in a stick of dynamite. That coffer in which you imprisoned the Devil and took with you, the wick burning in its inside walls reaches the blasting cap of the coffer's bottom made with explosive material after twenty minutes journey, and boom...." If Filipa would not have wiggled out then we would not also have had to do this drama of imprisoning the Devil."

"That's fine Bilzebub, even though you return all their colonies to these ten New-Gods, I will continue with this war." Lon said glaring scowling at the Devil.

The *Devil* whose face had been scorched with the coffer's blast, said. "When the colonies will be returned, the agreement made by Kaylos, according to which the other Vio-Crazy colonies cannot assist Ros and his ally colonies in this war will automatically be cancelled. And after that if you make this insolence, then the entire Vio-Crazy group will be standing against you."

Before the *'wind'* filled with the threats of the Nile River going away could proceed further, *Solon (Apotheosis' Chairman),* astounded with separate invitations from *'Daarck'* and *'Filipa'* for the same location Egypt, having arrived, he quietly stopped right there in the temptation of experiencing the balminess of unprecedented mysterious revelations.

"Solon, please explain to this son of the God. He will have to finally go away from the place where the Devil is present." Saying this, Paras started a video in the mini-pad and gave the pad in Solon's hand. Daarck bent towards Lord de Ros and said in a soft voice, "Don't worry Ros, this meeting was different from the meeting for which you tried to acquire the video through the Goblin Spirit." When the disappointed Solon finally handed over the mini-pad to Lon, Daarck went and stood beside Lon. When the un-match symbol flashed on the screen of the mini-pad between Lon's fingers which was matching his aura, Lon raised his head questioningly to Daarck. Daarck asked him to look towards the screen again. *Daarck* was now shaking hands with him and Solon in the video. As soon as Daarck took off his gloves after shaking hands, as if setting fire to all aspirations of Lon, a smiley chanting *'Aura is in tune'*, *'Aura is in tune'* popped up with a clang. Daarck winked and said slowly, "We had borne the terror of failure many times during the production of the chemical-gloves to bring down the effect of the Aura medicine. The second one of the original tapes is currently safe on the Master Galaxy. So go, and start preparing for a new conspiracy like the Walk of Life. Who knows, this time you actually might get success."

It was very surprising for everyone present there to see Apotheosis' Chairman Solon*zx* himself in a horror-struck disposition. Going near Daarck who was mending the broken cords of the Violin held in Malachi's hand, Solon told him in a poisonous tone, "Tell me the price of both the tapes?" Before Daarck could give any response, moving aside the crowd of Satanics and coming forward in the style of a Guardian-Angel, Filipa said, "Probably I will be able to make Daarck understand now," She handed Anjeolmac, that she had pressed in her armpit, over to Antonio and coming extremely close to Daarck she put her cheek on his cheek. She slowly said in a love-rapt voice, "Keep mercy on them Daarck... Why don't the laughing faces attract you? Why doesn't becoming the cause of happiness of billions of people of countless planets thrill you? Filipa moved her cheek from his cheek and not seeing any change in Daarck's expressionless countenance despite that, she finally said in a harsh tone, "You will not even be able to assess how painful it will be to lose you forever, Daarck. Yet I will do this." Moving behind with determination, she took Anjeolmac from Antonio and extending it towards Solon she said in his ear, "This is the one that Apotheosis is searching." When Daarck quickly moved close to Filipa in order to stop her from speaking further, Filipa said, "I have not called Solon here alone. He has come here with his whole personal army."

Daarck held Solon's hand and pulling him to one side, he said, "I will give you the original copies of both the tapes in exchange of this Anjeolmac. When I say, reach there with Filipa and this box, but please go away from here right away."

"I apologize, Lon." Turning towards Lon standing far, Solon said, "I should have become more modern with respect to the security against someone like Daarck." Saying this, he took big leaps as if measuring the land and going near Filipa, he picked her up and flew far in the direction of his air-craft.

Daarck initiated the melody of the Re-built Tune and as the ten New-Gods started manifesting in their physical bodies, the Satanics standing behind them, loaded the *'chip'* using the guns in the internal part of their brains. The manifested New-Gods waved their hands here and there in the pleasure of being alive and as soon as their glance fell on *'Lord de Ros'* who was standing in front of them, they all went forward to attack him together. Coming and standing in the middle, Daarck said as he extended a three paged Menithus Agreement and *'Lazo'* pen beneath nose of *'Malesty'*, "Not now, what is important right now is your freedom that will find you many ways to take revenge against Ros."

"What is all this?" Malesty opened his mouth and hid the happiness of the assurance that he could speak.

The Devil came in front of Malesty and giving a shoddy smile, he said, "The *'Devil Family'* had taken part in this battle for the sole purpose of getting freedom for all of you. In order to prove, that there was no role whatsoever of the Devil Family in the *Walk of Life* conspiracy that had been plotted against all of you. Just see, we are even betraying Lon for your rights in order to return your colonies to you. Just let us all sign on this Menithus having some insignificant conditions that is standing between you and your freedom, and your mega empire will be awaiting you."

Malesty now started reading the details of the Menithus Agreement loudly.

"During the subsequent 10 years, neither one of these ten freed colonies cannot attack the *'Devil Family'* or Lord de Ros' Colony *'Cons Lydia Dyaan'* either individually or jointly. After that, for an unspecified duration, the armies of the *'Devil Family'* will be bound to give Ros unconditional assistance with its entire capability in the attacks done by anyone on *'Lydia Dyaan'*. The conditions will be automatically cancelled in the situation of an attack being done either by Ros or the Devil Family on any one of these ten colonies. From the asteroids in your possession, all of you ten New-Gods will have to give one planet each of your own choice to Ros. And along with that all ten of your traitorous Chairmen as well..."

"We will wait for ten years, Ros. And after that we will obliterate your existence." Saying this, Malesty signed and passed on the Menithus towards the other New-God.

"This is foolishness." Lon said, "Before the end of ten years the Devil Family and Ros will have united together and would have prepared armies through the '*Walk of Life*' Project Discs that could eliminate all your armies and will also have won over your colonies by then."

"Oh really," Malesty replied to Lon, crunching his teeth to his traitorous Chairman *Dustin*, "If at all they want our Colonies, then what is the reason behind returning them to us and releasing us?"

"That is exactly what I am unable to understand." Saying this, Lon sighed. His head had started reeling. "O Heavenly Father... Finally even the truth is getting defeated here." Mumbling, as Lon went his way, far away on the stage of the Pyramid complex like an *'Ultimate Party Spot on the Earth'*, the pop-rock party had suddenly subsided and a *'ten... nine... eight... seven...'* countdown welcoming the new year had begun. Along with bidding adieu to the year filled with sweet and sour memories of tsunami, storms and financial difficulties expressing the hope of a better year, the Presidents of all the countries had done leadership of the crowd for this countdown to enter the new year. Amidst magnificent fireworks, a heart rendering music and prayer started there. But how would the guests writing their own wishes and sending the lanterns in the sky know that on their ground itself, the defeated Gods standing helplessly at the side, themselves were especially in need of prayers right now.

The alieonic crowd silently watching the sky sparkling with unlimited sky-shot crackers and the burning *'Welcome 2020'* digits with empty, desolate eyes, slowly and gradually went their own way.

*

After three weeks. On Colony Nebel Shift's toy-planet 'Illicit Daliance' of New-God Malesty who had been released.

"I have come to seek forgiveness for my sins." Lon said folding his hands and standing like a criminal before the jury in front of all those ten *'New-Gods'* along with *Malesty* who had been released, "Put aside whatever happened between us, but let's get together and bury the *axe of revenge* now."

"Say whatever you want to very clearly." Malesty growled.

"After getting released, all of you have got nuclear wars started on twenty-five of your *Toy Planets*, together. These innocent people of the Toy Planets are not at all responsible for what happened with you. What would you get by taking revenge against them? Tell me the price to stop this dictatorship of the third world..?"

"Price....? Grinding his teeth, *'Malesty'* went forward and pushed Lon on his chest, "Bastard, you and your bloody *'Metal Casting'* will not be able to pay the price even after being auctioned."

"You bloody cause of destruction...!" Another New-God *'Murat'* now fumed at Lon in a painful voice, "What has your *Daarck* done with us by fitting that chip in our heads? What kind of an effect of that chip is this…? Consider the intoxication of one bottle of alcohol is not even equivalent to one sip. Nothing has changed, yet it is as if there is no taste left in life..." Before Murat could speak further, a Win-Maker soldier who had suddenly come there in magician-like clothes and hat said:

"My lords, we are on *Water-guard's (A country of Illicit Daliance)* land that is considered to be the most pious."

This statue that has been made by carving a big rock is not a God's statue, but is that of the *'Holy Father'* Salas who bestowed freedom to the youth by crashing Water-guard's orthodox and strangling constitution. As a symbol of respect to this President of Water-guard, many couples of this country get tied with the marriage-knot at this place every year. The whole country is watching a live broadcast of this ceremony." Laughing slyly, the Win-Maker soldier gestured towards the row of majestic looking brides.

After Malesty signaled the Win-Maker to go away from there, another New-God said taking Murat's matter further, "Our minds are burning in the ocean of an endless yearning. How much ever pleasure you enjoy, still more, still more... Ahh what is this...!" His venting of anger was still going on when rubbing his hands, Murat spoke up gesturing towards the brides, "Really this time we should have fun indeed."

"The man famous with the name of The Welder, standing opposite on the head position far away in the garden had just completed the spells protecting from vanity, evil-eye and all kinds of disasters announced the couples wedded husband and wife when the Win-Makers who had been waiting ran screaming Hooray. They started the fiasco of this bestiality, through which the New-Gods were expecting to derive some pleasure, by slaughtering the guards. Amidst the inundation of the blood of bridegrooms who had come out on the ground to protect their brides in this open regime of live-rape and the screams of the brides who looked like a tonic to revitalize the gardens, every single corner of Lon's mind suddenly shone up with the speed of a big bang. Laughing, crying, sullenness, praising… taking a confusion of many feelings altogether, Lon's mind started plunging in the moat of indicative words- "In their entire plan there is no need of the aura-transplant even in the dreams…" After remembering Filipa's words, finally Lon who had suddenly awakened from the scene of the Devil taking out his one feet long tongue and licking Malesty's forehead, mumbled, "The Big Bang Mystery of the Century…" And immediately transforming himself into a saucer, he flew towards the ground to save the brides.

*

"Galaxy L3 North, the Devil's Asteroid Minikin 011 in the Boltman Region"

Such a drizzle of illusory brightness was pouring there that it could not be ascertained whether this is day or night. When Daarck went down two steps to reach upto the *Shikara (A Kashmiri Houseboat)* in the lake starting from the foothills of the mountain on which the *'castle'* broken from various places as if it was preferred by the Devil was located, and stopped to talk with Robrelco Fero; Lon, Solon, Filipa, Antonio and Benedict had reached there.

Disparaging the Satanics who were stopping them, Daarck spoke, "These guests following Lord de Ros' footsteps have come to get transferred from unfriendly to friendly relations. Let them come. Ultimately our back cannot bear the arrow of obstinate enemies like *Lon and Solon*."

All of them now came and stood in front of the *Devil*.

"We are giving you the first rank for this outstanding idea doling out effortless fun." After Lon said, Solon spoke, "There cannot be a more intelligent *person* than this on any other Galaxy. I am telling with certainty. No one would have ever even thought about servants manufacturing that one and only thing *fun* to achieve which all people in the world are always striving endlessly…" Now Lon spoke- "Why not, *WOW* it would actually be a wonder if this thought does not come in the Devil's mind. Both their voices were dripping with candor. "We bow in front of you Bilzebub. We salute you." Slowly stopping the claps both of them bent upto their waist in honor of the Devil's grandeur.

Coming absolutely close to the Devil, Robrelco Fero, Dervil and Daarck who looked like the prodigies of infinite pleasure as if they had taken a heavy dose of Morphine and were floating in the air, Lon said, "Not only will a new curriculum of the Satanic ideologies be started in all the knowledge-booths of my Colony Metal Casting, but his temples also will be established in the form of one more tribal-deity. Really, Due to this devilry of Bilzebub, the sorrow of defeat is gone away."

The Devil spoke, "Even then, when luck is not in the mood of meting out victory, even the best of diplomats are seen scuttling away in fright in confrontation against fools. And that matter is proved by our strategy that got delayed because of Filipa's misdeeds." Turning his glance to *Lon* from the mountains of marble towards the West, the Devil started narrating such a tale that would start with a wide smile -

"This entire mess of Walk of Life had been done with the sole purpose that we would get the ease of loading that chip in the minds of the New-Gods. The chip that has been fitted near the master hormone controller spot in the minds of the New-Gods, functions in this manner- "A nano-second before the realization of happiness and pleasure received by the New-God when the cellulose walls of the *New-God's* brain experiences the pleasure being generated in its central cerebral portion at the time of any type of event that gives him happiness, this *chip* that has been named *Heaven Transporter* steals away overall eighty percent of all their fun and broadcasts it via S. Station through a special frequency delivery system to the receiver chip that is fit in our head." The Devil added removing his hand from head, "The realization of being himself the emperor of many planets dawns on one of the portion of his brain, and the joy rising up there directly reaches our heads. Experience of acute sensitivity of joy and satisfaction at the climax of sexual intercourse in 60 different parts of the new-God's Ferocious brain, the relishing taste acquired from the flavours of savory entrées, alcohols generating pleasant experiences and the enjoyment of the impetuous swings of cocaine, to the extent that even eighty percent of the two seconds of relief acquired after a sneeze, this *"Heaven Transporter"* send to us after stealing.

When the Devil finished his talking, unable to stop a big smile, Daarck spoke, "And who would know this better than you Lon that the waves of pleasure rising up in the mind of a New-God are thousand times more in comparison to an ordinary person. An ordinary person cannot even imagine, the type of exquisite pleasure the minds of New-Gods can enjoy, during his entire life."

"Alright." Lon said nodding his head as if in agreement, "And a New-God is not even an ordinary person who can be caught any time to load the chip in his mind. So you developed the Tie-in and Re-built Tune, with which you could kidnap them through deceit and load the chip. Discovered the Mummy-Ointment, through which the body can be exchanged with someone in close proximity of the New-God in order to reach close to him. And finally if no tactic is useful, then in the end, loading the chip in the mind of the New-God by defeating and imprisoning him with the help of the army prepared through the Project Discs and then, giving the colonies back to them."

"Absolutely right..." Daarck said, "A long time ago, when *Lord de Ros* was taking Robrelco Fero's assistance in understanding his body's structure language, we slyly installed a *'Heaven Transporter'* in his mind and relished the taste of this ambrosia-liqueur for the first time. Ros tried out all alchemies including surgery to rid himself of the Heaven Transporter that could be switched off only after death. This was an extraordinary success for us. But the difficulty cropped up when Ros, who had changed the programming language and become immortal, blasted his body for getting rid of chip. When Ros' bodily molecules enjoined again, he had got freedom from the Heaven Transporter."

Swiftly blinking his eyes, Solon asked, "If Ros knew from the beginning that you are creating *Walk of Life* for this purpose only, then why did he not expose your ploy to Lon?"

"That was because Ros' intention was to expel us and steal this Heaven-Transporter program of ours. Ros is currently robbing pleasure of one of these ten New-Gods' brain. Ros had agreed to hand over those New-Gods to us as a result of this offer only.

"After relishing the taste of this thing once, we almost became insane after we stopped getting it. The next challenge for us was to produce such a chip, from which no New-God would ever get emancipation and for that it required the emergence of divine, heavenly and unthinkable intelligence power. After that, for descent such an unthinkable intelligence in Robrelco Fero's mind, a very big conflagration of Devil's worship was kindled. After giving millions of sacrifices and generating phenomenal mental powers, finally a thought giving the gift of exorbitant intellect was acquired. In which Robrelco Fero developed a chip made from human-flesh that would remain in the New-God's mind as his own constituent."

"You must have now understood how important it is to hide your intentions from the world, Lon! We took advantage of your world famous intentions of change the world" The Devil said smiling slyly, "It was enough to convey the thought of something like *'Walk of Life'* plan to you, so that you would get us to do what we wanted by paying us a price for it."

Listening to all the discussions attentively, Filipa standing with her face contorted exasperatedly, spoke up, "Did you understand now Lon, I was trying to tell you that you and Solon believe Daarck to be a hired gun, but the fact is that you yourselves have worked for him like a laborer without any charge."

"Alright. I am giving you a beautiful offer to finish off this matter right here." Lon spoke, "If the structure of the waves of pleasure derived from cruel demeanor and the pleasure derived in a straight forward way without harming anyone is similar, which will not make any difference to you then I am willing to replace my Chairmen with these ten New-Gods. You can unhesitatingly load the Heaven Transporter in their minds."

"And otherwise, the cruel Emperor Apotheosis will not want that anyone else also should have this *'Heavenly Technology'* of the Heaven Transporter apart from him." Solon threatened.

"Such a scene wherein someone stands in front of the Devil on Minikin and makes the desipience of threatening him is very rare." Saying this, Dervil moved forward.

"You leave that to me, Dervil." Saying this, *Daarck* invited Lon's small troupe to come into the boat as he looked at them with an expressive gaze. As the boat went a little further, leaving the Devil family behind, Solon moved the left side edge of his overcoat and taking out Anjeolmac, he extended it towards Daarck. After unblinkingly beholding Anjeolmac just like that for some time Daarck turned back to see the Devilish countryside that was now looking small. After switching on the *'Voice Cracking Machine' (to stop the conversation going on there from going out)*, he said, "I feel that before Filipa does something new, I should now tell the ultimate truth." Looking at a family of black ducks passing close by the Boat, he became silent for some time and after going far, he said:

"This ultimate truth of mine releases my image as a monster that is captivated in your eyes. One day when I promised myself to confer a pain free life to the visitors coming out to stroll for hundred, two hundred or five hundred years in the world, I did not have a single penny with me, and the investment was the destruction of such as Prestige, Apotheosis and the Owner Family's trinity for which an outright battle was impossible. A crazy eccentric having the belief that revolution is not possible without violence or dictatorship, burns a whole city, state or the entire country. Someone like *Antonio* on Earth-Eleven and someone like *Lon* on an entire Galaxy are seen becoming stupefied in favor of a conducive system for a liberal revolution. But my attempts are of the highest level." After smiling a little, he spoke further, "This matter is somewhat like this- Hardly any New-God will be there from all the six Galaxies of our cluster who will know that Apotheosis and Prestige also are nothing more special than high level servants. Yes, there is one power even above those two Directors. That is referred to by the name of Owner-Family."

Staring at the shores of the lake, when Solon now looked towards Daarck with a terrible shock, Daarck laughed and said, "Apotheosis' great Chairman Solon is present here, and he will be the one who will authenticate whether my story is true or not. The descendents of the *Owner-Family* with huge bodies and large brains are spread on several mysterious and hidden planets of the Master Galaxy where even our Directors cannot go without the permission of the Owner-Family. They are really very scary. These are people who have achieved peculiar accomplishments in such a science that could be called talismanic, who are claiming through a long tradition of centuries that they have invented the *basic elements of (Fire, Water, Air, Earth, Sky)* the *Material World (Physical World)*. They claim to be our God and looking at the science they have, its true." Giving Anjeolmac to Antonio, Daarck said further:

"This is actually that highest level, where strategies are decided that evil and good, which means that the conflict of both the Vio-Crazy and Off Idiotic groups would continue forever on our six Galaxies. And to do this, they prepare a graph-root. And according to the requirement of that graph-root, Prestige and Apotheosis relentlessly keep on doing pranks so that the *character-roots* of the Galaxies keep on wandering around that. The life exists on all the planets of all six of our Galaxies have entirely distinct methodologies, ceremonies, customs and all their inhabitants are totally different from each other. Always vulnerable towards the inevitable attraction of newness, they create a new graph-root after a session of some centuries and sometimes even within a few years. The Owner Family is very large. They exchange the Galaxies under each other's ownership for a short time. As the Vertical Seismograph Mass Pane dribbles the intensity of the earthquake, similarly, they design the new graph-root taking the reference of the samples prepared earlier by their sensory tool-crack machine that catches the different kinds of thought waves rising from the painful screams and happiness that is derived. The responsibility of making this progress on the appropriate track is fulfilled by the Directors."

"All of us are still small children in front of them, Daarck." Solon said, "Do you know what a graph-root is?"

"Not entirely." Feeling ashamed for ignorance, Daarck asked, "What is the reality of the graph-root?"

Solon said, "During a meeting with the head of the Owner Family, it was inquired by Apotheosis out of curiosity as to what would happen if we design a graph-root for the existence of only one group, either Idiotics or Vio-Crazys. Meaning, either just heaven all around or only hell on every planet, then the head said giving a very strange response: "These things are beyond your imagination. Just suppose I tell you that among several mysterious things necessary for sustaining this world, one of the things is also that it is through the waves generating and pulsating from the human sufferings and screams that several types of powers are acquired by the basic molecules with which the Physical World is made of, then you will not be able to believe it. Yet it is true. To quite an extent, the strength of the physical elements, that is necessary to preserve the world. And hence the existence of the Vio-Crazy New-Gods and the Devil is necessary. This means that the graph-root is a type of measurement. That shows in what quantity the creation of subtle waves rising from pain, suffering, violence, etc. should be done and in what quantity the waves of happiness and pleasure. They say that grief and suffering is an inevitable misfortune of the human beings. They say that they are compelled to accept these things also along with accepting the gift of life. And we do all this only as much as it is required to sustain the world. We don't have even a little interest in making anyone unhappy."

Solon said completing the topic, "Then this is the explanation of the Owner Family to safeguard evil and stop every planet from being transformed into heaven. Yet I am not convinced by this story of theirs. The mystery is surely of a different nature than this."

"So now let's get to the point." Daarck said, "The destruction of the Owner-Family is necessary for establishing everlasting heavenly governance on every planet. But the difficulty is that these people have the most optimized science and hence the most optimized weapons as well. Such weapons, that all the colonies of all the six Galaxies of our local cluster can hardly compare with even if they all get together to do so. Solon, I am telling the truth, right?"

"Every single word…" Solon said, looking at Daarck with sparkling eyes.

"The destruction of this Owner Family can be done in only one way." Daarck said, "By getting them to fight against each other. But before that, it is necessary to acquire their science that controls the elements that initiate alterations in the Physical World. Through which the five elements are maintained. Or else there will be a catastrophe. The quantity of entertainment that these Owner Family members require to remain normal is thousands of time more than the creatures having any type of cerebral composition across all the Galaxies. If the size of our brains can be compared with a tennis-ball, the brain of an Owner Family member can be compared with a football. Even though a very big portion of the Galaxy comes in share of each family member, the complaint of crisis for enjoyment and fun is constantly hanging on their lips. This crisis can transform their small, insignificant internal conflicts into a terrible enmity for something like *Heaven Transporter.*

The woman known by the name of *'Mithalia'*, who has the *beauty fancied by fairies (Such beauty that is scarcely there even amongst fairies, a beauty to acquire which even the fairies keep on dreaming)*, was to get entry into the world of the Owner Family only after she would exchange her body with one Director through the Mummy-Ointment. And after that, Mithalia was going to take the *Heaven Transporter Chip* to the head of the Owner Family and was going to start an internal dispute between them. But that woman *'Mithalia'* got involved into other passions altogether. So now you must have understood why the invention of all the things like the Mummy-Ointment, Tie-in and Re-built Tunes, Aura Transformation Germ, Heaven-Transporter etc. has been done. We are on the test level for Heaven-Transporter. The members of the Owner Family to whom we will give the Heaven-Transporter technology, will do with the other Owner Family members that which we are currently doing with the *New-Gods* of those ten colonies and in that way they will invite each other's destruction."

"Oops…." Filipa said, biting her tongue between the teeth, "Couldn't you raise this curtain from the mystery earlier, at least I wouldn't have had to kill you."

Gesturing to take the boat towards the narrow waterway near the *'Host of Hell'* standing with weird darts on the Western shores to take the souls of several dead Satanics into the other world, Daarck said, "Looking at the kind of resources available with the Owner-Family, it is better for this mission that the secret of this Ultimate revolutionary mission reaches as few minds as possible.

"After all who is Daarck? Who is Mithalia? Who is Filipa? From which bloody world do they come? When the hell this partnership of trinity started…?" Experiencing moments of relief after ages when Lon asked as if unable to believe that it was time to deploy the stinking rogue on Daarck, *(An occasion to hand over all the worries of a Heavenly revolution to Daarck)* then Antonio spoke, "The description of the Messiah who will come with *two beautiful wings (Filipa and Mithalia)* for the establishment of a new World-order mentioned in the priest's book Lexicaptive, a prediction has been made that the period of revelation of the original truth of that Messiah will be determined only after that great revolution.

Finally Daarck's melodious voice echoed as if the traditional songs of spring, "Otherwise it is only known to my heart that the intoxication I have to forget the pain of the harsh law of the Universe is euphoric above all intoxication." When a spate of smiles surged forth on Filipa's countenance that was swishing in the water of the lake at the spot where the reflection of colorful lights shining in the sky was falling, Daarck said completing the sentence, "And hence I had no need of something like *'Heaven-Transporter'* for my own self."

*